Also by Owen King

Double Feature: A Novel

We're All in This Together: A Novella and Stories

Who Can Save Us Now? (coeditor)

Also by Mark Jude Poirier

Modern Ranch Living

Unsung Heroes of American Industry

Goats

Naked Pueblo

The Worst Years of Your Life (editor)

Intro to ALIEN INVASION

ILLUSTRATED BY NANCY AHN

OWEN KING AND
MARK JUDE POIRIER

SCRIBNER

New York   London   Toronto   Sydney   New Delhi

Scribner
An Imprint of Simon & Schuster, Inc.
1230 Avenue of the Americas
New York, NY 10020

First Scribner trade paperback edition September 2015

SCRIBNER and design are registered trademarks of the Gale Group, Inc.,
used under license by Simon & Schuster, Inc., the publisher of this work.

For information about special discounts for bulk purchases,
please contact Simon & Schuster Special Sales at 1-866-506-1949
or business@simonandschuster.com.

The Simon & Schuster Speakers Bureau can bring authors to your live event.
For more information or to book an event, contact the Simon & Schuster Speakers
Bureau at 866-248-3049 or visit our website at www.simonspeakers.com.

Manufactured in the United States of America

10 9 8 7 6 5 4 3 2

Library of Congress Control Number: 2014017627

ISBN 978-1-4767-6340-8
ISBN 978-1-4767-6342-2 (ebook)

For Joseph Hillstrom King & Madeline Minaudière . . .

and for Rose Davis (1970–2003)

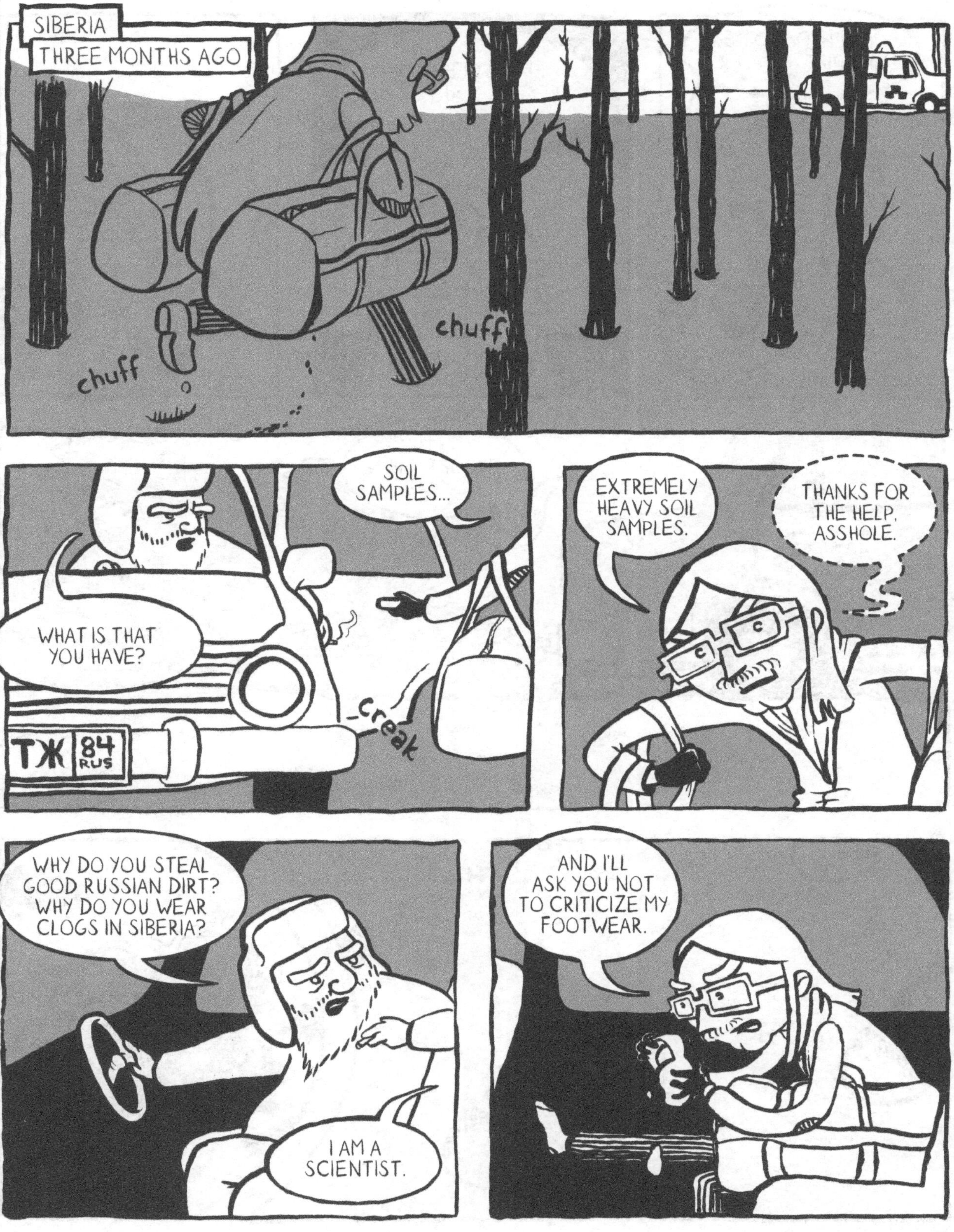
SIBERIA
THREE MONTHS AGO
chuff
chuff
SOIL SAMPLES...
WHAT IS THAT YOU HAVE?
creak
ТЖ 84 RUS
EXTREMELY HEAVY SOIL SAMPLES.
THANKS FOR THE HELP, ASSHOLE.
WHY DO YOU STEAL GOOD RUSSIAN DIRT? WHY DO YOU WEAR CLOGS IN SIBERIA?
I AM A SCIENTIST.
AND I'LL ASK YOU NOT TO CRITICIZE MY FOOTWEAR.

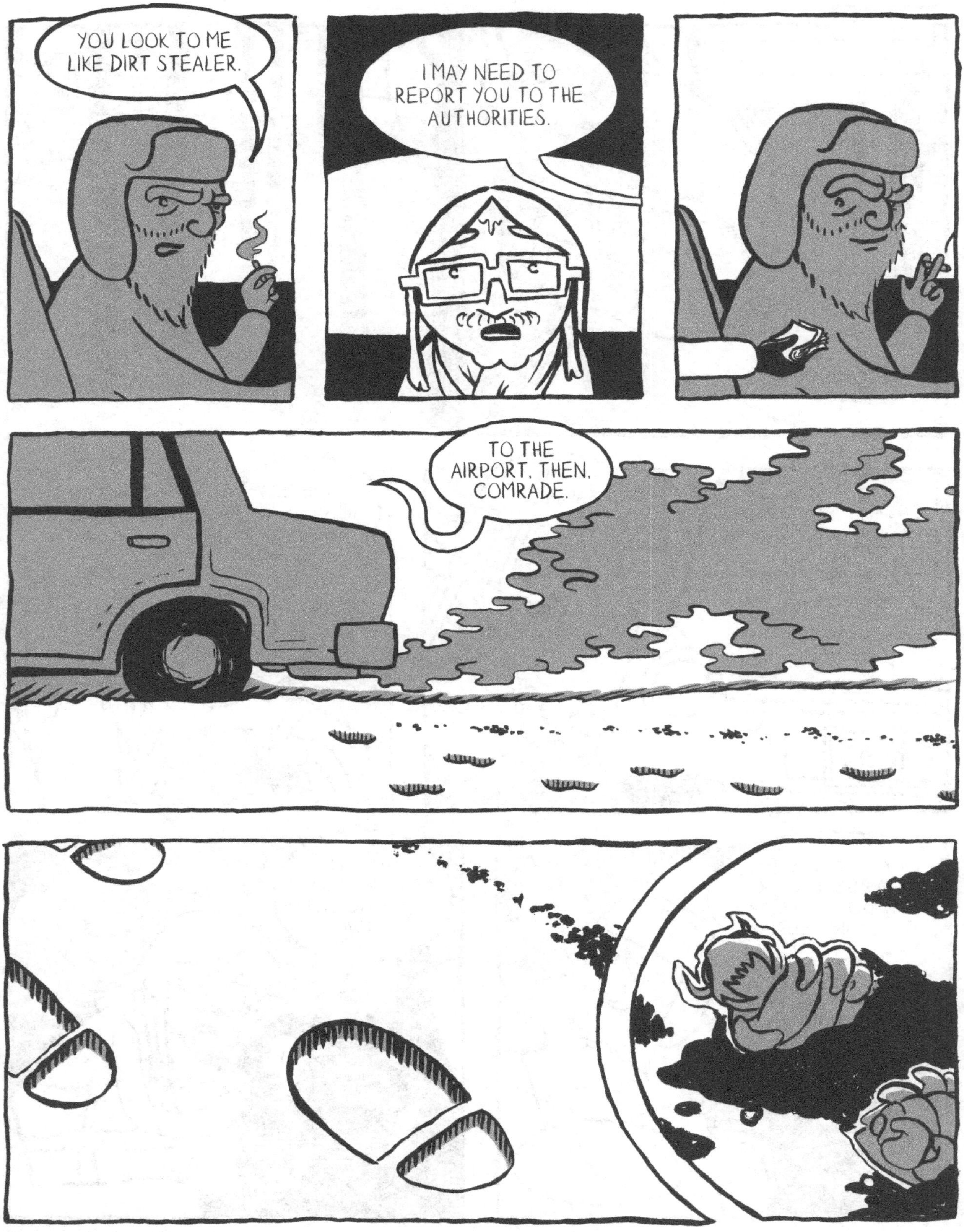
YOU LOOK TO ME LIKE DIRT STEALER.
I MAY NEED TO REPORT YOU TO THE AUTHORITIES.
TO THE AIRPORT, THEN, COMRADE.

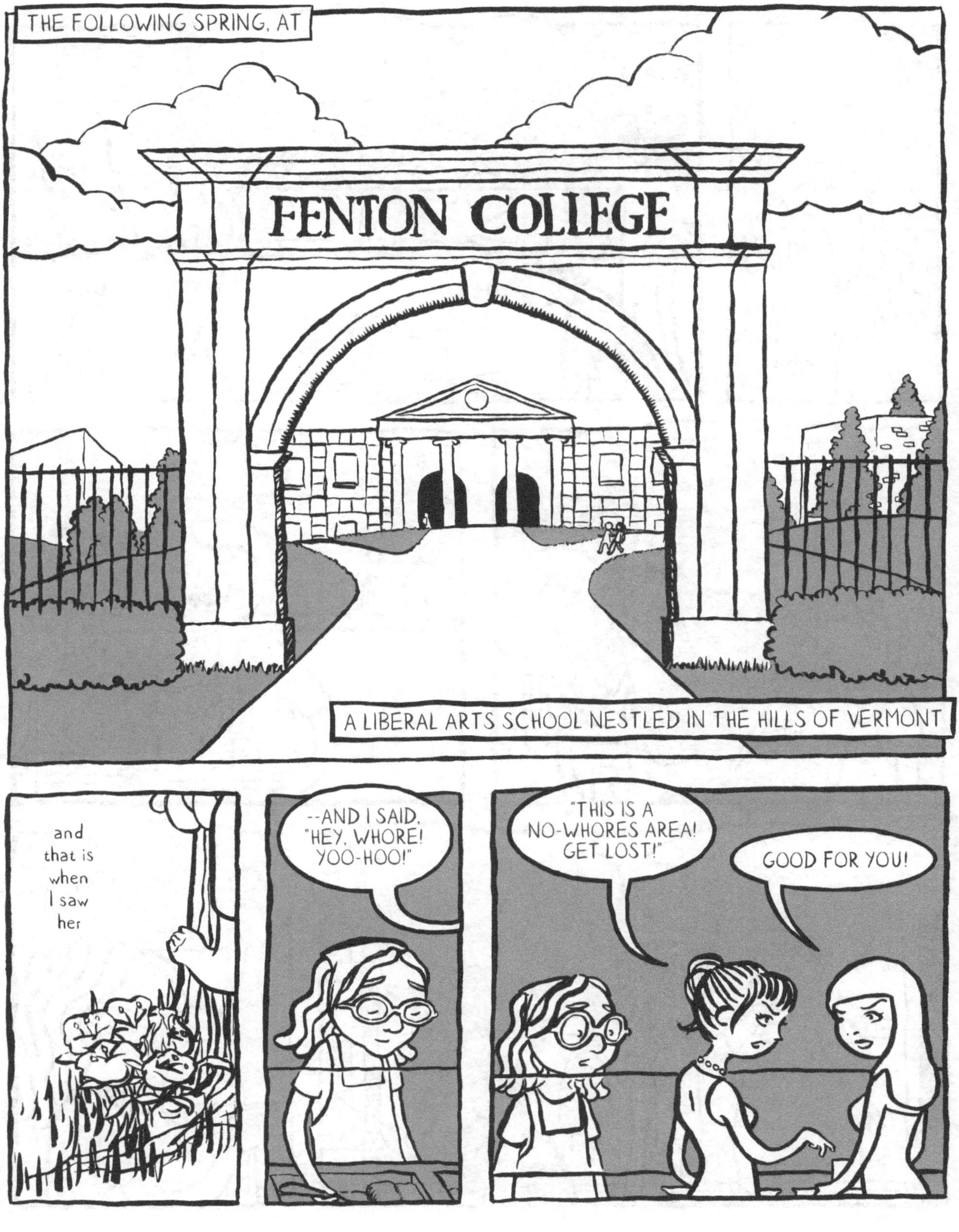
THE FOLLOWING SPRING, AT
FENTON COLLEGE
A LIBERAL ARTS SCHOOL NESTLED IN THE HILLS OF VERMONT
and that is when I saw her
--AND I SAID, "HEY, WHORE! YOO-HOO!"
"THIS IS A NO-WHORES AREA! GET LOST!"
GOOD FOR YOU!

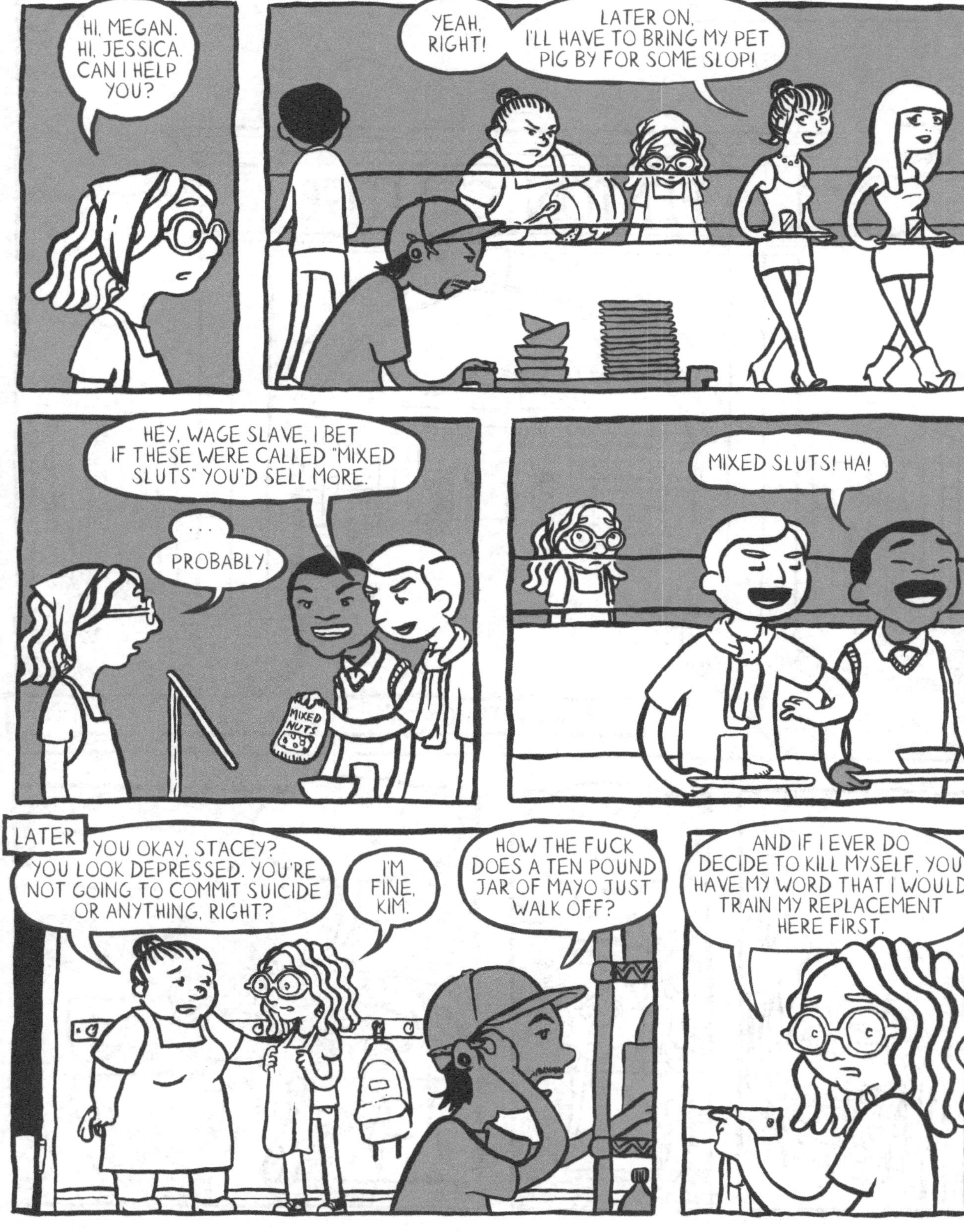
HI, MEGAN. HI, JESSICA. CAN I HELP YOU?
YEAH, RIGHT!
LATER ON, I'LL HAVE TO BRING MY PET PIG BY FOR SOME SLOP!
HEY, WAGE SLAVE, I BET IF THESE WERE CALLED "MIXED SLUTS" YOU'D SELL MORE.
MIXED NUTS
. . . PROBABLY.
MIXED SLUTS! HA!
LATER
YOU OKAY, STACEY? YOU LOOK DEPRESSED. YOU'RE NOT GOING TO COMMIT SUICIDE OR ANYTHING, RIGHT?
I'M FINE, KIM.
HOW THE FUCK DOES A TEN POUND JAR OF MAYO JUST WALK OFF?
AND IF I EVER DO DECIDE TO KILL MYSELF, YOU HAVE MY WORD THAT I WOULD TRAIN MY REPLACEMENT HERE FIRST.

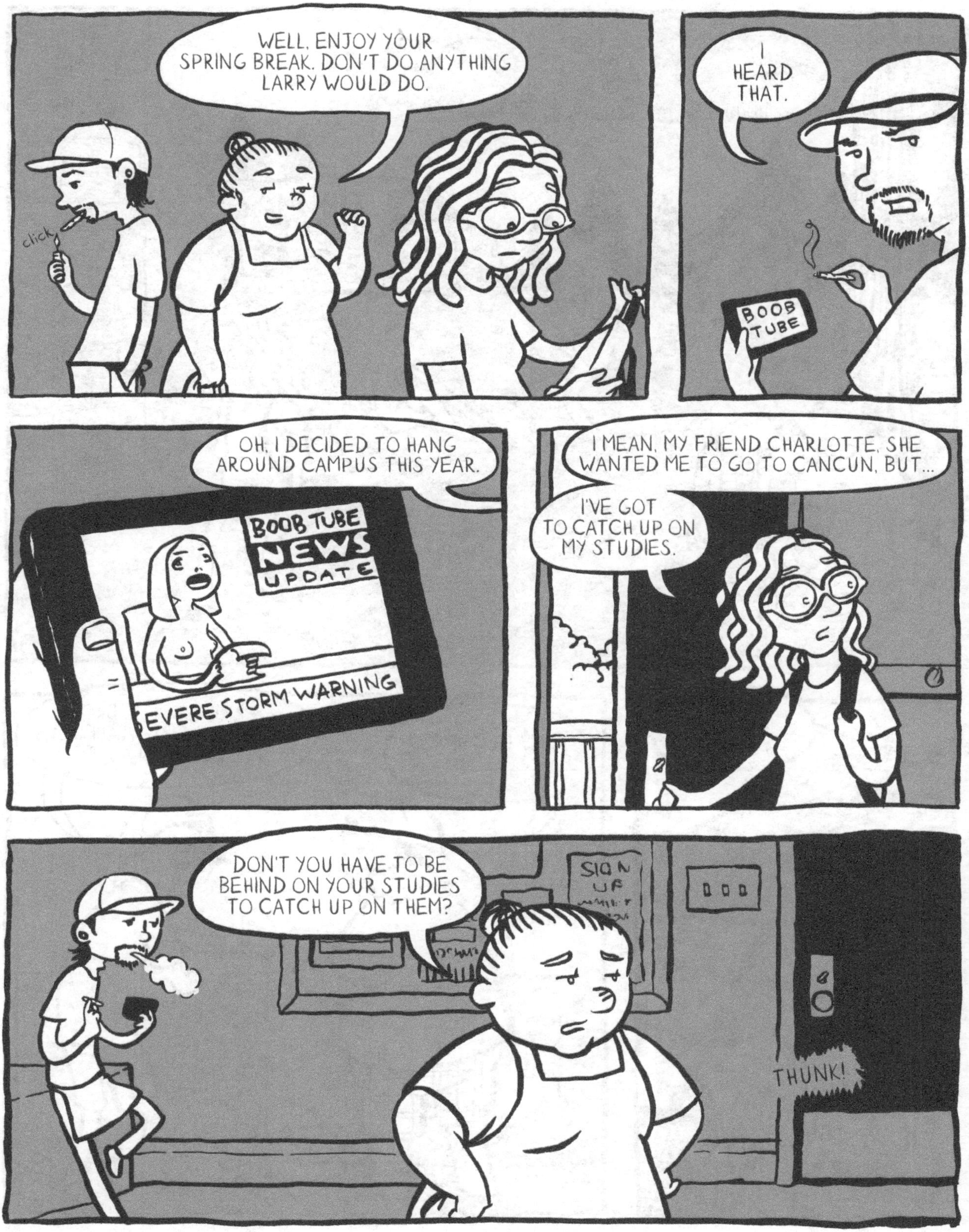
WELL, ENJOY YOUR SPRING BREAK. DON'T DO ANYTHING LARRY WOULD DO.
click
I HEARD THAT.
BOOB TUBE
OH, I DECIDED TO HANG AROUND CAMPUS THIS YEAR.
BOOB TUBE NEWS UPDATE
SEVERE STORM WARNING
I MEAN, MY FRIEND CHARLOTTE, SHE WANTED ME TO GO TO CANCUN, BUT...
I'VE GOT TO CATCH UP ON MY STUDIES.
DON'T YOU HAVE TO BE BEHIND ON YOUR STUDIES TO CATCH UP ON THEM?
SIGN UP
THUNK!

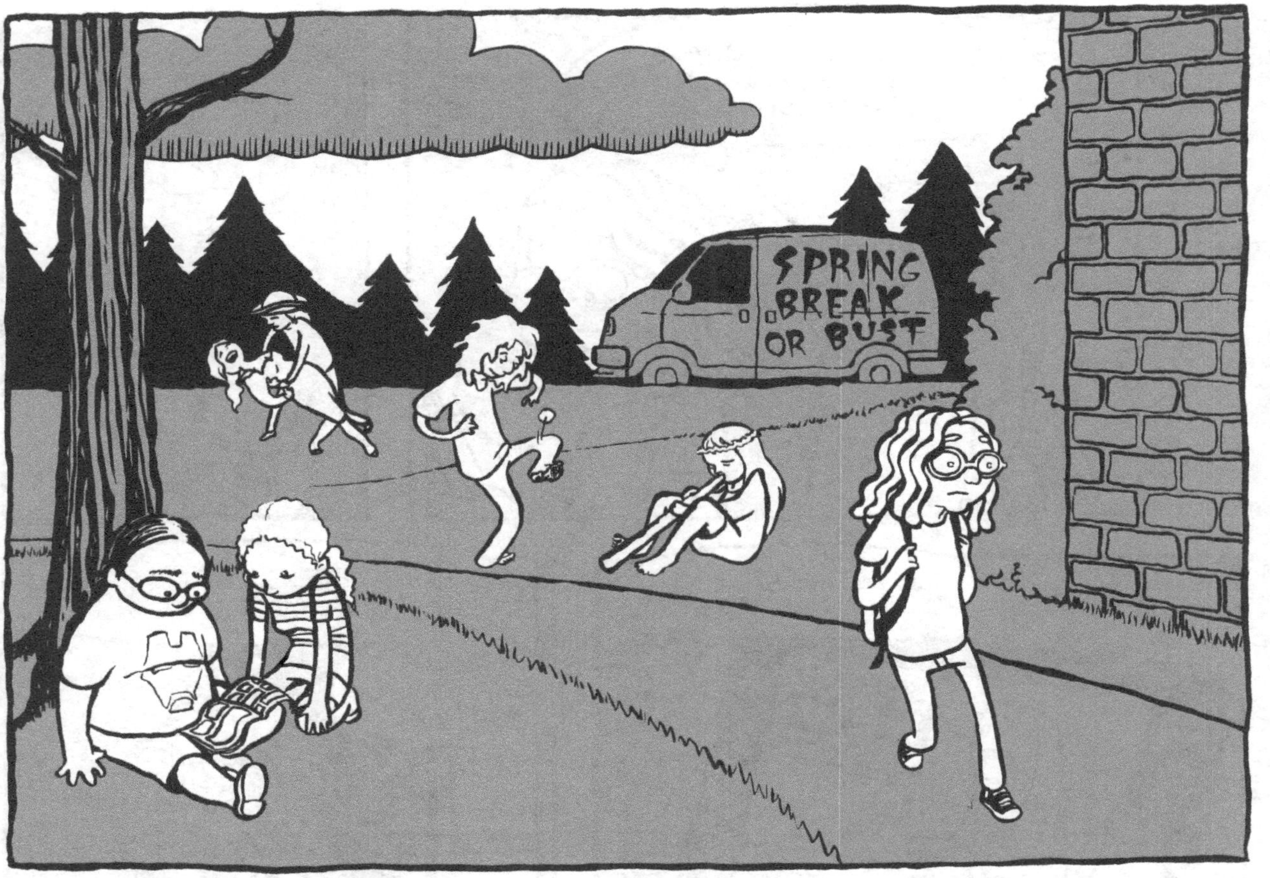
SPRING BREAK OR BUST

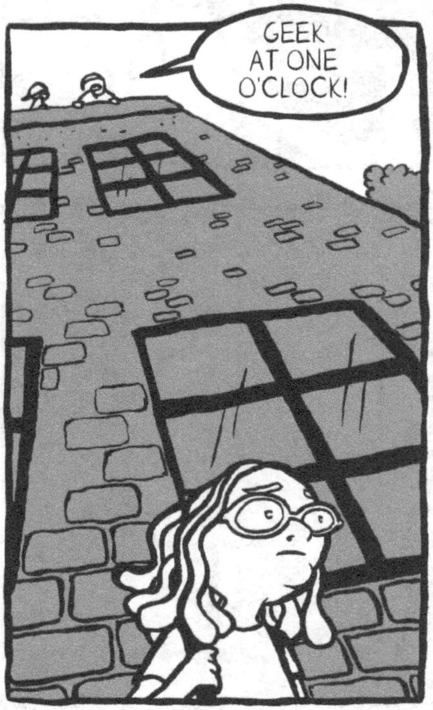
GEEK AT ONE O'CLOCK!

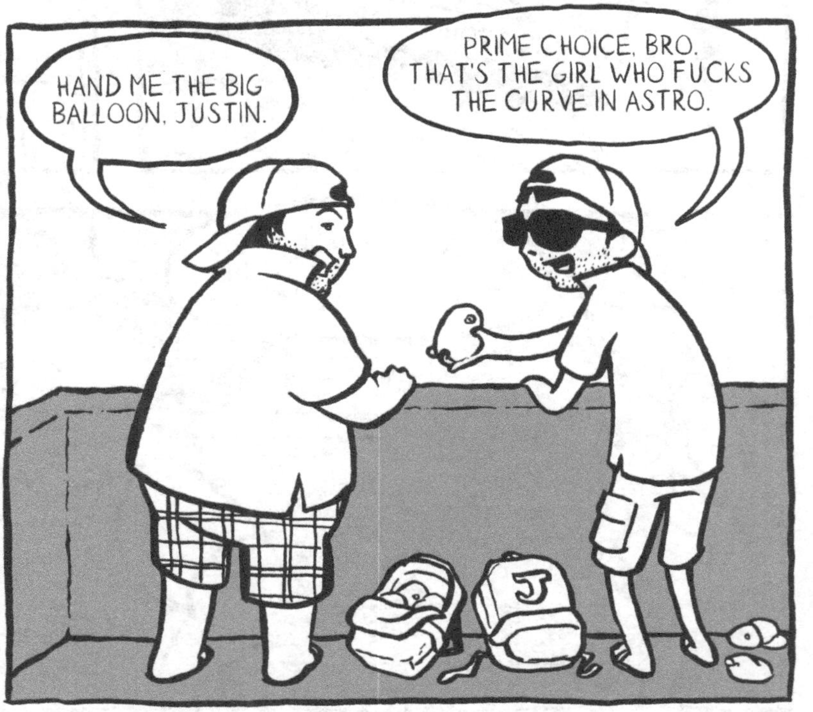
HAND ME THE BIG BALLOON, JUSTIN.
PRIME CHOICE, BRO. THAT'S THE GIRL WHO FUCKS THE CURVE IN ASTRO.

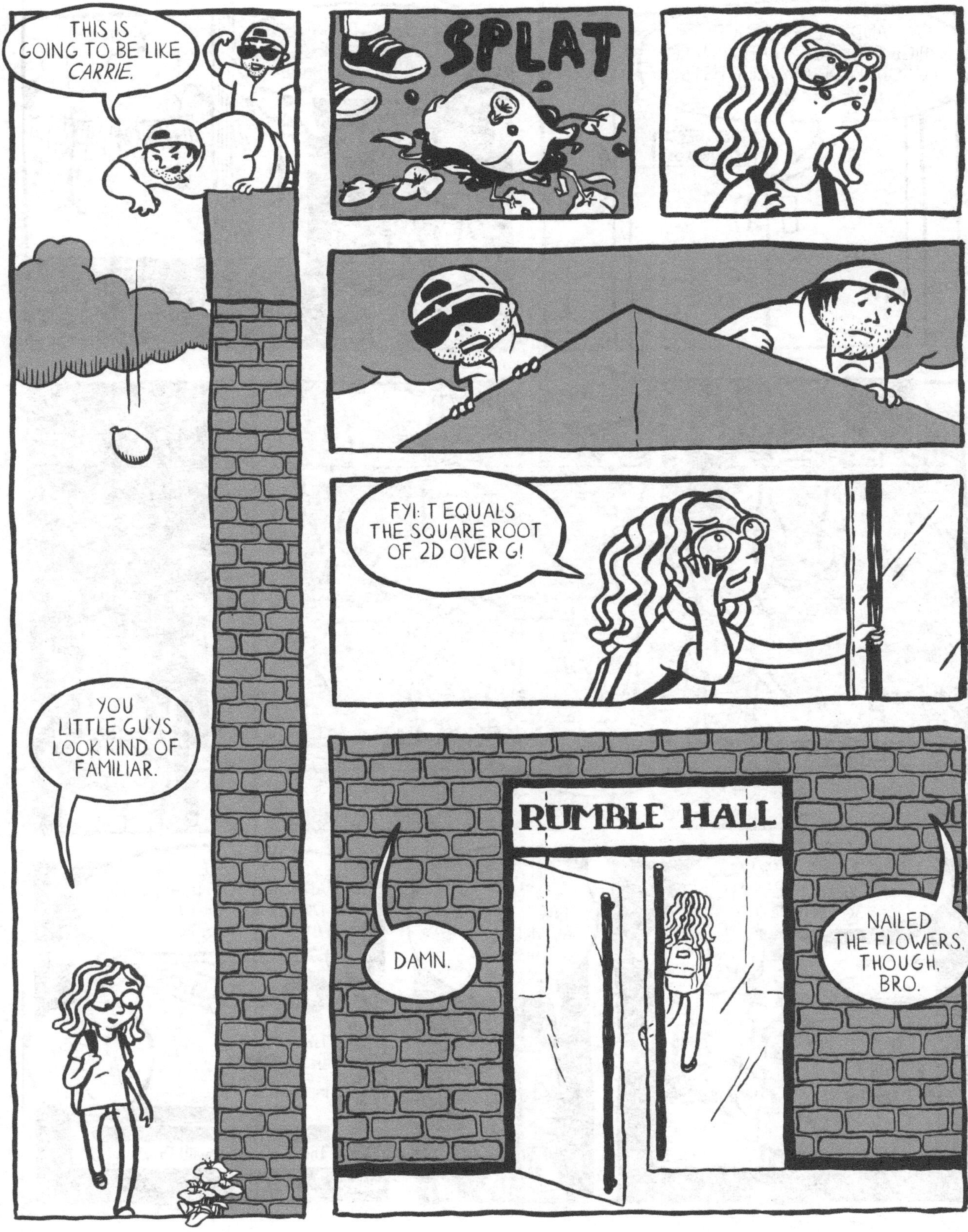
THIS IS GOING TO BE LIKE *CARRIE*.
YOU LITTLE GUYS LOOK KIND OF FAMILIAR.
SPLAT
FYI: T EQUALS THE SQUARE ROOT OF 2D OVER G!
RUMBLE HALL
DAMN.
NAILED THE FLOWERS, THOUGH, BRO.

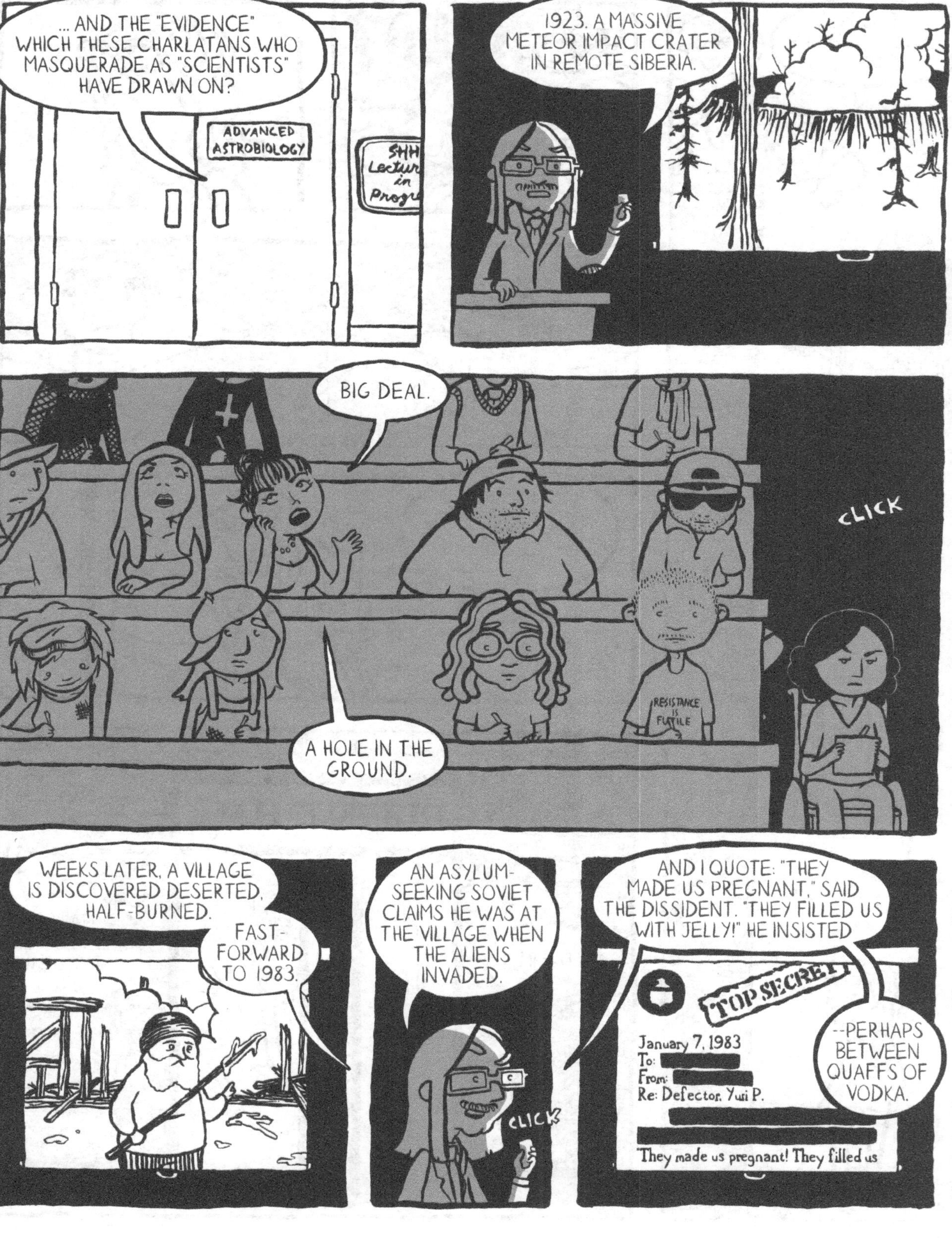

... AND THE "EVIDENCE" WHICH THESE CHARLATANS WHO MASQUERADE AS "SCIENTISTS" HAVE DRAWN ON?
ADVANCED ASTROBIOLOGY
1923. A MASSIVE METEOR IMPACT CRATER IN REMOTE SIBERIA.
BIG DEAL.
CLICK
RESISTANCE IS FUTILE
A HOLE IN THE GROUND.
WEEKS LATER, A VILLAGE IS DISCOVERED DESERTED, HALF-BURNED.
FAST-FORWARD TO 1983.
AN ASYLUM-SEEKING SOVIET CLAIMS HE WAS AT THE VILLAGE WHEN THE ALIENS INVADED.
CLICK
AND I QUOTE: "THEY MADE US PREGNANT," SAID THE DISSIDENT. "THEY FILLED US WITH JELLY!" HE INSISTED
TOP SECRET
January 7, 1983
To: [redacted]
From: [redacted]
Re: Defector, Yuri P.
[redacted]
"They made us pregnant! They filled us
--PERHAPS BETWEEN QUAFFS OF VODKA.

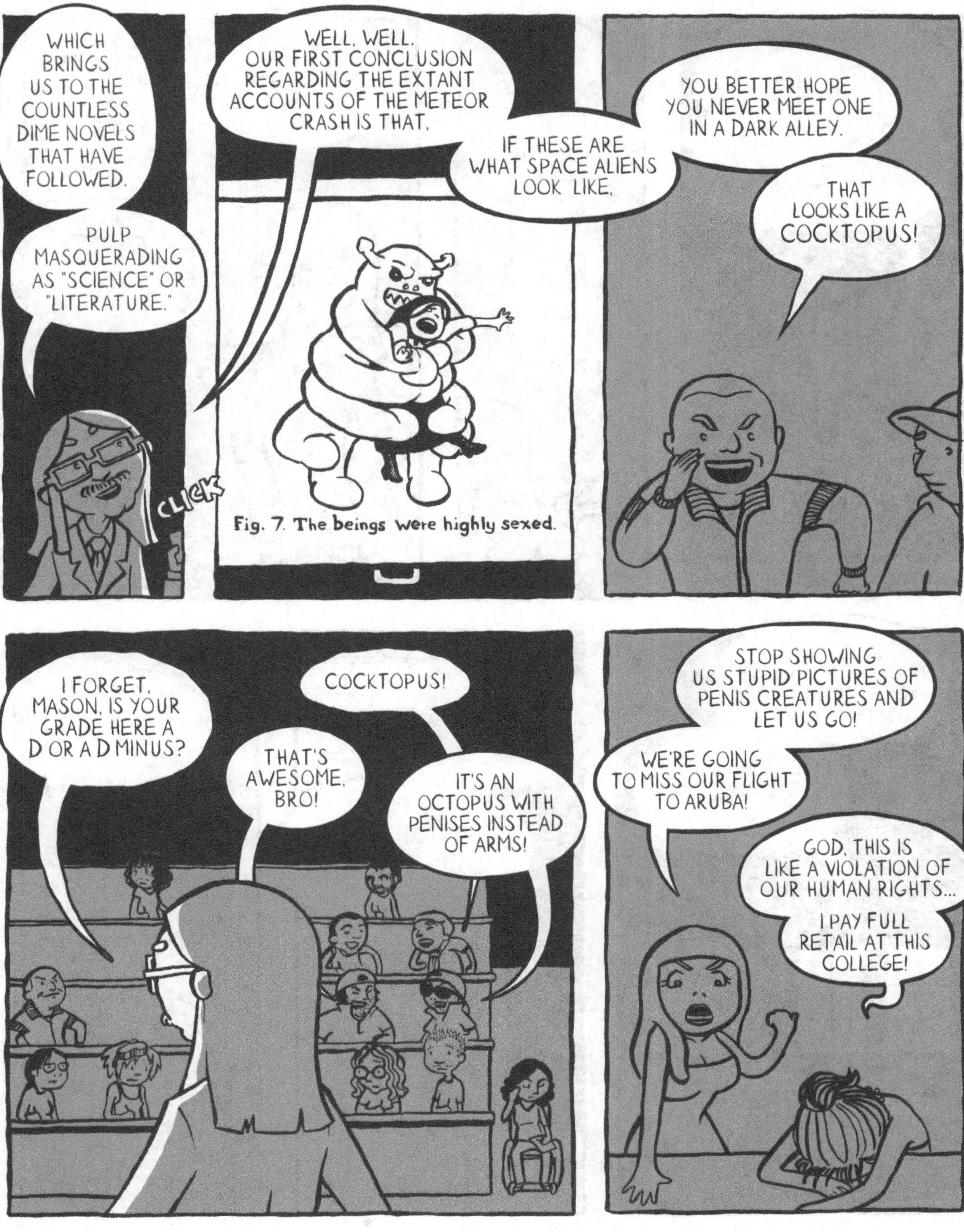

WHICH BRINGS US TO THE COUNTLESS DIME NOVELS THAT HAVE FOLLOWED.
PULP MASQUERADING AS "SCIENCE" OR "LITERATURE."
CLICK
WELL, WELL. OUR FIRST CONCLUSION REGARDING THE EXTANT ACCOUNTS OF THE METEOR CRASH IS THAT,
Fig. 7. The beings were highly sexed.
IF THESE ARE WHAT SPACE ALIENS LOOK LIKE,
YOU BETTER HOPE YOU NEVER MEET ONE IN A DARK ALLEY.
THAT LOOKS LIKE A COCKTOPUS!
I FORGET, MASON, IS YOUR GRADE HERE A D OR A D MINUS?
COCKTOPUS!
THAT'S AWESOME, BRO!
IT'S AN OCTOPUS WITH PENISES INSTEAD OF ARMS!
STOP SHOWING US STUPID PICTURES OF PENIS CREATURES AND LET US GO!
WE'RE GOING TO MISS OUR FLIGHT TO ARUBA!
GOD, THIS IS LIKE A VIOLATION OF OUR HUMAN RIGHTS...
I PAY FULL RETAIL AT THIS COLLEGE!

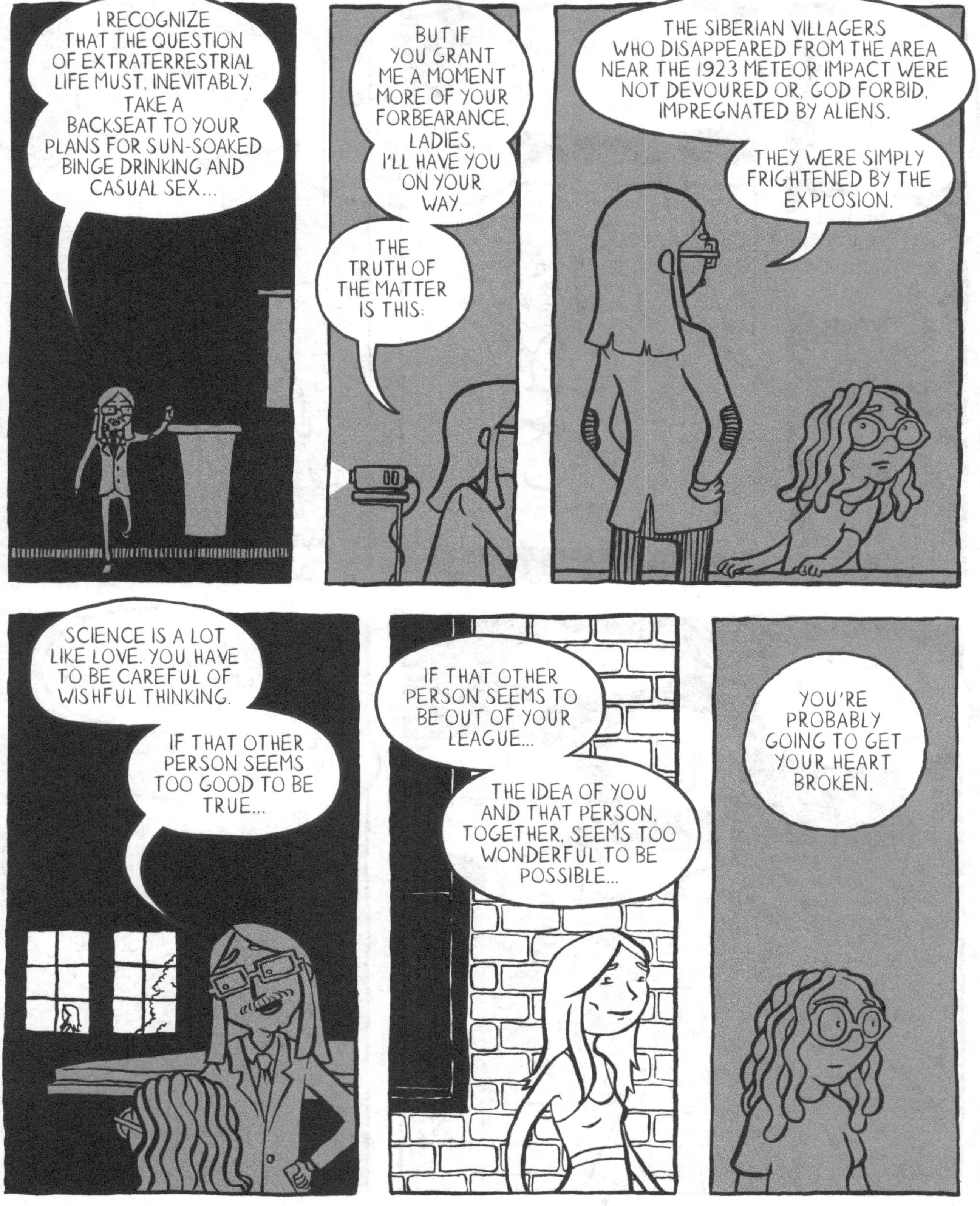
I RECOGNIZE THAT THE QUESTION OF EXTRATERRESTRIAL LIFE MUST, INEVITABLY, TAKE A BACKSEAT TO YOUR PLANS FOR SUN-SOAKED BINGE DRINKING AND CASUAL SEX...
BUT IF YOU GRANT ME A MOMENT MORE OF YOUR FORBEARANCE, LADIES, I'LL HAVE YOU ON YOUR WAY.
THE TRUTH OF THE MATTER IS THIS:
THE SIBERIAN VILLAGERS WHO DISAPPEARED FROM THE AREA NEAR THE 1923 METEOR IMPACT WERE NOT DEVOURED OR, GOD FORBID, IMPREGNATED BY ALIENS.
THEY WERE SIMPLY FRIGHTENED BY THE EXPLOSION.
SCIENCE IS A LOT LIKE LOVE. YOU HAVE TO BE CAREFUL OF WISHFUL THINKING.
IF THAT OTHER PERSON SEEMS TOO GOOD TO BE TRUE...
IF THAT OTHER PERSON SEEMS TO BE OUT OF YOUR LEAGUE...
THE IDEA OF YOU AND THAT PERSON, TOGETHER, SEEMS TOO WONDERFUL TO BE POSSIBLE...
YOU'RE PROBABLY GOING TO GET YOUR HEART BROKEN.

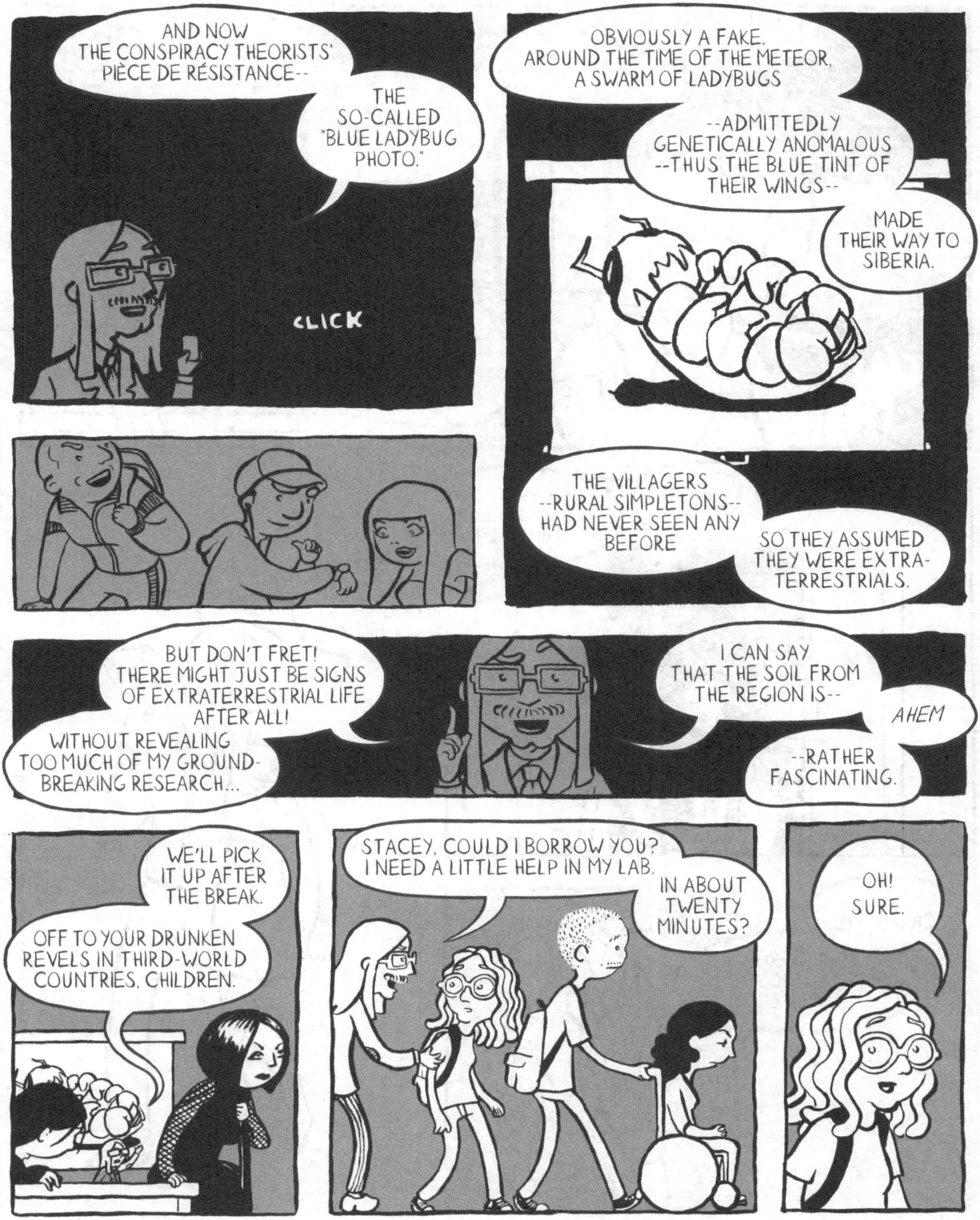
AND NOW THE CONSPIRACY THEORISTS' PIÈCE DE RÉSISTANCE--
THE SO-CALLED "BLUE LADYBUG PHOTO."
CLICK
OBVIOUSLY A FAKE. AROUND THE TIME OF THE METEOR, A SWARM OF LADYBUGS
--ADMITTEDLY GENETICALLY ANOMALOUS --THUS THE BLUE TINT OF THEIR WINGS--
MADE THEIR WAY TO SIBERIA.
THE VILLAGERS --RURAL SIMPLETONS-- HAD NEVER SEEN ANY BEFORE
SO THEY ASSUMED THEY WERE EXTRA-TERRESTRIALS.
BUT DON'T FRET! THERE MIGHT JUST BE SIGNS OF EXTRATERRESTRIAL LIFE AFTER ALL!
WITHOUT REVEALING TOO MUCH OF MY GROUND-BREAKING RESEARCH...
I CAN SAY THAT THE SOIL FROM THE REGION IS--
AHEM
--RATHER FASCINATING.
WE'LL PICK IT UP AFTER THE BREAK.
OFF TO YOUR DRUNKEN REVELS IN THIRD-WORLD COUNTRIES, CHILDREN.
STACEY, COULD I BORROW YOU? I NEED A LITTLE HELP IN MY LAB.
IN ABOUT TWENTY MINUTES?
OH! SURE.

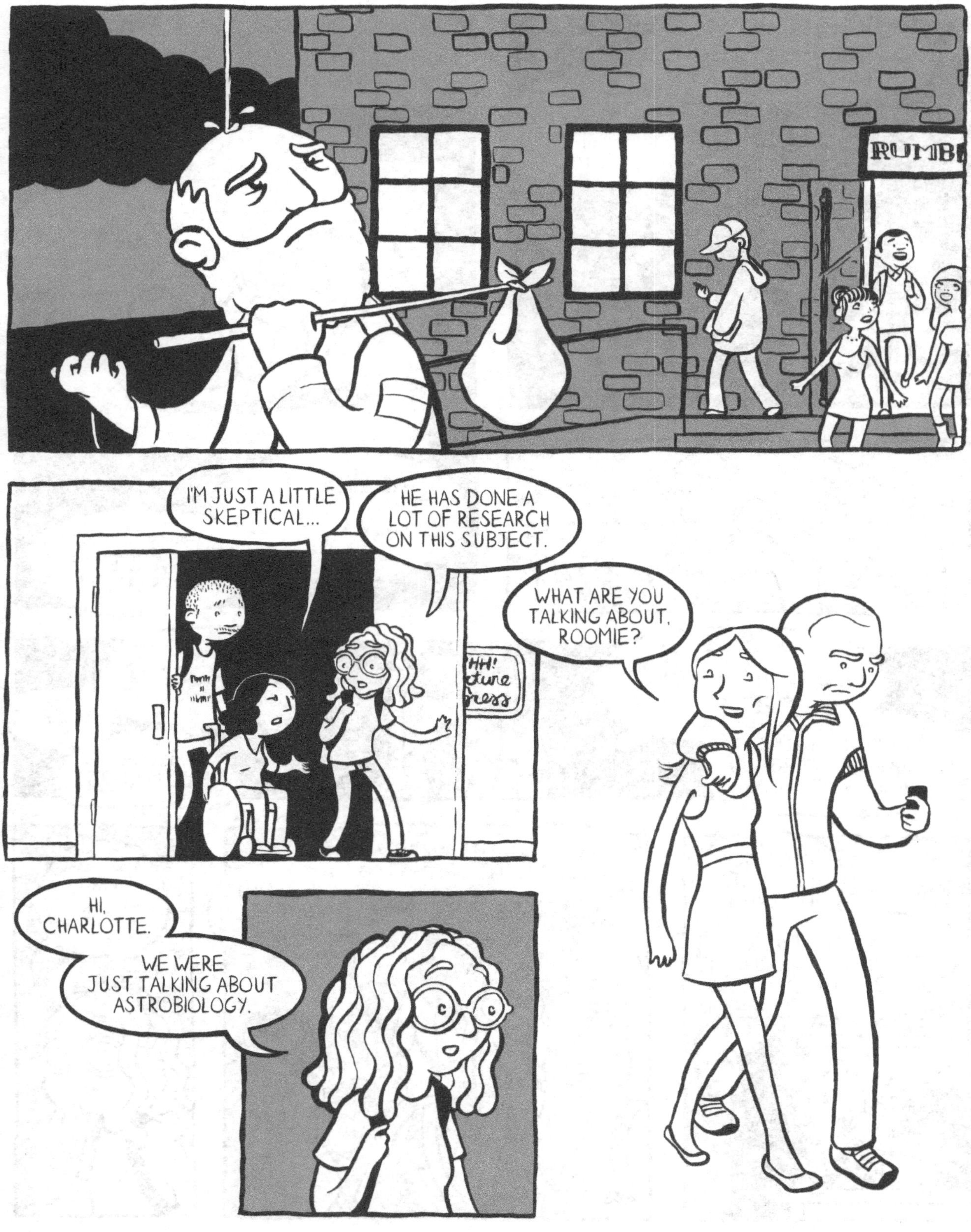
RUMB
I'M JUST A LITTLE SKEPTICAL...
HE HAS DONE A LOT OF RESEARCH ON THIS SUBJECT.
WHAT ARE YOU TALKING ABOUT, ROOMIE?
HI, CHARLOTTE.
WE WERE JUST TALKING ABOUT ASTROBIOLOGY.

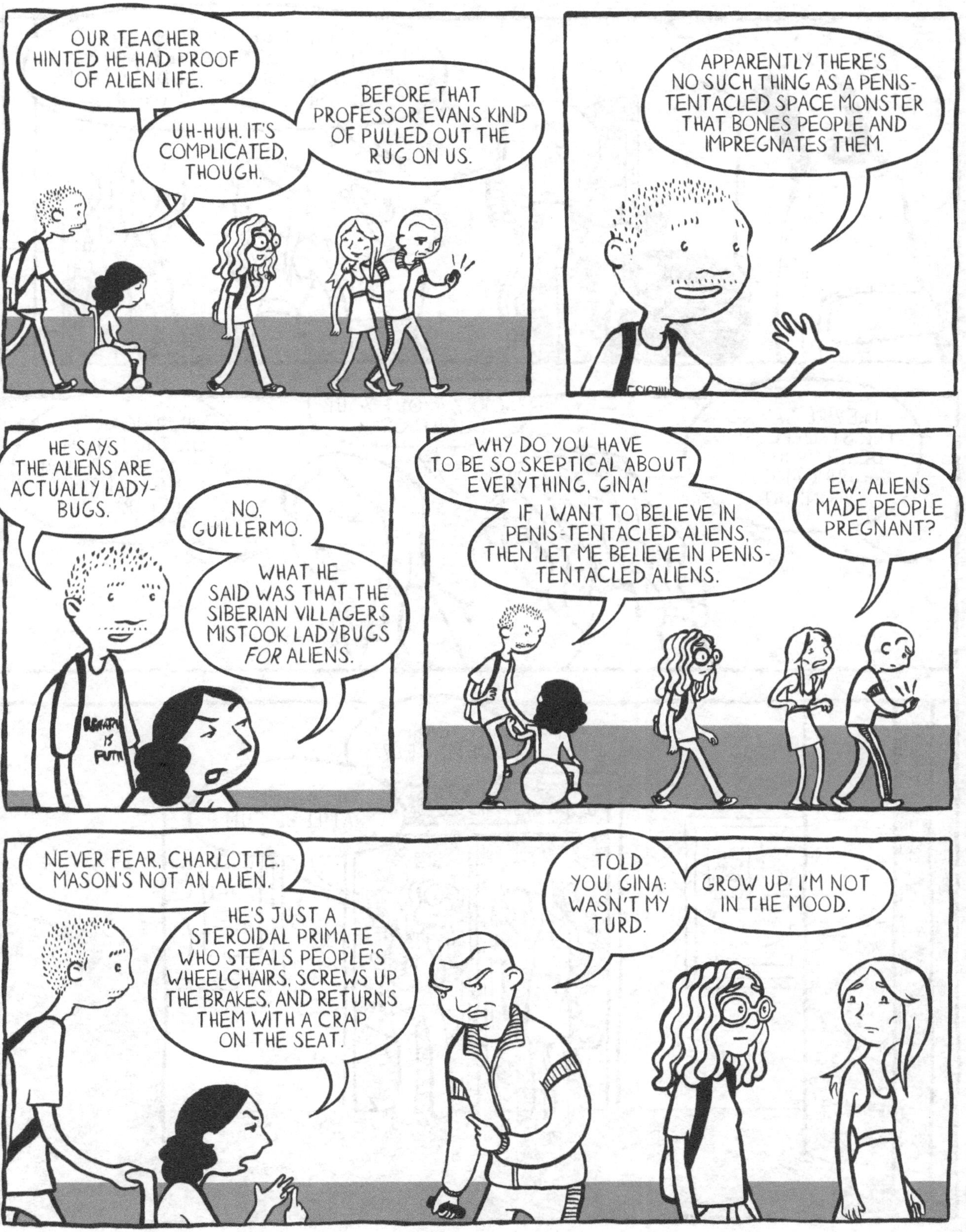
OUR TEACHER HINTED HE HAD PROOF OF ALIEN LIFE.
UH-HUH. IT'S COMPLICATED, THOUGH.
BEFORE THAT PROFESSOR EVANS KIND OF PULLED OUT THE RUG ON US.
APPARENTLY THERE'S NO SUCH THING AS A PENIS-TENTACLED SPACE MONSTER THAT BONES PEOPLE AND IMPREGNATES THEM.
HE SAYS THE ALIENS ARE ACTUALLY LADY-BUGS.
NO, GUILLERMO.
WHAT HE SAID WAS THAT THE SIBERIAN VILLAGERS MISTOOK LADYBUGS *FOR* ALIENS.
WHY DO YOU HAVE TO BE SO SKEPTICAL ABOUT EVERYTHING, GINA!
IF I WANT TO BELIEVE IN PENIS-TENTACLED ALIENS, THEN LET ME BELIEVE IN PENIS-TENTACLED ALIENS.
EW. ALIENS MADE PEOPLE PREGNANT?
NEVER FEAR, CHARLOTTE. MASON'S NOT AN ALIEN.
HE'S JUST A STEROIDAL PRIMATE WHO STEALS PEOPLE'S WHEELCHAIRS, SCREWS UP THE BRAKES, AND RETURNS THEM WITH A CRAP ON THE SEAT.
TOLD YOU, GINA: WASN'T MY TURD.
GROW UP. I'M NOT IN THE MOOD.

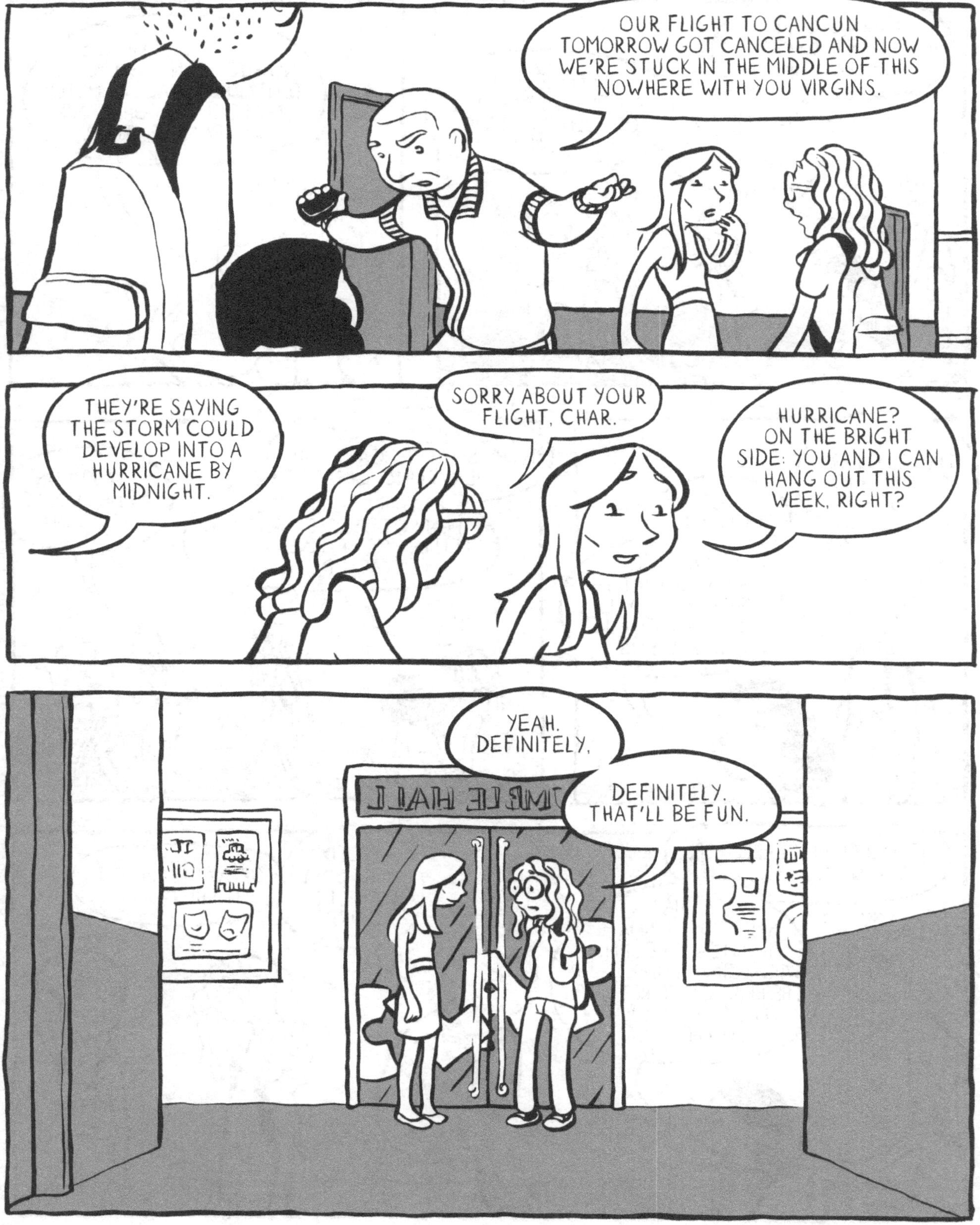
OUR FLIGHT TO CANCUN TOMORROW GOT CANCELED AND NOW WE'RE STUCK IN THE MIDDLE OF THIS NOWHERE WITH YOU VIRGINS.
THEY'RE SAYING THE STORM COULD DEVELOP INTO A HURRICANE BY MIDNIGHT.
SORRY ABOUT YOUR FLIGHT, CHAR.
HURRICANE? ON THE BRIGHT SIDE: YOU AND I CAN HANG OUT THIS WEEK, RIGHT?
YEAH. DEFINITELY.
DEFINITELY. THAT'LL BE FUN.

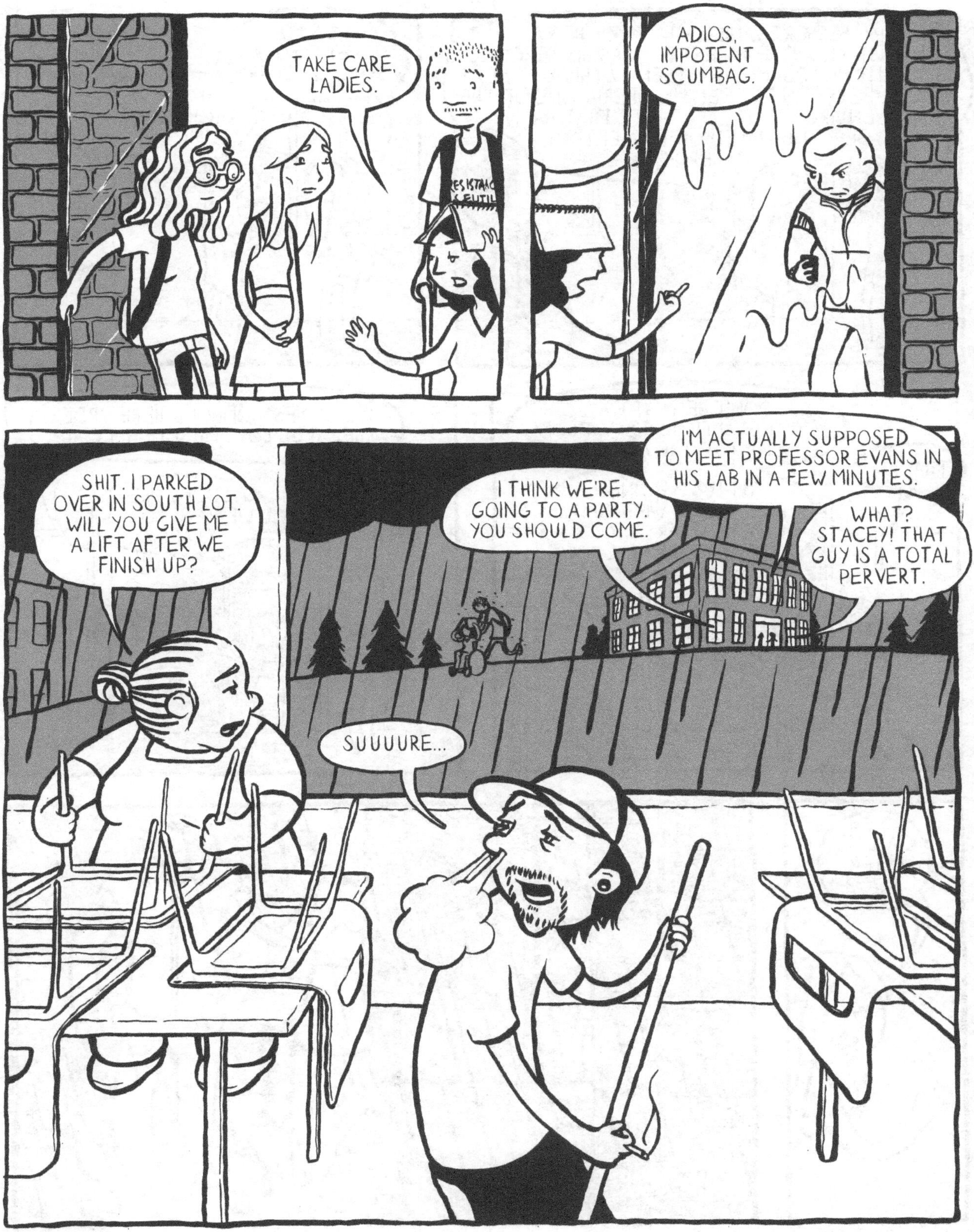
TAKE CARE, LADIES.
ADIOS, IMPOTENT SCUMBAG.
SHIT. I PARKED OVER IN SOUTH LOT. WILL YOU GIVE ME A LIFT AFTER WE FINISH UP?
I THINK WE'RE GOING TO A PARTY. YOU SHOULD COME.
I'M ACTUALLY SUPPOSED TO MEET PROFESSOR EVANS IN HIS LAB IN A FEW MINUTES.
WHAT? STACEY! THAT GUY IS A TOTAL PERVERT.
SUUUURE...

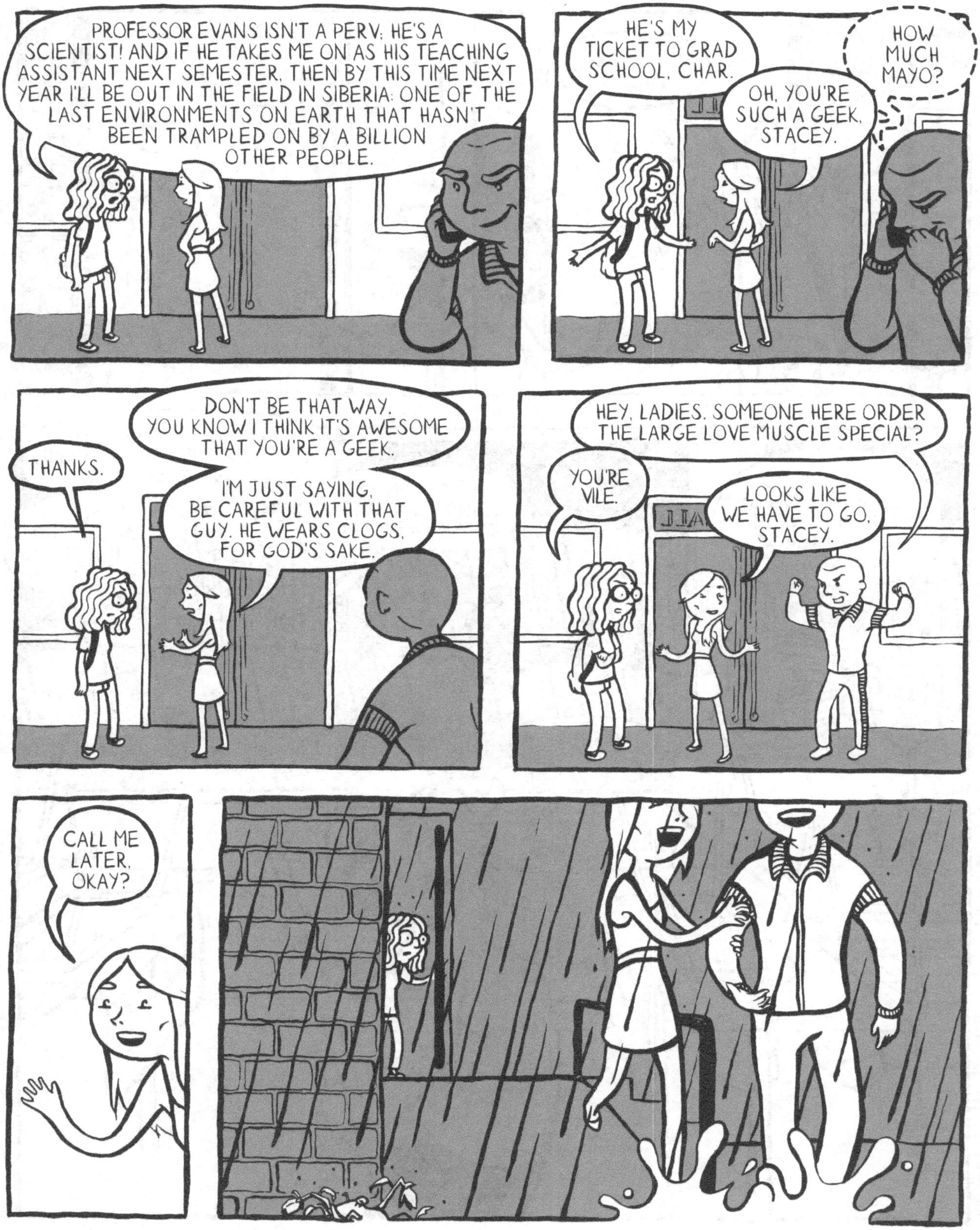
PROFESSOR EVANS ISN'T A PERV; HE'S A SCIENTIST! AND IF HE TAKES ME ON AS HIS TEACHING ASSISTANT NEXT SEMESTER, THEN BY THIS TIME NEXT YEAR I'LL BE OUT IN THE FIELD IN SIBERIA: ONE OF THE LAST ENVIRONMENTS ON EARTH THAT HASN'T BEEN TRAMPLED ON BY A BILLION OTHER PEOPLE.
HE'S MY TICKET TO GRAD SCHOOL, CHAR.
OH, YOU'RE SUCH A GEEK, STACEY.
HOW MUCH MAYO?
THANKS.
DON'T BE THAT WAY. YOU KNOW I THINK IT'S AWESOME THAT YOU'RE A GEEK.
I'M JUST SAYING, BE CAREFUL WITH THAT GUY. HE WEARS CLOGS, FOR GOD'S SAKE.
HEY, LADIES. SOMEONE HERE ORDER THE LARGE LOVE MUSCLE SPECIAL?
YOU'RE VILE.
LOOKS LIKE WE HAVE TO GO, STACEY.
CALL ME LATER, OKAY?

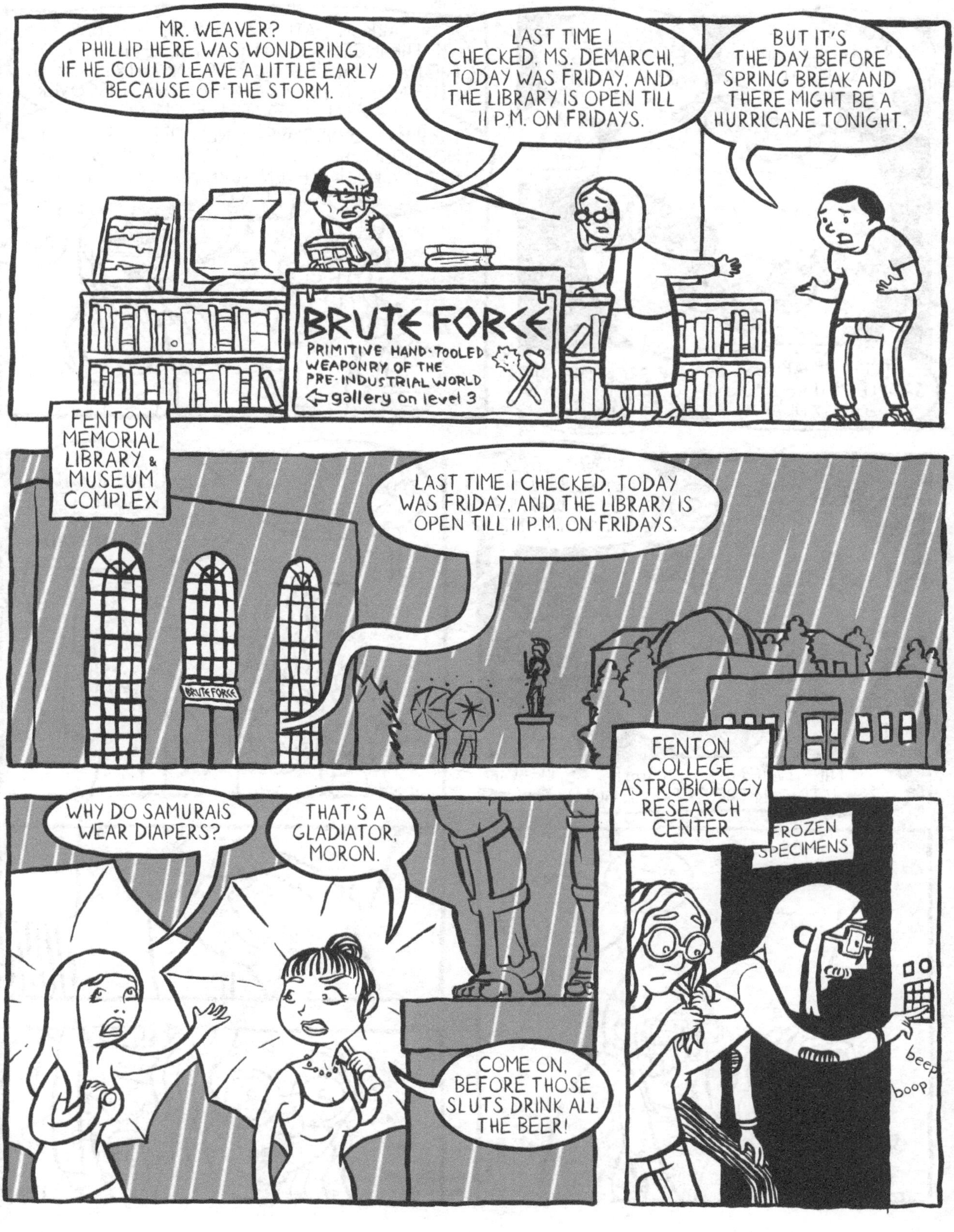
MR. WEAVER? PHILLIP HERE WAS WONDERING IF HE COULD LEAVE A LITTLE EARLY BECAUSE OF THE STORM.
LAST TIME I CHECKED, MS. DEMARCHI, TODAY WAS FRIDAY, AND THE LIBRARY IS OPEN TILL 11 P.M. ON FRIDAYS.
BUT IT'S THE DAY BEFORE SPRING BREAK AND THERE MIGHT BE A HURRICANE TONIGHT.
BRUTE FORCE
PRIMITIVE HAND-TOOLED WEAPONRY OF THE PRE-INDUSTRIAL WORLD
gallery on level 3
FENTON MEMORIAL LIBRARY & MUSEUM COMPLEX
LAST TIME I CHECKED, TODAY WAS FRIDAY, AND THE LIBRARY IS OPEN TILL 11 P.M. ON FRIDAYS.
BRUTE FORCE
FENTON COLLEGE ASTROBIOLOGY RESEARCH CENTER
WHY DO SAMURAIS WEAR DIAPERS?
THAT'S A GLADIATOR, MORON.
COME ON, BEFORE THOSE SLUTS DRINK ALL THE BEER!
FROZEN SPECIMENS
beep
boop

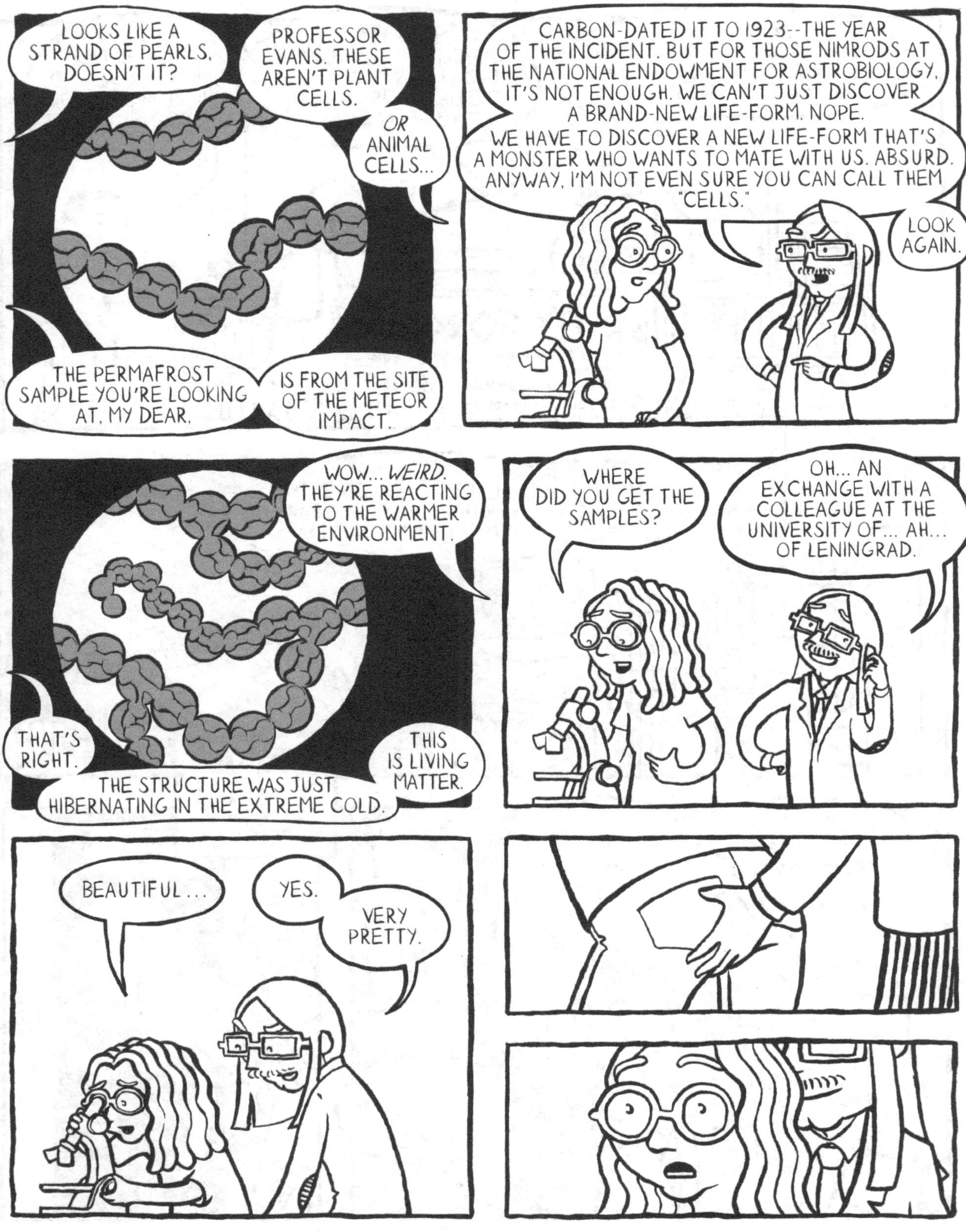
LOOKS LIKE A STRAND OF PEARLS, DOESN'T IT?
PROFESSOR EVANS. THESE AREN'T PLANT CELLS.
OR ANIMAL CELLS...
THE PERMAFROST SAMPLE YOU'RE LOOKING AT, MY DEAR,
IS FROM THE SITE OF THE METEOR IMPACT.
CARBON-DATED IT TO 1923--THE YEAR OF THE INCIDENT. BUT FOR THOSE NIMRODS AT THE NATIONAL ENDOWMENT FOR ASTROBIOLOGY, IT'S NOT ENOUGH. WE CAN'T JUST DISCOVER A BRAND-NEW LIFE-FORM. NOPE.
WE HAVE TO DISCOVER A NEW LIFE-FORM THAT'S A MONSTER WHO WANTS TO MATE WITH US. ABSURD. ANYWAY, I'M NOT EVEN SURE YOU CAN CALL THEM "CELLS."
LOOK AGAIN.
WOW... *WEIRD.* THEY'RE REACTING TO THE WARMER ENVIRONMENT.
THAT'S RIGHT.
THE STRUCTURE WAS JUST HIBERNATING IN THE EXTREME COLD.
THIS IS LIVING MATTER.
WHERE DID YOU GET THE SAMPLES?
OH... AN EXCHANGE WITH A COLLEAGUE AT THE UNIVERSITY OF... AH... OF LENINGRAD.
BEAUTIFUL...
YES.
VERY PRETTY.

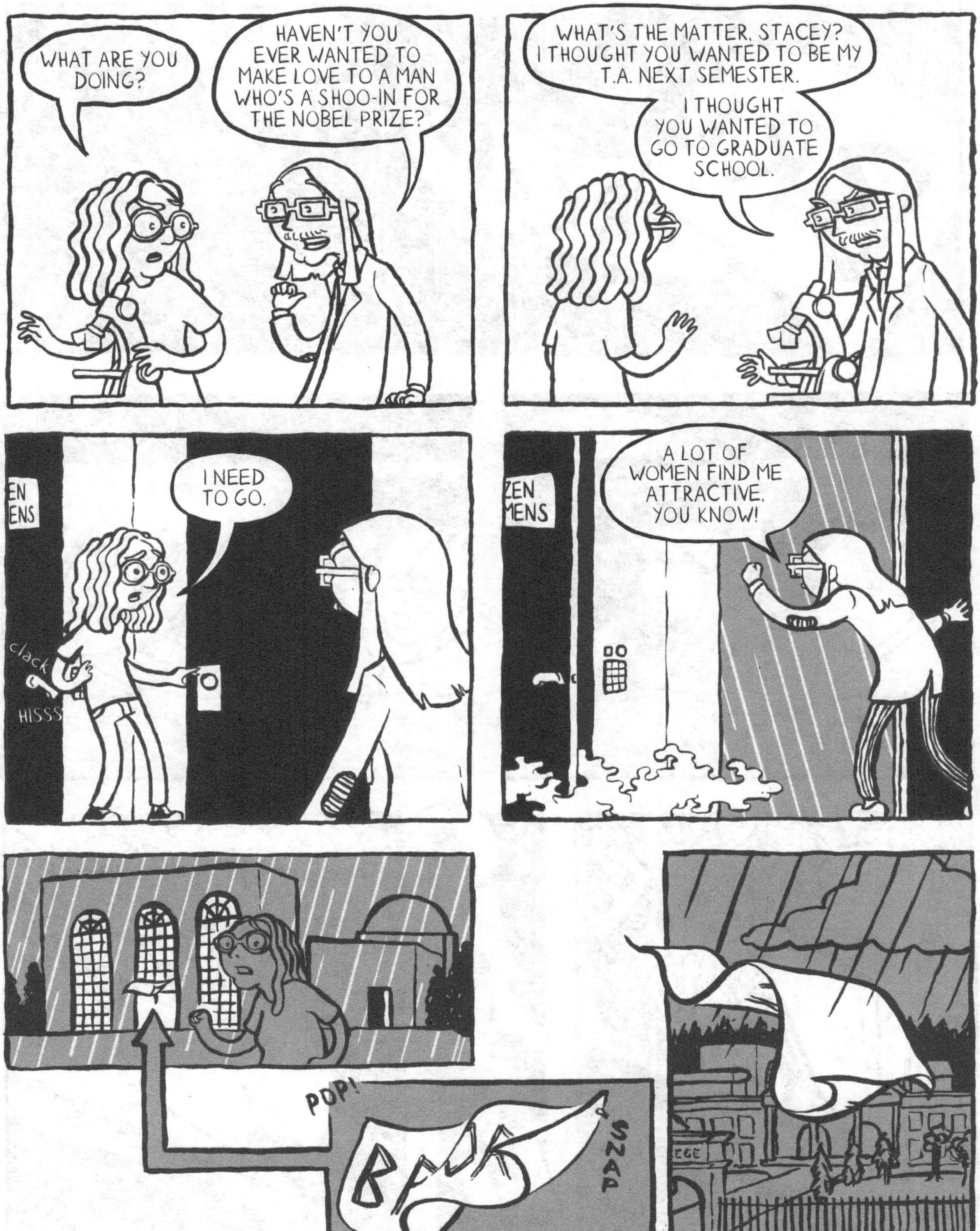
WHAT ARE YOU DOING?
HAVEN'T YOU EVER WANTED TO MAKE LOVE TO A MAN WHO'S A SHOO-IN FOR THE NOBEL PRIZE?
WHAT'S THE MATTER, STACEY? I THOUGHT YOU WANTED TO BE MY T.A. NEXT SEMESTER.
I THOUGHT YOU WANTED TO GO TO GRADUATE SCHOOL.
I NEED TO GO.
clack
HISSS
A LOT OF WOMEN FIND ME ATTRACTIVE, YOU KNOW!
POP!
SNAP

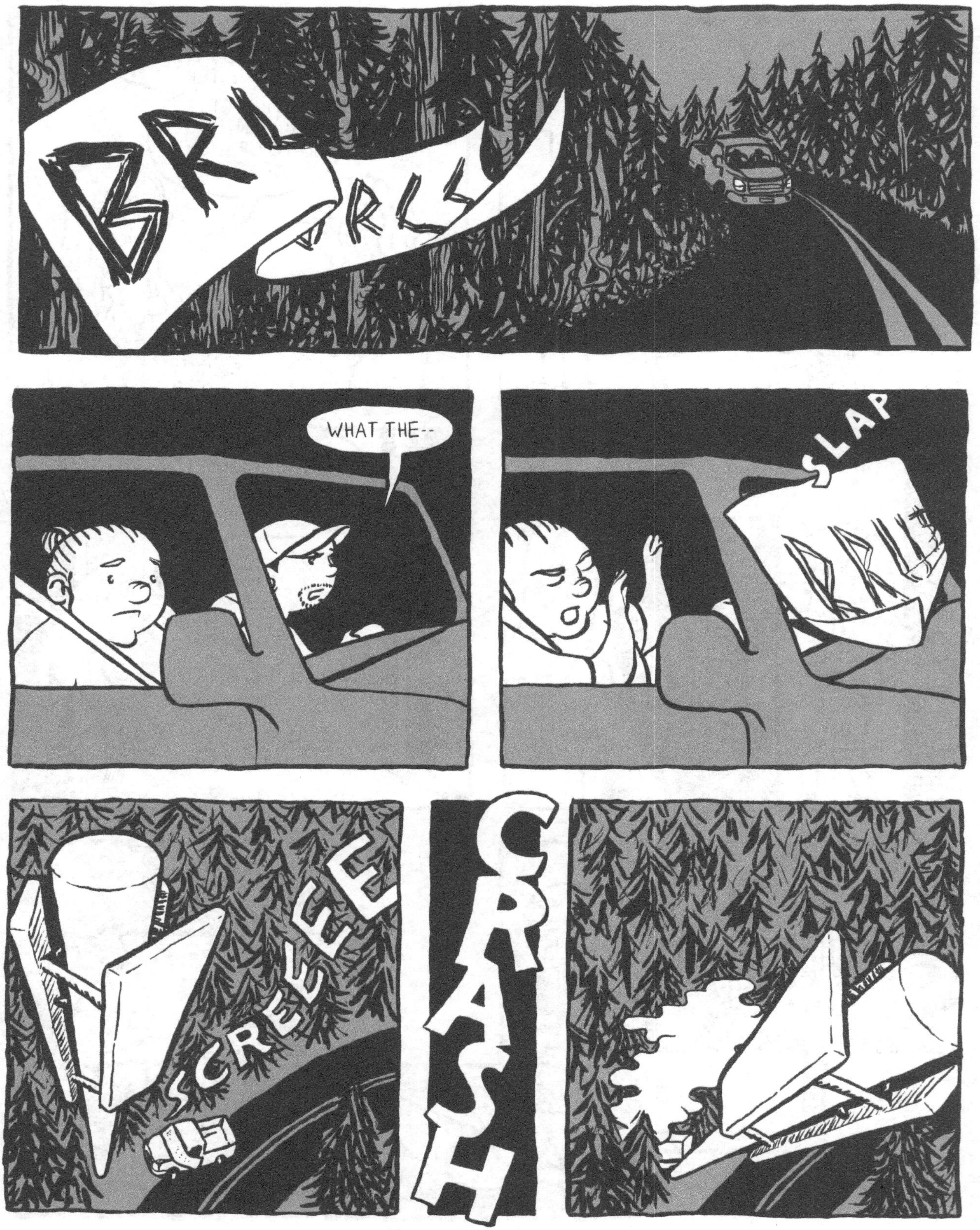
WHAT THE--
SLAP
CRASH

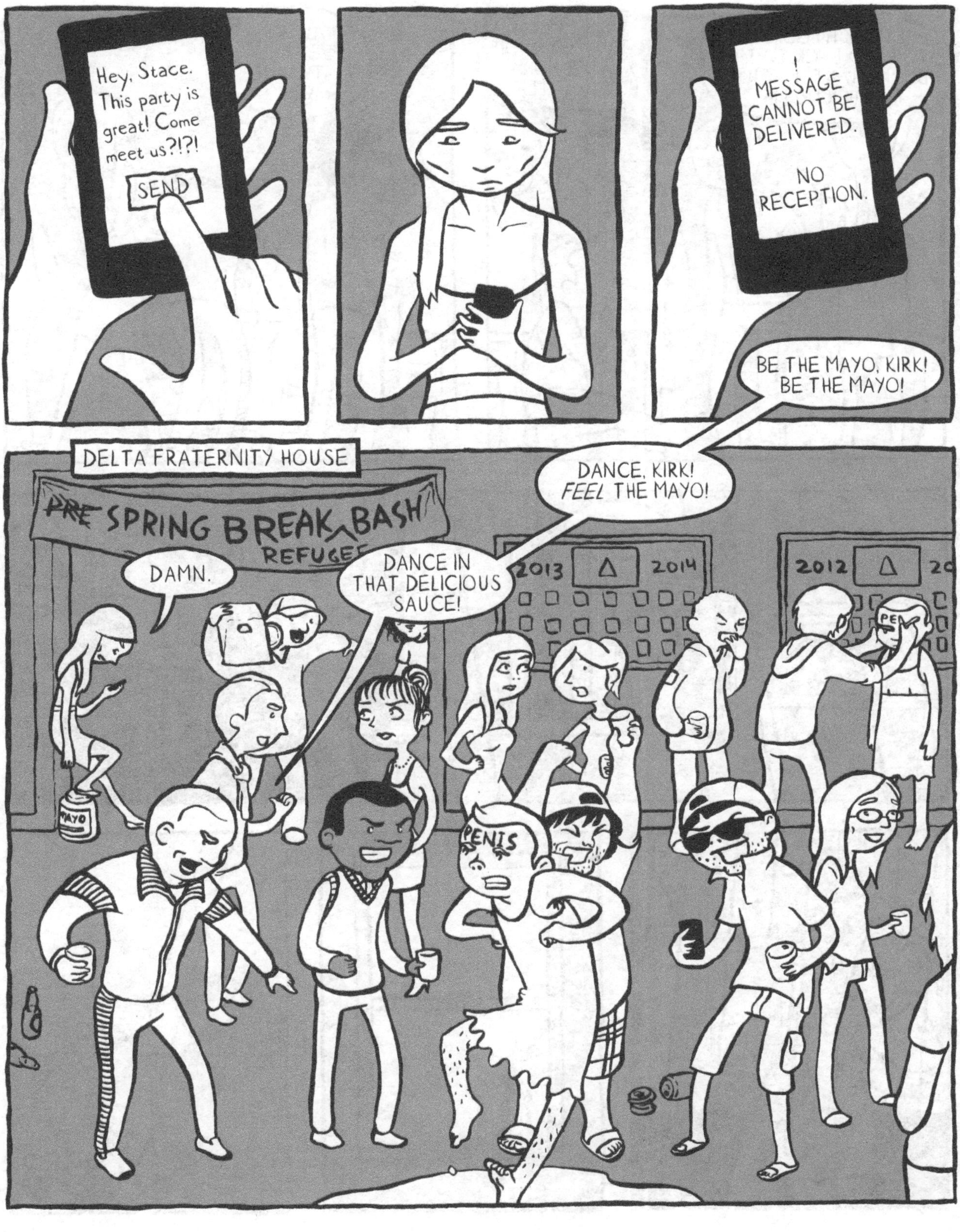
Hey, Stace. This party is great! Come meet us?!?!
SEND
!
MESSAGE CANNOT BE DELIVERED.
NO RECEPTION.
DELTA FRATERNITY HOUSE
~~PRE~~ SPRING BREAK BASH
REFUGE
DAMN.
DANCE IN THAT DELICIOUS SAUCE!
DANCE, KIRK! *FEEL* THE MAYO!
BE THE MAYO, KIRK! BE THE MAYO!
2013 Δ 2014
2012 Δ
MAYO
PENIS

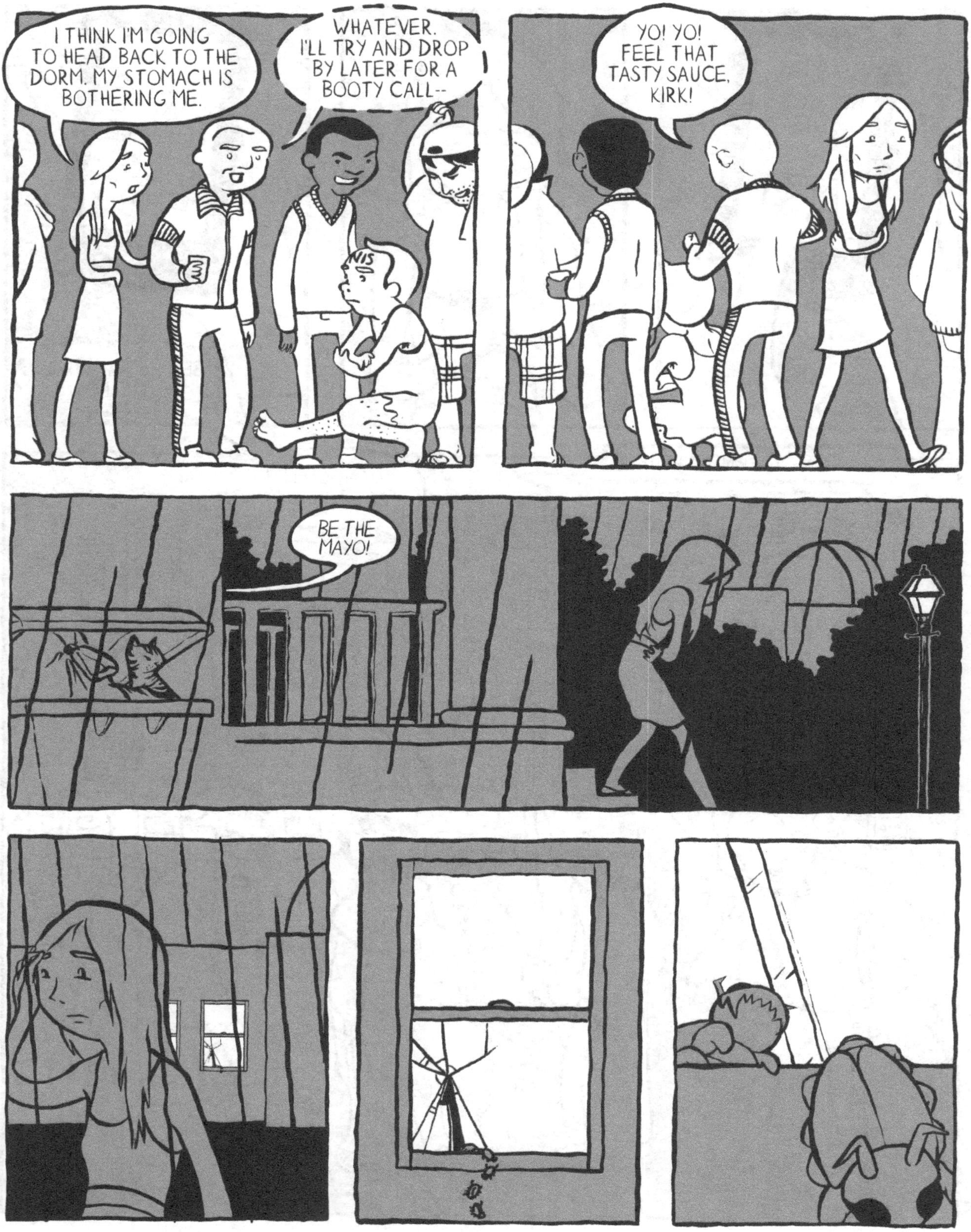
I THINK I'M GOING TO HEAD BACK TO THE DORM. MY STOMACH IS BOTHERING ME.
WHATEVER. I'LL TRY AND DROP BY LATER FOR A BOOTY CALL--
YO! YO! FEEL THAT TASTY SAUCE, KIRK!
BE THE MAYO!

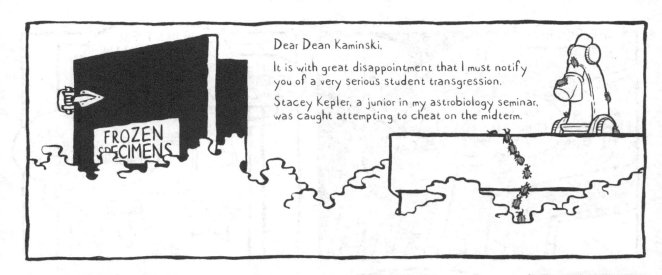

Dear Dean Kaminski,

It is with great disappointment that I must notify you of a very serious student transgression.

Stacey Kepler, a junior in my astrobiology seminar, was caught attempting to cheat on the midterm.

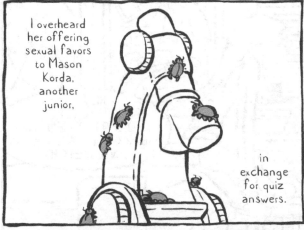

I overheard her offering sexual favors to Mason Korda, another junior,

in exchange for quiz answers.

RESIDENT PROFESSOR'S QUARTERS, HENSLEY HALL

Moreover,

it was clear that this was not the first time they had made such an arrangement.

My recommendation is for immediate expulsion of this despicable whore.

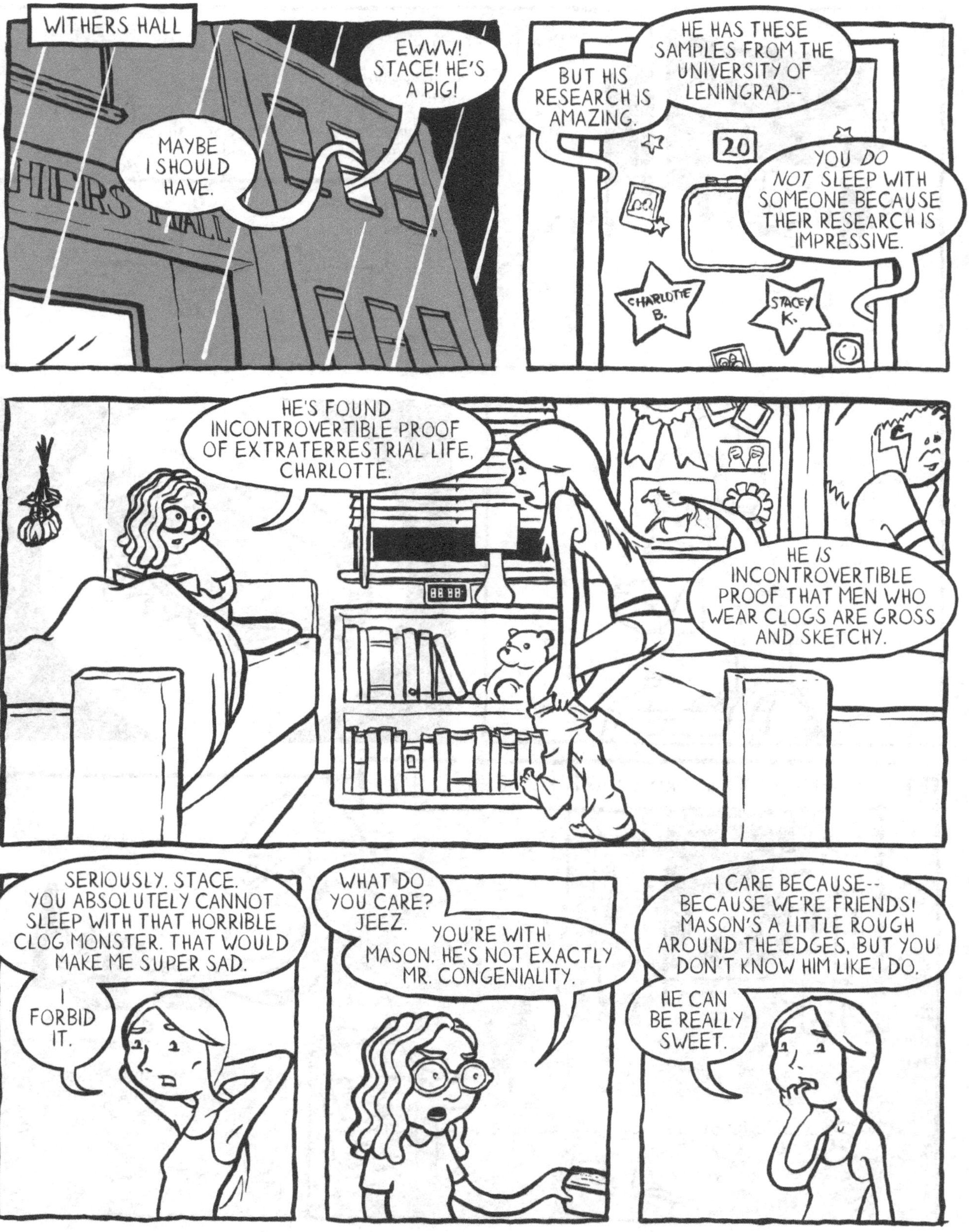
WITHERS HALL
MAYBE I SHOULD HAVE.
EWWW! STACE! HE'S A PIG!
BUT HIS RESEARCH IS AMAZING.
HE HAS THESE SAMPLES FROM THE UNIVERSITY OF LENINGRAD--
YOU *DO NOT* SLEEP WITH SOMEONE BECAUSE THEIR RESEARCH IS IMPRESSIVE.
20
CHARLOTTE B.
STACEY K.
HE'S FOUND INCONTROVERTIBLE PROOF OF EXTRATERRESTRIAL LIFE, CHARLOTTE.
HE *IS* INCONTROVERTIBLE PROOF THAT MEN WHO WEAR CLOGS ARE GROSS AND SKETCHY.
SERIOUSLY. STACE. YOU ABSOLUTELY CANNOT SLEEP WITH THAT HORRIBLE CLOG MONSTER. THAT WOULD MAKE ME SUPER SAD.
I FORBID IT.
WHAT DO YOU CARE? JEEZ.
YOU'RE WITH MASON. HE'S NOT EXACTLY MR. CONGENIALITY.
I CARE BECAUSE-- BECAUSE WE'RE FRIENDS! MASON'S A LITTLE ROUGH AROUND THE EDGES, BUT YOU DON'T KNOW HIM LIKE I DO.
HE CAN BE REALLY SWEET.

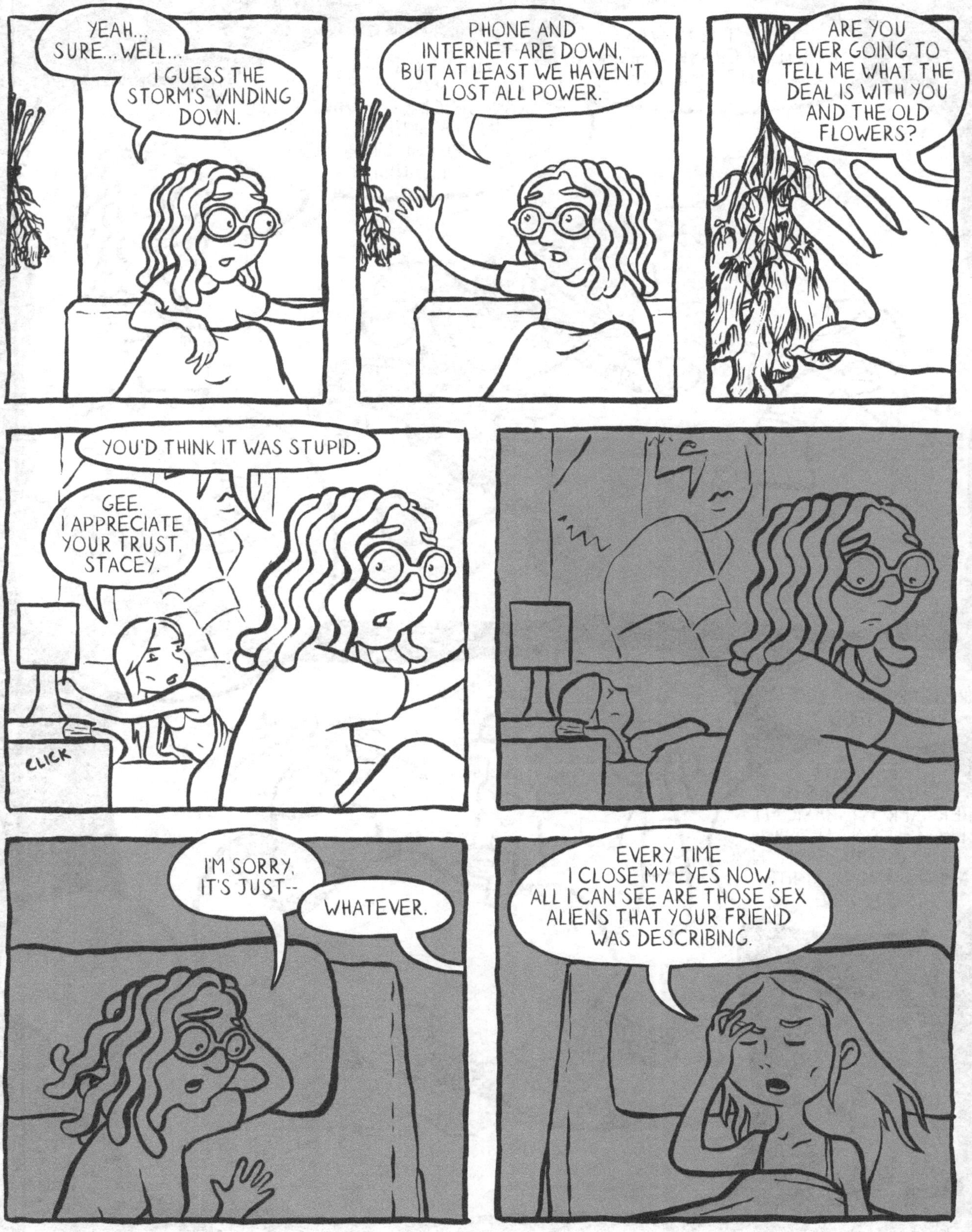
YEAH... SURE... WELL...
I GUESS THE STORM'S WINDING DOWN.
PHONE AND INTERNET ARE DOWN, BUT AT LEAST WE HAVEN'T LOST ALL POWER.
ARE YOU EVER GOING TO TELL ME WHAT THE DEAL IS WITH YOU AND THE OLD FLOWERS?
YOU'D THINK IT WAS STUPID.
GEE. I APPRECIATE YOUR TRUST, STACEY.
CLICK
I'M SORRY, IT'S JUST--
WHATEVER.
EVERY TIME I CLOSE MY EYES NOW, ALL I CAN SEE ARE THOSE SEX ALIENS THAT YOUR FRIEND WAS DESCRIBING.

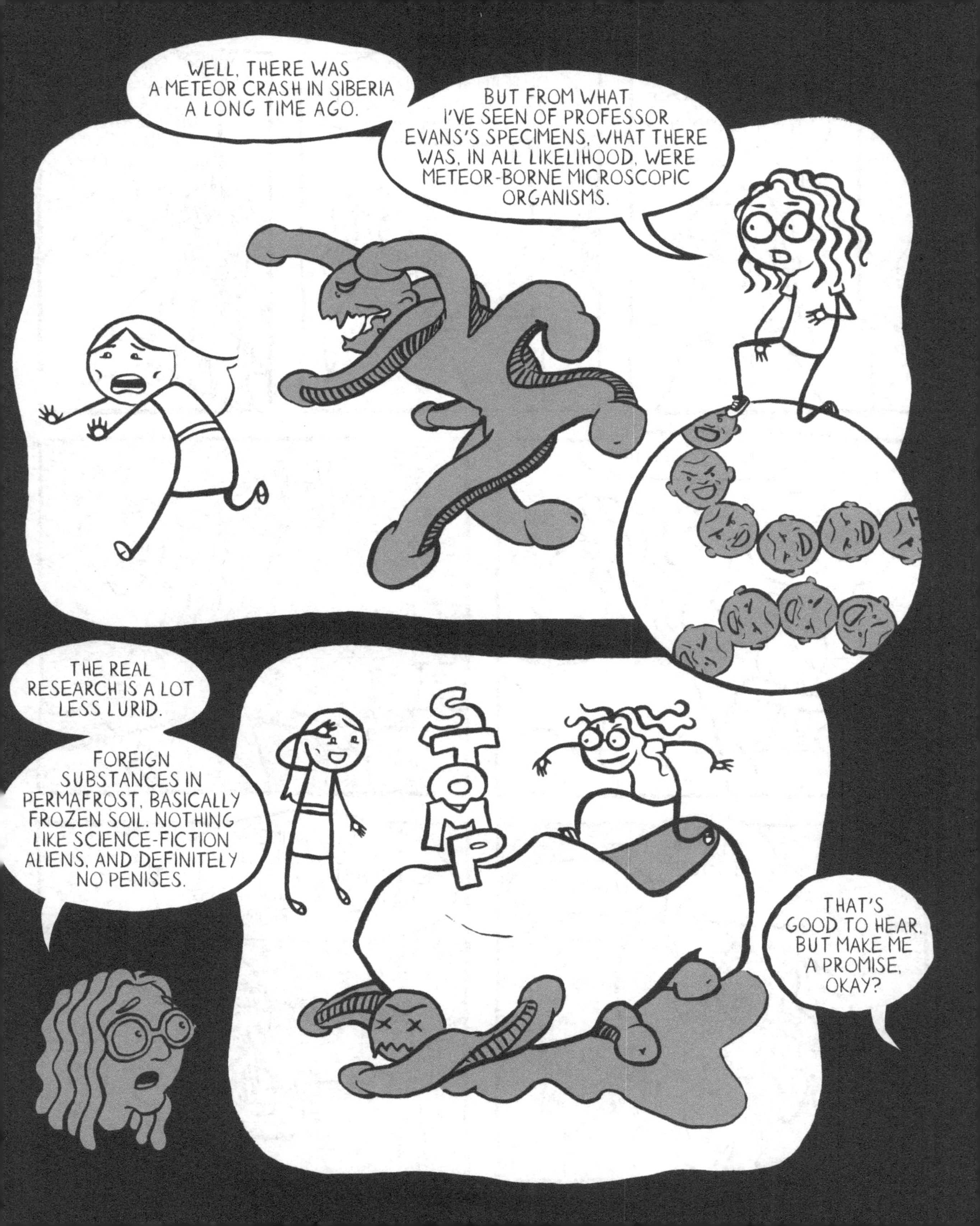
WELL, THERE WAS A METEOR CRASH IN SIBERIA A LONG TIME AGO.
BUT FROM WHAT I'VE SEEN OF PROFESSOR EVANS'S SPECIMENS, WHAT THERE WAS, IN ALL LIKELIHOOD, WERE METEOR-BORNE MICROSCOPIC ORGANISMS.
THE REAL RESEARCH IS A LOT LESS LURID.
FOREIGN SUBSTANCES IN PERMAFROST, BASICALLY FROZEN SOIL. NOTHING LIKE SCIENCE-FICTION ALIENS, AND DEFINITELY NO PENISES.
STOMP
THAT'S GOOD TO HEAR, BUT MAKE ME A PROMISE, OKAY?

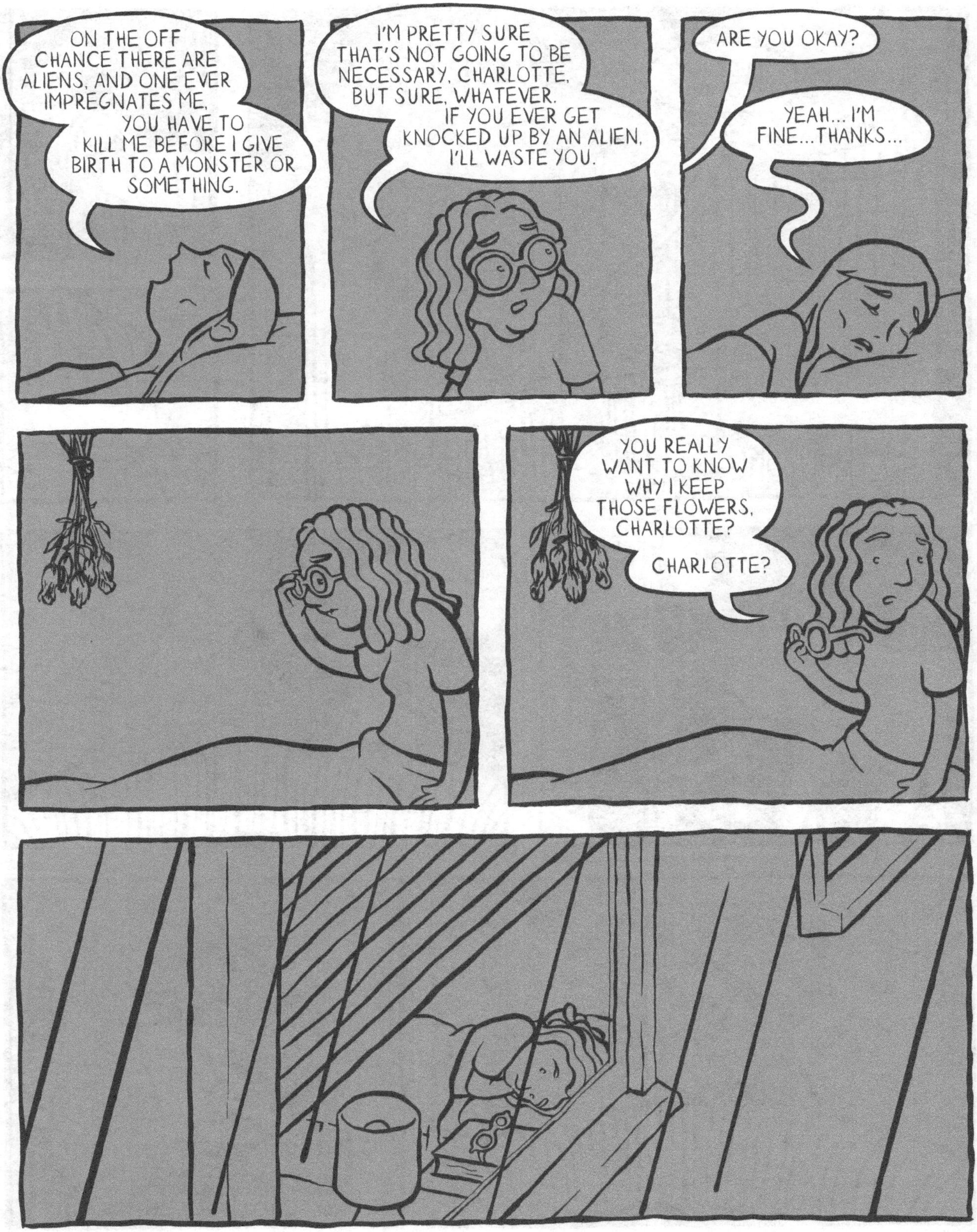
ON THE OFF CHANCE THERE ARE ALIENS, AND ONE EVER IMPREGNATES ME, YOU HAVE TO KILL ME BEFORE I GIVE BIRTH TO A MONSTER OR SOMETHING.
I'M PRETTY SURE THAT'S NOT GOING TO BE NECESSARY, CHARLOTTE, BUT SURE, WHATEVER. IF YOU EVER GET KNOCKED UP BY AN ALIEN, I'LL WASTE YOU.
ARE YOU OKAY?
YEAH... I'M FINE... THANKS...
YOU REALLY WANT TO KNOW WHY I KEEP THOSE FLOWERS, CHARLOTTE?
CHARLOTTE?

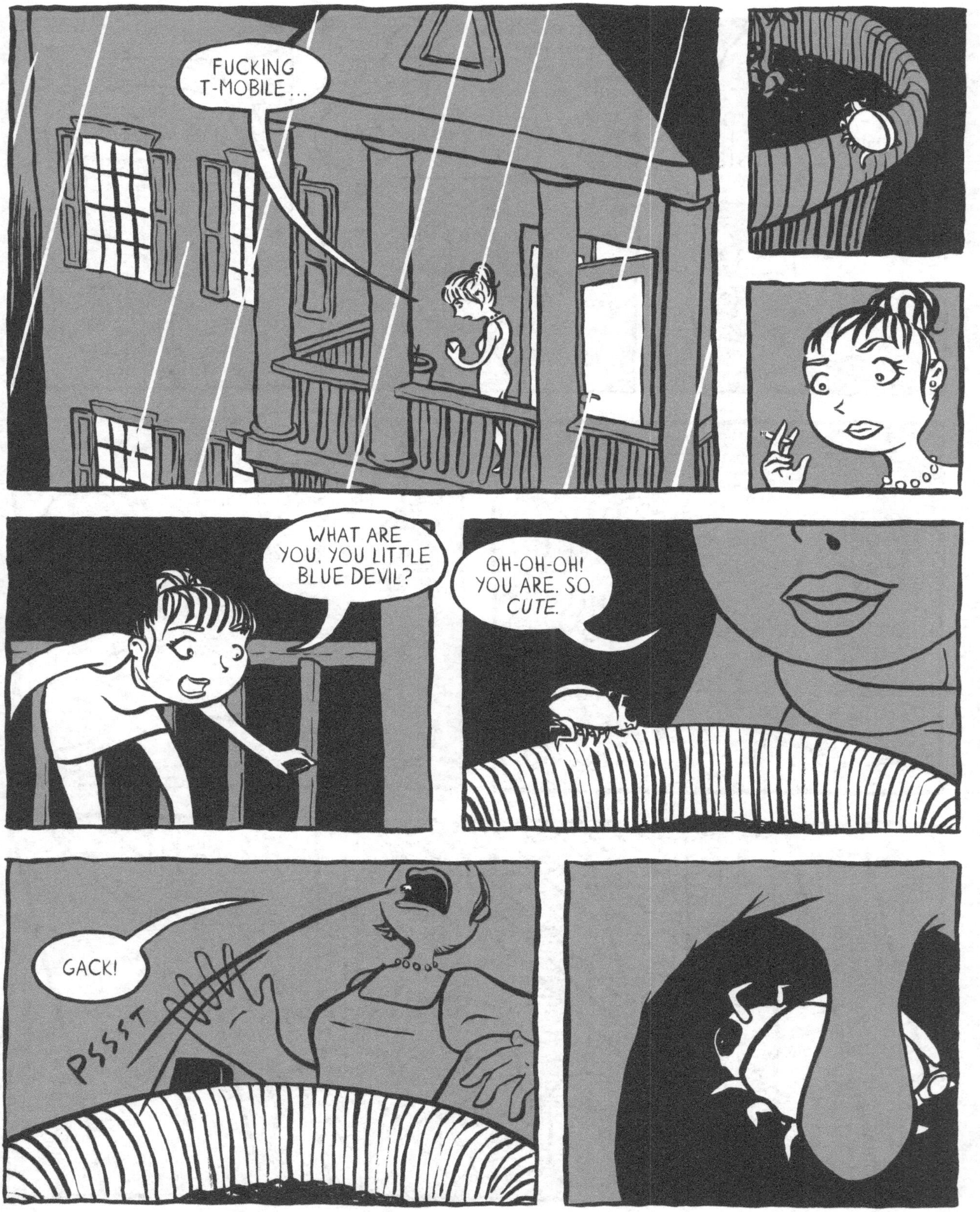
FUCKING T-MOBILE...
WHAT ARE YOU, YOU LITTLE BLUE DEVIL?
OH-OH-OH! YOU ARE. SO. *CUTE*.
GACK!
PSSST

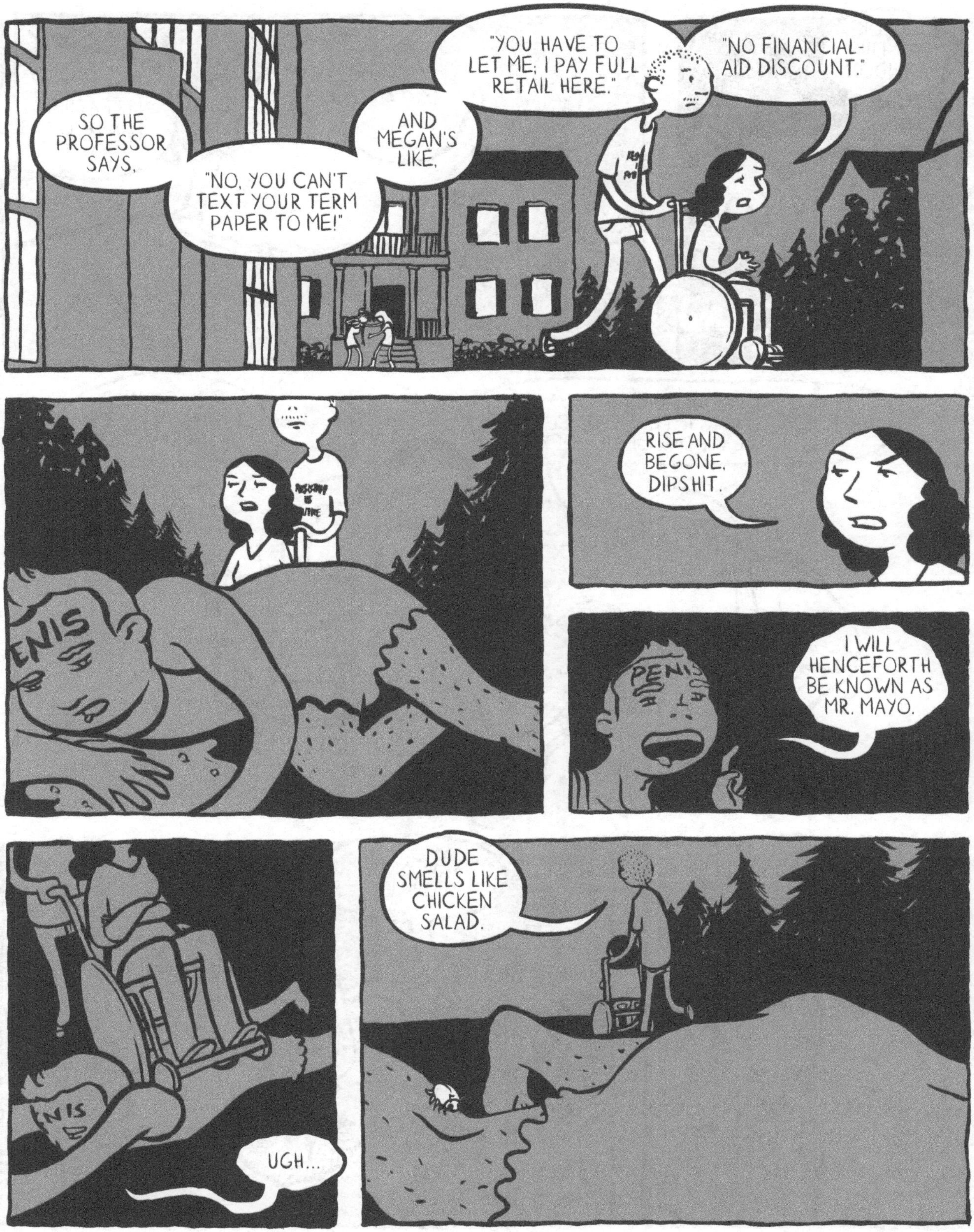
SO THE PROFESSOR SAYS,
"NO, YOU CAN'T TEXT YOUR TERM PAPER TO ME!"
AND MEGAN'S LIKE,
"YOU HAVE TO LET ME; I PAY FULL RETAIL HERE."
"NO FINANCIAL-AID DISCOUNT."
RISE AND BEGONE, DIPSHIT.
I WILL HENCEFORTH BE KNOWN AS MR. MAYO.
UGH...
DUDE SMELLS LIKE CHICKEN SALAD.

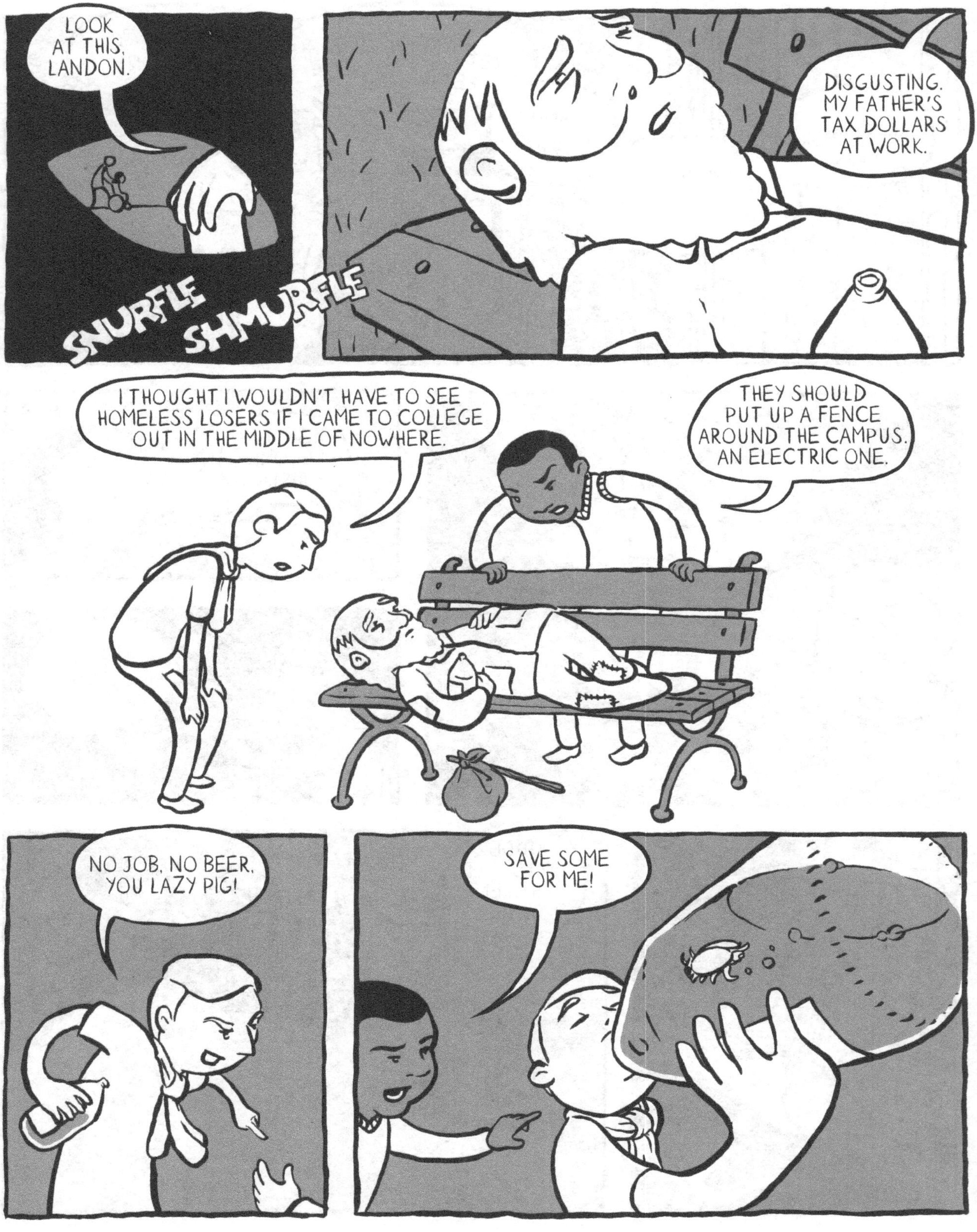
LOOK AT THIS, LANDON.
SNURFLE SHMURFLE
DISGUSTING. MY FATHER'S TAX DOLLARS AT WORK.
I THOUGHT I WOULDN'T HAVE TO SEE HOMELESS LOSERS IF I CAME TO COLLEGE OUT IN THE MIDDLE OF NOWHERE.
THEY SHOULD PUT UP A FENCE AROUND THE CAMPUS. AN ELECTRIC ONE.
NO JOB, NO BEER, YOU LAZY PIG!
SAVE SOME FOR ME!

FENTON MEMORIAL LIBRARY

THE DEEP STACKS

WHO'S THERE? LIBRARY CLOSES AT 11 P.M. ON FRIDAYS. I WARNED YOU KIDS ABOUT FOOLING AROUND IN THE STACKS.

THIS IS A SANCTUARY OF LEARNING, NOT A BORDELLO.

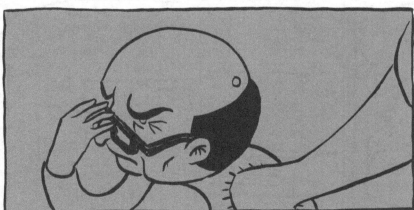

CLICK

AAAAAAAH!

SNAP

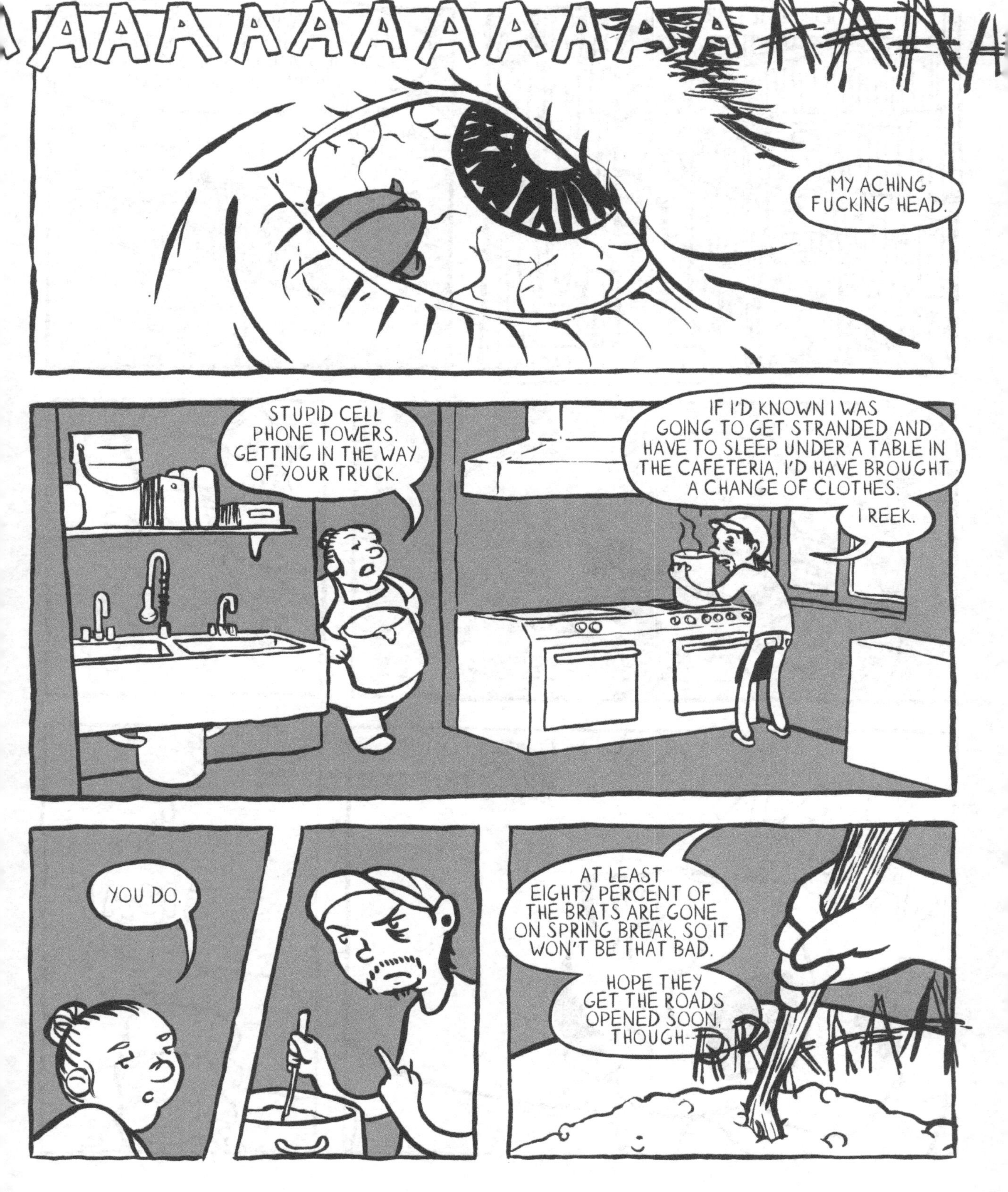
AAAAAAAAAAAAAAA
MY ACHING FUCKING HEAD.
STUPID CELL PHONE TOWERS. GETTING IN THE WAY OF YOUR TRUCK.
IF I'D KNOWN I WAS GOING TO GET STRANDED AND HAVE TO SLEEP UNDER A TABLE IN THE CAFETERIA, I'D HAVE BROUGHT A CHANGE OF CLOTHES.
I REEK.
YOU DO.
AT LEAST EIGHTY PERCENT OF THE BRATS ARE GONE ON SPRING BREAK, SO IT WON'T BE THAT BAD.
HOPE THEY GET THE ROADS OPENED SOON, THOUGH--
BRRAAAA

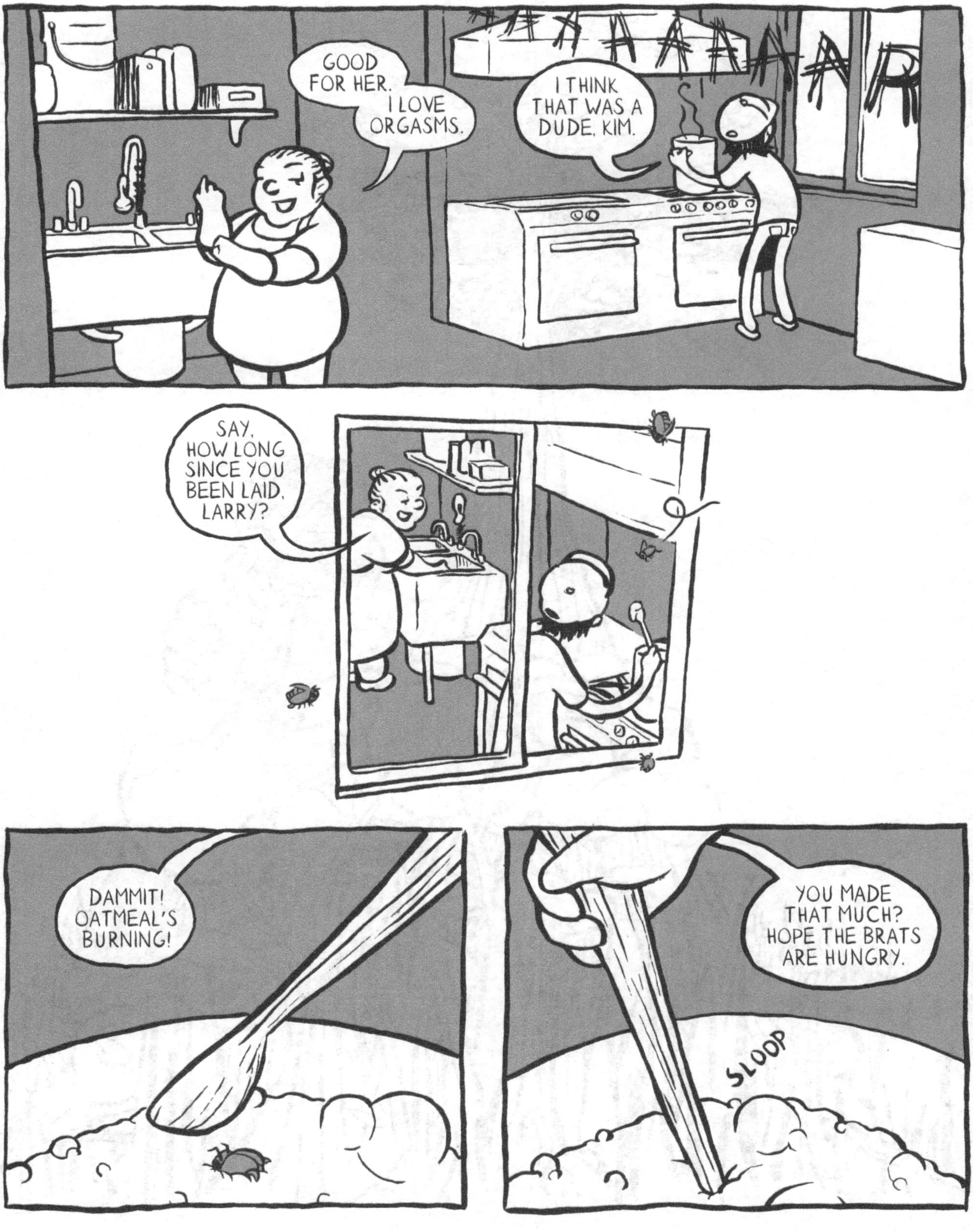

GOOD FOR HER. I LOVE ORGASMS.
I THINK THAT WAS A DUDE, KIM.
SAY, HOW LONG SINCE YOU BEEN LAID, LARRY?
DAMMIT! OATMEAL'S BURNING!
YOU MADE THAT MUCH? HOPE THE BRATS ARE HUNGRY.
SLOOP

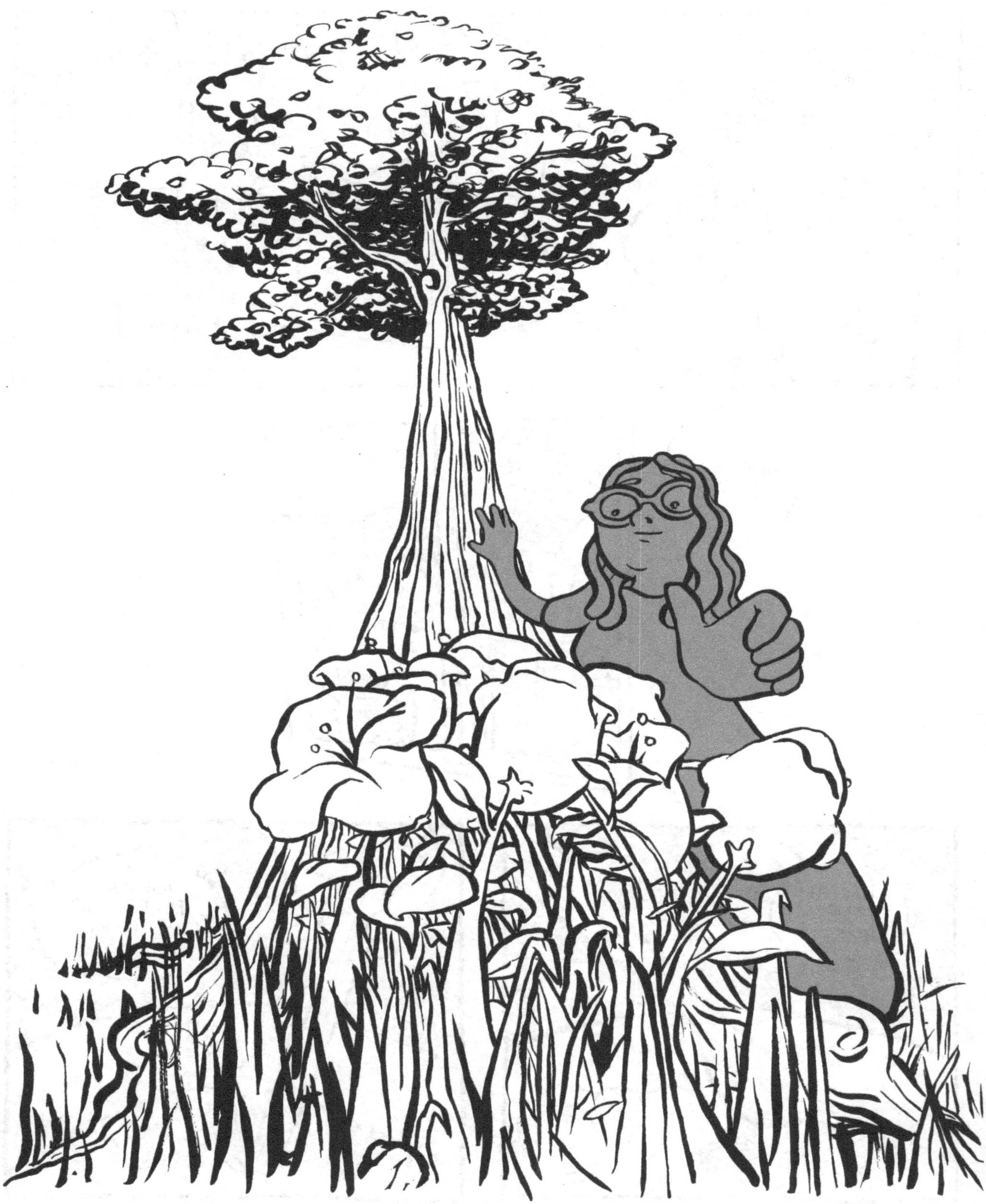

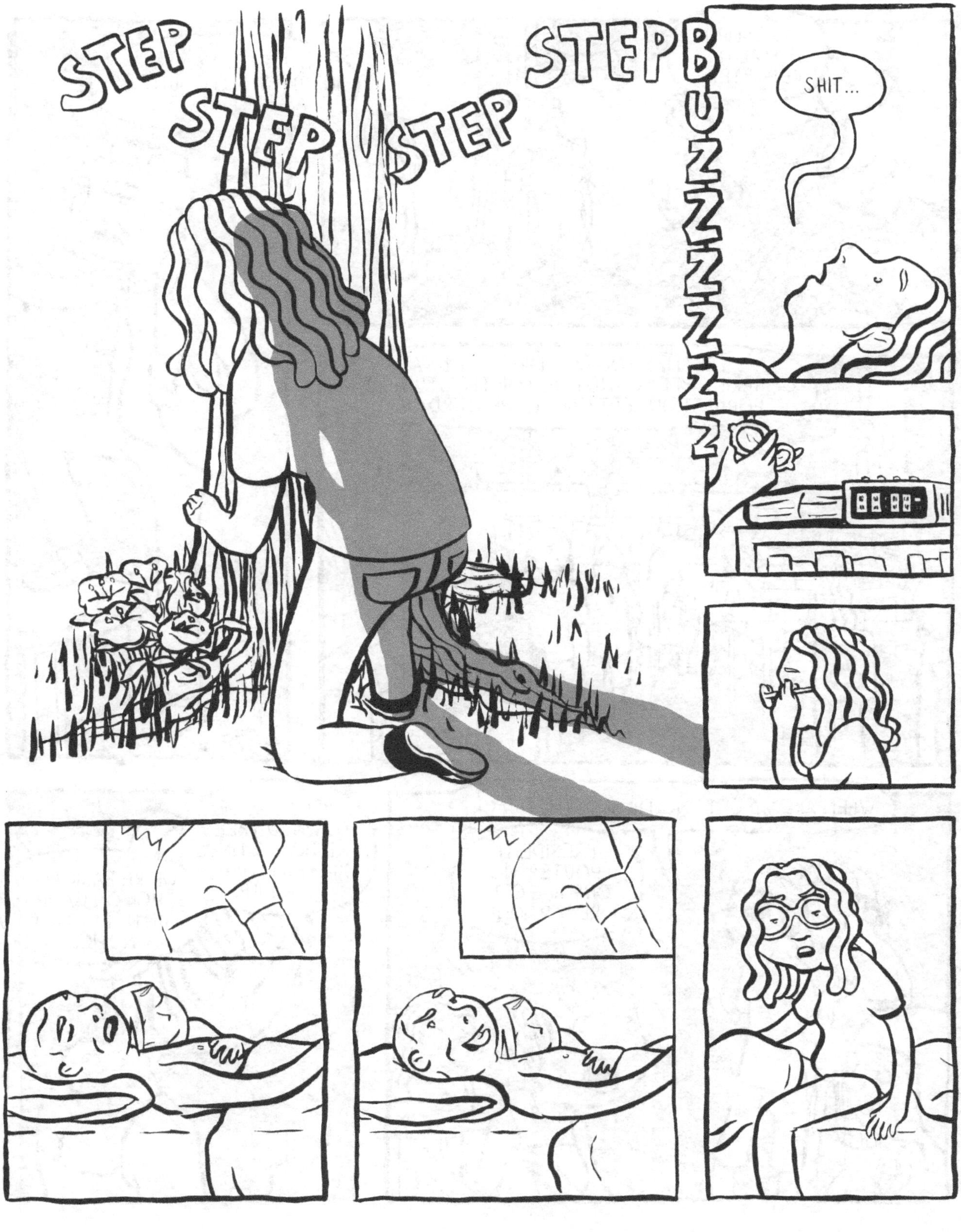
STEP
STEP
STEP
STEP
BUZZZZZZZ
SHIT...

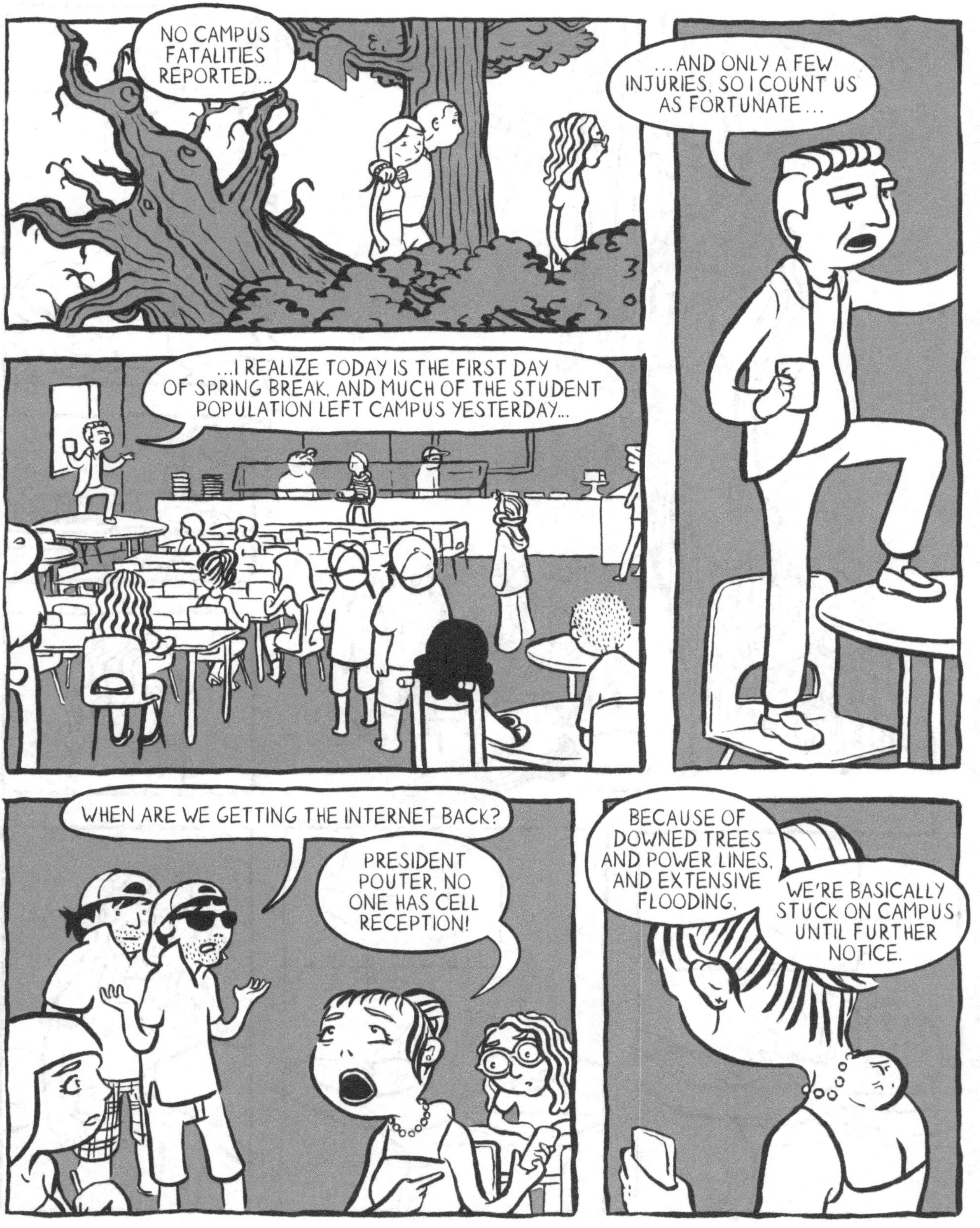
NO CAMPUS FATALITIES REPORTED...
...AND ONLY A FEW INJURIES, SO I COUNT US AS FORTUNATE...
...I REALIZE TODAY IS THE FIRST DAY OF SPRING BREAK, AND MUCH OF THE STUDENT POPULATION LEFT CAMPUS YESTERDAY...
WHEN ARE WE GETTING THE INTERNET BACK?
PRESIDENT POUTER, NO ONE HAS CELL RECEPTION!
BECAUSE OF DOWNED TREES AND POWER LINES, AND EXTENSIVE FLOODING,
WE'RE BASICALLY STUCK ON CAMPUS UNTIL FURTHER NOTICE.

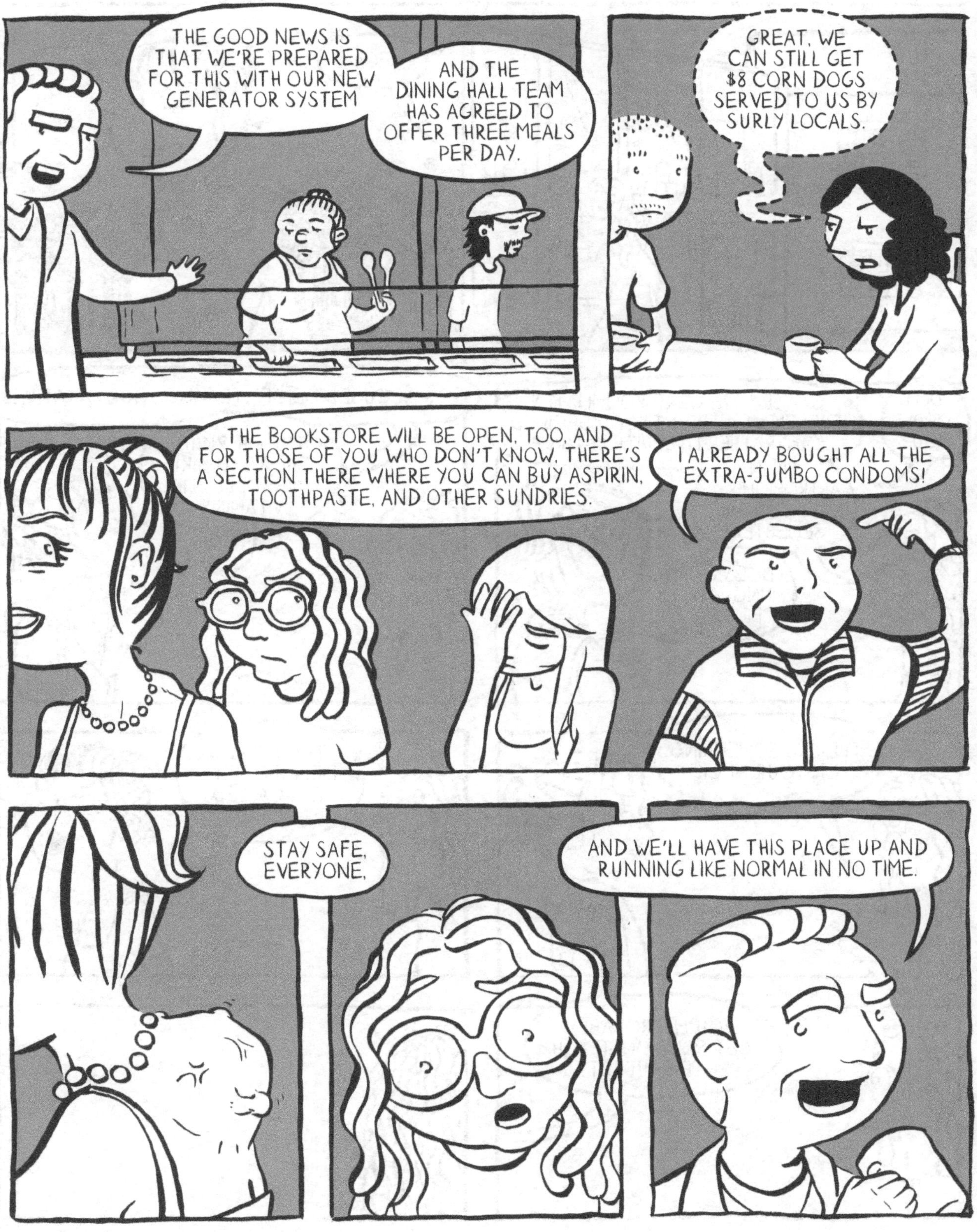
THE GOOD NEWS IS THAT WE'RE PREPARED FOR THIS WITH OUR NEW GENERATOR SYSTEM
AND THE DINING HALL TEAM HAS AGREED TO OFFER THREE MEALS PER DAY.
GREAT, WE CAN STILL GET $8 CORN DOGS SERVED TO US BY SURLY LOCALS.
THE BOOKSTORE WILL BE OPEN, TOO, AND FOR THOSE OF YOU WHO DON'T KNOW, THERE'S A SECTION THERE WHERE YOU CAN BUY ASPIRIN, TOOTHPASTE, AND OTHER SUNDRIES.
I ALREADY BOUGHT ALL THE EXTRA-JUMBO CONDOMS!
STAY SAFE, EVERYONE,
AND WE'LL HAVE THIS PLACE UP AND RUNNING LIKE NORMAL IN NO TIME.

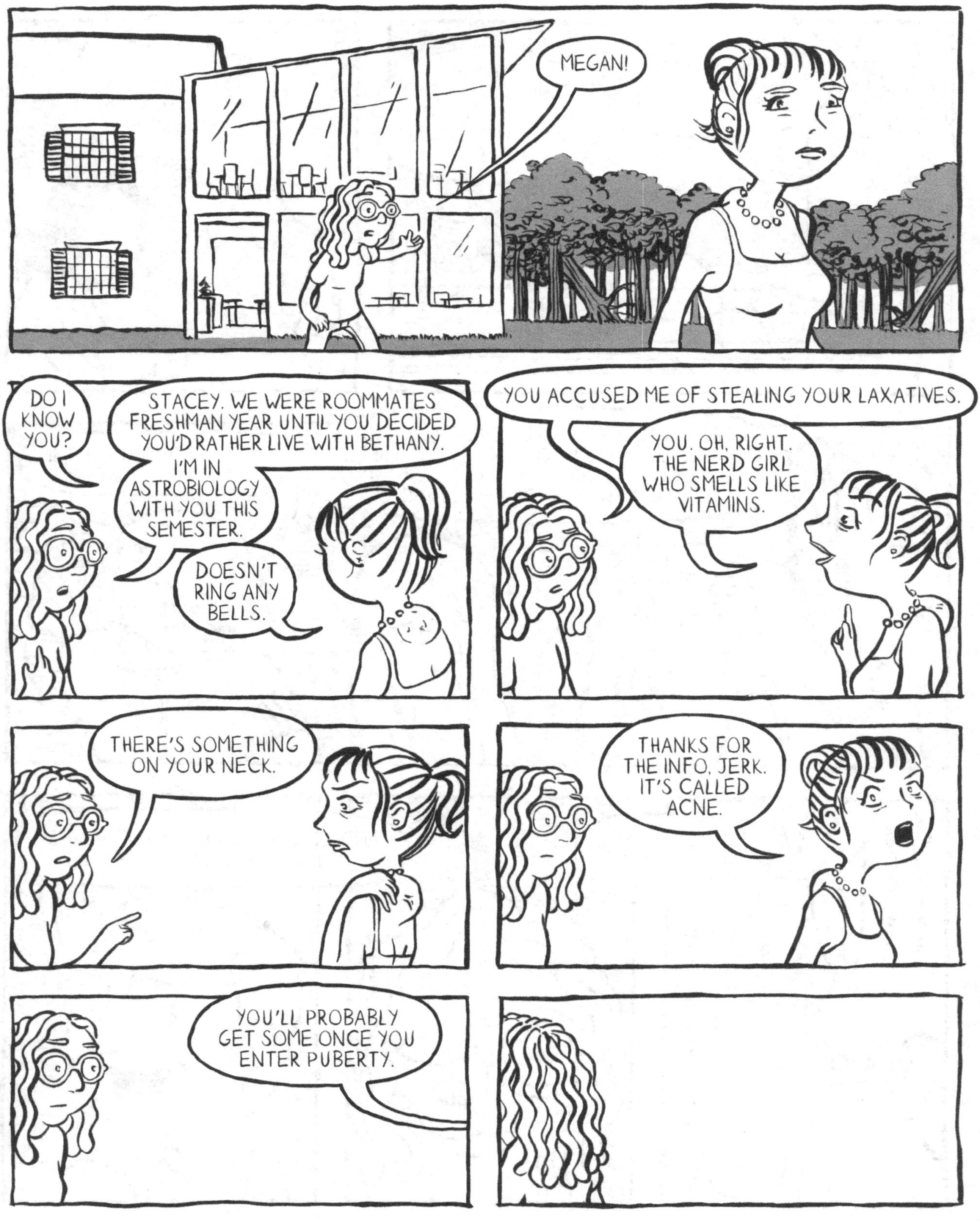
MEGAN!
DO I KNOW YOU?
STACEY. WE WERE ROOMMATES FRESHMAN YEAR UNTIL YOU DECIDED YOU'D RATHER LIVE WITH BETHANY.
I'M IN ASTROBIOLOGY WITH YOU THIS SEMESTER.
DOESN'T RING ANY BELLS.
YOU ACCUSED ME OF STEALING YOUR LAXATIVES.
YOU. OH, RIGHT. THE NERD GIRL WHO SMELLS LIKE VITAMINS.
THERE'S SOMETHING ON YOUR NECK.
THANKS FOR THE INFO, JERK. IT'S CALLED ACNE.
YOU'LL PROBABLY GET SOME ONCE YOU ENTER PUBERTY.

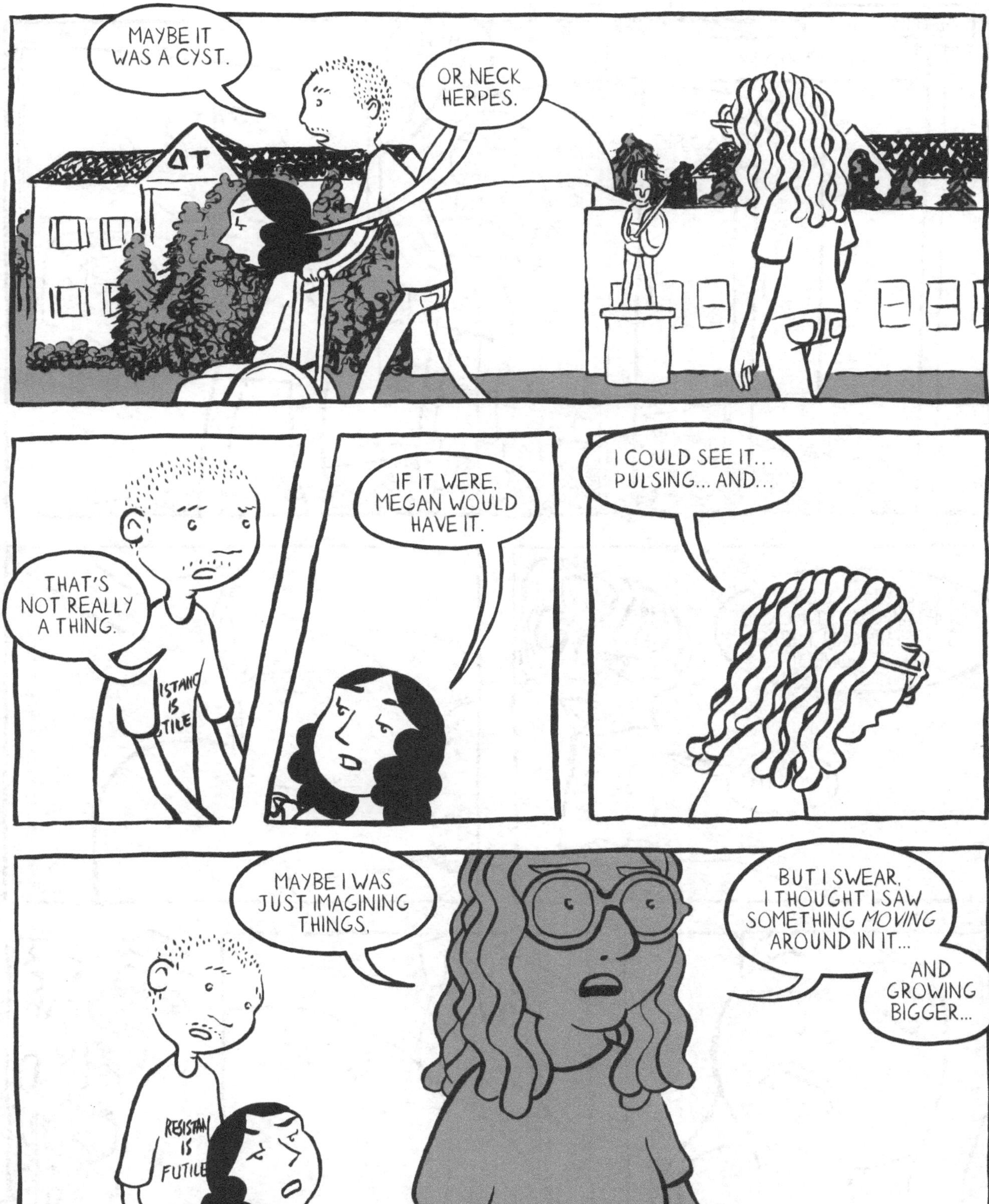
MAYBE IT WAS A CYST.
OR NECK HERPES.
ΔT
THAT'S NOT REALLY A THING.
IF IT WERE, MEGAN WOULD HAVE IT.
I COULD SEE IT... PULSING... AND...
MAYBE I WAS JUST IMAGINING THINGS,
BUT I SWEAR, I THOUGHT I SAW SOMETHING *MOVING* AROUND IN IT...
AND GROWING BIGGER...
RESISTAN IS FUTILE

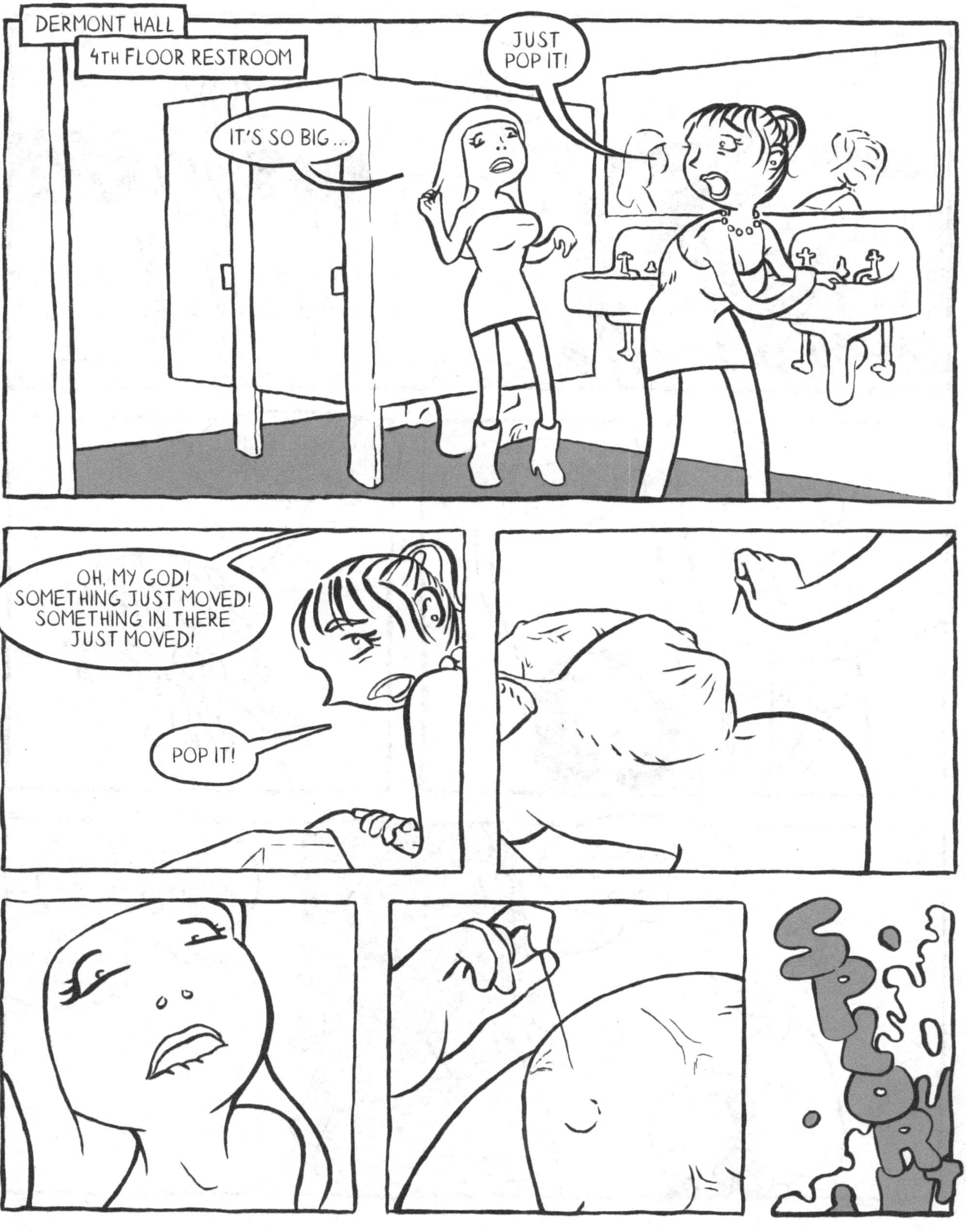

DERMONT HALL
4TH FLOOR RESTROOM
JUST POP IT!
IT'S SO BIG...
OH, MY GOD! SOMETHING JUST MOVED! SOMETHING IN THERE JUST MOVED!
POP IT!
SPLORT

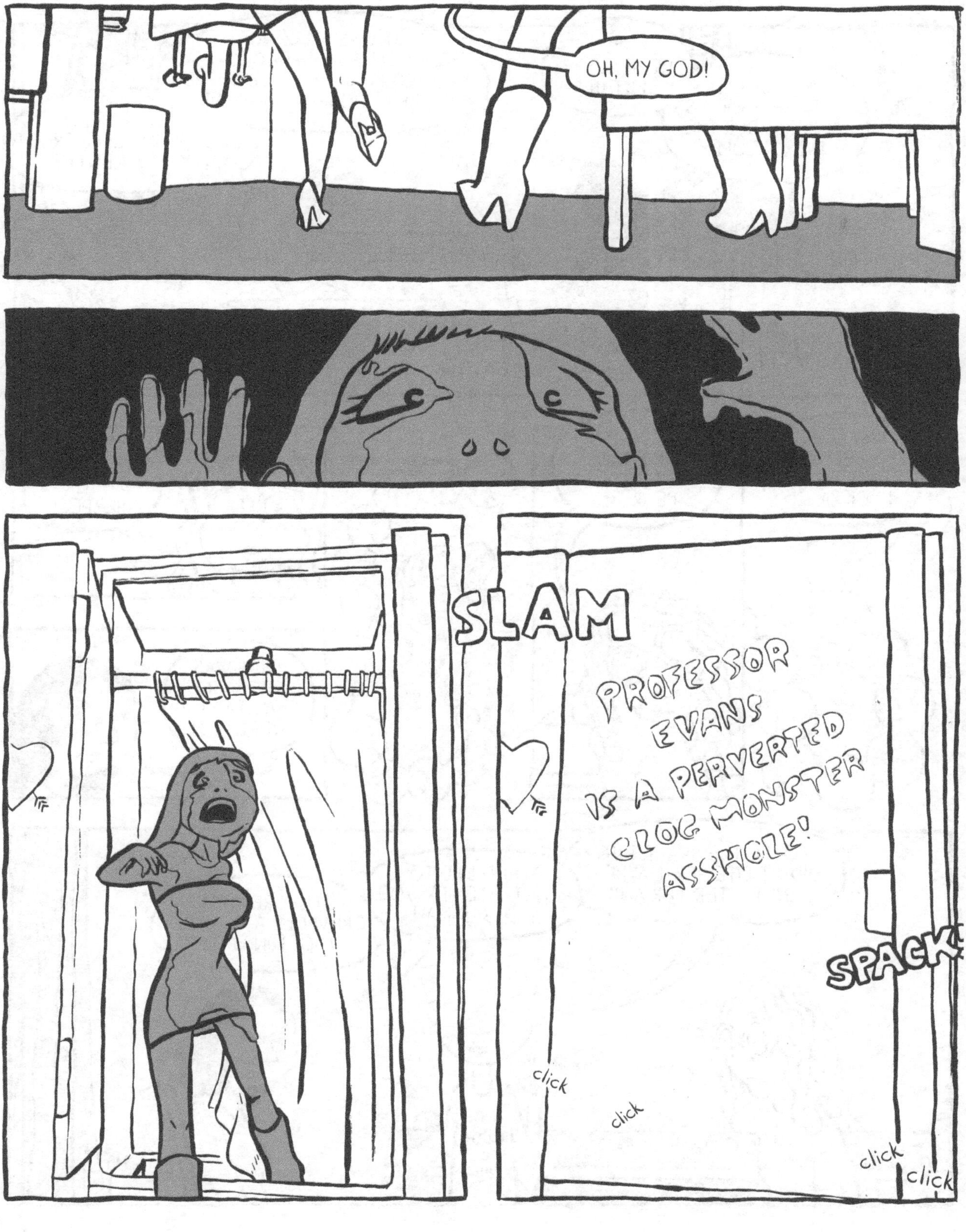
OH, MY GOD!
SLAM
PROFESSOR EVANS IS A PERVERTED CLOG MONSTER ASSHOLE!
SPACK!
click
click
click
click

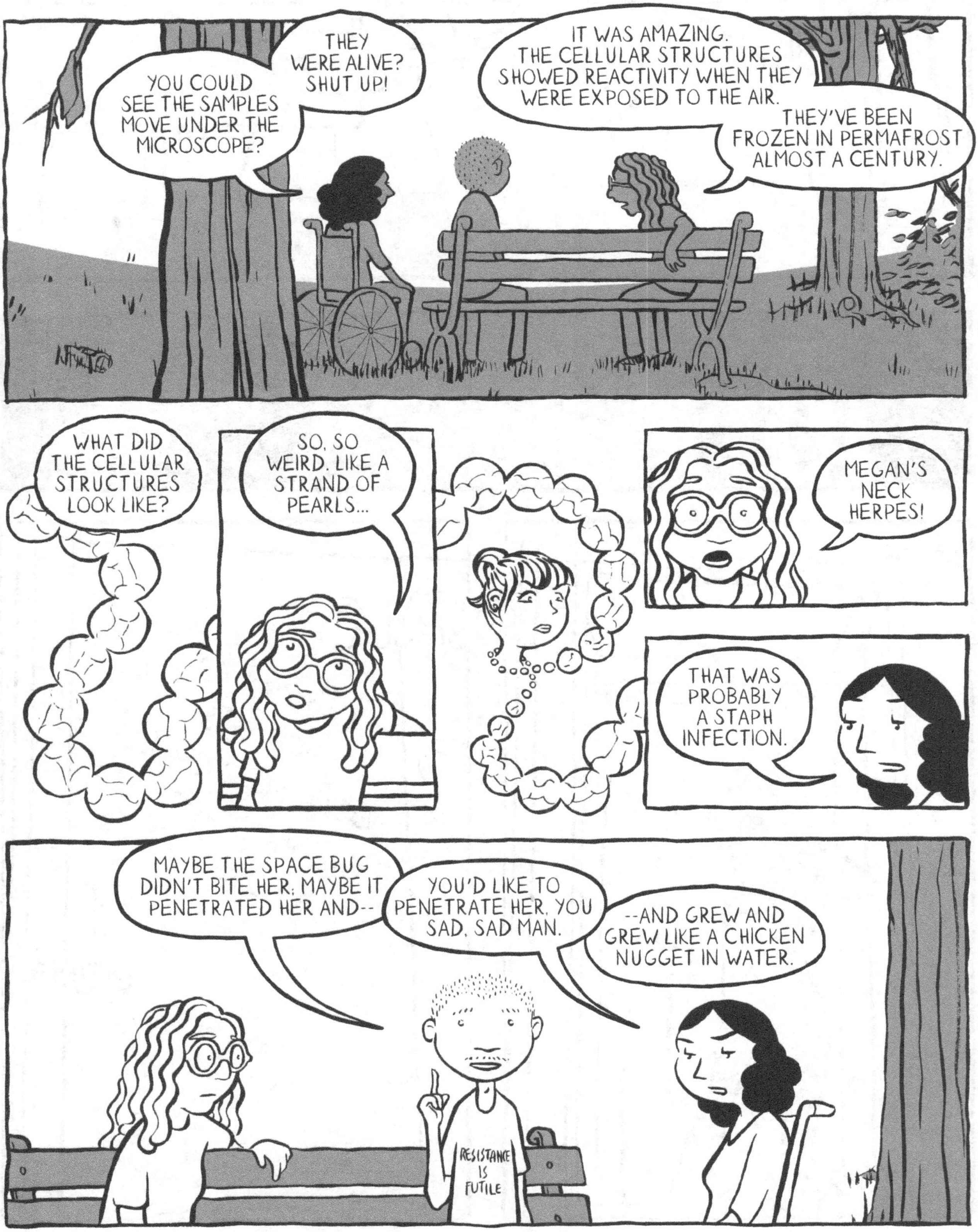
YOU COULD SEE THE SAMPLES MOVE UNDER THE MICROSCOPE?
THEY WERE ALIVE? SHUT UP!
IT WAS AMAZING. THE CELLULAR STRUCTURES SHOWED REACTIVITY WHEN THEY WERE EXPOSED TO THE AIR.
THEY'VE BEEN FROZEN IN PERMAFROST ALMOST A CENTURY.
WHAT DID THE CELLULAR STRUCTURES LOOK LIKE?
SO, SO WEIRD. LIKE A STRAND OF PEARLS...
MEGAN'S NECK HERPES!
THAT WAS PROBABLY A STAPH INFECTION.
MAYBE THE SPACE BUG DIDN'T BITE HER; MAYBE IT PENETRATED HER AND--
YOU'D LIKE TO PENETRATE HER, YOU SAD, SAD MAN.
--AND GREW AND GREW LIKE A CHICKEN NUGGET IN WATER.
RESISTANCE IS FUTILE

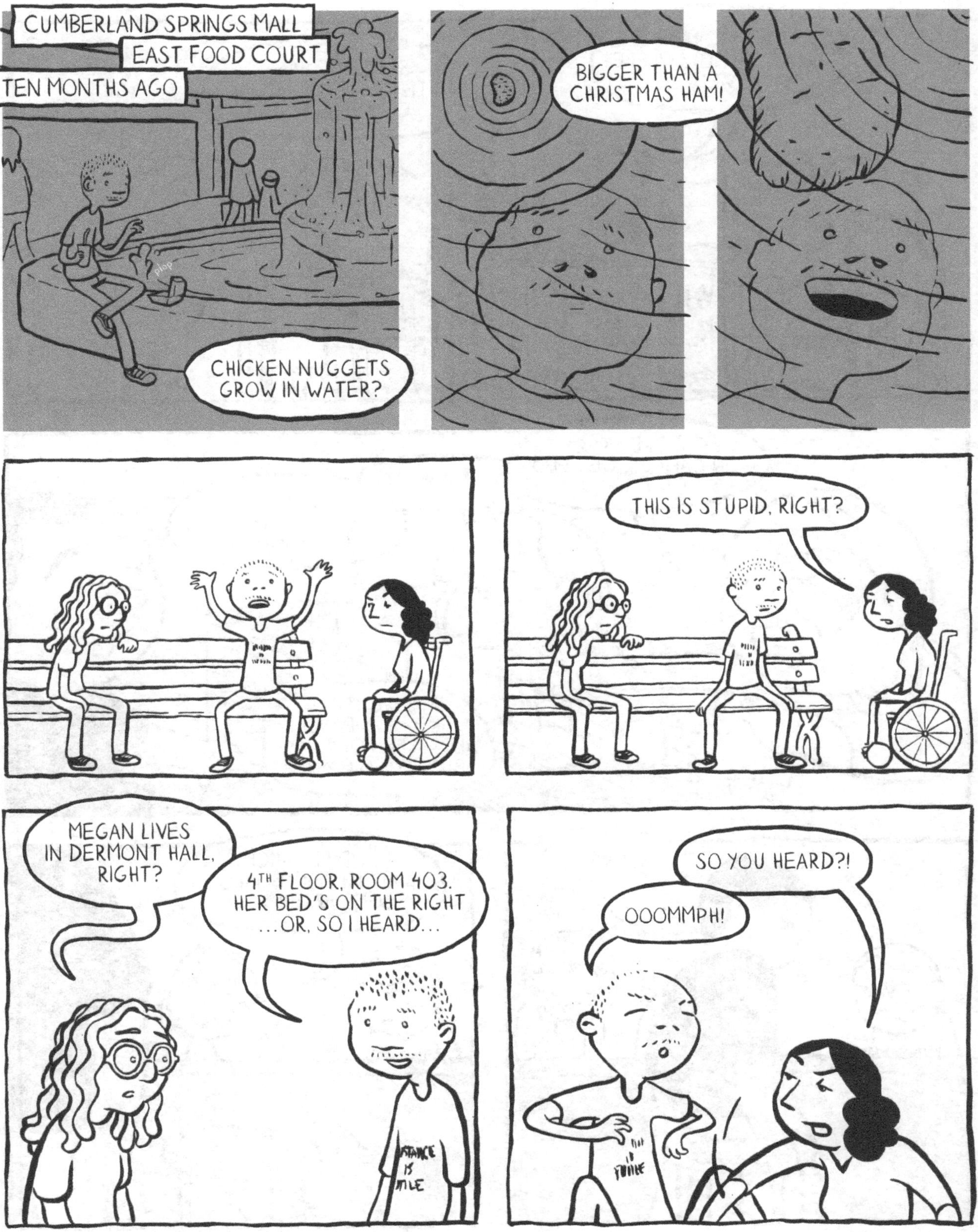
CUMBERLAND SPRINGS MALL
EAST FOOD COURT
TEN MONTHS AGO
CHICKEN NUGGETS GROW IN WATER?
BIGGER THAN A CHRISTMAS HAM!
THIS IS STUPID, RIGHT?
MEGAN LIVES IN DERMONT HALL, RIGHT?
4TH FLOOR, ROOM 403. HER BED'S ON THE RIGHT ...OR, SO I HEARD...
SO YOU HEARD?!
OOOMMPH!

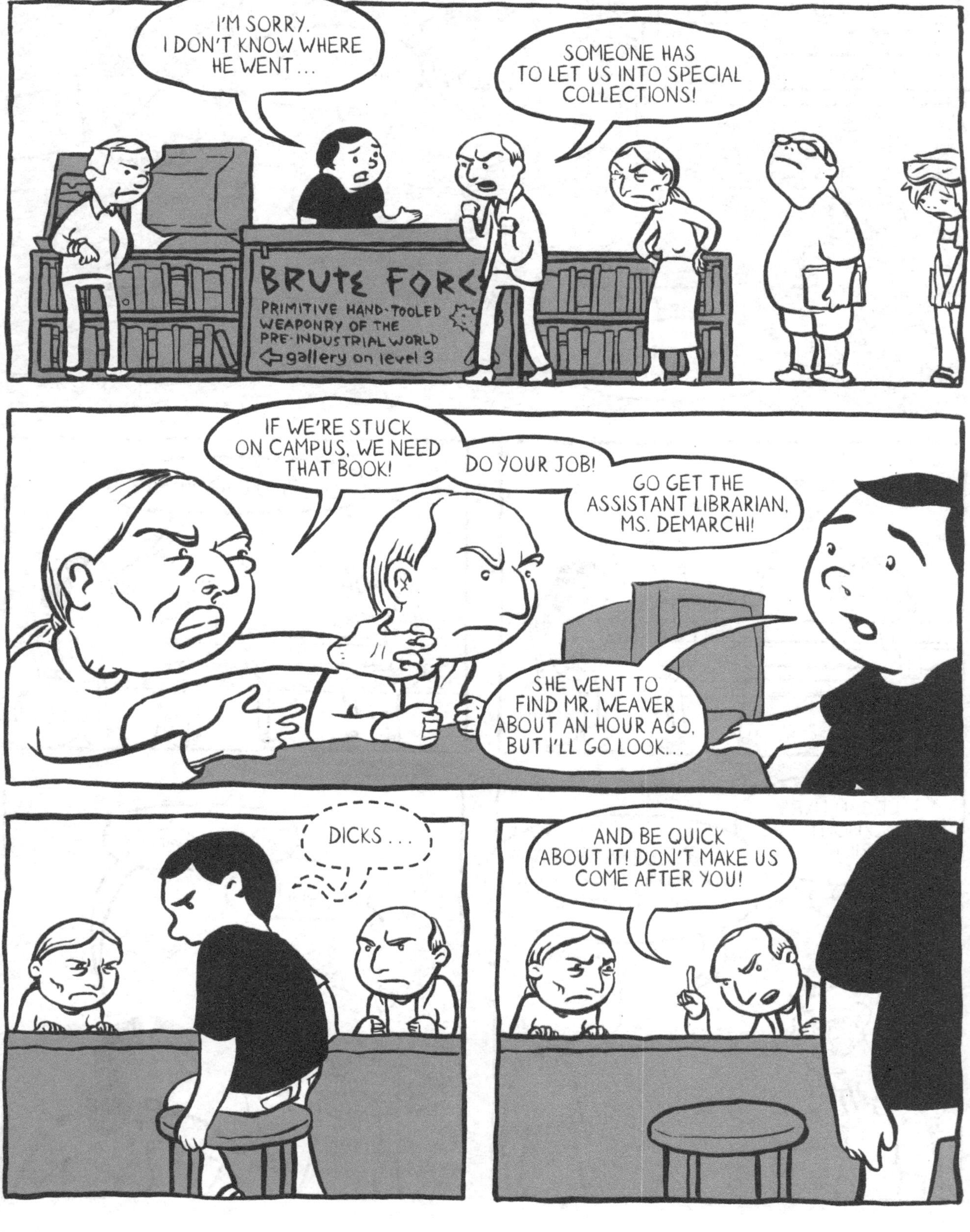
I'M SORRY. I DON'T KNOW WHERE HE WENT...
SOMEONE HAS TO LET US INTO SPECIAL COLLECTIONS!
BRUTE FORC
PRIMITIVE HAND-TOOLED WEAPONRY OF THE PRE-INDUSTRIAL WORLD
gallery on level 3
IF WE'RE STUCK ON CAMPUS, WE NEED THAT BOOK!
DO YOUR JOB!
GO GET THE ASSISTANT LIBRARIAN, MS. DEMARCHI!
SHE WENT TO FIND MR. WEAVER ABOUT AN HOUR AGO, BUT I'LL GO LOOK...
DICKS . . .
AND BE QUICK ABOUT IT! DON'T MAKE US COME AFTER YOU!

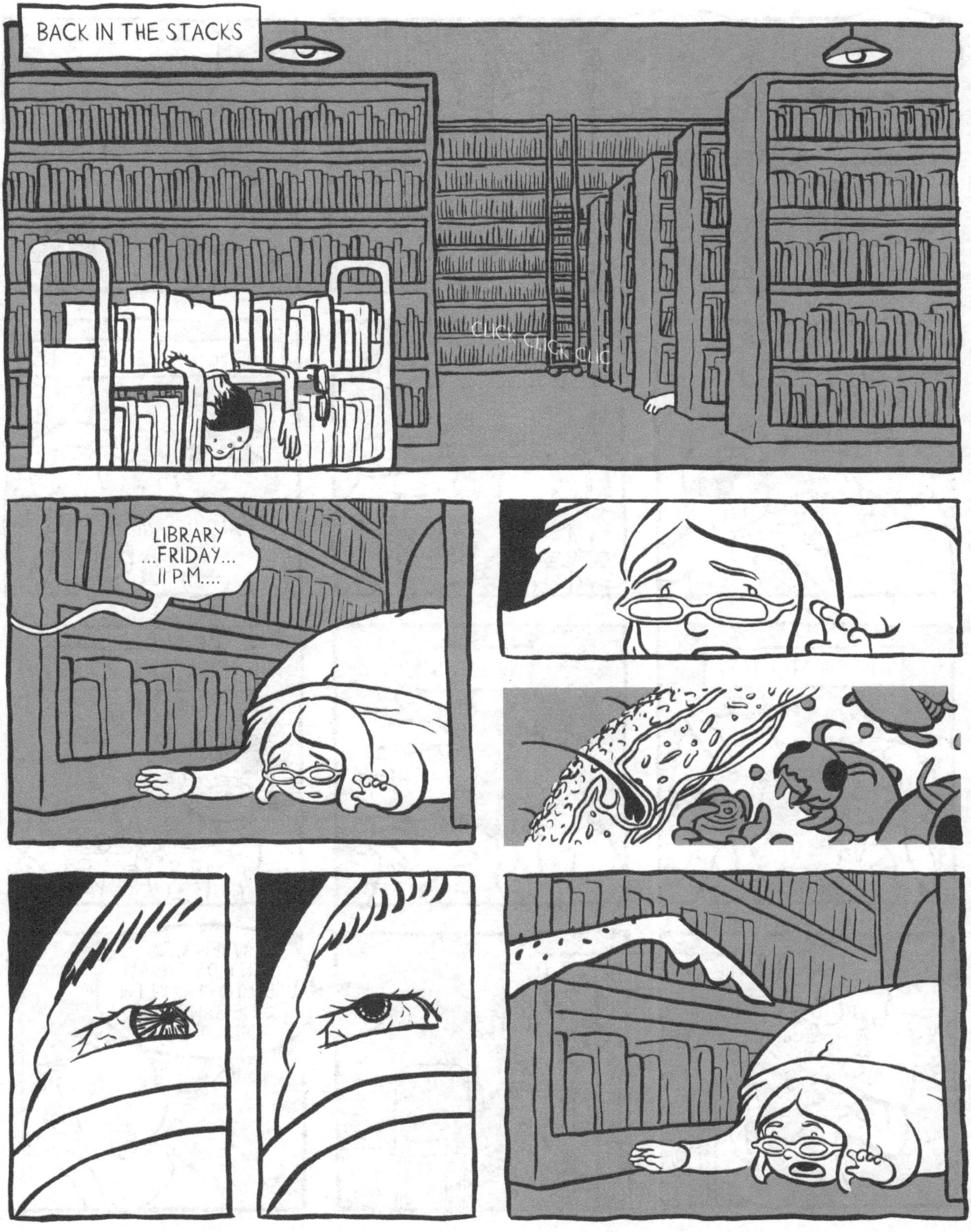
BACK IN THE STACKS
CLICK CLICK CLIC
LIBRARY ...FRIDAY... 11 P.M....

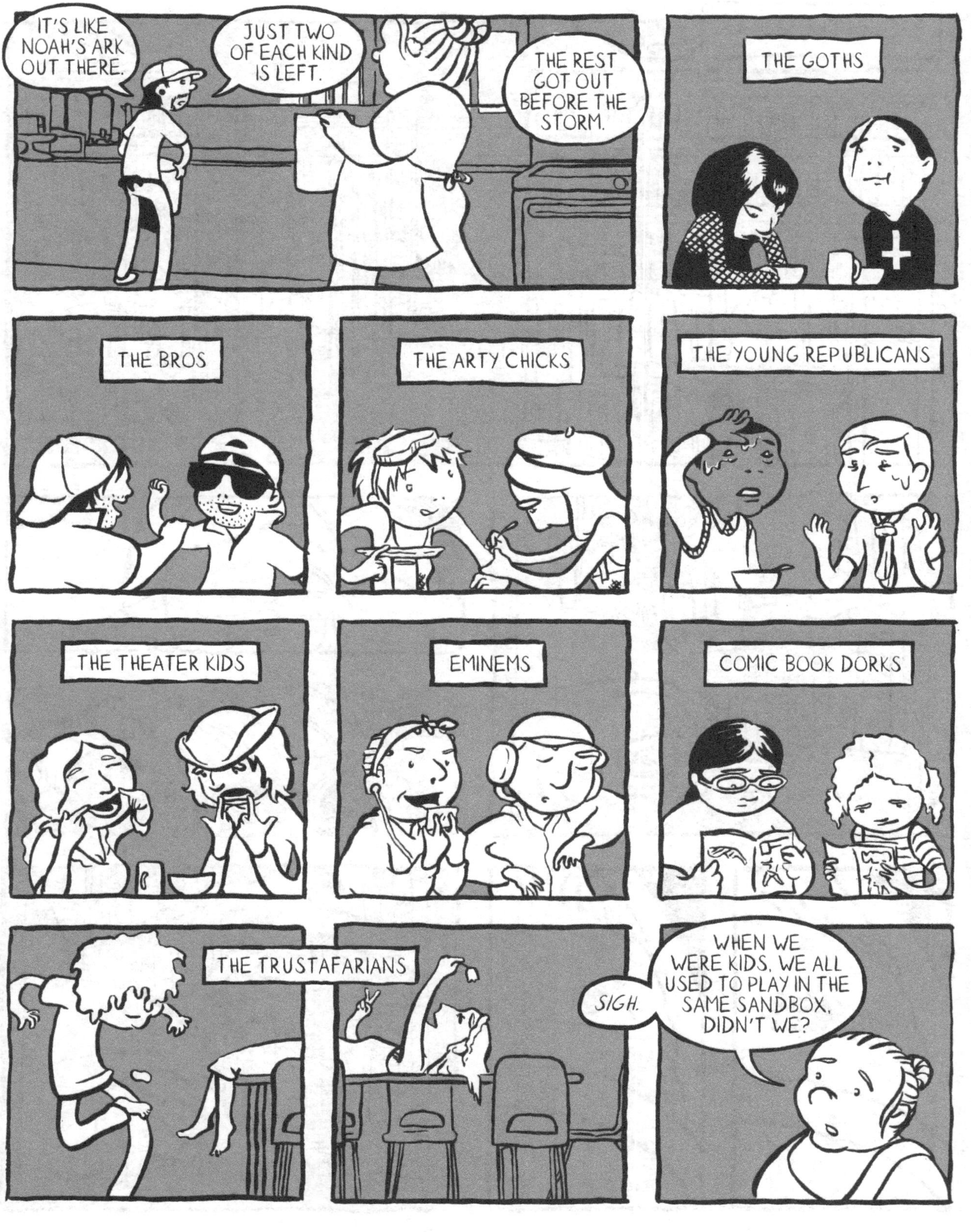
IT'S LIKE NOAH'S ARK OUT THERE.
JUST TWO OF EACH KIND IS LEFT.
THE REST GOT OUT BEFORE THE STORM.
THE GOTHS
THE BROS
THE ARTY CHICKS
THE YOUNG REPUBLICANS
THE THEATER KIDS
EMINEMS
COMIC BOOK DORKS
THE TRUSTAFARIANS
SIGH.
WHEN WE WERE KIDS, WE ALL USED TO PLAY IN THE SAME SANDBOX, DIDN'T WE?

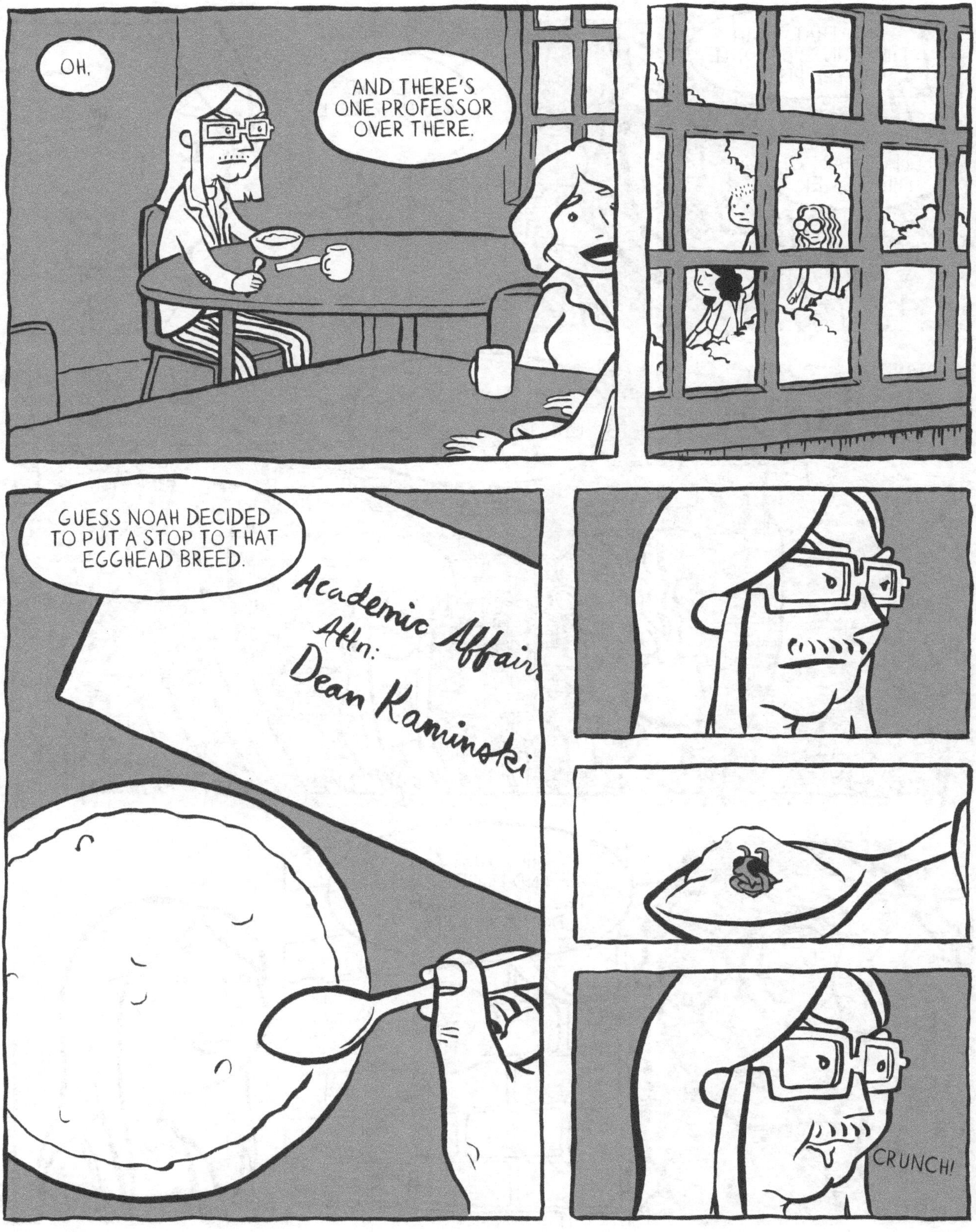

OH.
AND THERE'S ONE PROFESSOR OVER THERE.
GUESS NOAH DECIDED TO PUT A STOP TO THAT EGGHEAD BREED.
Academic Affair
Attn:
Dean Kaminski
CRUNCH!

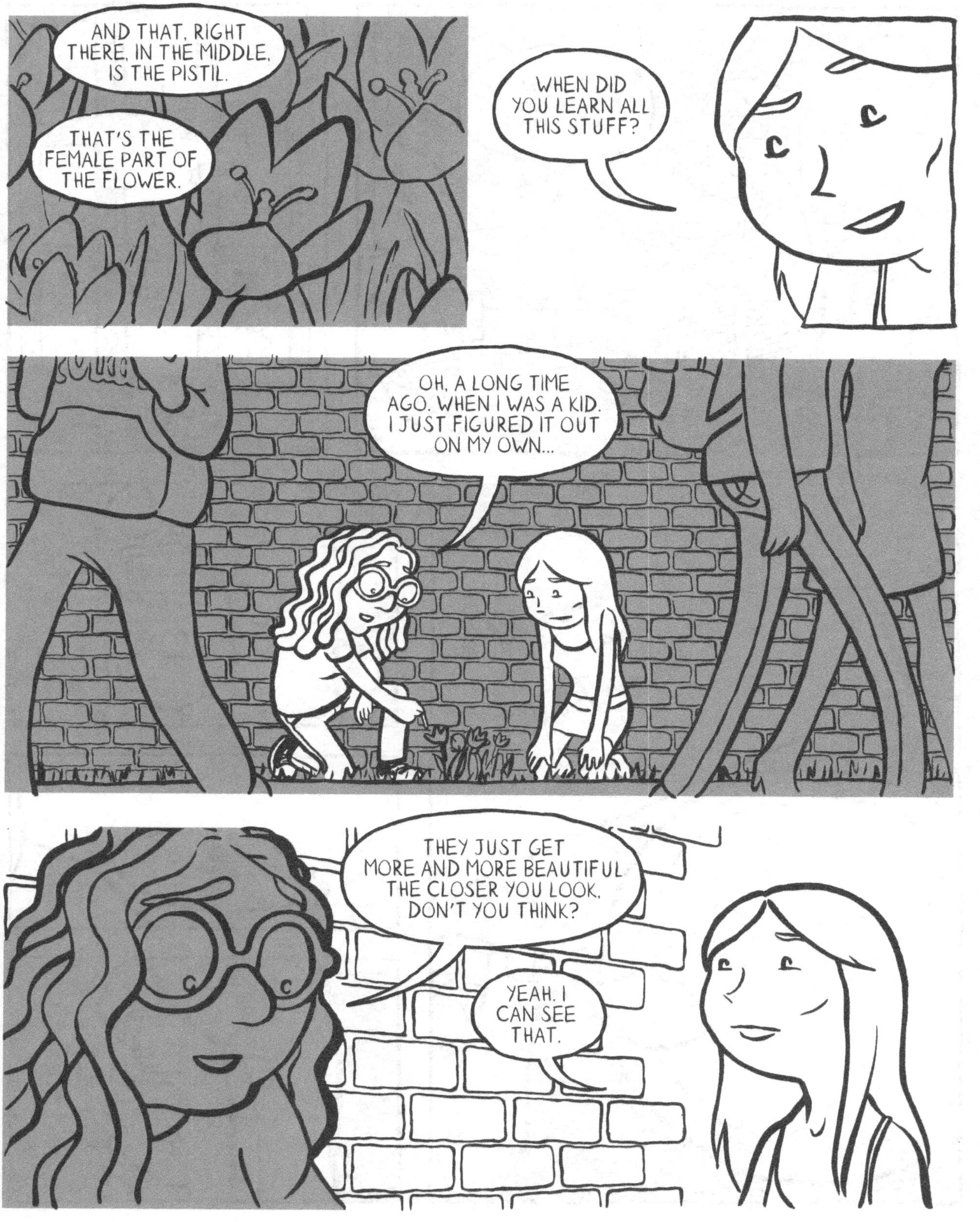
AND THAT, RIGHT THERE, IN THE MIDDLE, IS THE PISTIL.
THAT'S THE FEMALE PART OF THE FLOWER.
WHEN DID YOU LEARN ALL THIS STUFF?
OH, A LONG TIME AGO. WHEN I WAS A KID. I JUST FIGURED IT OUT ON MY OWN...
THEY JUST GET MORE AND MORE BEAUTIFUL THE CLOSER YOU LOOK, DON'T YOU THINK?
YEAH. I CAN SEE THAT.

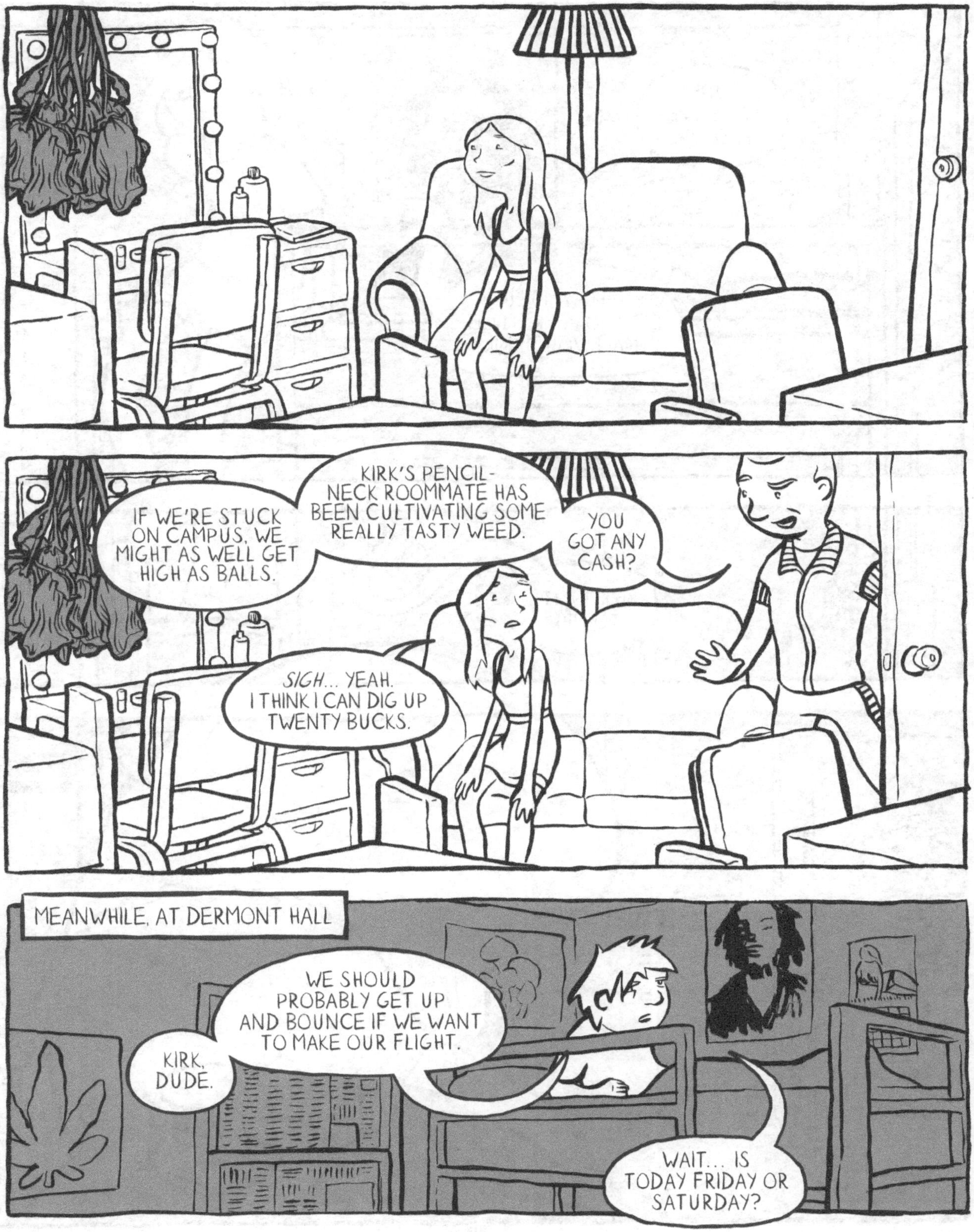
IF WE'RE STUCK ON CAMPUS, WE MIGHT AS WELL GET HIGH AS BALLS.
KIRK'S PENCIL-NECK ROOMMATE HAS BEEN CULTIVATING SOME REALLY TASTY WEED.
YOU GOT ANY CASH?
SIGH... YEAH. I THINK I CAN DIG UP TWENTY BUCKS.
MEANWHILE, AT DERMONT HALL
KIRK, DUDE.
WE SHOULD PROBABLY GET UP AND BOUNCE IF WE WANT TO MAKE OUR FLIGHT.
WAIT... IS TODAY FRIDAY OR SATURDAY?

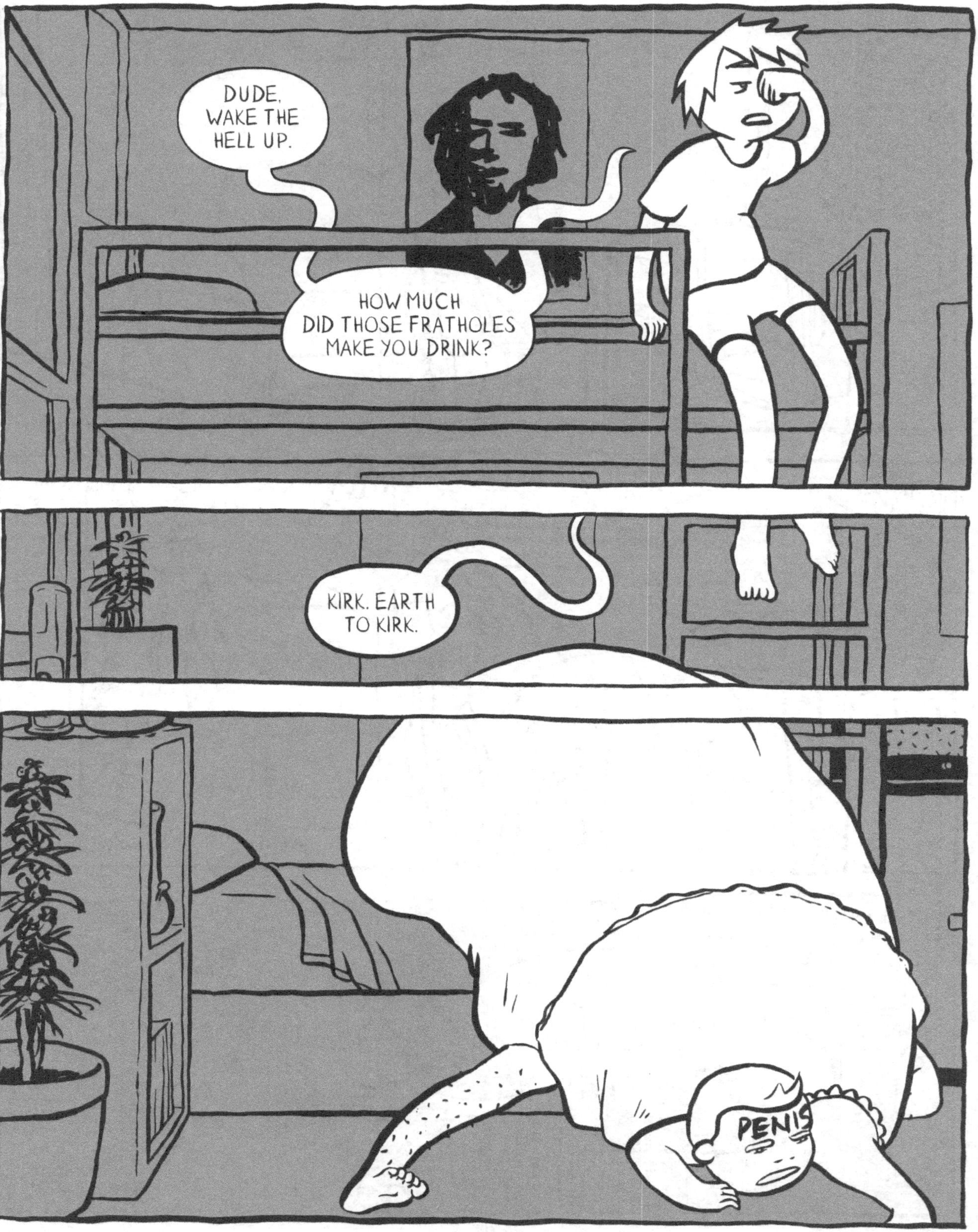
DUDE, WAKE THE HELL UP.
HOW MUCH DID THOSE FRATHOLES MAKE YOU DRINK?
KIRK. EARTH TO KIRK.
PENIS

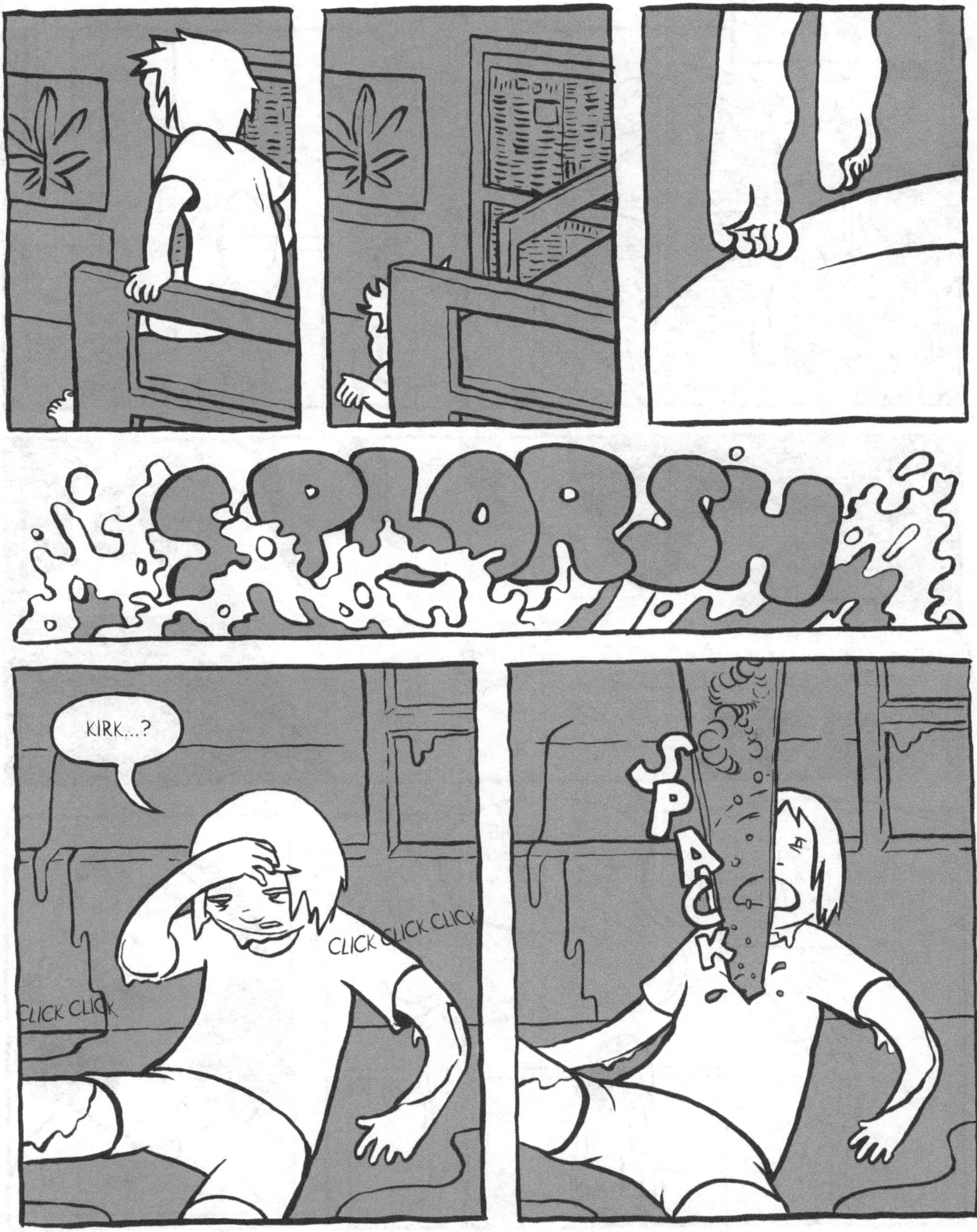
SPLORSH
KIRK...?
CLICK CLICK CLICK
CLICK CLICK
SPACK

BACK AT THE LAB

BLUE... JUST LIKE THE RUSSIANS SAID...

ARE YOU CRAZY? WHAT IF THERE'S SOME SORT OF ALIEN VIRUS ON THEM?

WE'VE ALREADY BREATHED IT IN IF THERE IS.

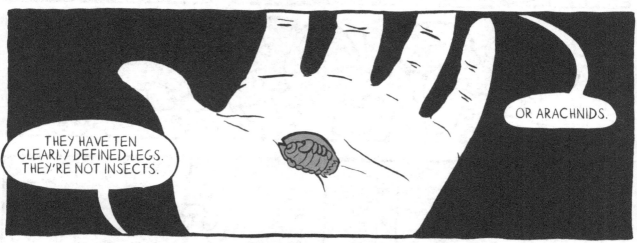

THEY HAVE TEN CLEARLY DEFINED LEGS. THEY'RE NOT INSECTS.

OR ARACHNIDS.

THEY'RE DRY AND DEAD AND THEY WEREN'T HERE LAST NIGHT, WHICH MEANS THEY HAVE A REALLY SHORT LIFE CYCLE. WHICH IS GOOD.

UNLESS THE STORIES ABOUT THE MATURE FORM ARE TRUE.

THE "HIGHLY-SEXED" MATURE FORM.

THE COCKTOPUS...

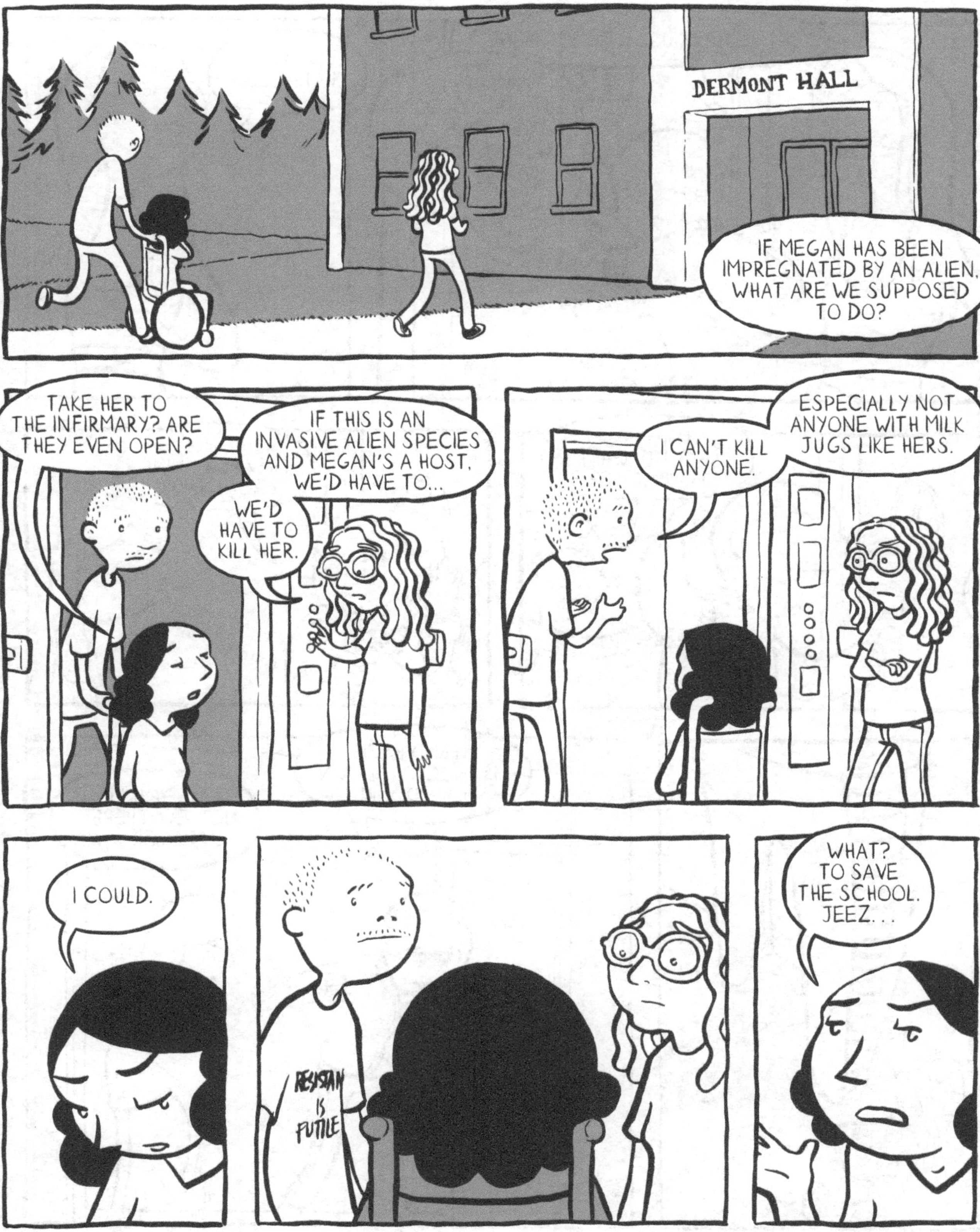
DERMONT HALL
IF MEGAN HAS BEEN IMPREGNATED BY AN ALIEN, WHAT ARE WE SUPPOSED TO DO?
TAKE HER TO THE INFIRMARY? ARE THEY EVEN OPEN?
IF THIS IS AN INVASIVE ALIEN SPECIES AND MEGAN'S A HOST, WE'D HAVE TO...
WE'D HAVE TO KILL HER.
I CAN'T KILL ANYONE.
ESPECIALLY NOT ANYONE WITH MILK JUGS LIKE HERS.
I COULD.
RESISTAN IS FUTILE
WHAT? TO SAVE THE SCHOOL. JEEZ. . .

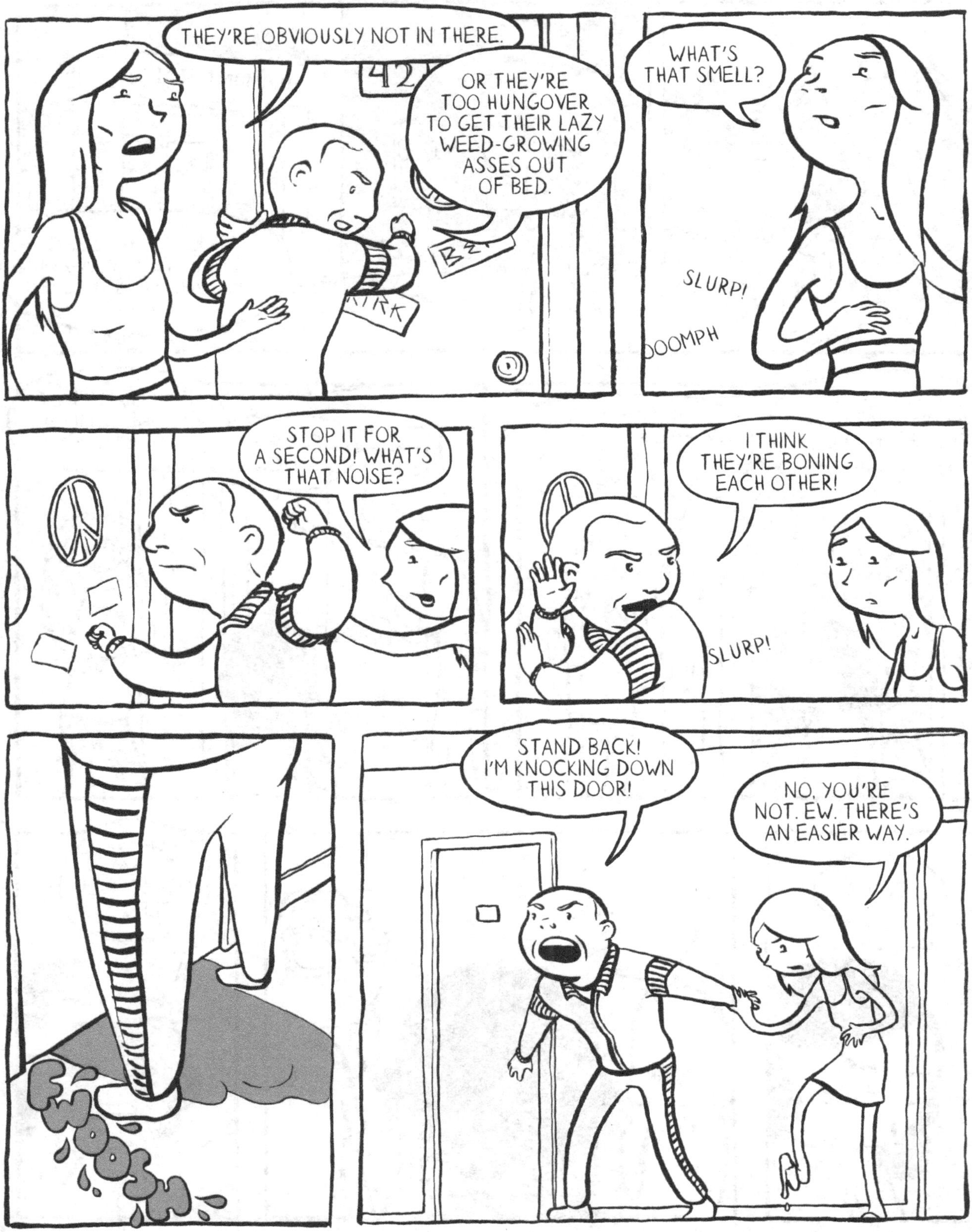
THEY'RE OBVIOUSLY NOT IN THERE.
OR THEY'RE TOO HUNGOVER TO GET THEIR LAZY WEED-GROWING ASSES OUT OF BED.
42
KIRK
WHAT'S THAT SMELL?
SLURP!
OOMPH
STOP IT FOR A SECOND! WHAT'S THAT NOISE?
I THINK THEY'RE BONING EACH OTHER!
SLURP!
FWOOSH
STAND BACK! I'M KNOCKING DOWN THIS DOOR!
NO, YOU'RE NOT. EW. THERE'S AN EASIER WAY.

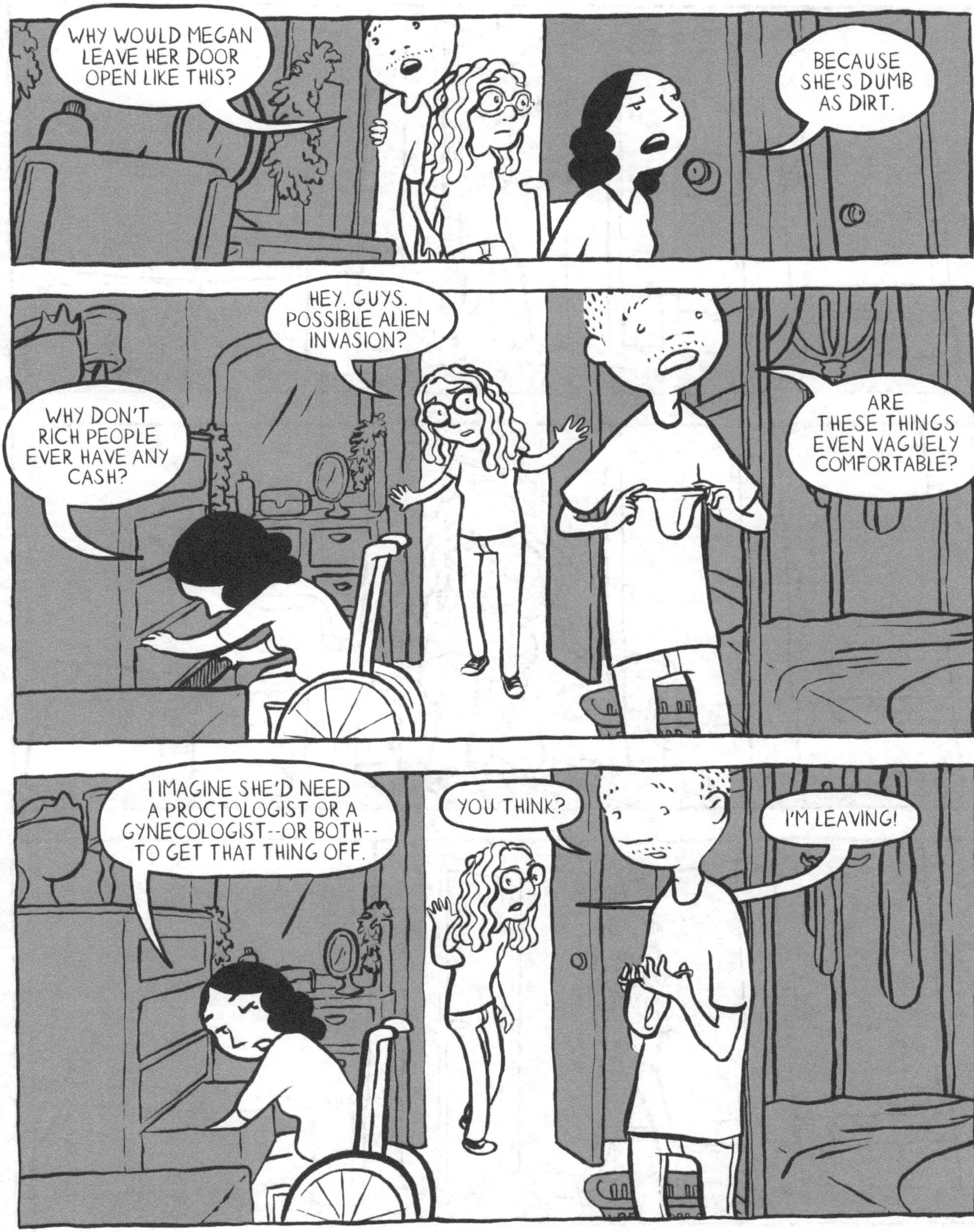
WHY WOULD MEGAN LEAVE HER DOOR OPEN LIKE THIS?
BECAUSE SHE'S DUMB AS DIRT.
HEY. GUYS. POSSIBLE ALIEN INVASION?
WHY DON'T RICH PEOPLE EVER HAVE ANY CASH?
ARE THESE THINGS EVEN VAGUELY COMFORTABLE?
I IMAGINE SHE'D NEED A PROCTOLOGIST OR A GYNECOLOGIST--OR BOTH--TO GET THAT THING OFF.
YOU THINK?
I'M LEAVING!

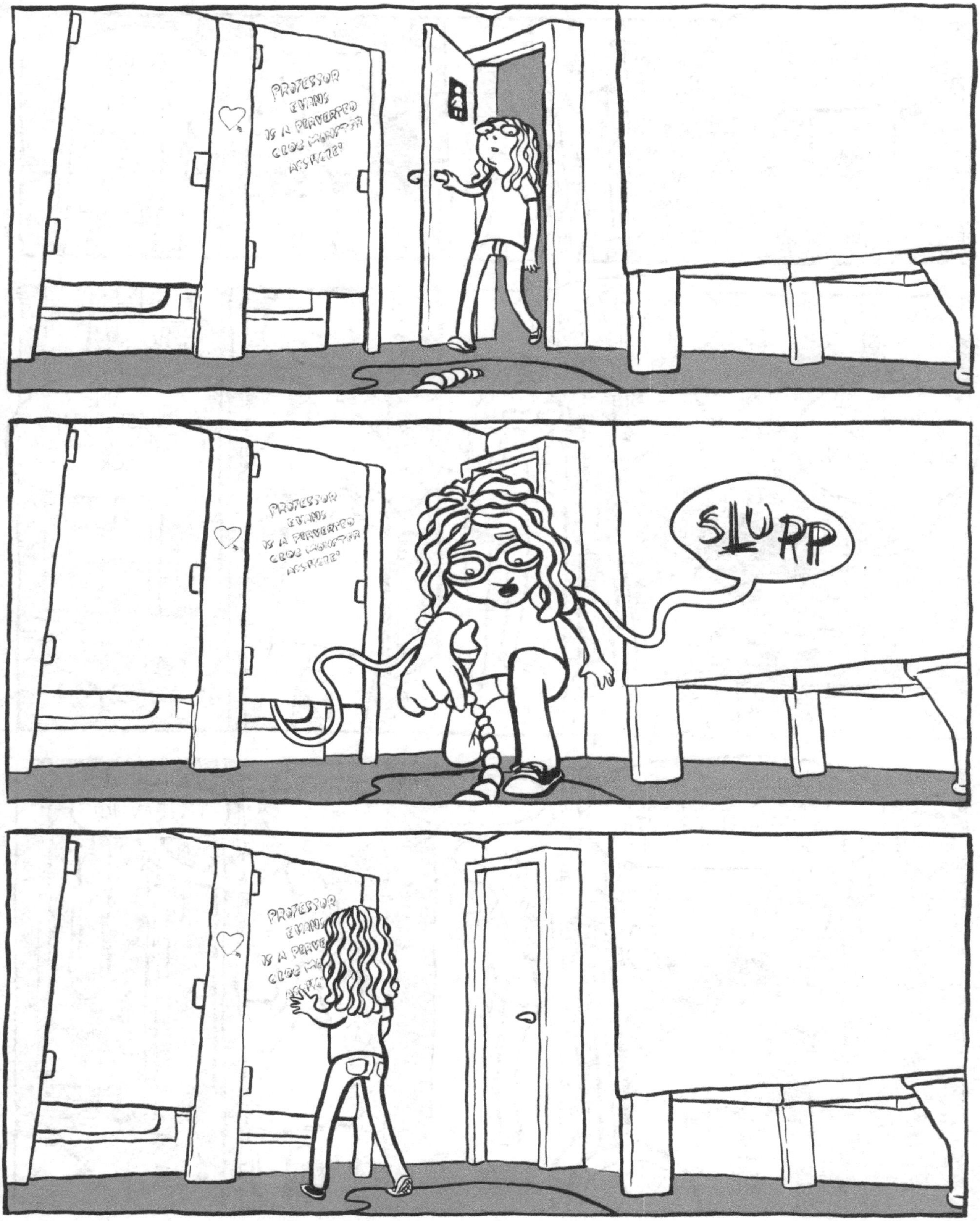
PROFESSOR EVANS IS A PERVERTED
SLURP

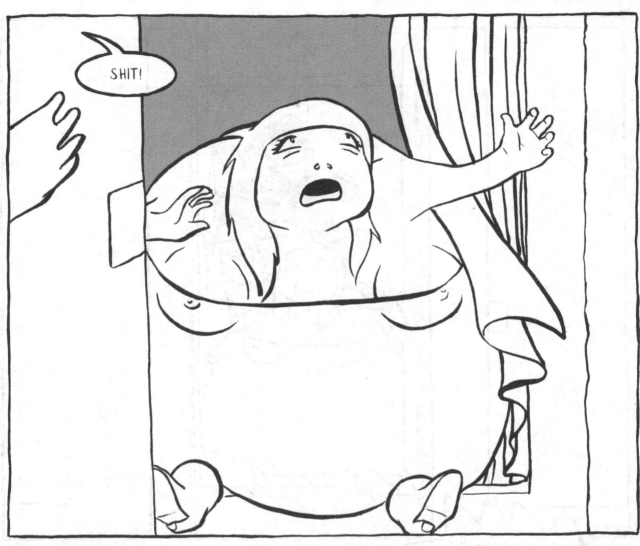

SHIT!

STAY HERE. I'LL GO FOR HELP!

RU...RU... RUUUUUUN...

RAHAR!!

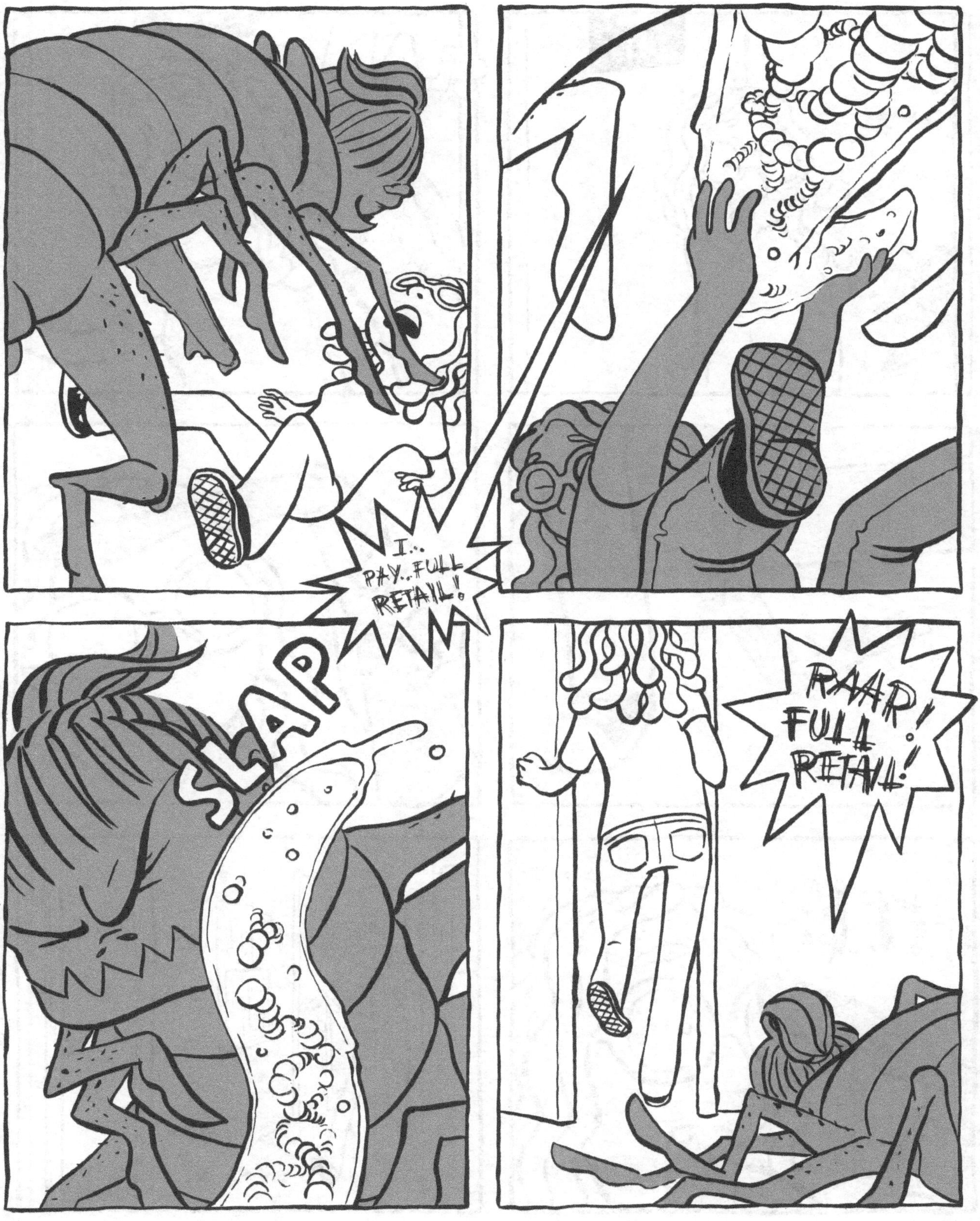

I... PAY... FULL RETAIL!
SLAP
RAAR! FULL RETAIL!

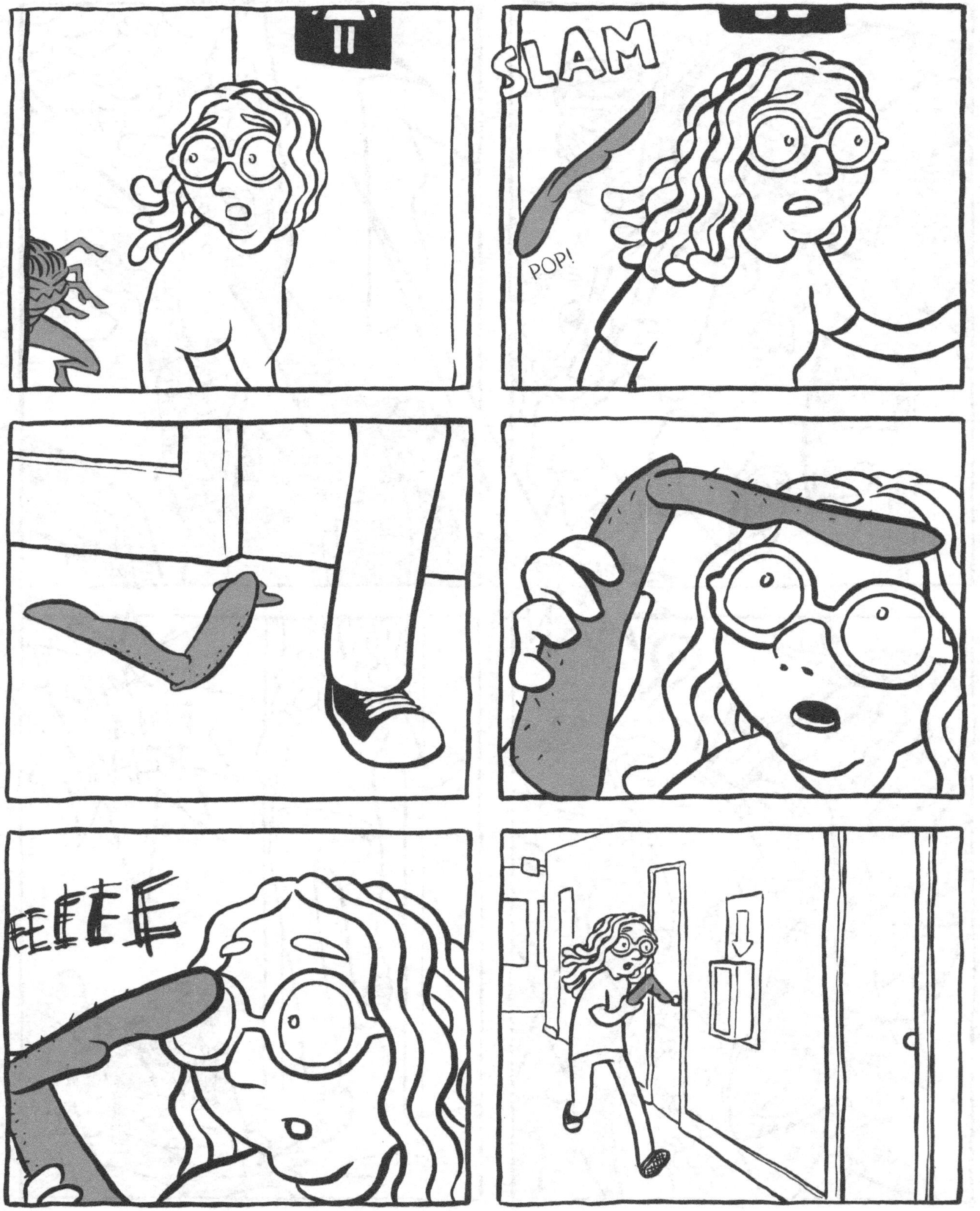
SLAM
POP!
EEEEE

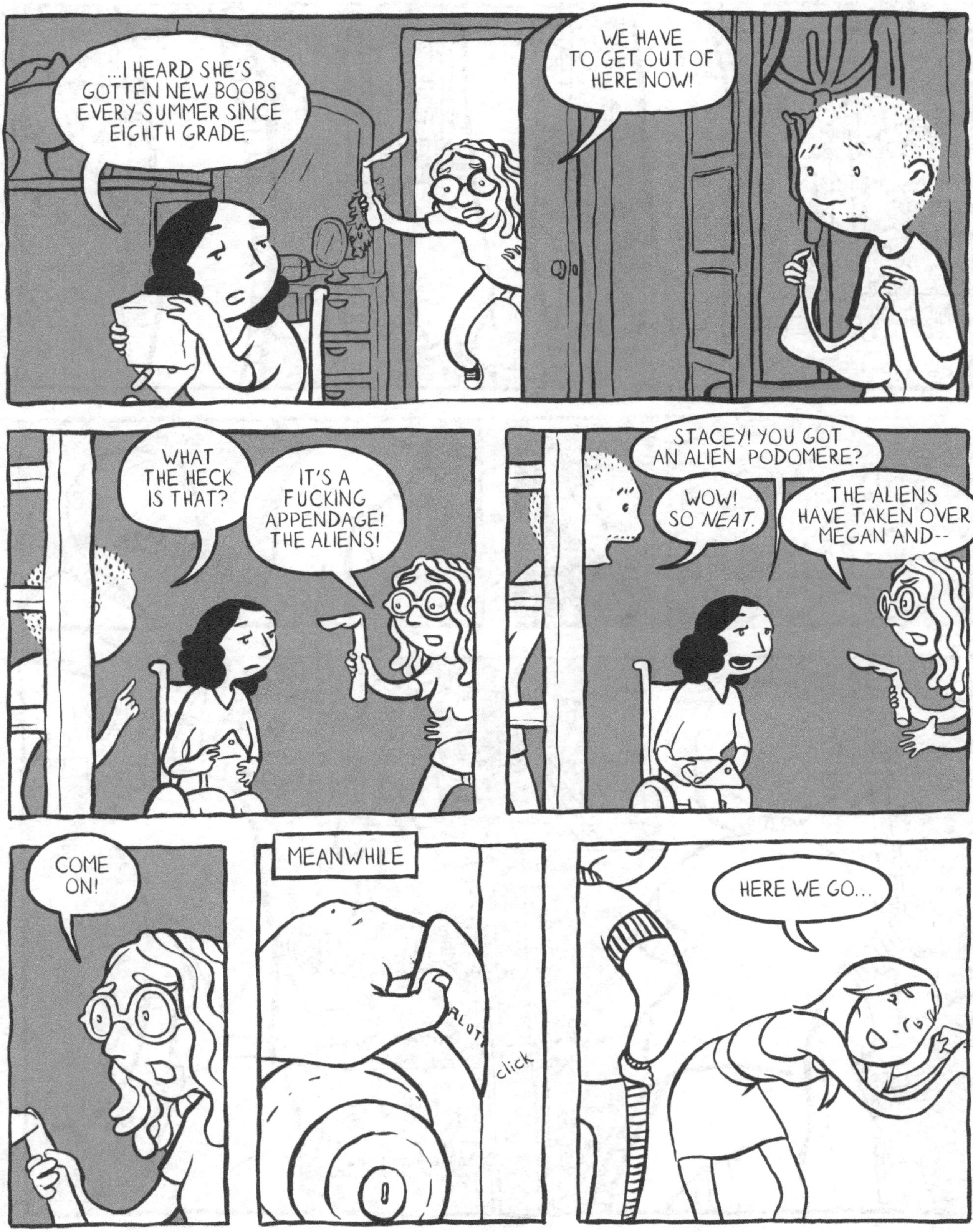
...I HEARD SHE'S GOTTEN NEW BOOBS EVERY SUMMER SINCE EIGHTH GRADE.
WE HAVE TO GET OUT OF HERE NOW!
WHAT THE HECK IS THAT?
IT'S A FUCKING APPENDAGE! THE ALIENS!
STACEY! YOU GOT AN ALIEN PODOMERE?
WOW! SO *NEAT*.
THE ALIENS HAVE TAKEN OVER MEGAN AND--
COME ON!
MEANWHILE
click
HERE WE GO...

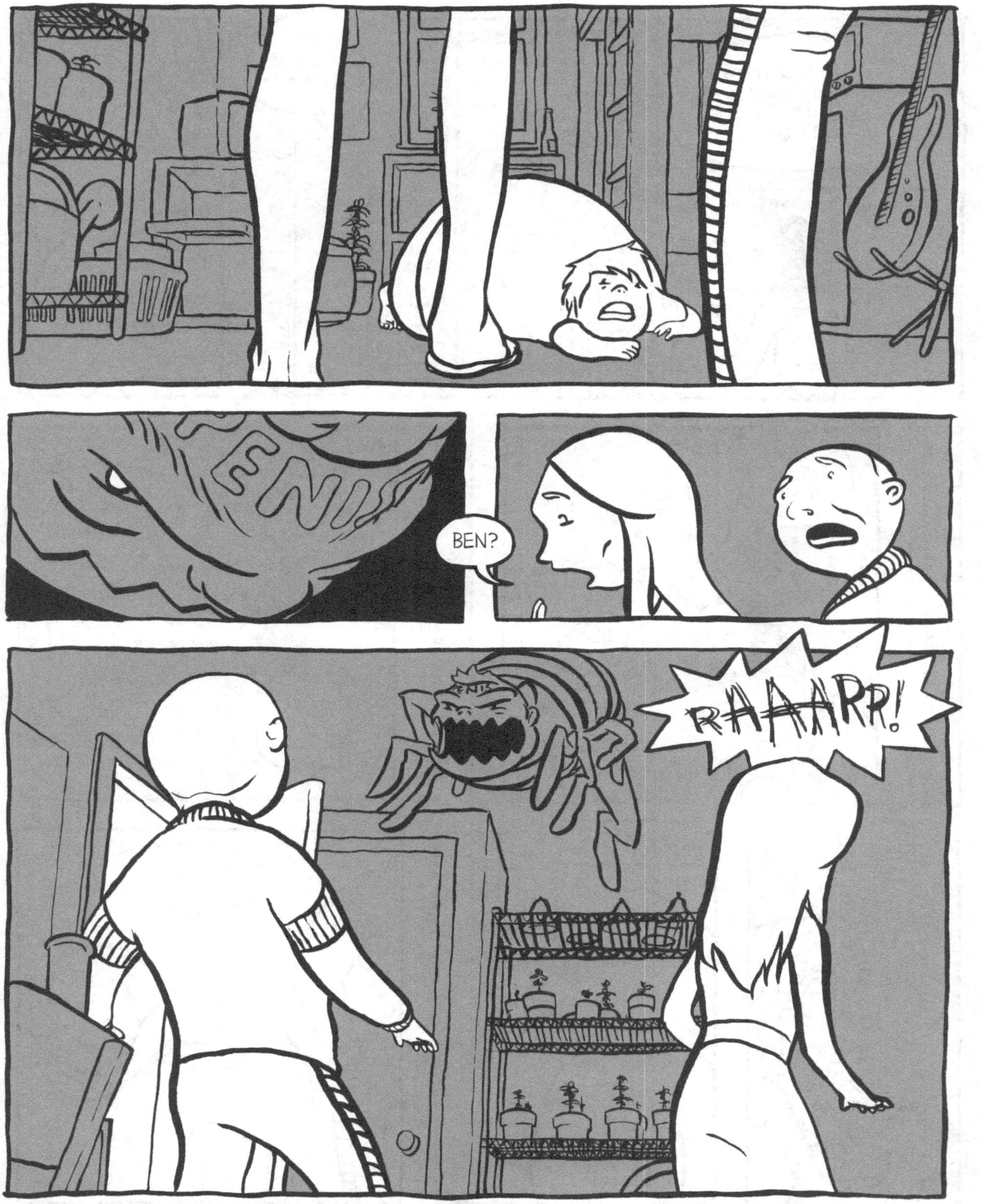
PENI
BEN?
PENIS
RAAARR!

AAAAAA
AAA

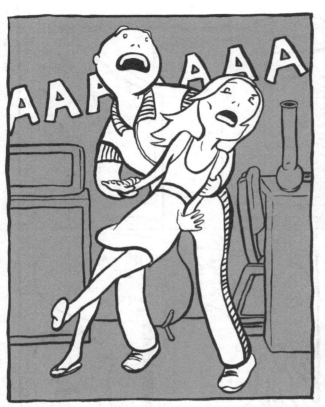

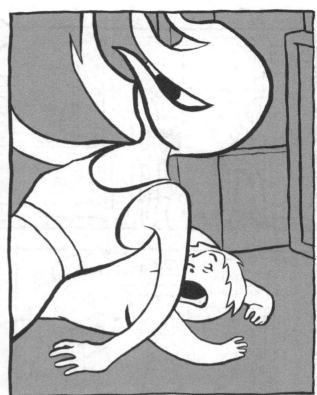

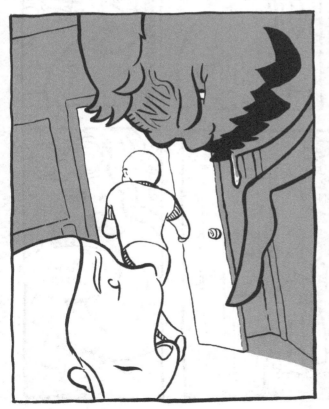

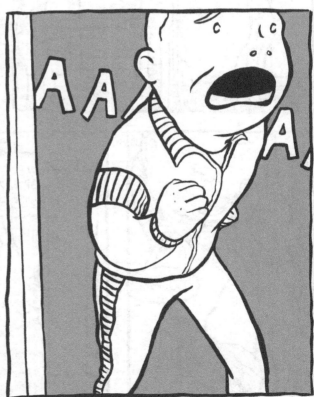

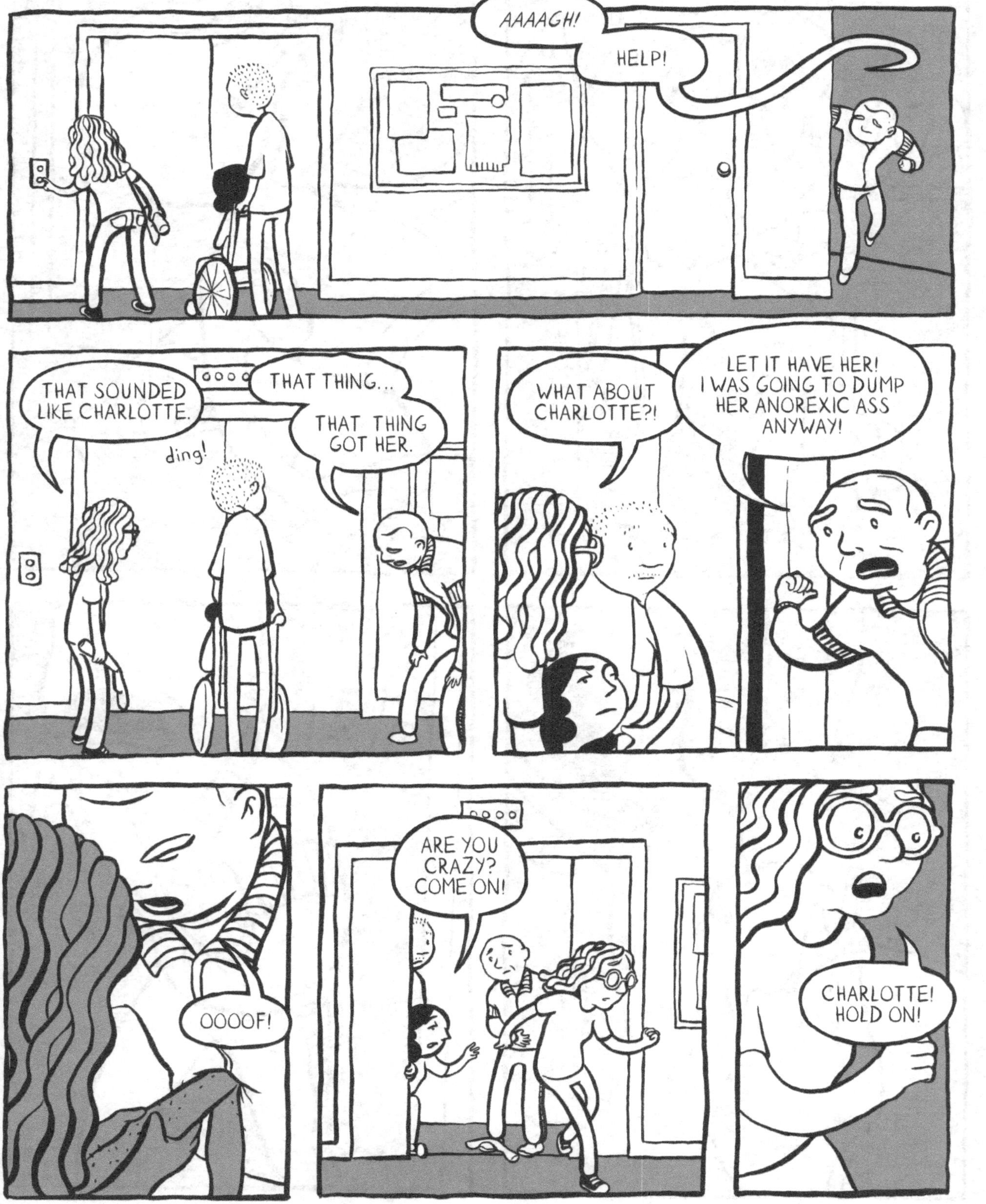
AAAAGH!
HELP!
THAT SOUNDED LIKE CHARLOTTE.
ding!
THAT THING...
THAT THING GOT HER.
WHAT ABOUT CHARLOTTE?!
LET IT HAVE HER! I WAS GOING TO DUMP HER ANOREXIC ASS ANYWAY!
OOOOF!
ARE YOU CRAZY? COME ON!
CHARLOTTE! HOLD ON!

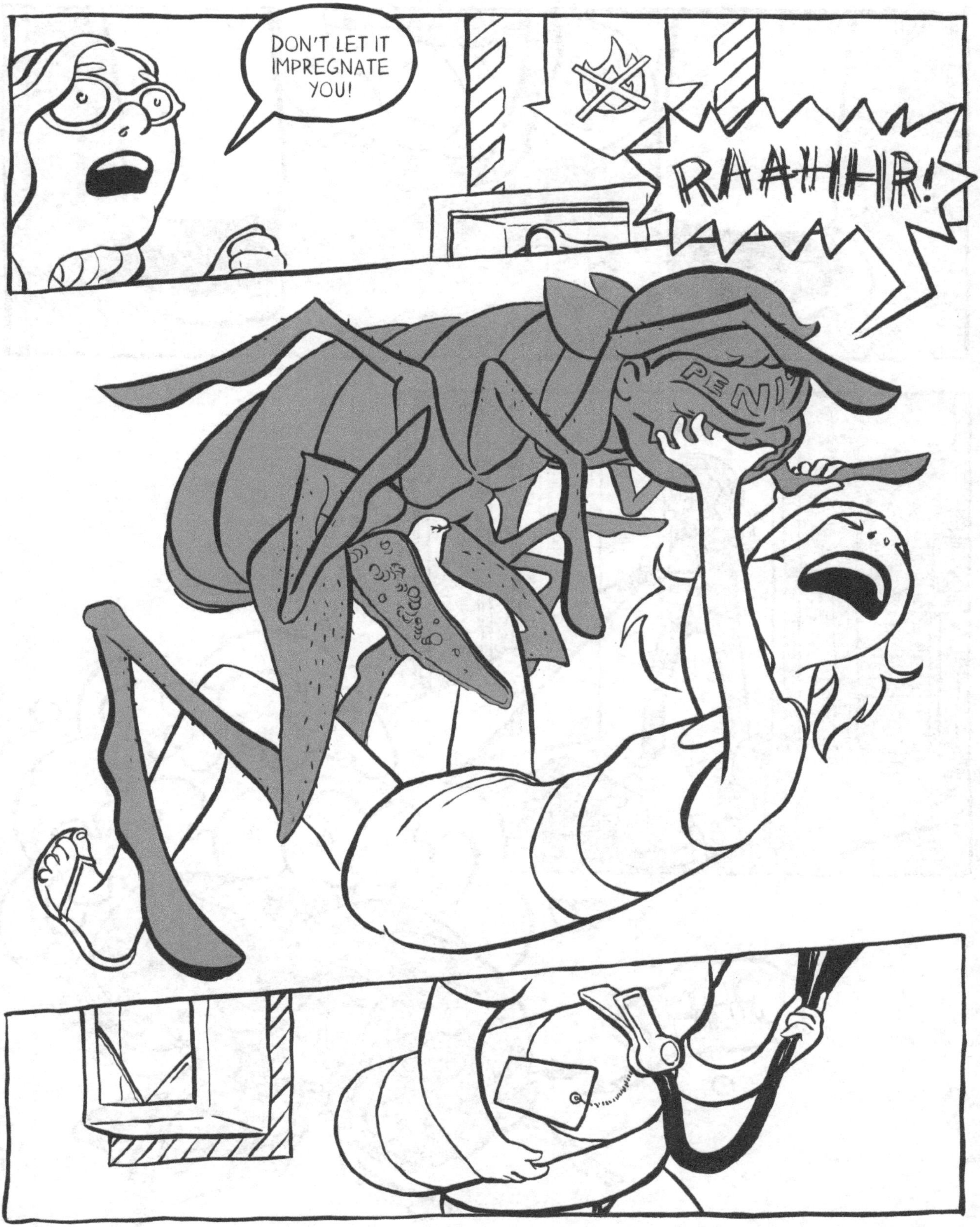
DON'T LET IT IMPREGNATE YOU!
RAAHHR!

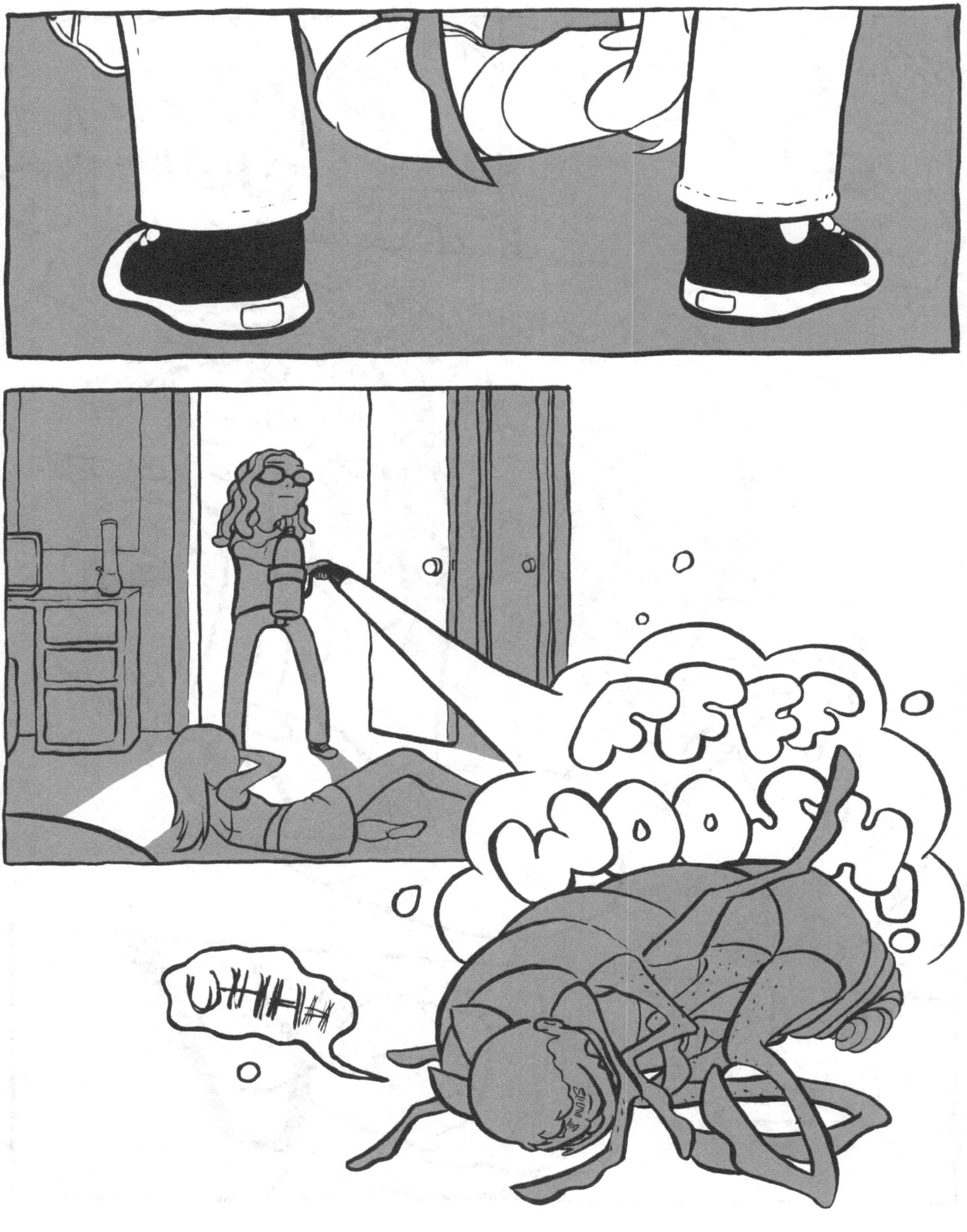
FFFF
WOOSH!
UHHHH

CRACK
PEN

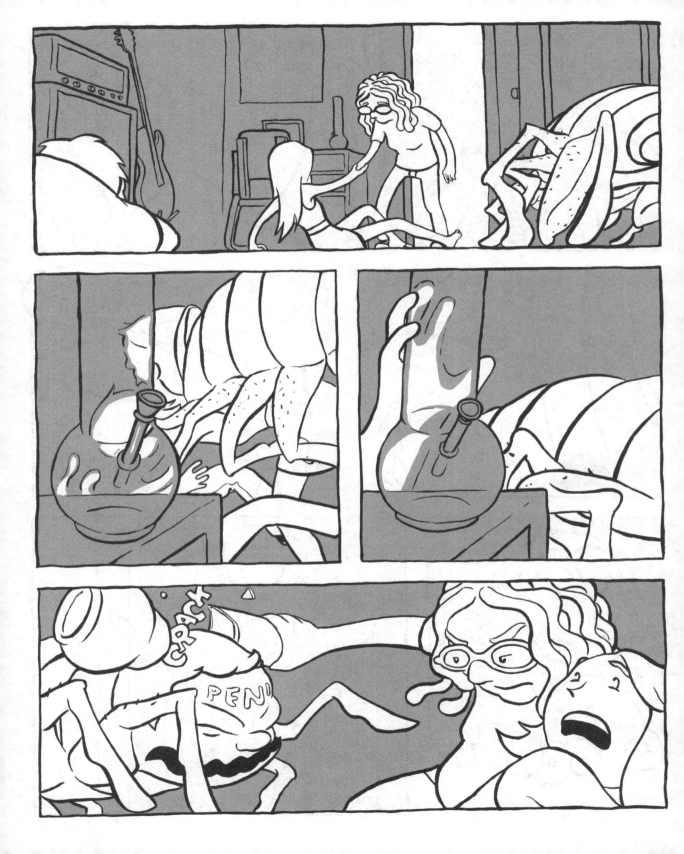

HEY, BEN?

I'M SORRY. YOU'VE BEEN INFECTED. I CAN'T LET YOU MATURE.

OH. DAMN.

GLOOORP

ARE YOU OKAY?
NO, STACEY, I AM *NOT* OKAY!
THERE ARE PARTS OF AN EXPLODED GUY IN MY HAIR!
creak
MEGAN? OH, MY GOD!
JUST KEEP RUNNING!
RAAR
RETAIL!

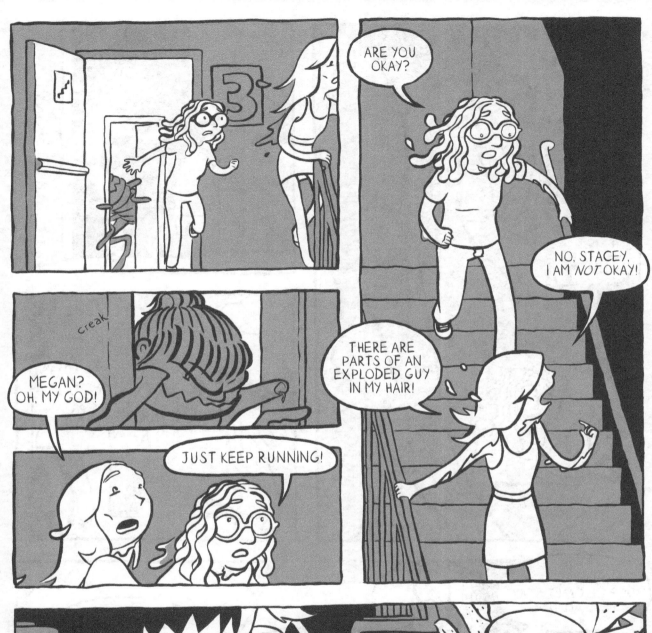

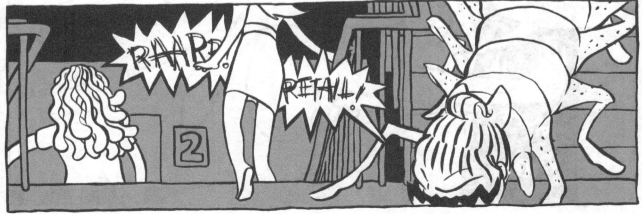

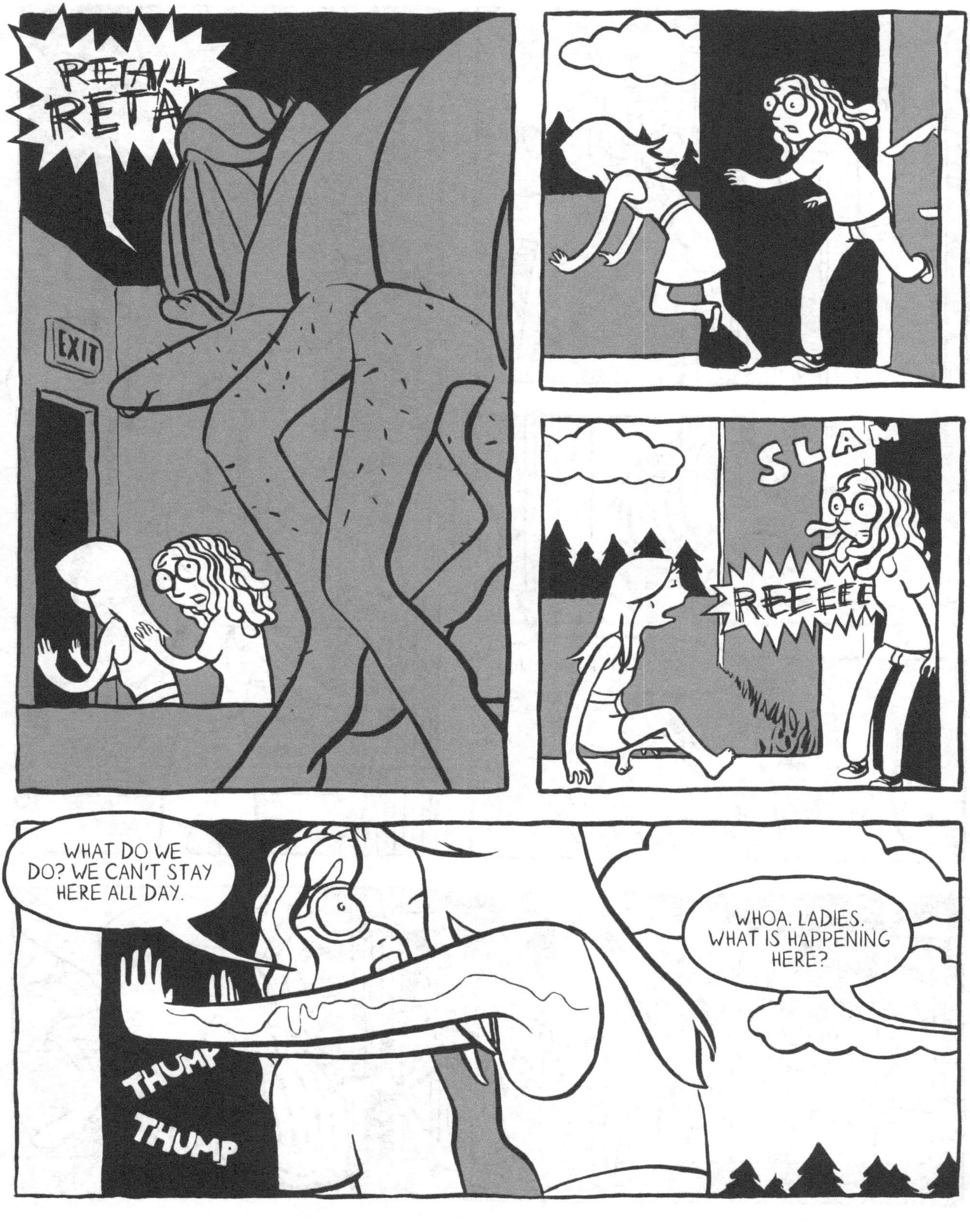
RETA!!
RETA
EXIT
SLAM
REEEEE
WHAT DO WE DO? WE CAN'T STAY HERE ALL DAY.
THUMP
THUMP
WHOA. LADIES. WHAT IS HAPPENING HERE?

QUICK! GO FOR HELP! THERE'S BEEN A - AN OUTBREAK!

AND THEN HIDE! GET IN YOUR ROOM AND LOCK THE DOORS!

OUTBREAK? THESE CHICKS APPEAR TO BE TWEAKING, BRO.

HEY, CHARLOTTE. HOW'D YOU GET ALL THAT STANK ON YOU?

IT'S A MONSTER! IT USED TO BE MEGAN DUNLOP!

WE'RE HAVING A HURRICANE REFUGEE BASH OVER IN BECKER. WHY DON'T YOU CLEAN UP AND COME OVER. LEAVE MASON AT HOME.

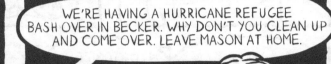

MEGAN DUNLOP IS A MEGABITCH.

REEETAIL!!

HOT, THOUGH.

BACK IN THE ELEVATOR

STUCK. UNBELIEVABLE.

IT'S GOING TO GET US!

THIS SUCKS.

MASON! GROW A VAGINA ALREADY AND CLIMB UP THROUGH THE HATCH.

I'M NOT SITTING IN THIS ELEVATOR A SECOND LONGER THAN I HAVE TO.

I CAN'T... I CAN'T...

WHY DON'T I GIVE IT A SHOT?

RESISTANCE IS FUTILE

OOOPS! FORGOT I HAD THAT!

RESISTANCE IS FUTILE

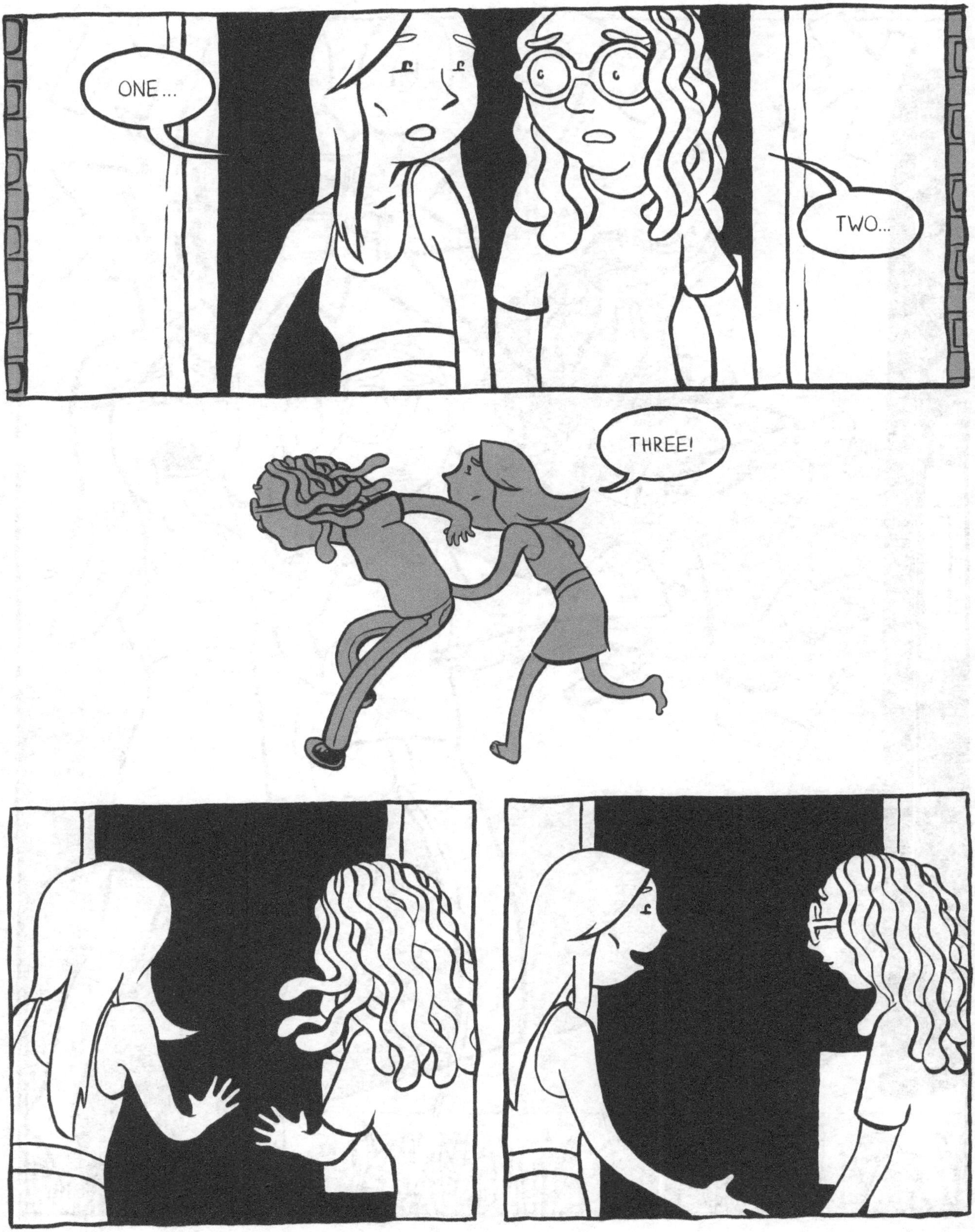
ONE...
TWO...
THREE!

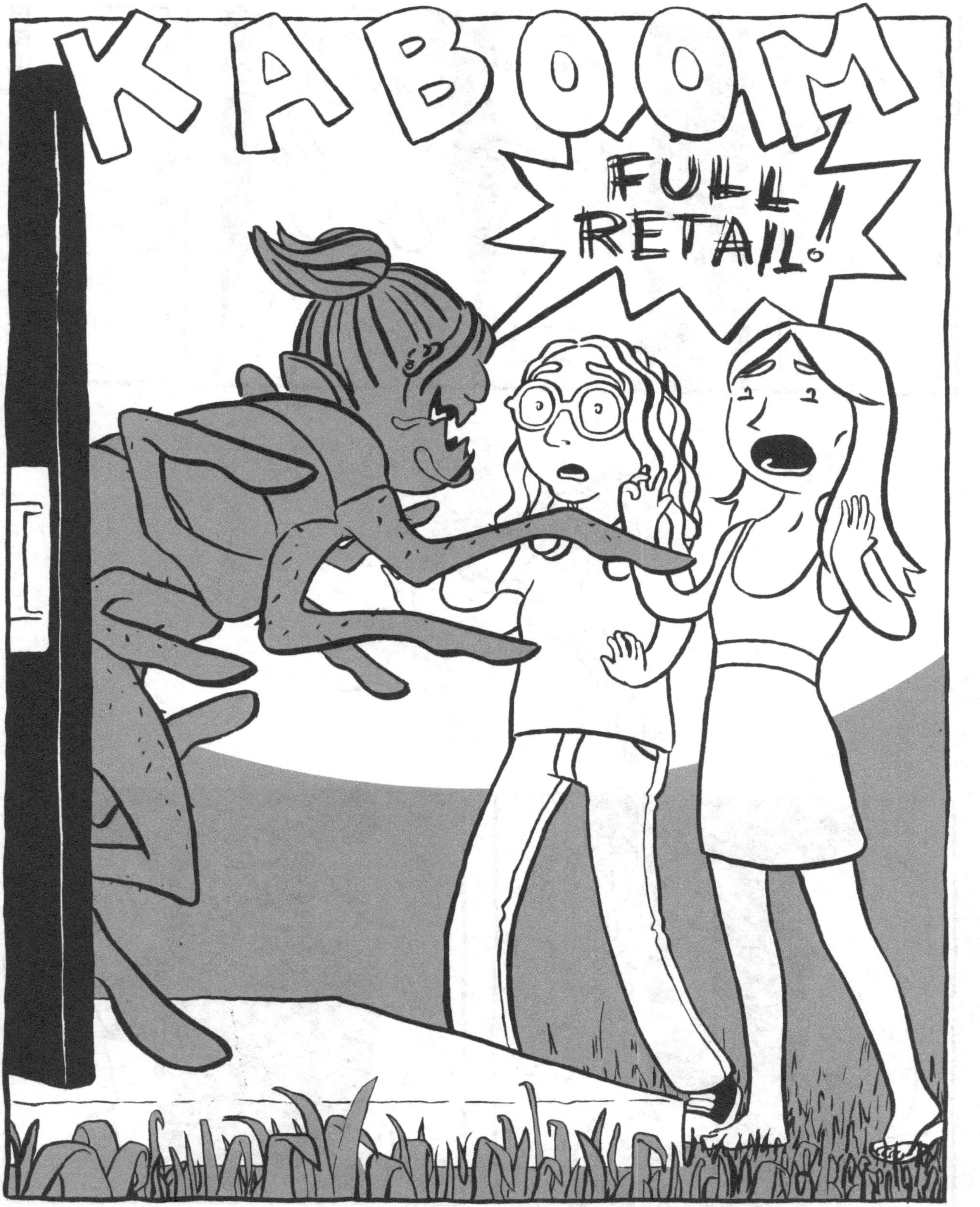
KABOOM
FULL RETAIL!

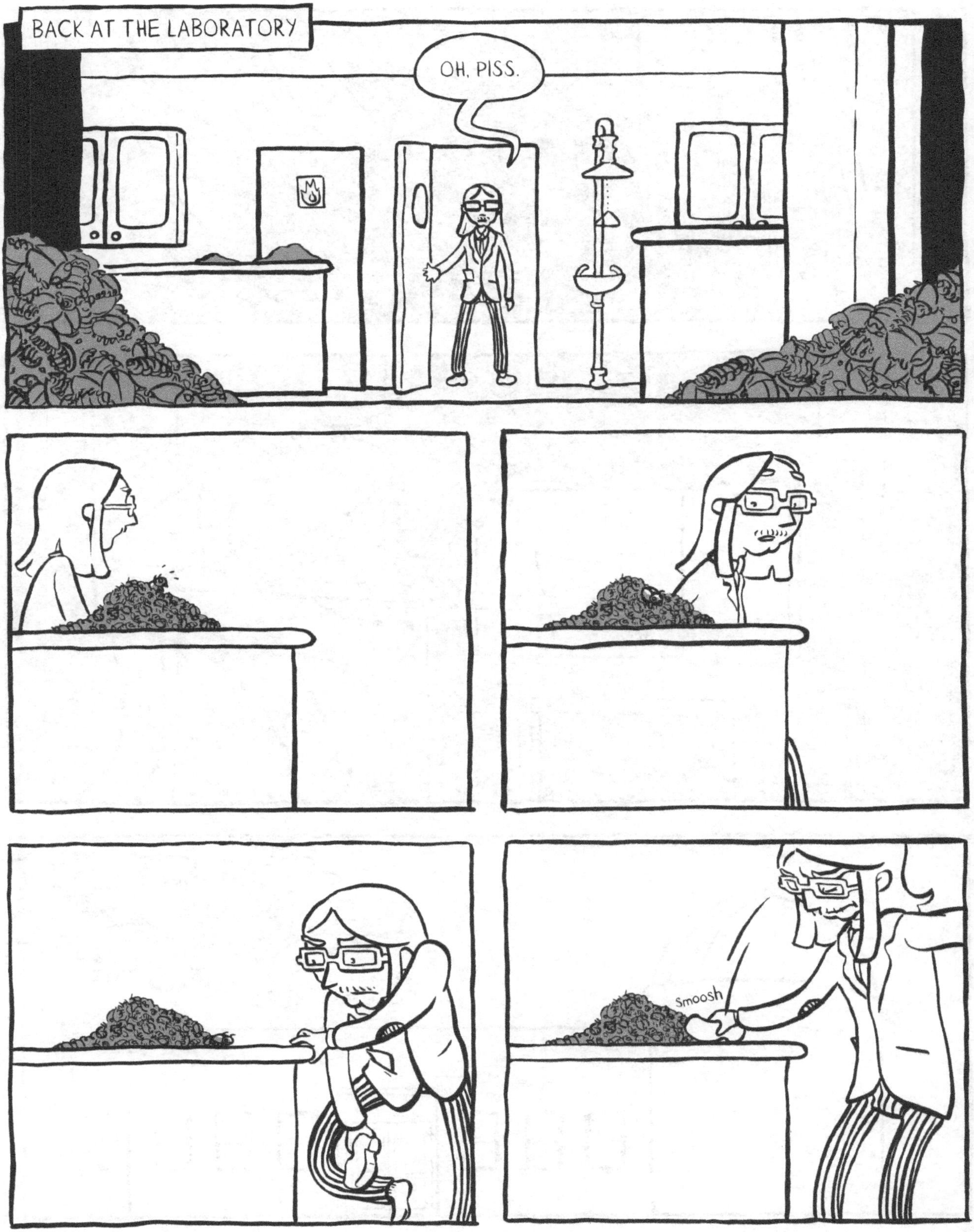
BACK AT THE LABORATORY
OH, PISS.
smoosh

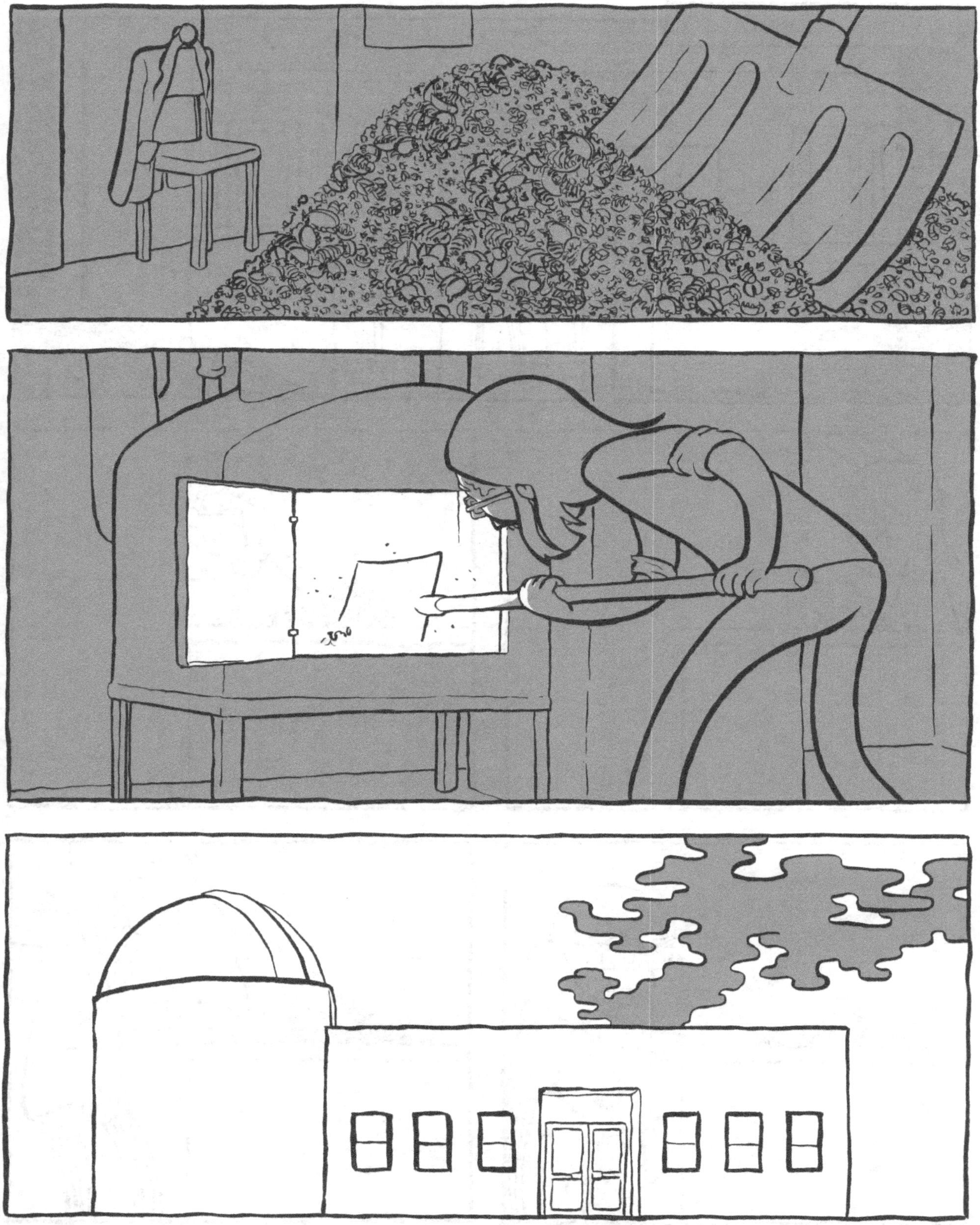

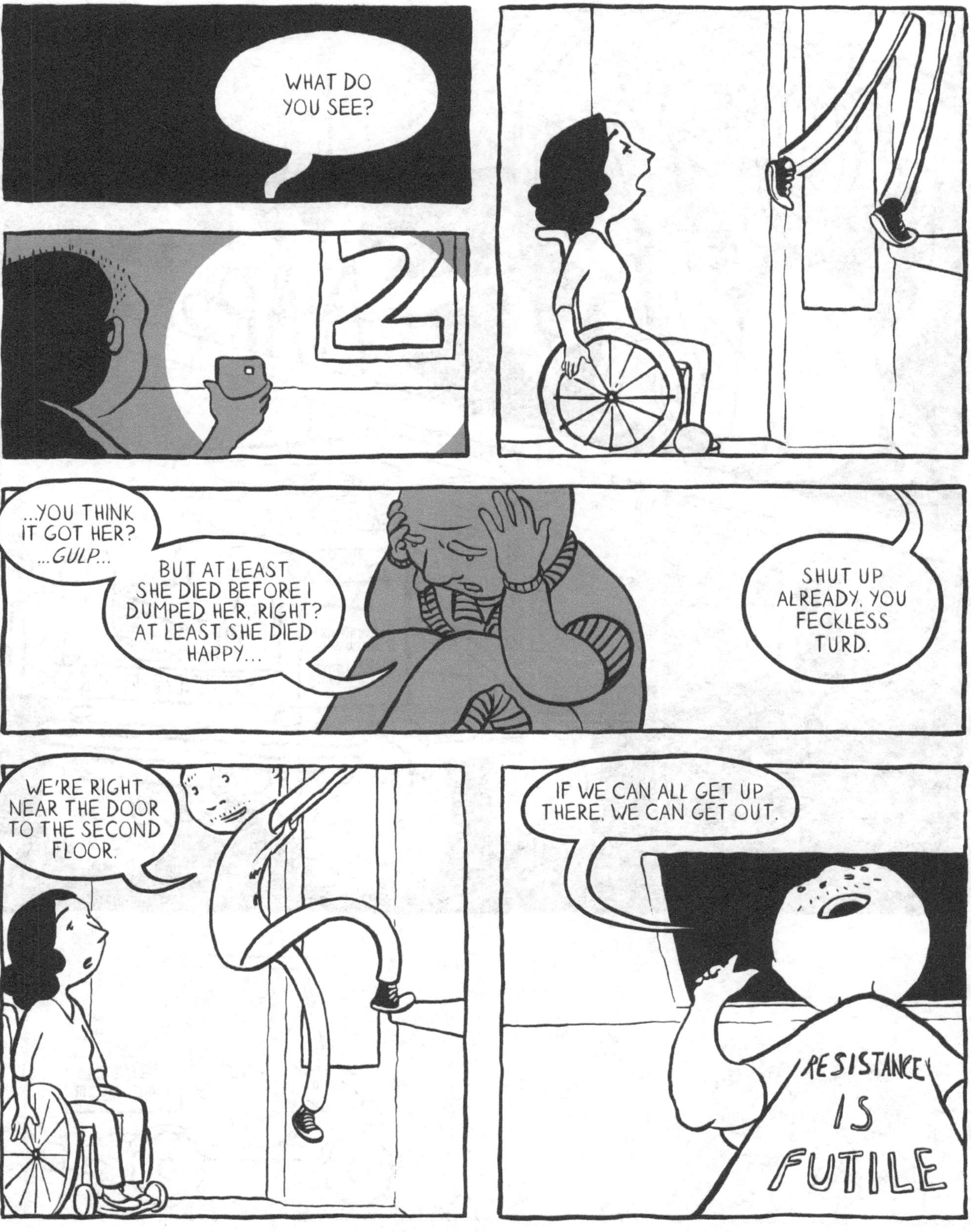
WHAT DO YOU SEE?
...YOU THINK IT GOT HER? ...*GULP*...
BUT AT LEAST SHE DIED BEFORE I DUMPED HER, RIGHT? AT LEAST SHE DIED HAPPY...
SHUT UP ALREADY, YOU FECKLESS TURD.
WE'RE RIGHT NEAR THE DOOR TO THE SECOND FLOOR.
IF WE CAN ALL GET UP THERE, WE CAN GET OUT.
RESISTANCE IS FUTILE

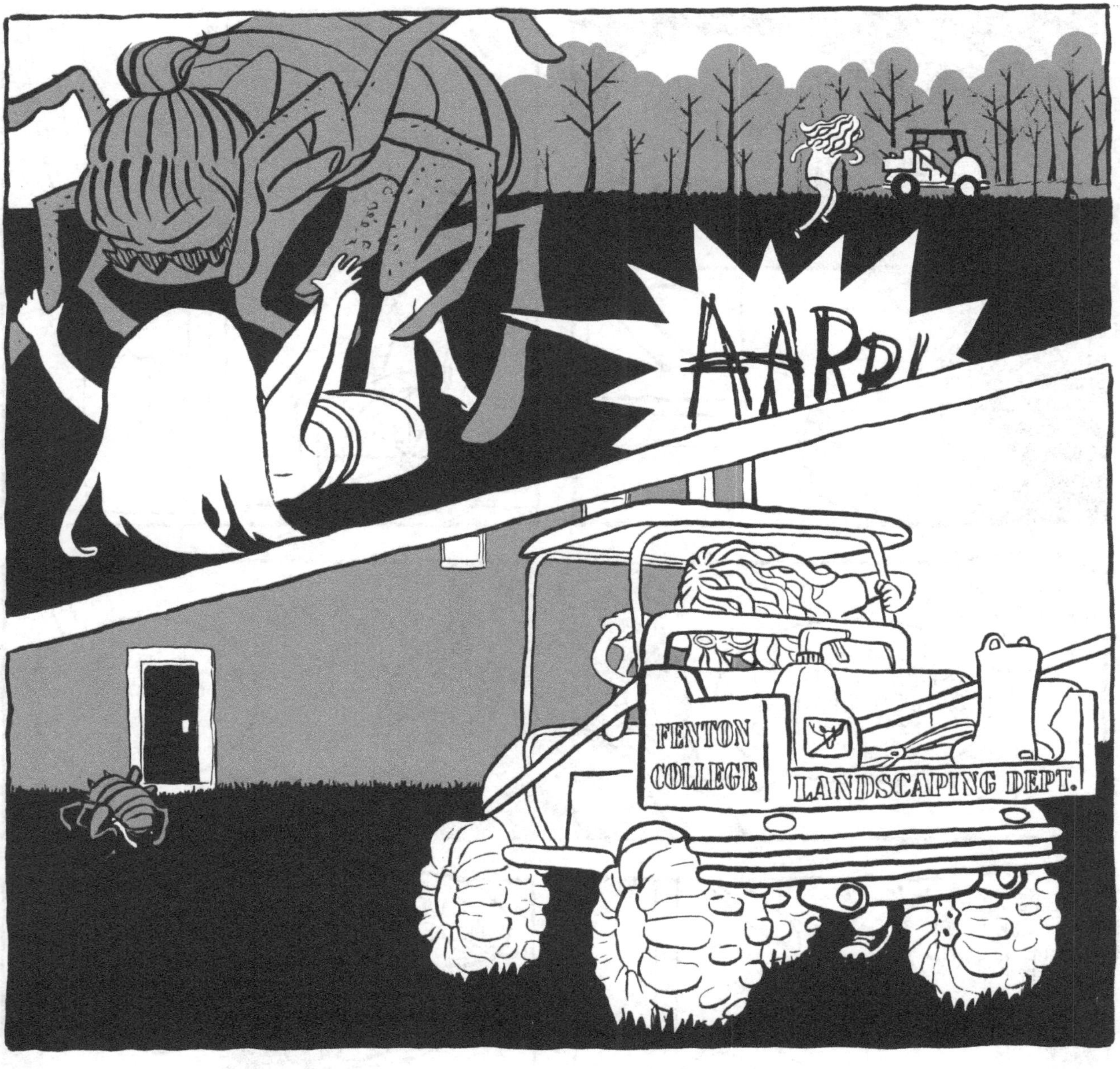
AAR
FENTON COLLEGE
LANDSCAPING DEPT.

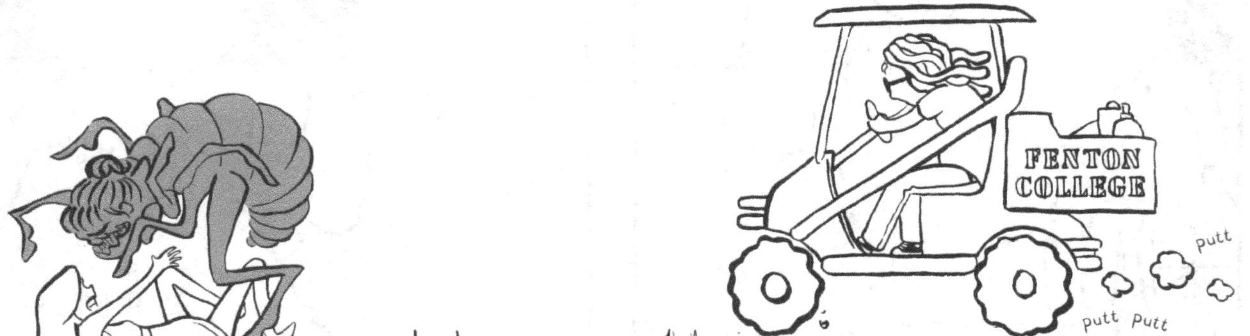
FENTON COLLEGE
putt
putt putt

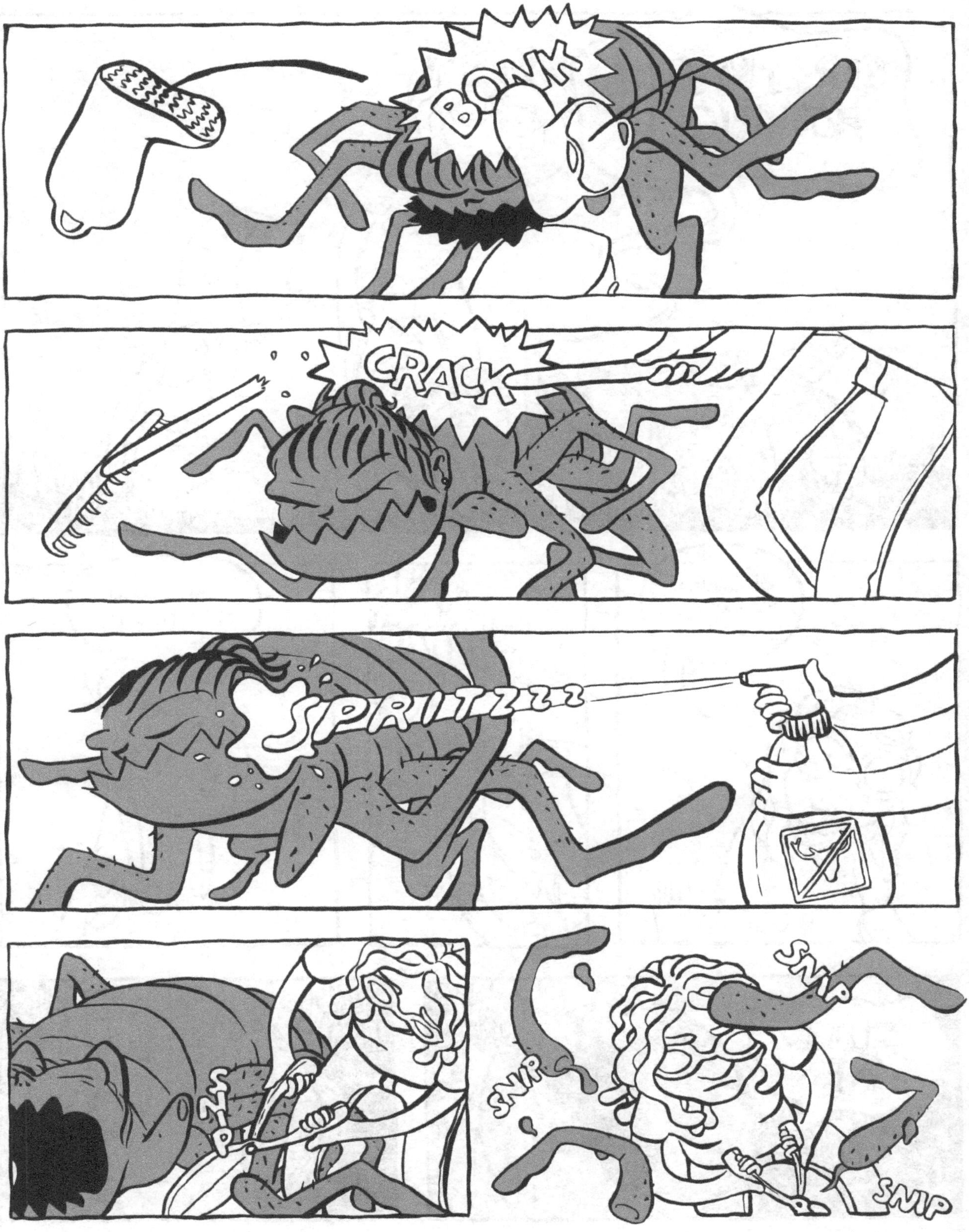
BONK
CRACK
SPRITZZZZ
SNIP
SNIP
SNIP
SNIP

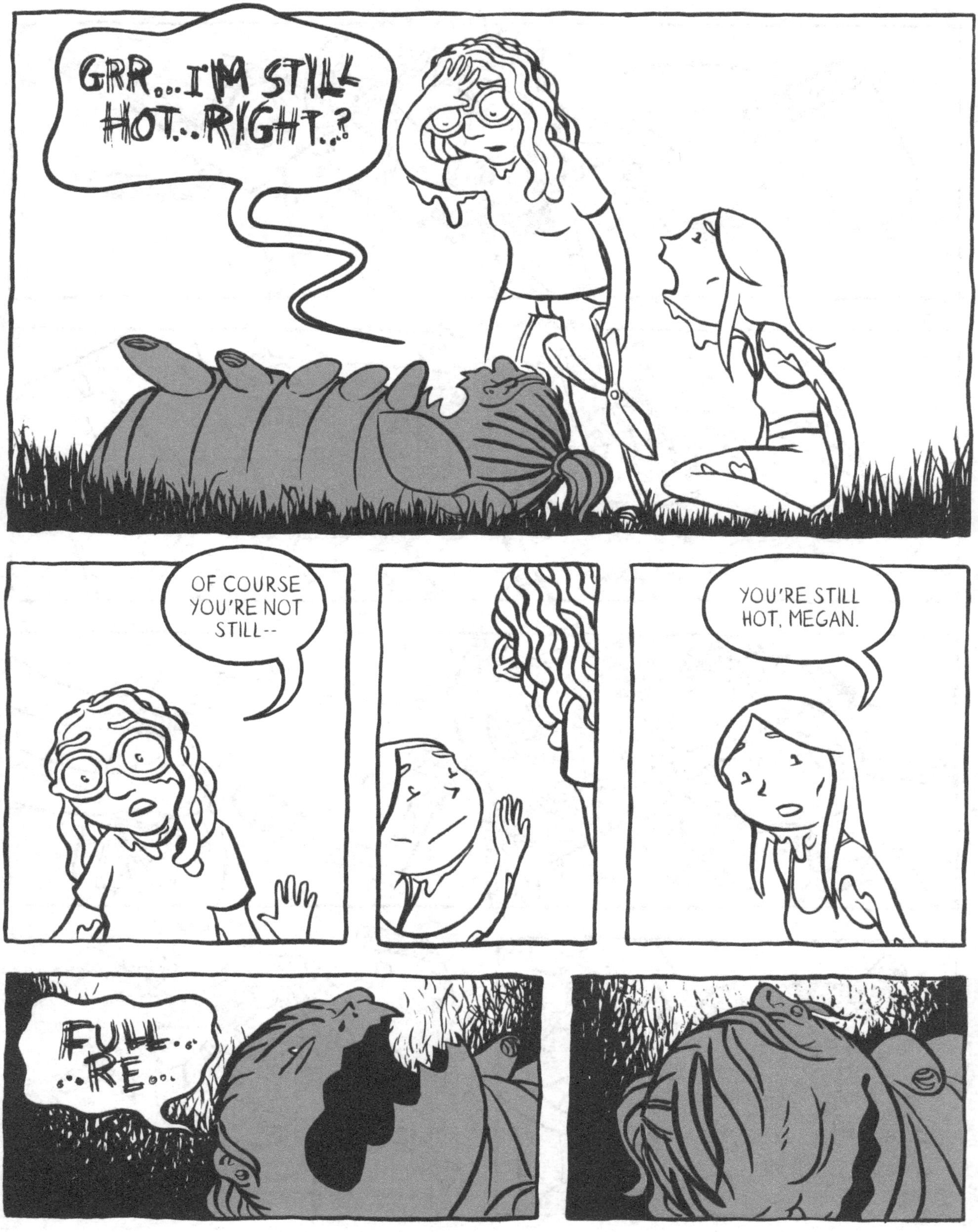
GRR... I'M STILL HOT... RIGHT..?
OF COURSE YOU'RE NOT STILL--
YOU'RE STILL HOT, MEGAN.
FULL... ...RE...

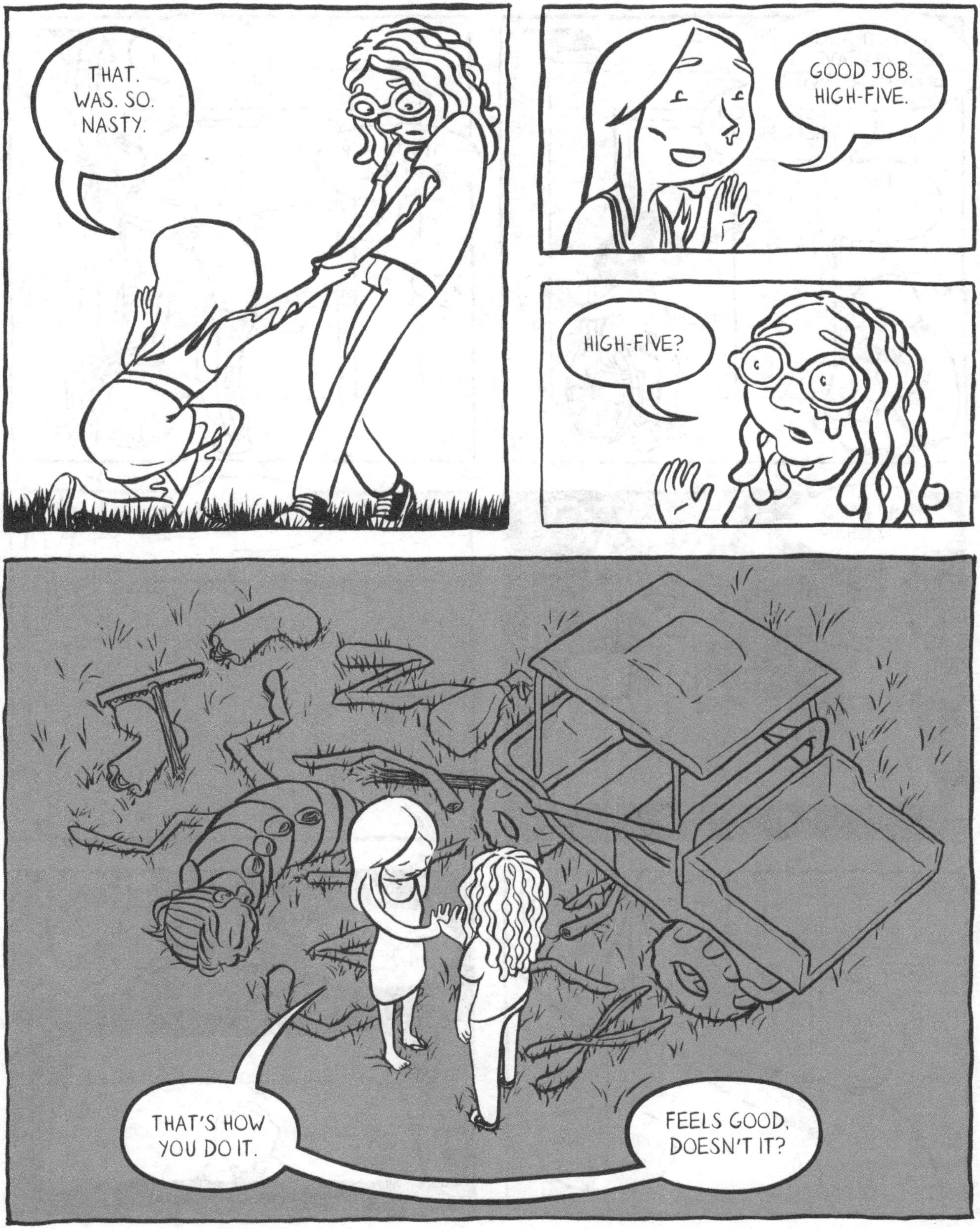
THAT. WAS. SO. NASTY.
GOOD JOB. HIGH-FIVE.
HIGH-FIVE?
THAT'S HOW YOU DO IT.
FEELS GOOD, DOESN'T IT?

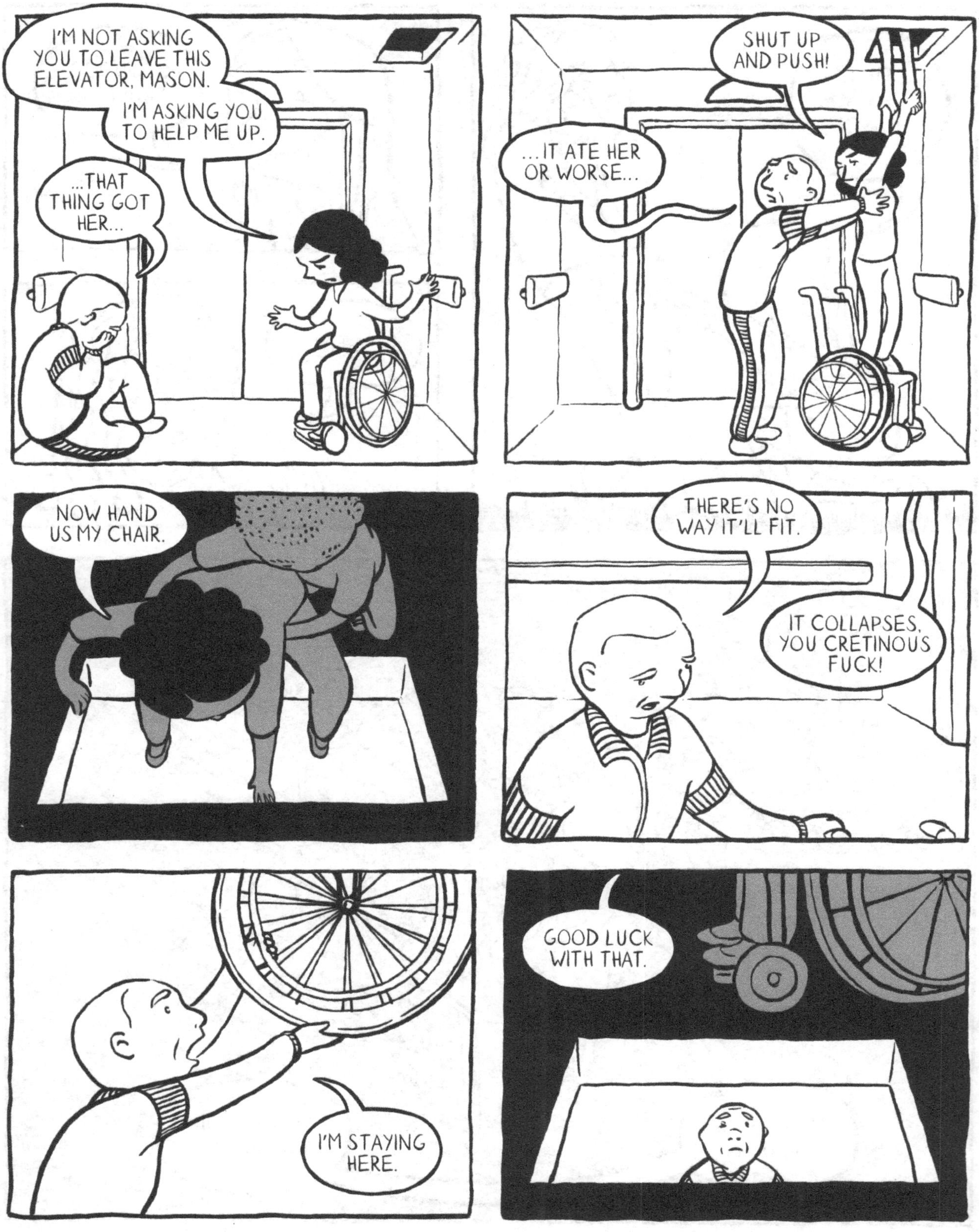
I'M NOT ASKING YOU TO LEAVE THIS ELEVATOR, MASON.
I'M ASKING YOU TO HELP ME UP.
...THAT THING GOT HER...
SHUT UP AND PUSH!
...IT ATE HER OR WORSE...
NOW HAND US MY CHAIR.
THERE'S NO WAY IT'LL FIT.
IT COLLAPSES, YOU CRETINOUS FUCK!
I'M STAYING HERE.
GOOD LUCK WITH THAT.

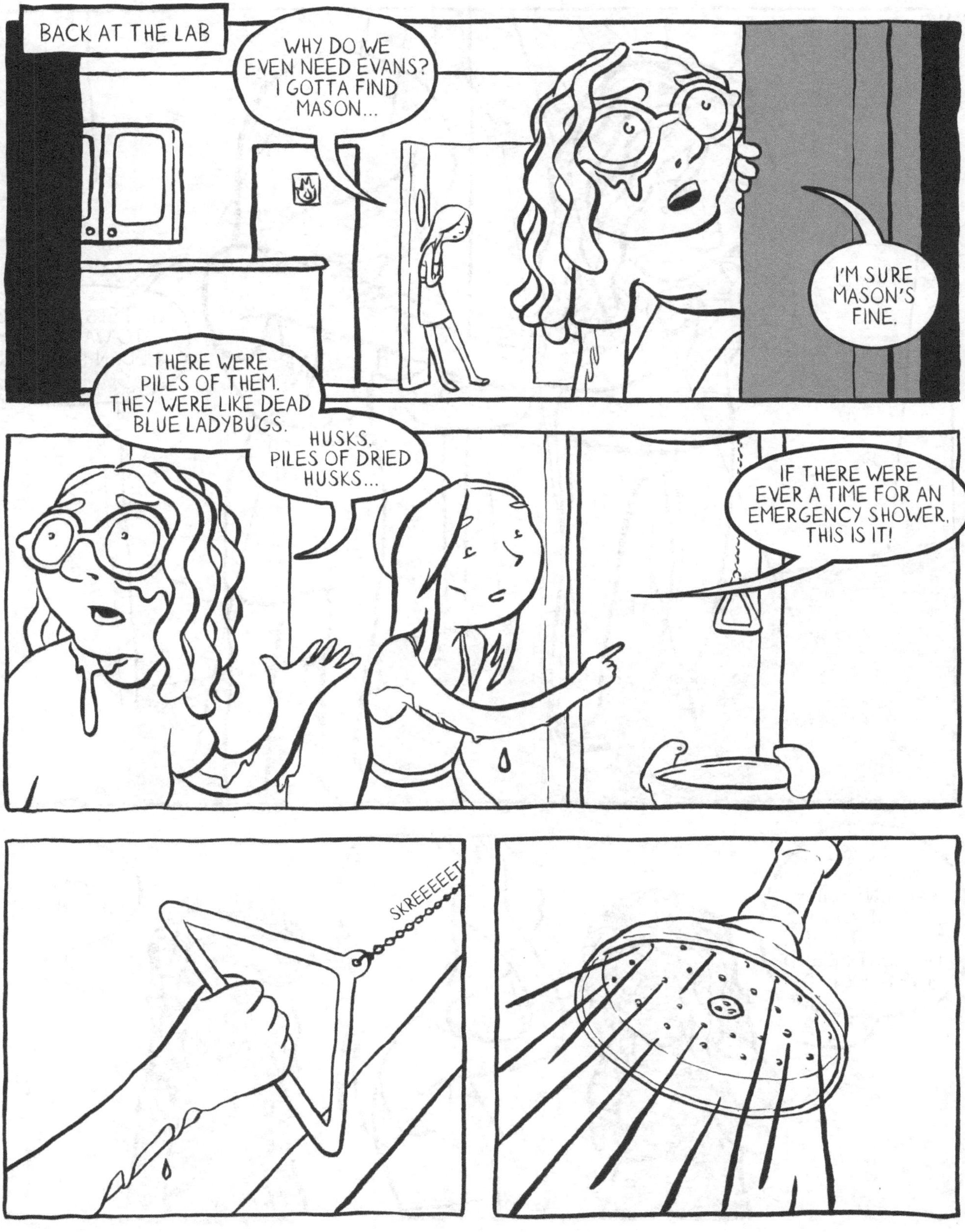
BACK AT THE LAB
WHY DO WE EVEN NEED EVANS? I GOTTA FIND MASON...
I'M SURE MASON'S FINE.
THERE WERE PILES OF THEM. THEY WERE LIKE DEAD BLUE LADYBUGS.
HUSKS. PILES OF DRIED HUSKS...
IF THERE WERE EVER A TIME FOR AN EMERGENCY SHOWER, THIS IS IT!
SKREEEEEET

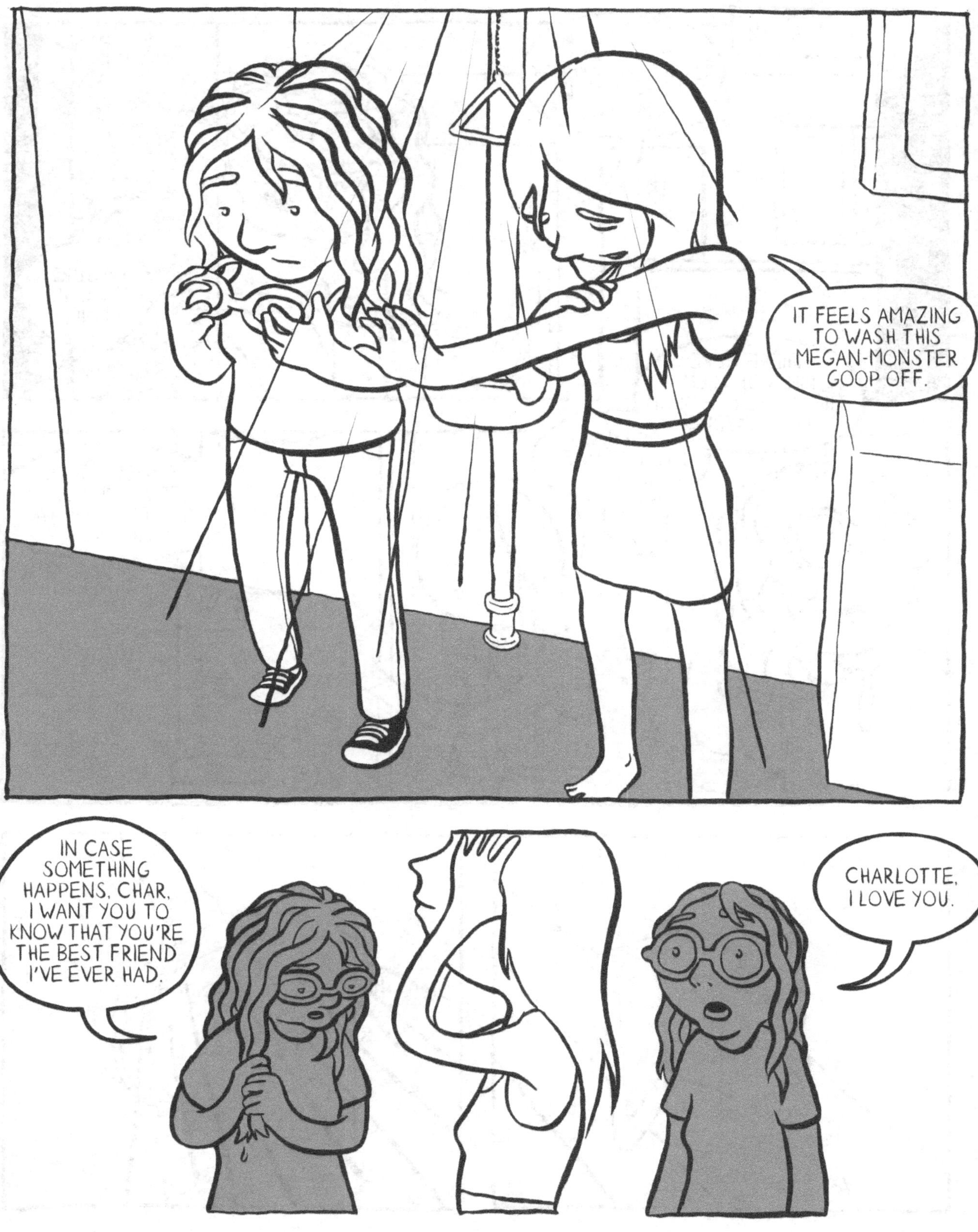
IT FEELS AMAZING TO WASH THIS MEGAN-MONSTER GOOP OFF.
IN CASE SOMETHING HAPPENS, CHAR, I WANT YOU TO KNOW THAT YOU'RE THE BEST FRIEND I'VE EVER HAD.
CHARLOTTE, I LOVE YOU.

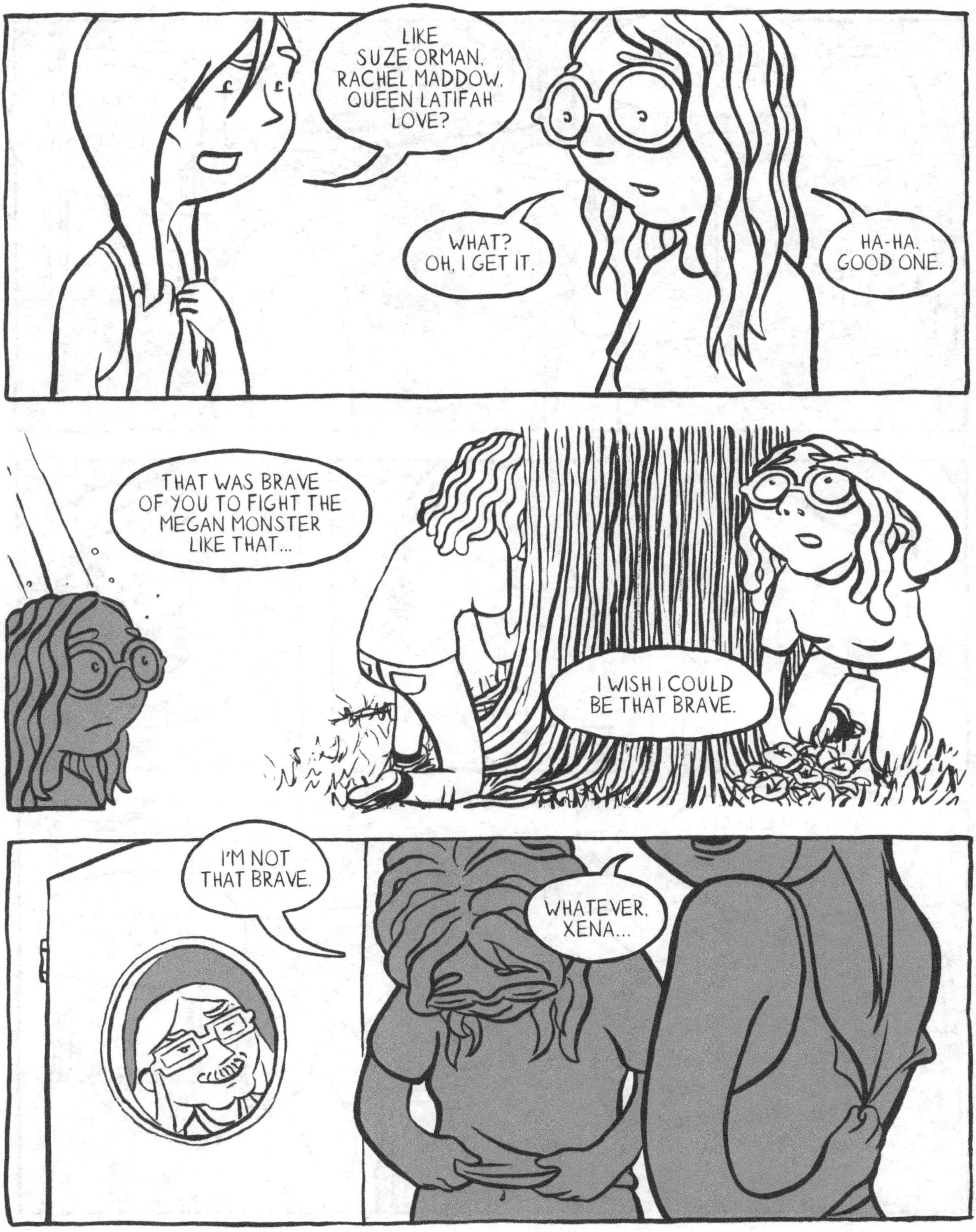
LIKE SUZE ORMAN, RACHEL MADDOW, QUEEN LATIFAH LOVE?
WHAT? OH, I GET IT.
HA-HA. GOOD ONE.
THAT WAS BRAVE OF YOU TO FIGHT THE MEGAN MONSTER LIKE THAT...
I WISH I COULD BE THAT BRAVE.
I'M NOT THAT BRAVE.
WHATEVER, XENA...

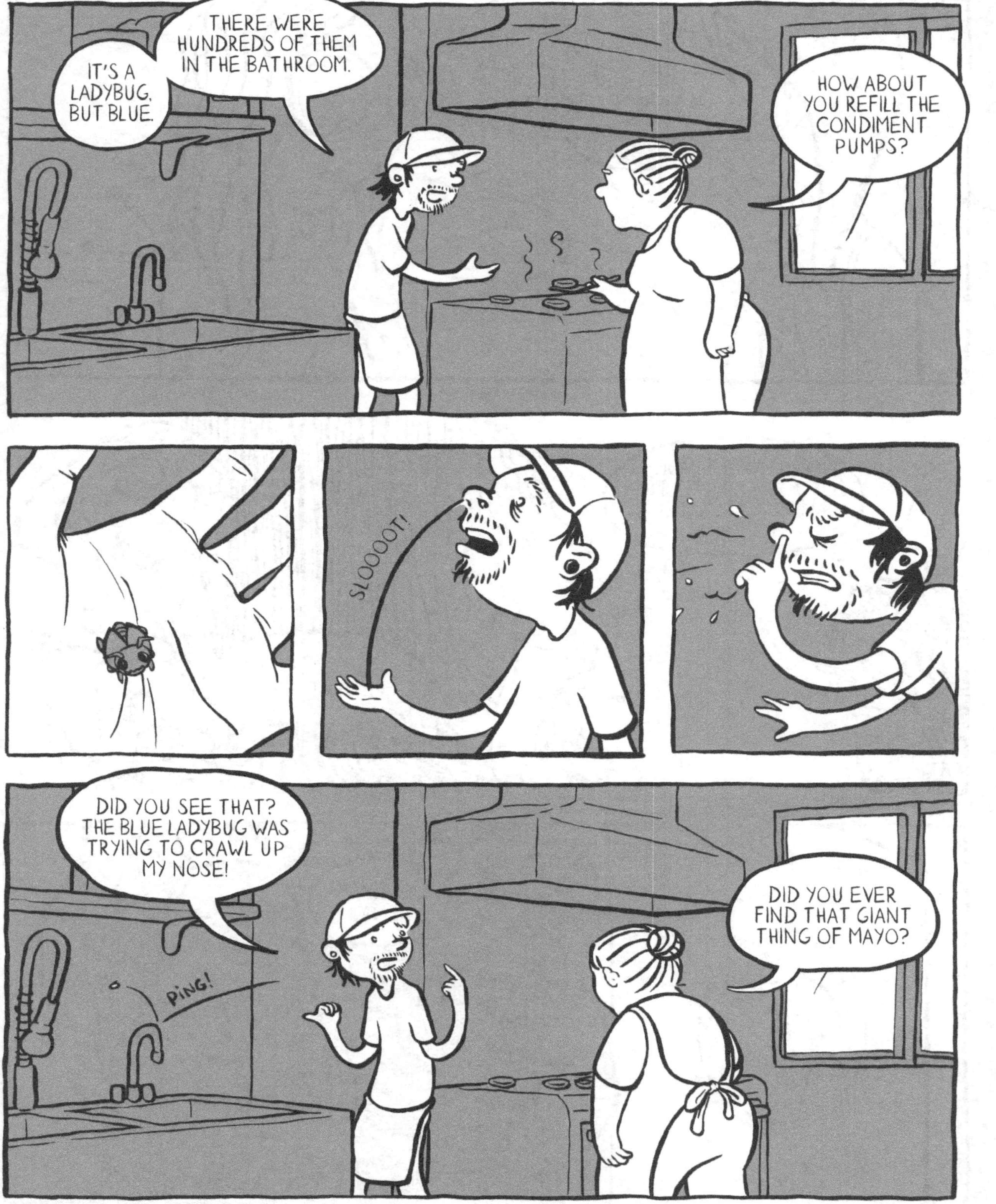
IT'S A LADYBUG, BUT BLUE.
THERE WERE HUNDREDS OF THEM IN THE BATHROOM.
HOW ABOUT YOU REFILL THE CONDIMENT PUMPS?
SLOOOOT!
DID YOU SEE THAT? THE BLUE LADYBUG WAS TRYING TO CRAWL UP MY NOSE!
PING!
DID YOU EVER FIND THAT GIANT THING OF MAYO?

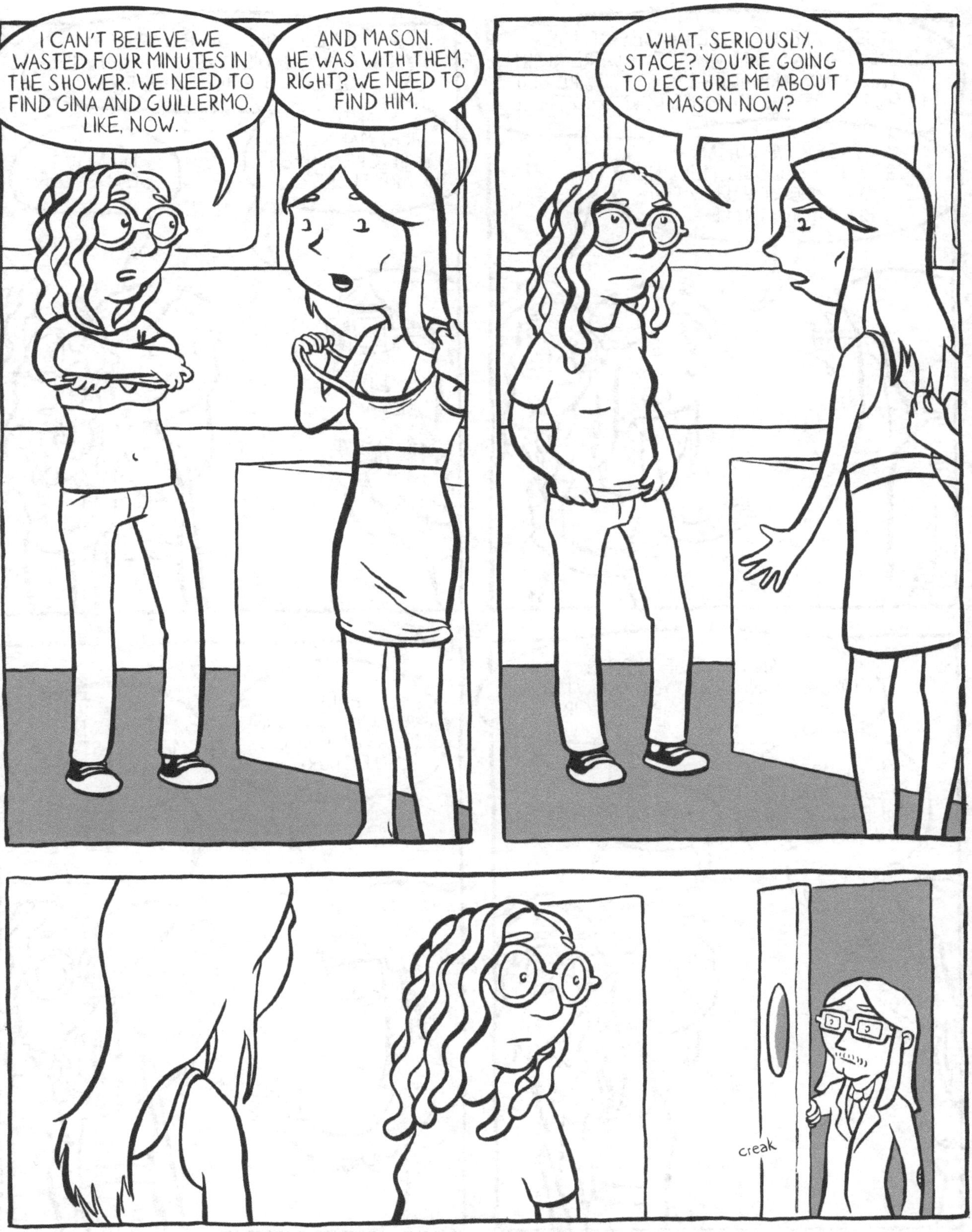

I CAN'T BELIEVE WE WASTED FOUR MINUTES IN THE SHOWER. WE NEED TO FIND GINA AND GUILLERMO. LIKE, NOW.
AND MASON. HE WAS WITH THEM, RIGHT? WE NEED TO FIND HIM.
WHAT, SERIOUSLY, STACE? YOU'RE GOING TO LECTURE ME ABOUT MASON NOW?
creak

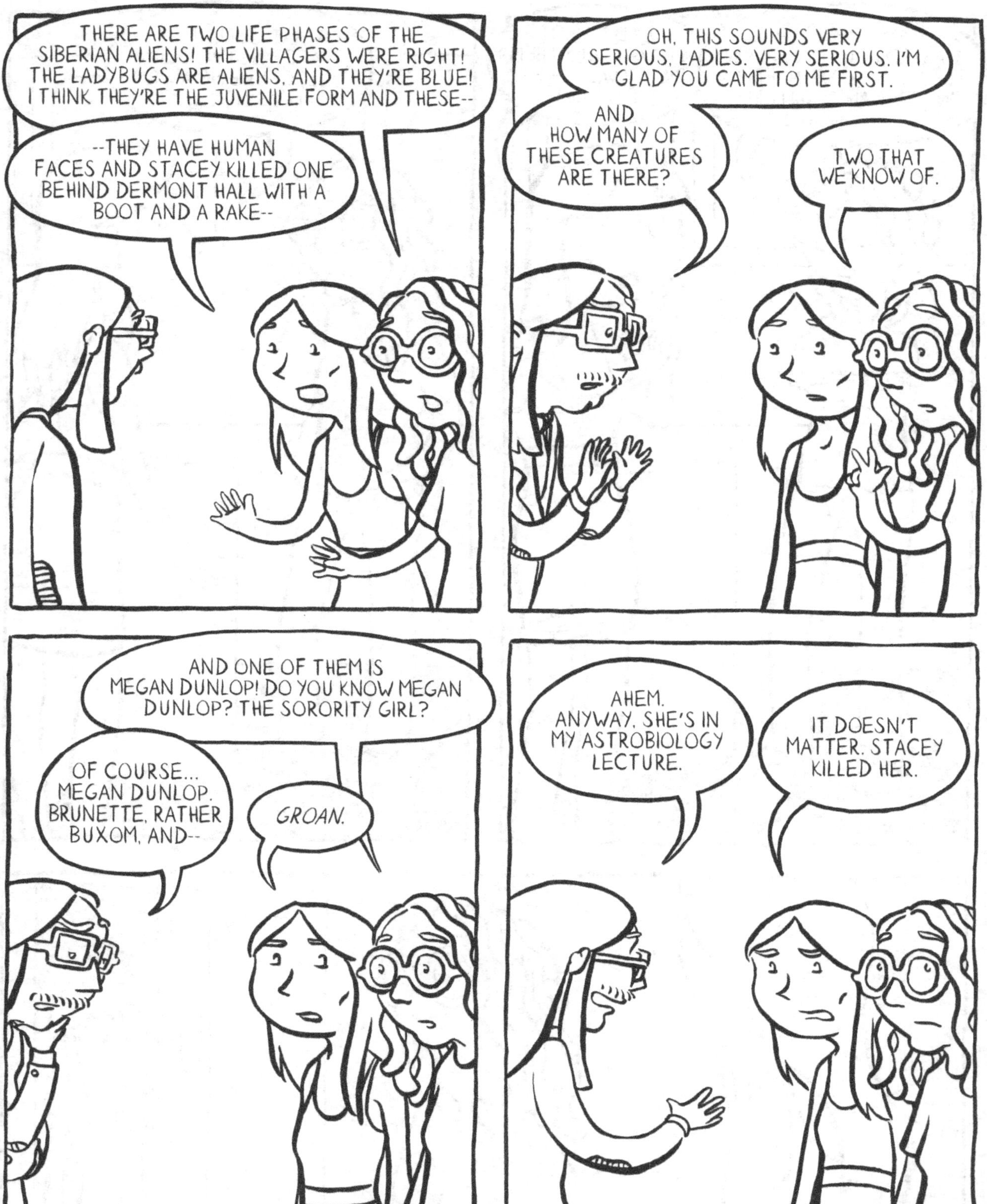
THERE ARE TWO LIFE PHASES OF THE SIBERIAN ALIENS! THE VILLAGERS WERE RIGHT! THE LADYBUGS ARE ALIENS, AND THEY'RE BLUE! I THINK THEY'RE THE JUVENILE FORM AND THESE--
--THEY HAVE HUMAN FACES AND STACEY KILLED ONE BEHIND DERMONT HALL WITH A BOOT AND A RAKE--
OH, THIS SOUNDS VERY SERIOUS, LADIES. VERY SERIOUS. I'M GLAD YOU CAME TO ME FIRST.
AND HOW MANY OF THESE CREATURES ARE THERE?
TWO THAT WE KNOW OF.
AND ONE OF THEM IS MEGAN DUNLOP! DO YOU KNOW MEGAN DUNLOP? THE SORORITY GIRL?
OF COURSE... MEGAN DUNLOP. BRUNETTE, RATHER BUXOM, AND--
GROAN.
AHEM. ANYWAY, SHE'S IN MY ASTROBIOLOGY LECTURE.
IT DOESN'T MATTER. STACEY KILLED HER.

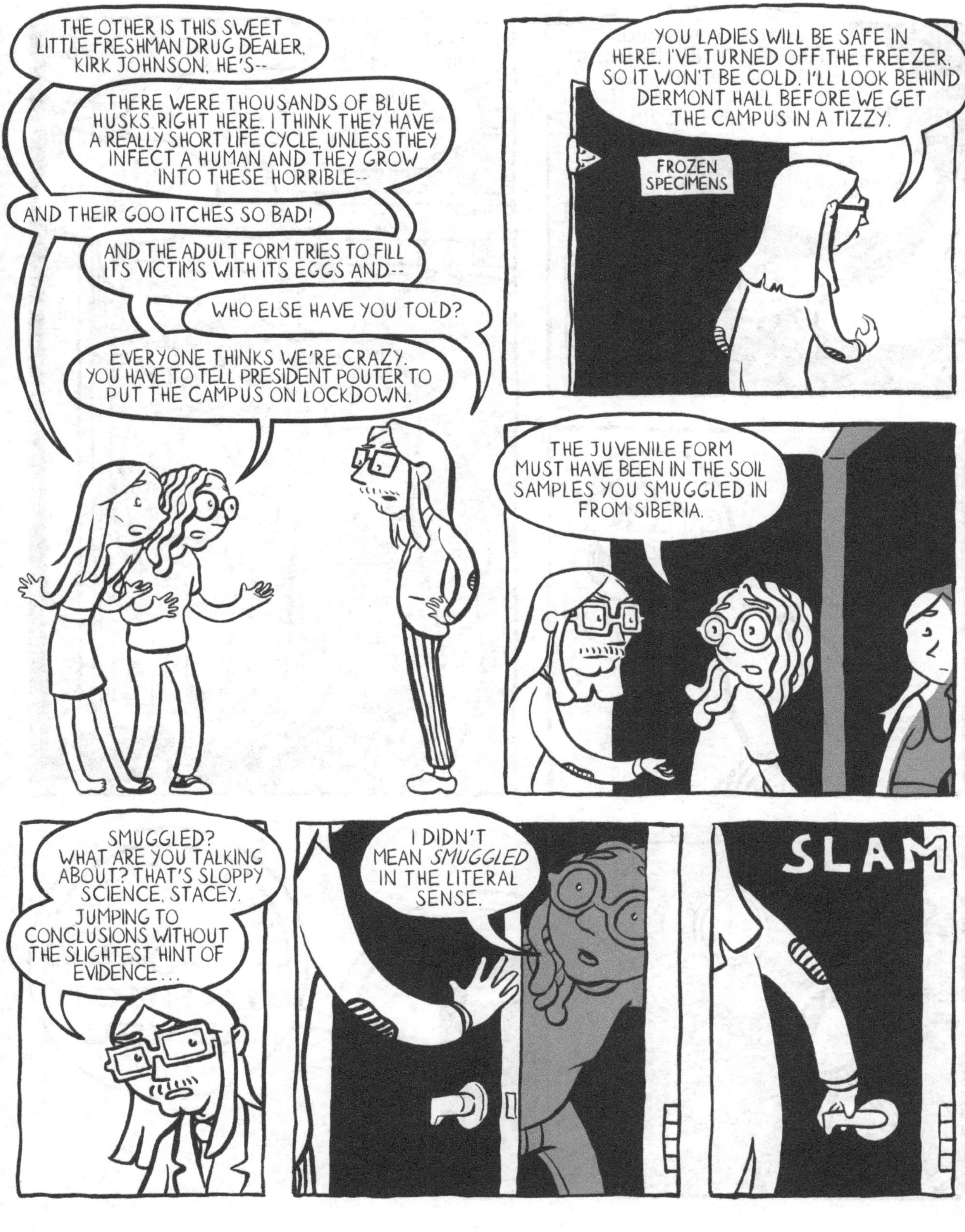
THE OTHER IS THIS SWEET LITTLE FRESHMAN DRUG DEALER, KIRK JOHNSON, HE'S--
THERE WERE THOUSANDS OF BLUE HUSKS RIGHT HERE. I THINK THEY HAVE A REALLY SHORT LIFE CYCLE, UNLESS THEY INFECT A HUMAN AND THEY GROW INTO THESE HORRIBLE--
AND THEIR GOO ITCHES SO BAD!
AND THE ADULT FORM TRIES TO FILL ITS VICTIMS WITH ITS EGGS AND--
WHO ELSE HAVE YOU TOLD?
EVERYONE THINKS WE'RE CRAZY. YOU HAVE TO TELL PRESIDENT POUTER TO PUT THE CAMPUS ON LOCKDOWN.
YOU LADIES WILL BE SAFE IN HERE. I'VE TURNED OFF THE FREEZER, SO IT WON'T BE COLD. I'LL LOOK BEHIND DERMONT HALL BEFORE WE GET THE CAMPUS IN A TIZZY.
FROZEN SPECIMENS
THE JUVENILE FORM MUST HAVE BEEN IN THE SOIL SAMPLES YOU SMUGGLED IN FROM SIBERIA.
SMUGGLED? WHAT ARE YOU TALKING ABOUT? THAT'S SLOPPY SCIENCE, STACEY.
JUMPING TO CONCLUSIONS WITHOUT THE SLIGHTEST HINT OF EVIDENCE...
I DIDN'T MEAN *SMUGGLED* IN THE LITERAL SENSE.
SLAM

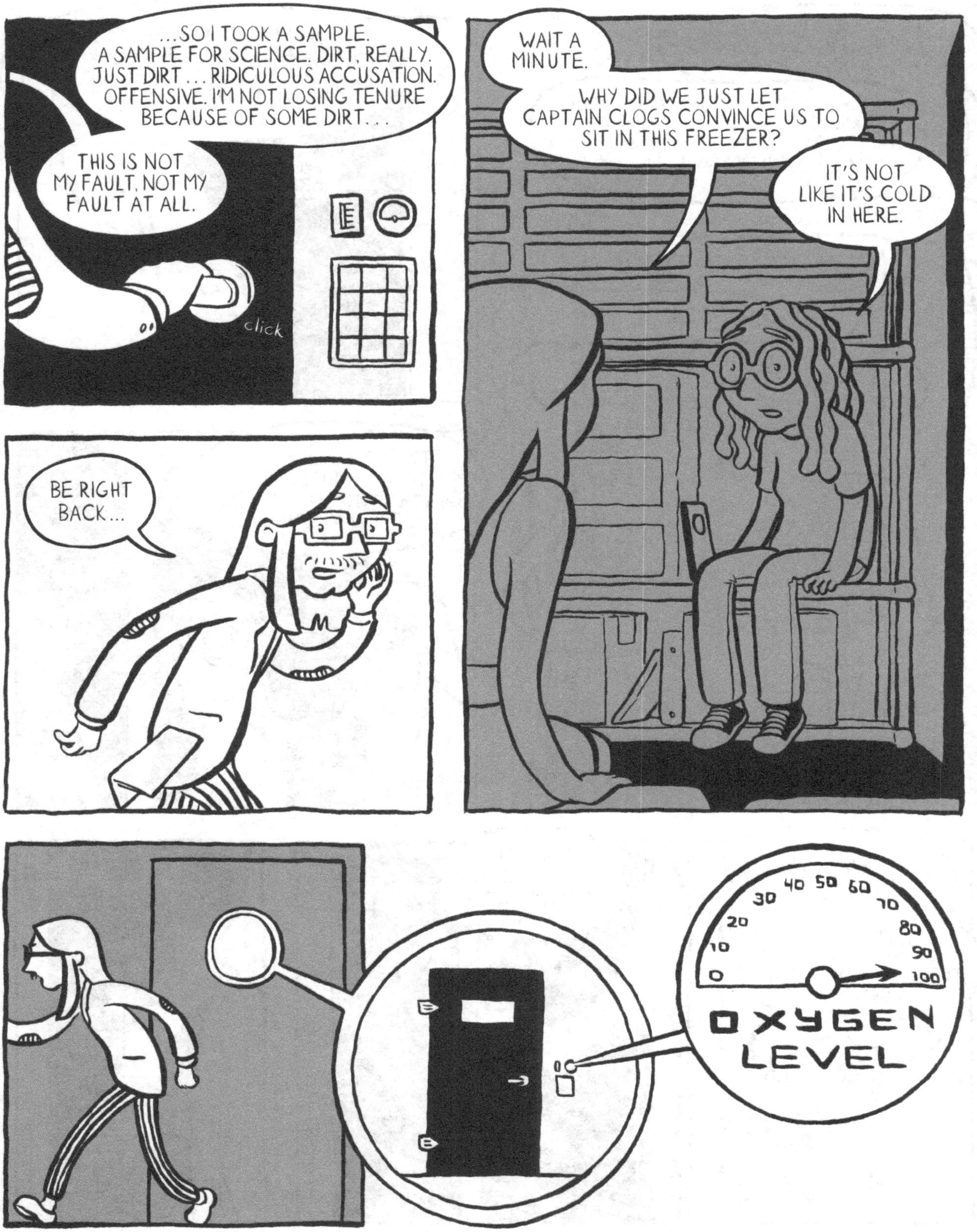
...SO I TOOK A SAMPLE. A SAMPLE FOR SCIENCE. DIRT, REALLY. JUST DIRT... RIDICULOUS ACCUSATION. OFFENSIVE. I'M NOT LOSING TENURE BECAUSE OF SOME DIRT...
THIS IS NOT MY FAULT, NOT MY FAULT AT ALL.
click
WAIT A MINUTE.
WHY DID WE JUST LET CAPTAIN CLOGS CONVINCE US TO SIT IN THIS FREEZER?
IT'S NOT LIKE IT'S COLD IN HERE.
BE RIGHT BACK...
0 10 20 30 40 50 60 70 80 90 100
OXYGEN LEVEL

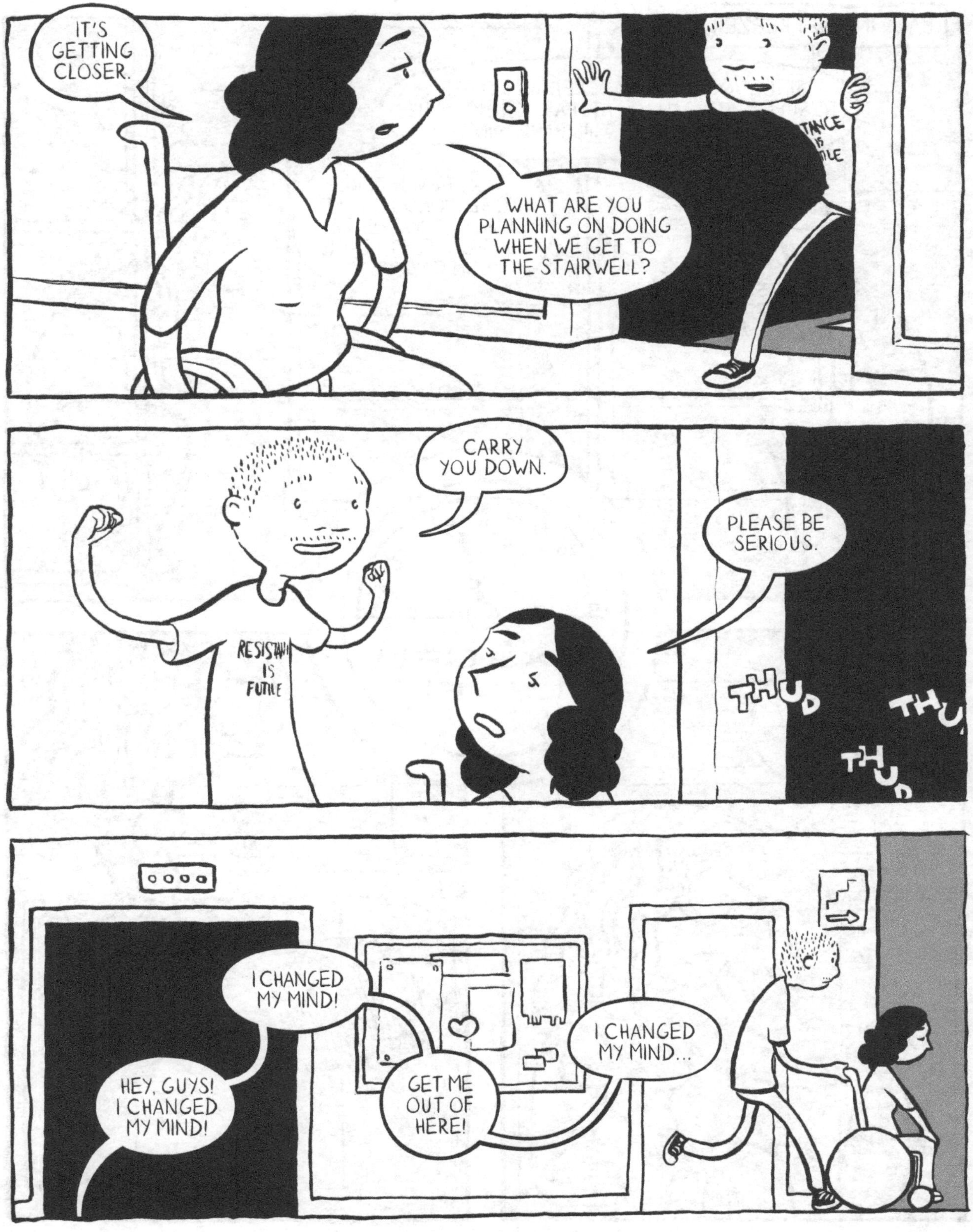
IT'S GETTING CLOSER.
WHAT ARE YOU PLANNING ON DOING WHEN WE GET TO THE STAIRWELL?
CARRY YOU DOWN.
PLEASE BE SERIOUS.
THUD
THUD
HEY, GUYS! I CHANGED MY MIND!
I CHANGED MY MIND!
GET ME OUT OF HERE!
I CHANGED MY MIND...

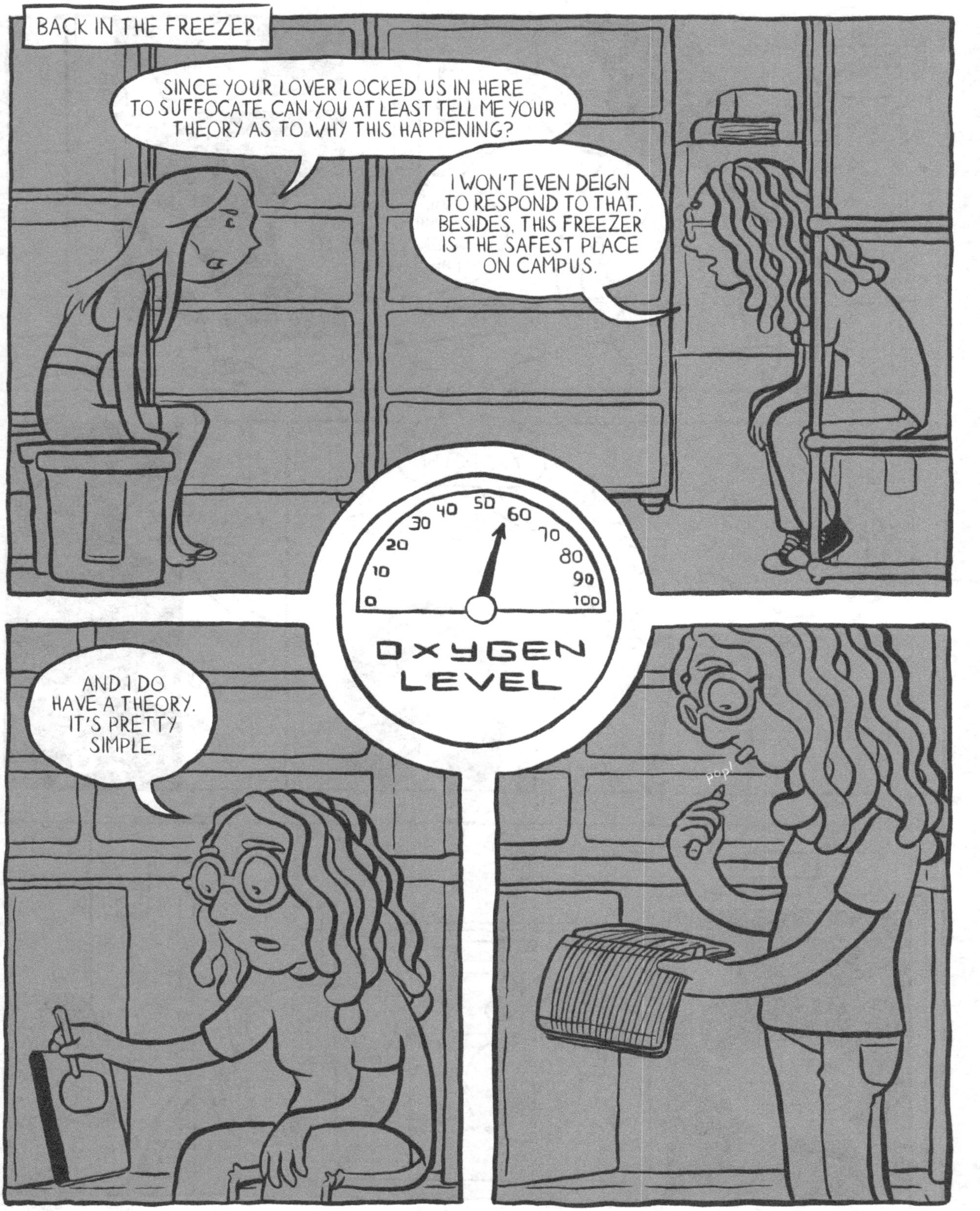
BACK IN THE FREEZER
SINCE YOUR LOVER LOCKED US IN HERE TO SUFFOCATE, CAN YOU AT LEAST TELL ME YOUR THEORY AS TO WHY THIS HAPPENING?
I WON'T EVEN DEIGN TO RESPOND TO THAT. BESIDES, THIS FREEZER IS THE SAFEST PLACE ON CAMPUS.
0 10 20 30 40 50 60 70 80 90 100
OXYGEN LEVEL
AND I DO HAVE A THEORY. IT'S PRETTY SIMPLE.
POP!

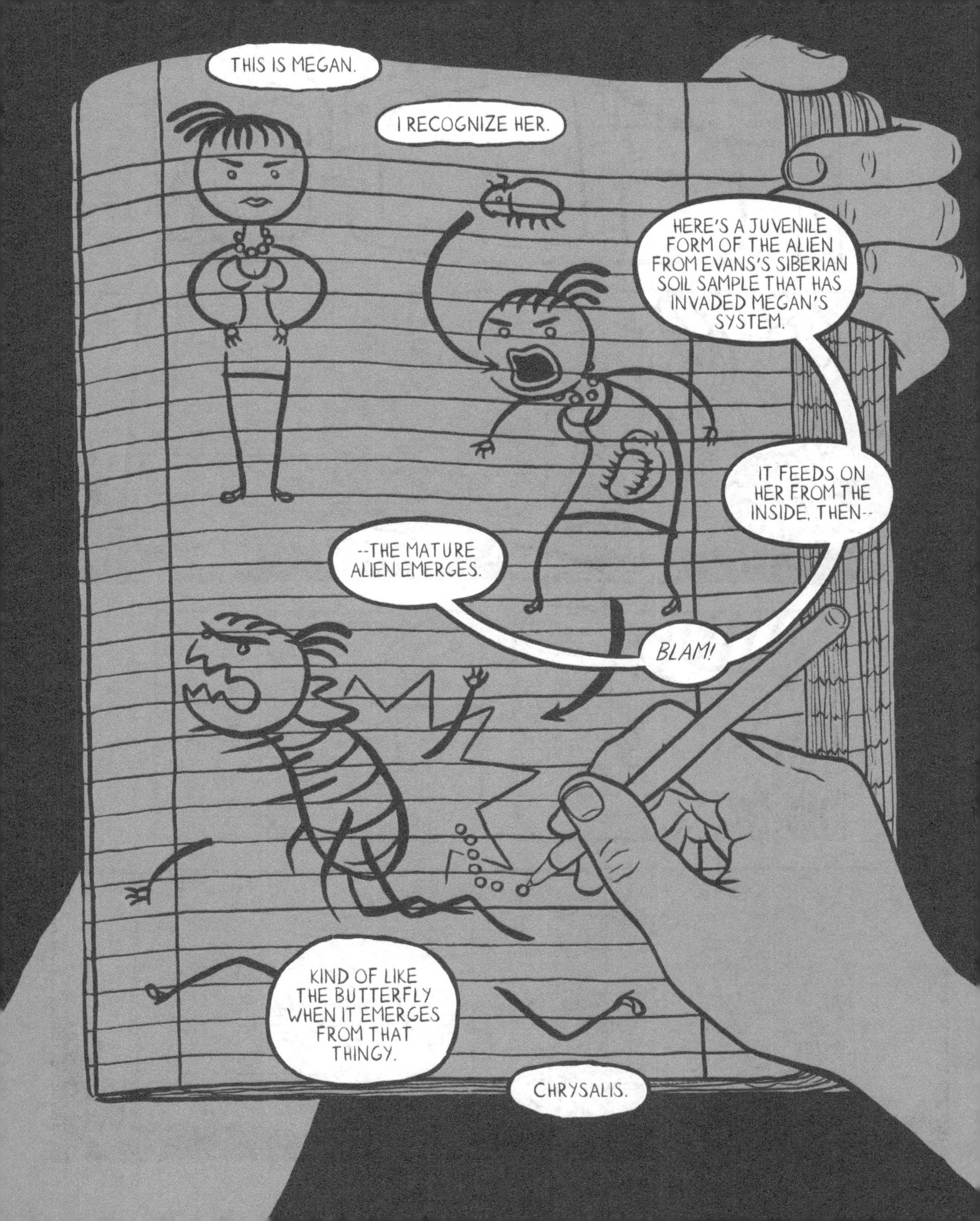
THIS IS MEGAN.
I RECOGNIZE HER.
HERE'S A JUVENILE FORM OF THE ALIEN FROM EVANS'S SIBERIAN SOIL SAMPLE THAT HAS INVADED MEGAN'S SYSTEM.
IT FEEDS ON HER FROM THE INSIDE, THEN--
--THE MATURE ALIEN EMERGES.
BLAM!
KIND OF LIKE THE BUTTERFLY WHEN IT EMERGES FROM THAT THINGY.
CHRYSALIS.

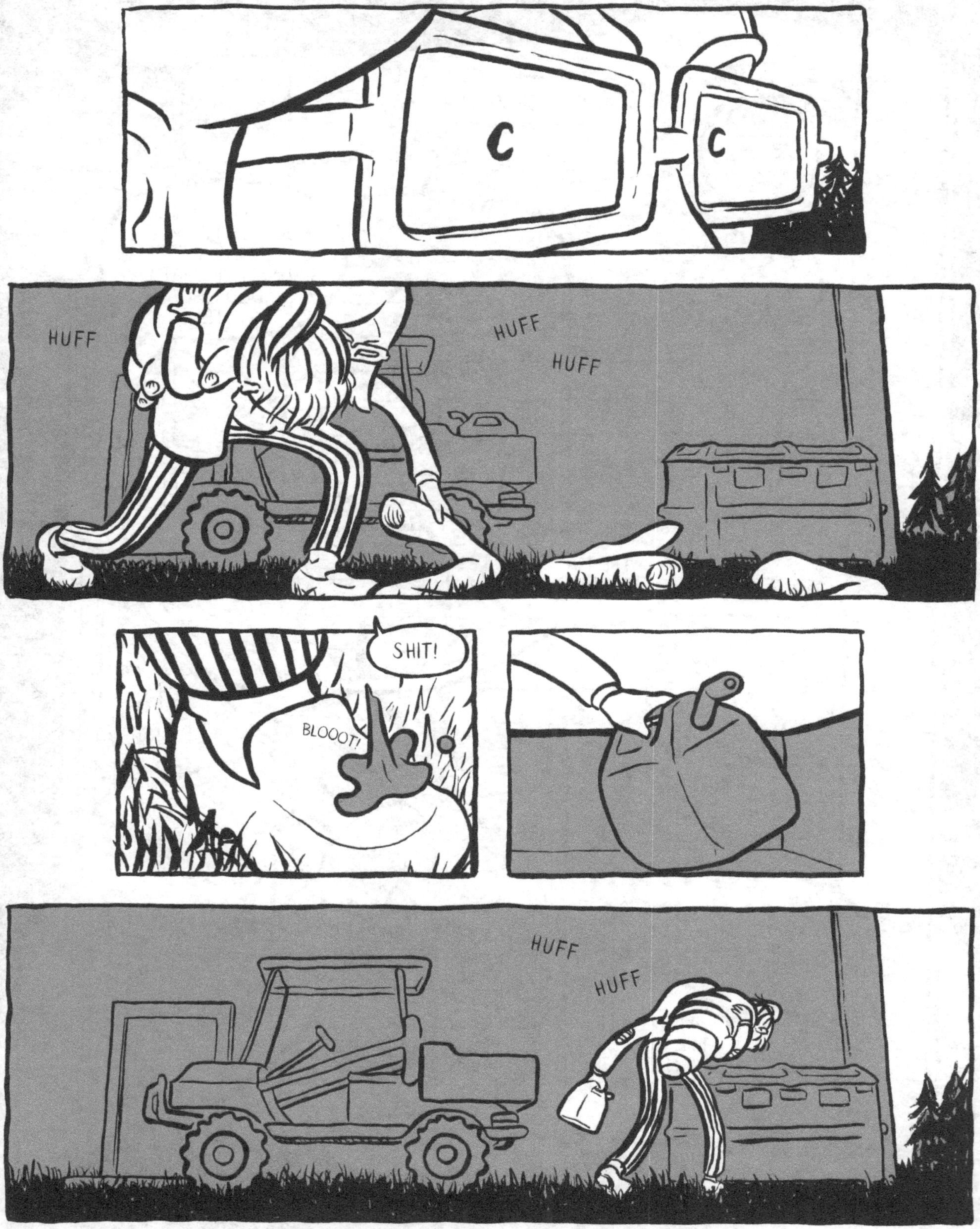
HUFF
HUFF
HUFF
SHIT!
BLOOOT!
HUFF
HUFF

glub
blub
CHIFFF
ONE DOWN.

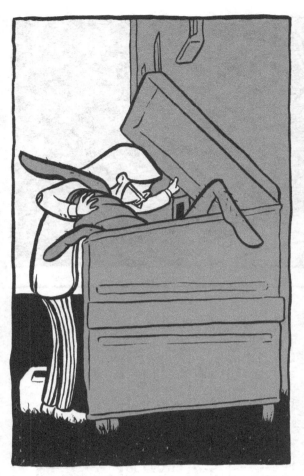

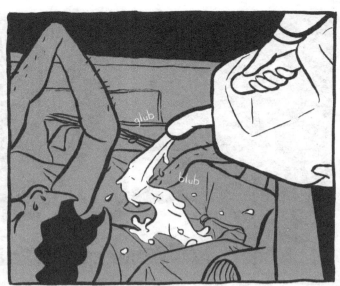

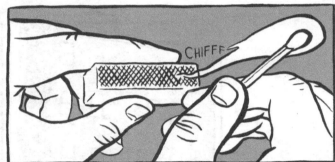

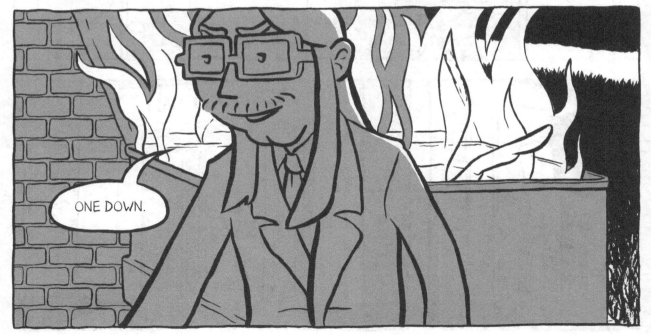

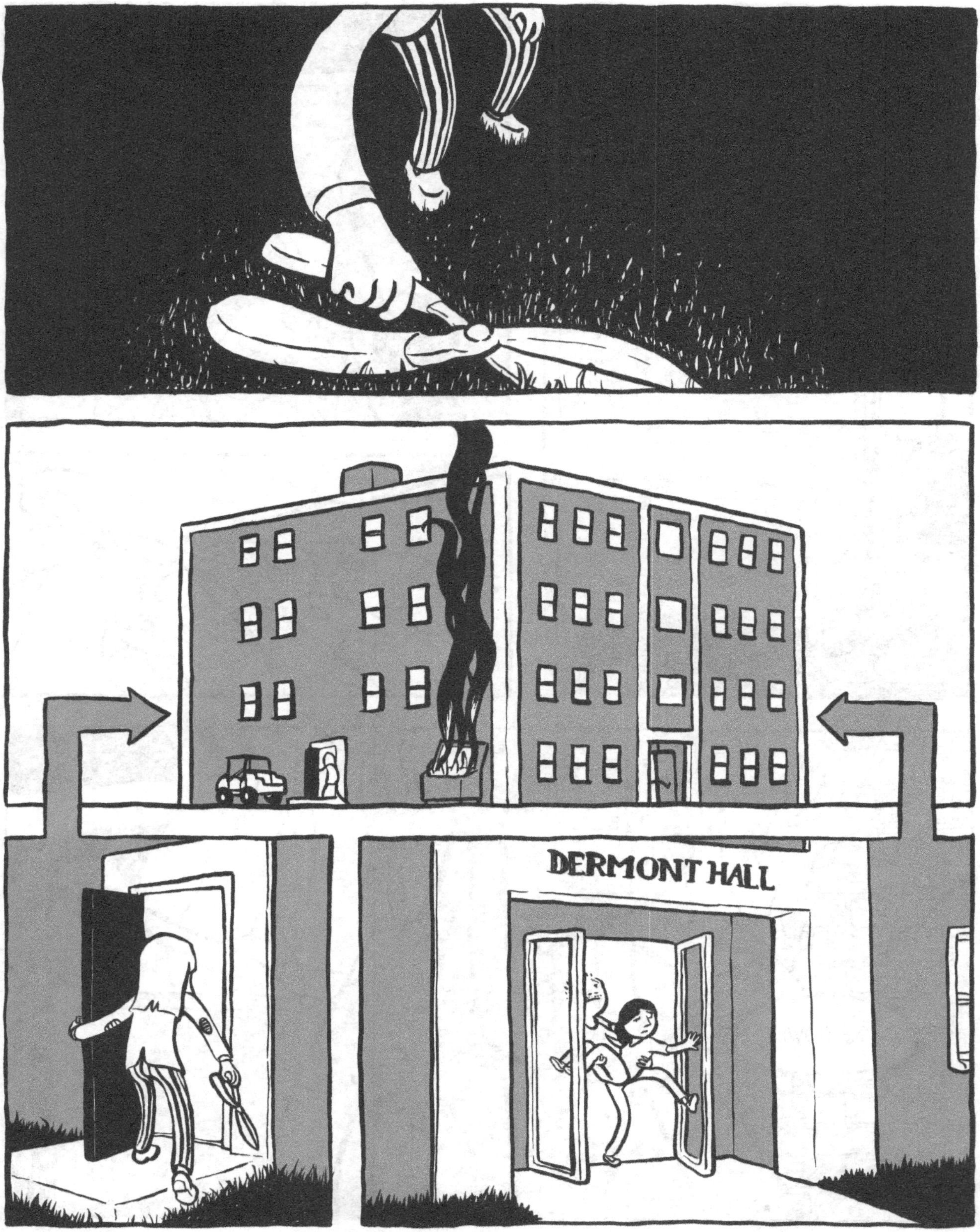
DERMONT HALL

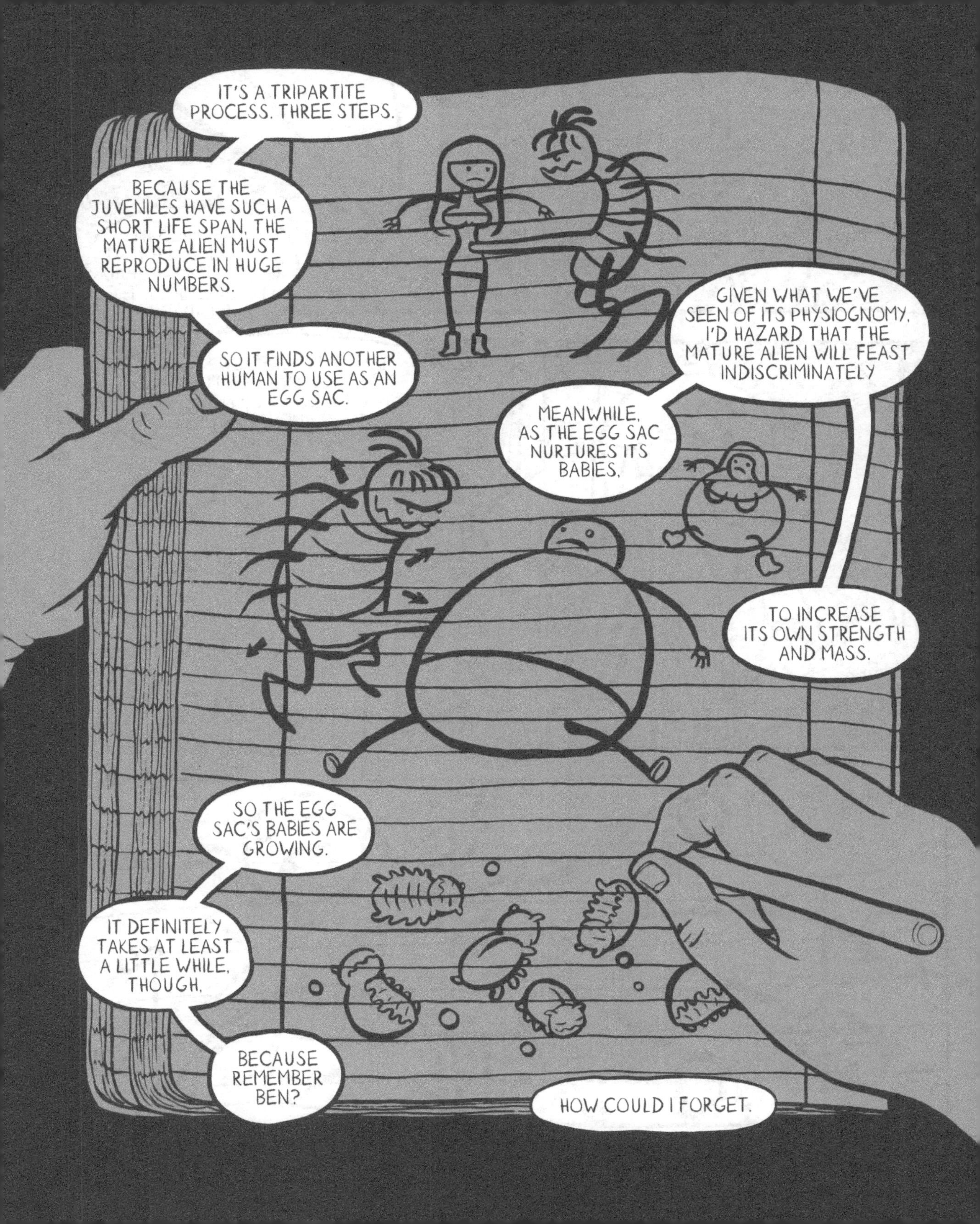
IT'S A TRIPARTITE PROCESS. THREE STEPS.
BECAUSE THE JUVENILES HAVE SUCH A SHORT LIFE SPAN, THE MATURE ALIEN MUST REPRODUCE IN HUGE NUMBERS.
SO IT FINDS ANOTHER HUMAN TO USE AS AN EGG SAC.
GIVEN WHAT WE'VE SEEN OF ITS PHYSIOGNOMY, I'D HAZARD THAT THE MATURE ALIEN WILL FEAST INDISCRIMINATELY
MEANWHILE, AS THE EGG SAC NURTURES ITS BABIES,
TO INCREASE ITS OWN STRENGTH AND MASS.
SO THE EGG SAC'S BABIES ARE GROWING.
IT DEFINITELY TAKES AT LEAST A LITTLE WHILE, THOUGH,
BECAUSE REMEMBER BEN?
HOW COULD I FORGET.

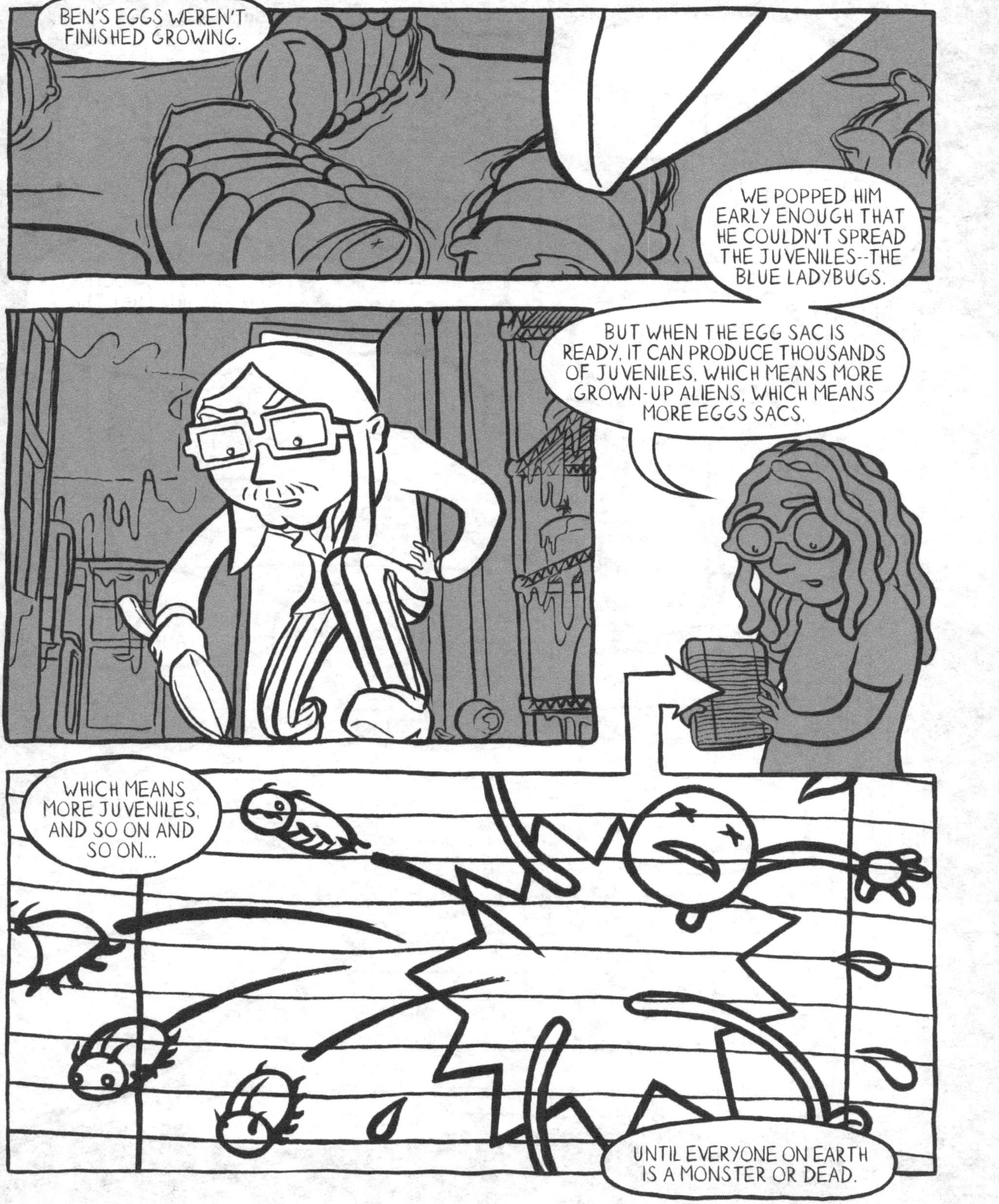
BEN'S EGGS WEREN'T FINISHED GROWING.
WE POPPED HIM EARLY ENOUGH THAT HE COULDN'T SPREAD THE JUVENILES--THE BLUE LADYBUGS.
BUT WHEN THE EGG SAC IS READY, IT CAN PRODUCE THOUSANDS OF JUVENILES, WHICH MEANS MORE GROWN-UP ALIENS, WHICH MEANS MORE EGGS SACS,
WHICH MEANS MORE JUVENILES, AND SO ON AND SO ON...
UNTIL EVERYONE ON EARTH IS A MONSTER OR DEAD.

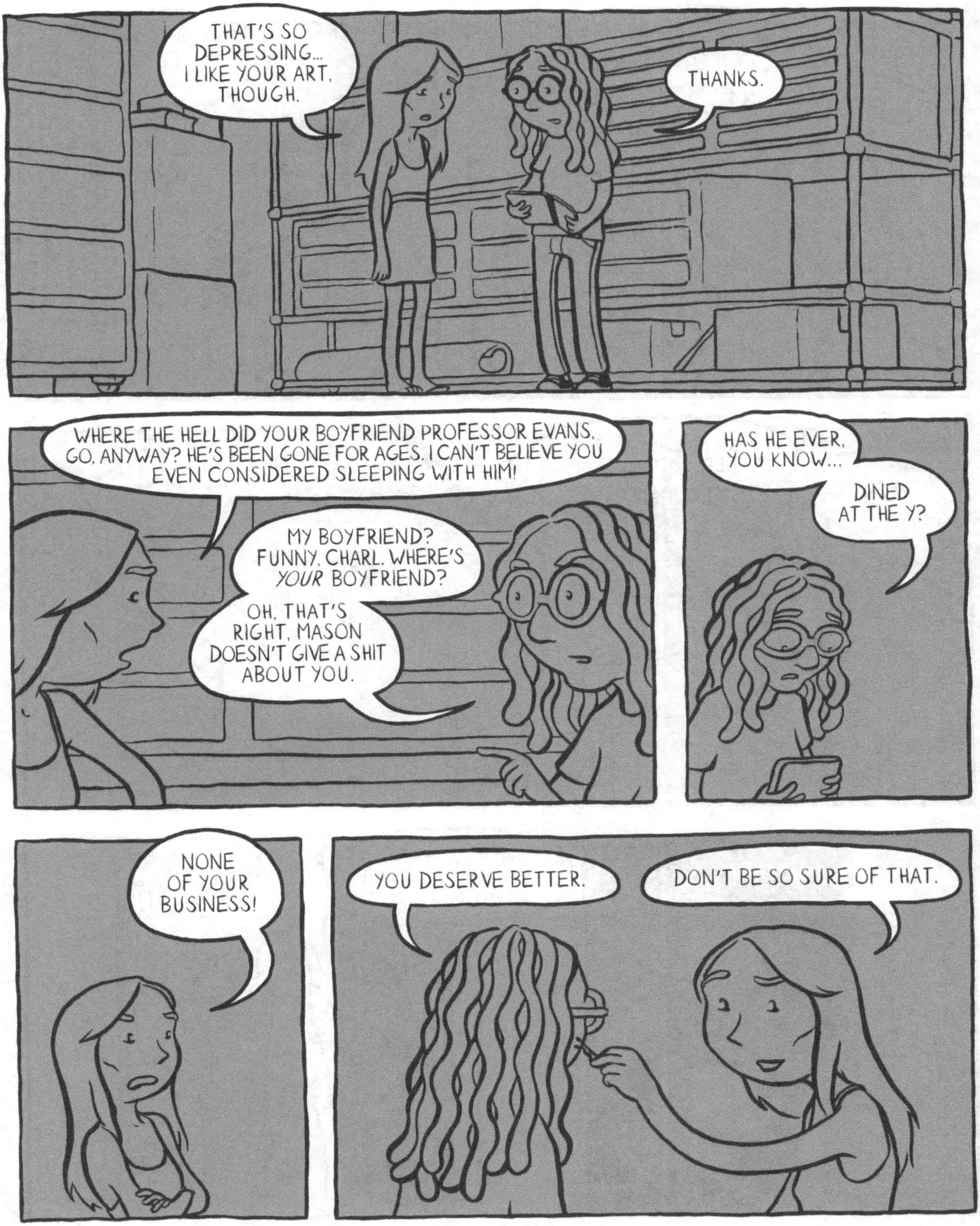
THAT'S SO DEPRESSING... I LIKE YOUR ART, THOUGH.
THANKS.
WHERE THE HELL DID YOUR BOYFRIEND PROFESSOR EVANS, GO, ANYWAY? HE'S BEEN GONE FOR AGES. I CAN'T BELIEVE YOU EVEN CONSIDERED SLEEPING WITH HIM!
MY BOYFRIEND? FUNNY, CHARL. WHERE'S *YOUR* BOYFRIEND?
OH, THAT'S RIGHT, MASON DOESN'T GIVE A SHIT ABOUT YOU.
HAS HE EVER, YOU KNOW...
DINED AT THE Y?
NONE OF YOUR BUSINESS!
YOU DESERVE BETTER.
DON'T BE SO SURE OF THAT.

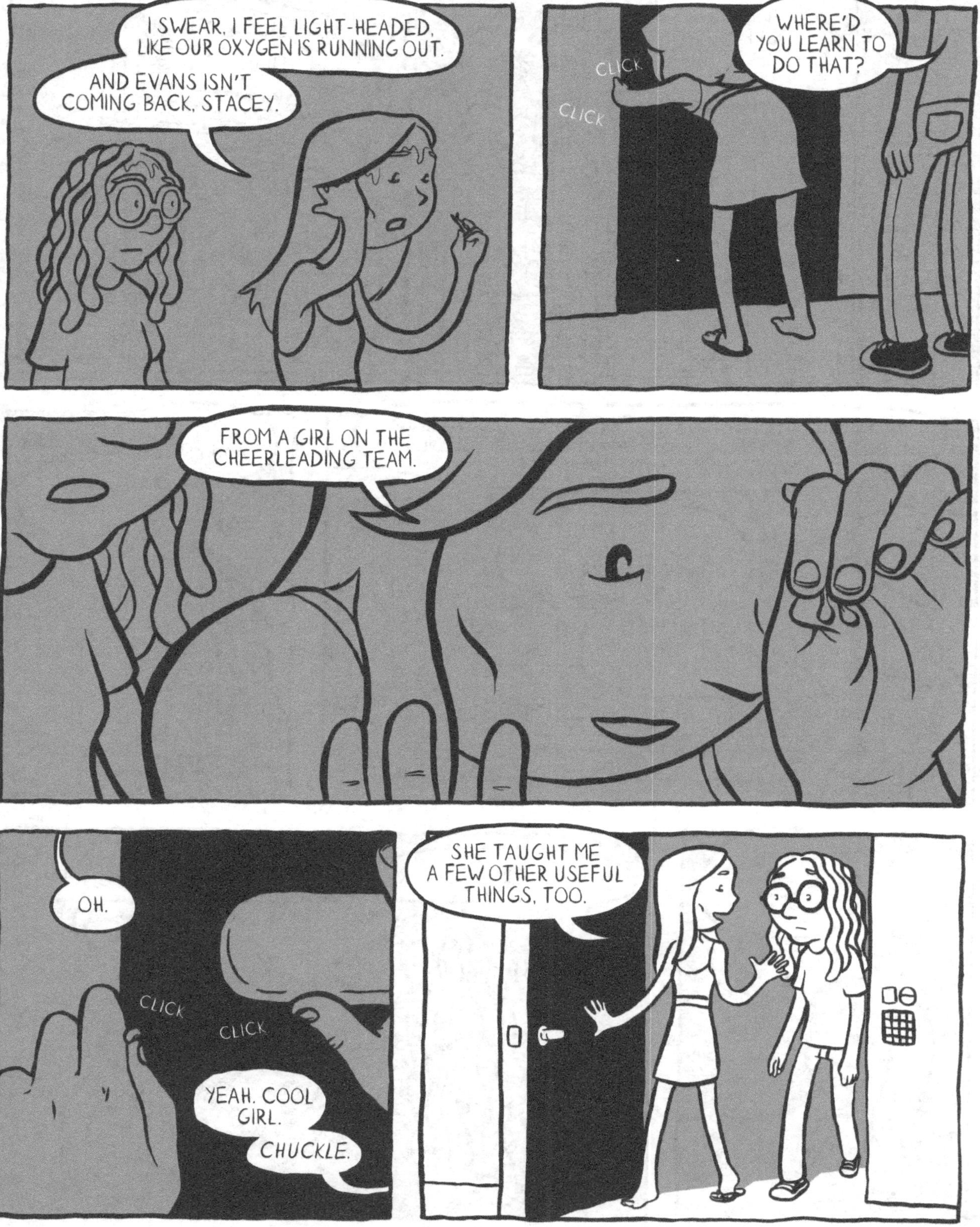
I SWEAR, I FEEL LIGHT-HEADED, LIKE OUR OXYGEN IS RUNNING OUT.
AND EVANS ISN'T COMING BACK, STACEY.
CLICK
CLICK
WHERE'D YOU LEARN TO DO THAT?
FROM A GIRL ON THE CHEERLEADING TEAM.
OH.
CLICK
CLICK
YEAH. COOL GIRL.
CHUCKLE.
SHE TAUGHT ME A FEW OTHER USEFUL THINGS, TOO.

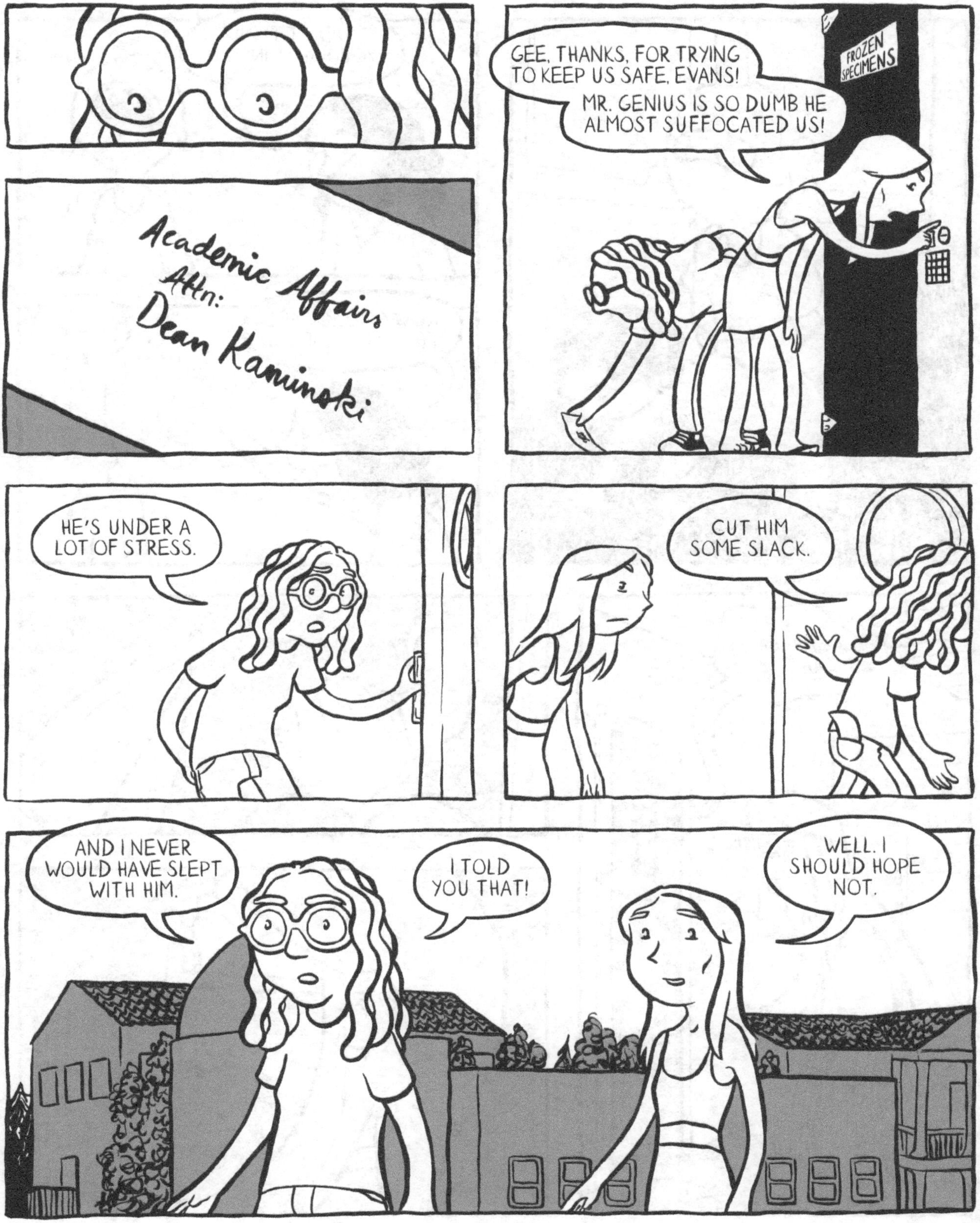
Academic Affairs
Attn:
Dean Kaminski
GEE, THANKS, FOR TRYING TO KEEP US SAFE, EVANS!
MR. GENIUS IS SO DUMB HE ALMOST SUFFOCATED US!
FROZEN SPECIMENS
HE'S UNDER A LOT OF STRESS.
CUT HIM SOME SLACK.
AND I NEVER WOULD HAVE SLEPT WITH HIM.
I TOLD YOU THAT!
WELL. I SHOULD HOPE NOT.

DIDN'T THINK YOU HAD IT IN YOU.

NOW GO BACK AND FETCH MY WHEELS.

SIGH.

OHHHHH... AHHH...

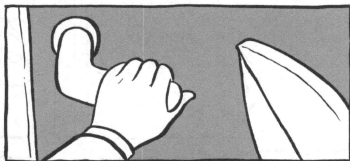

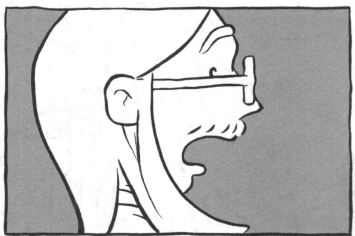

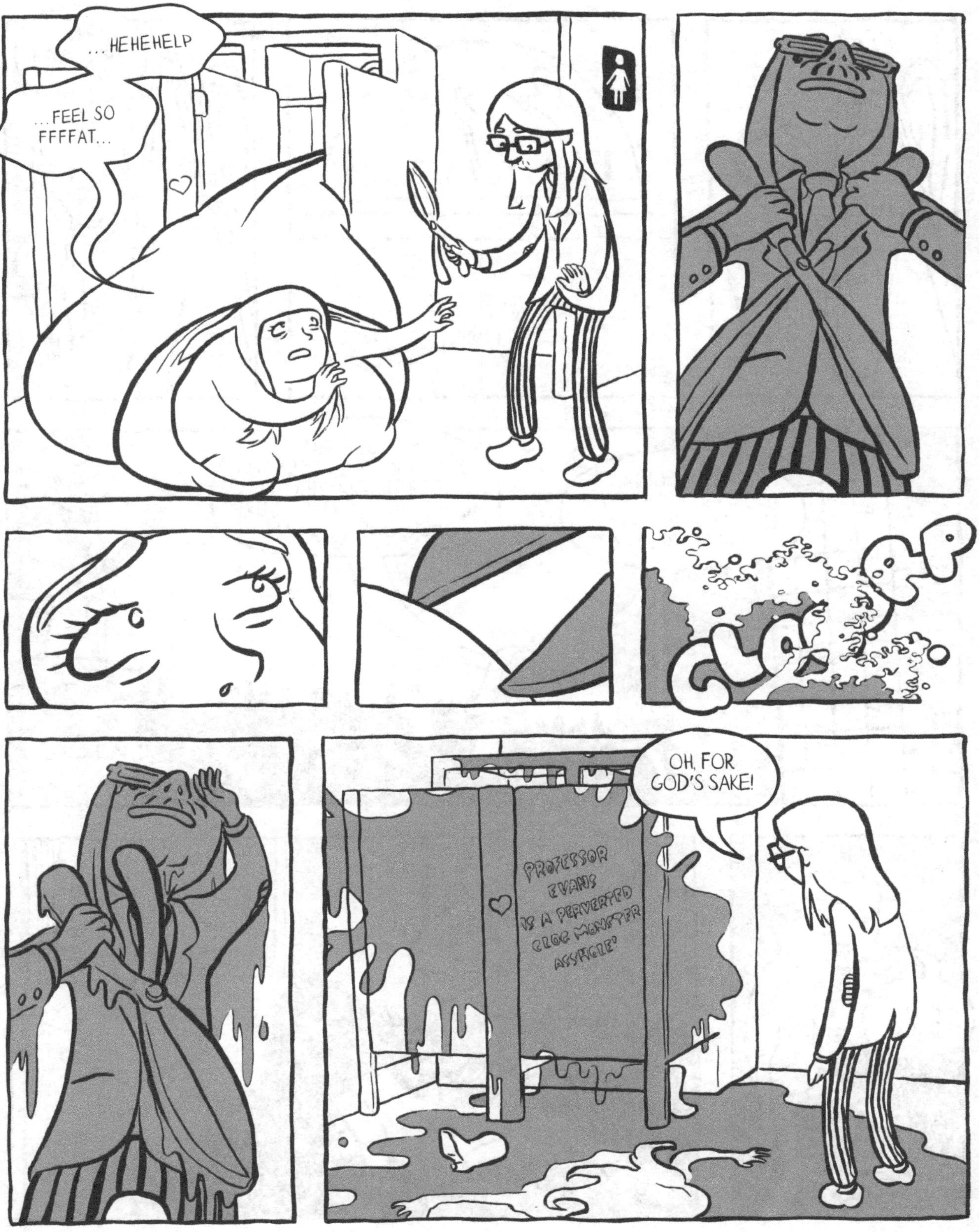
...HEHEHELP
...FEEL SO FFFFAT...
GLORP
PROFESSOR EVANS IS A PERVERTED CLOG MONSTER ASSHOLE!
OH, FOR GOD'S SAKE!

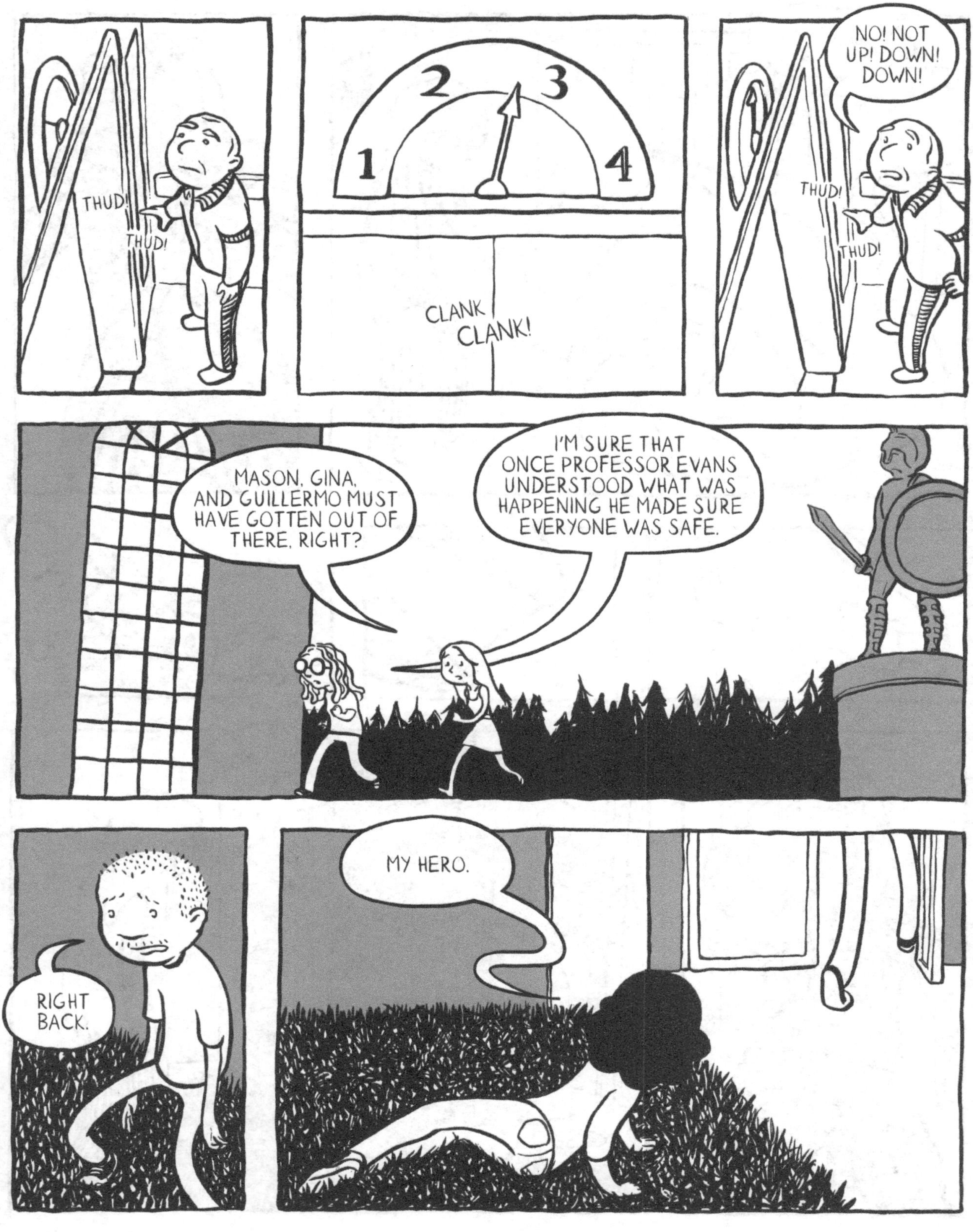
THUD!
THUD!
1 2 3 4
CLANK
CLANK!
NO! NOT UP! DOWN! DOWN!
THUD!
THUD!
MASON, GINA, AND GUILLERMO MUST HAVE GOTTEN OUT OF THERE, RIGHT?
I'M SURE THAT ONCE PROFESSOR EVANS UNDERSTOOD WHAT WAS HAPPENING HE MADE SURE EVERYONE WAS SAFE.
RIGHT BACK.
MY HERO.

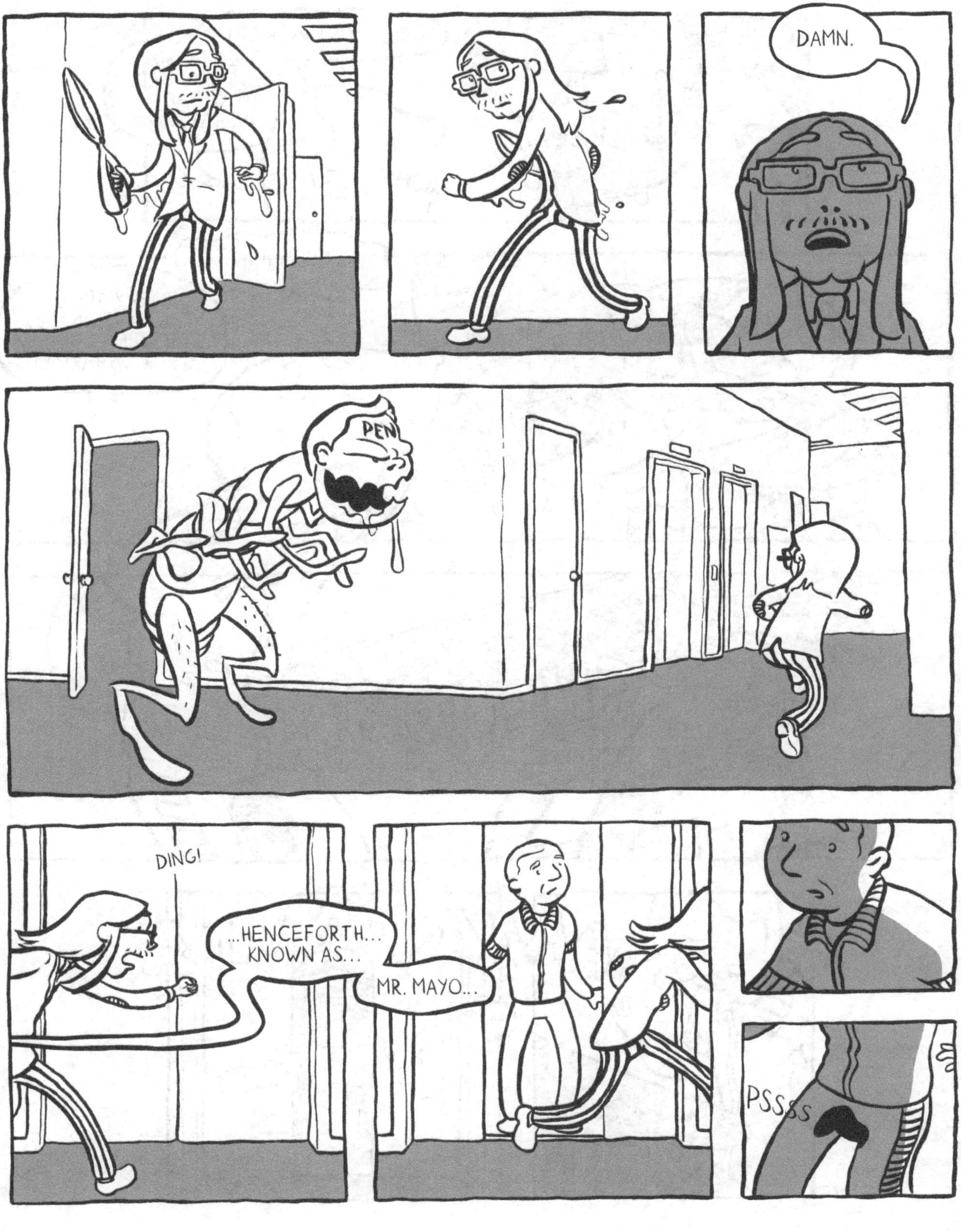
DAMN.
PEN
DING!
...HENCEFORTH... KNOWN AS...
MR. MAYO...
PSSSS

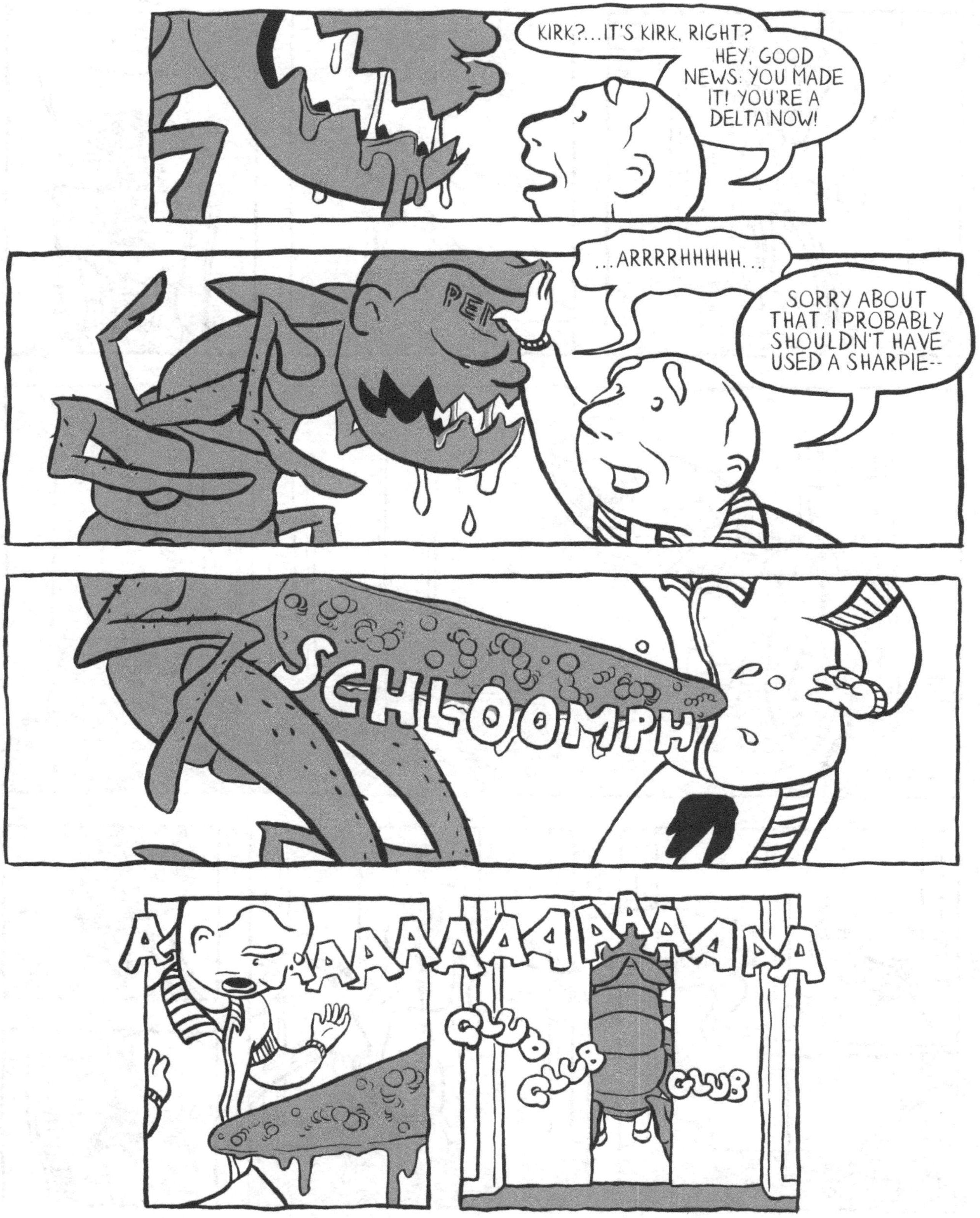

KIRK?...IT'S KIRK, RIGHT?
HEY, GOOD NEWS: YOU MADE IT! YOU'RE A DELTA NOW!
...ARRRRHHHHH...
SORRY ABOUT THAT. I PROBABLY SHOULDN'T HAVE USED A SHARPIE--
SCHLOOMPH
AAAAAAAAAAAAAAA
GLUB
GLUB
GLUB

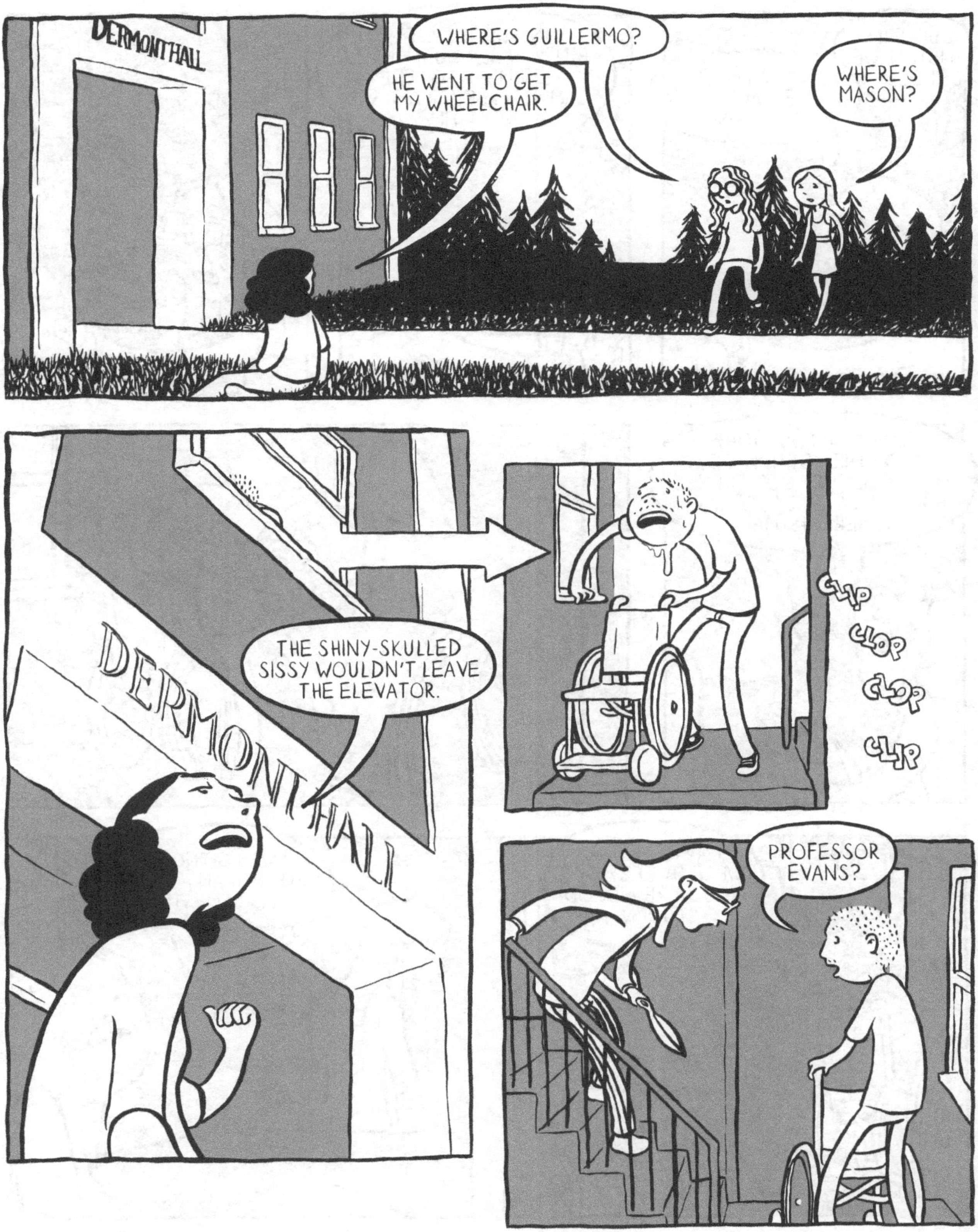
DERMONT HALL
WHERE'S GUILLERMO?
HE WENT TO GET MY WHEELCHAIR.
WHERE'S MASON?
DERMONT HALL
THE SHINY-SKULLED SISSY WOULDN'T LEAVE THE ELEVATOR.
CLOP
CLOP
CLIP
PROFESSOR EVANS?

GUILLERMO, LISTEN, WE NEED--

I KNOW, I KNOW. THERE'S ALIENS ON THE LOOSE.

NO DISRESPECT, BUT YOU SERIOUSLY NEED TO REMEMBER TO KEEP THE SAMPLE FREEZER CLOSED NEXT TIME.

HAVE YOU LOST YOUR MIND? THE HOTTEST GIRL IN SCHOOL JUST GOT TURNED INTO A HATE BEAST. THIS IS SERIOUS, MAN.

HO!

HO!

HO!

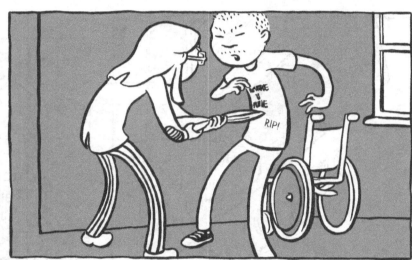

RIP!

I'M SORRY. YOU WERE DWEEBY, BUT YOU WERE A GOOD STUDENT.

I WAS GOING TO GIVE YOU AN A MINUS THIS SEMESTER.

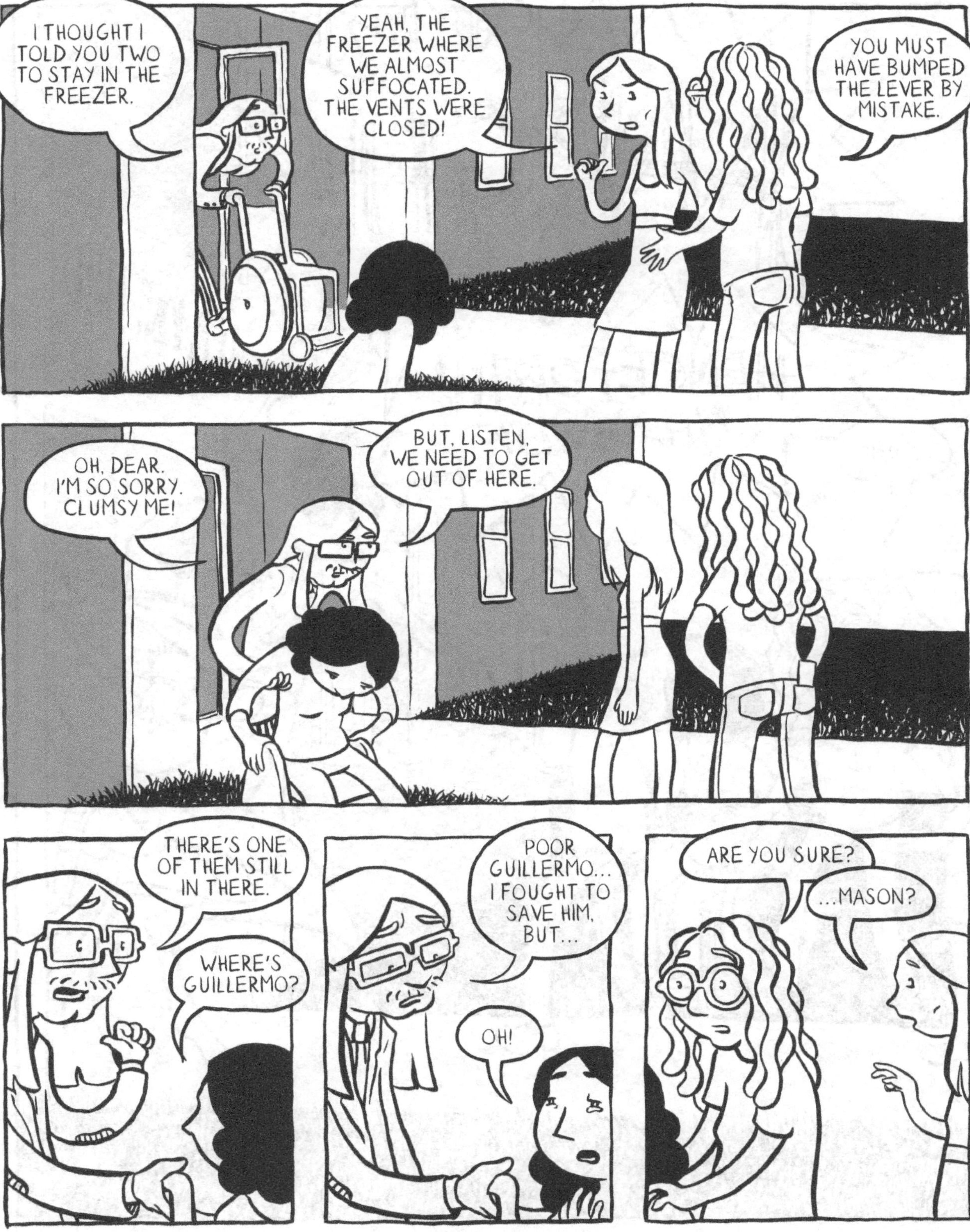
I THOUGHT I TOLD YOU TWO TO STAY IN THE FREEZER.
YEAH, THE FREEZER WHERE WE ALMOST SUFFOCATED. THE VENTS WERE CLOSED!
YOU MUST HAVE BUMPED THE LEVER BY MISTAKE.
OH, DEAR. I'M SO SORRY. CLUMSY ME!
BUT, LISTEN, WE NEED TO GET OUT OF HERE.
THERE'S ONE OF THEM STILL IN THERE.
WHERE'S GUILLERMO?
POOR GUILLERMO... I FOUGHT TO SAVE HIM, BUT...
OH!
ARE YOU SURE?
...MASON?

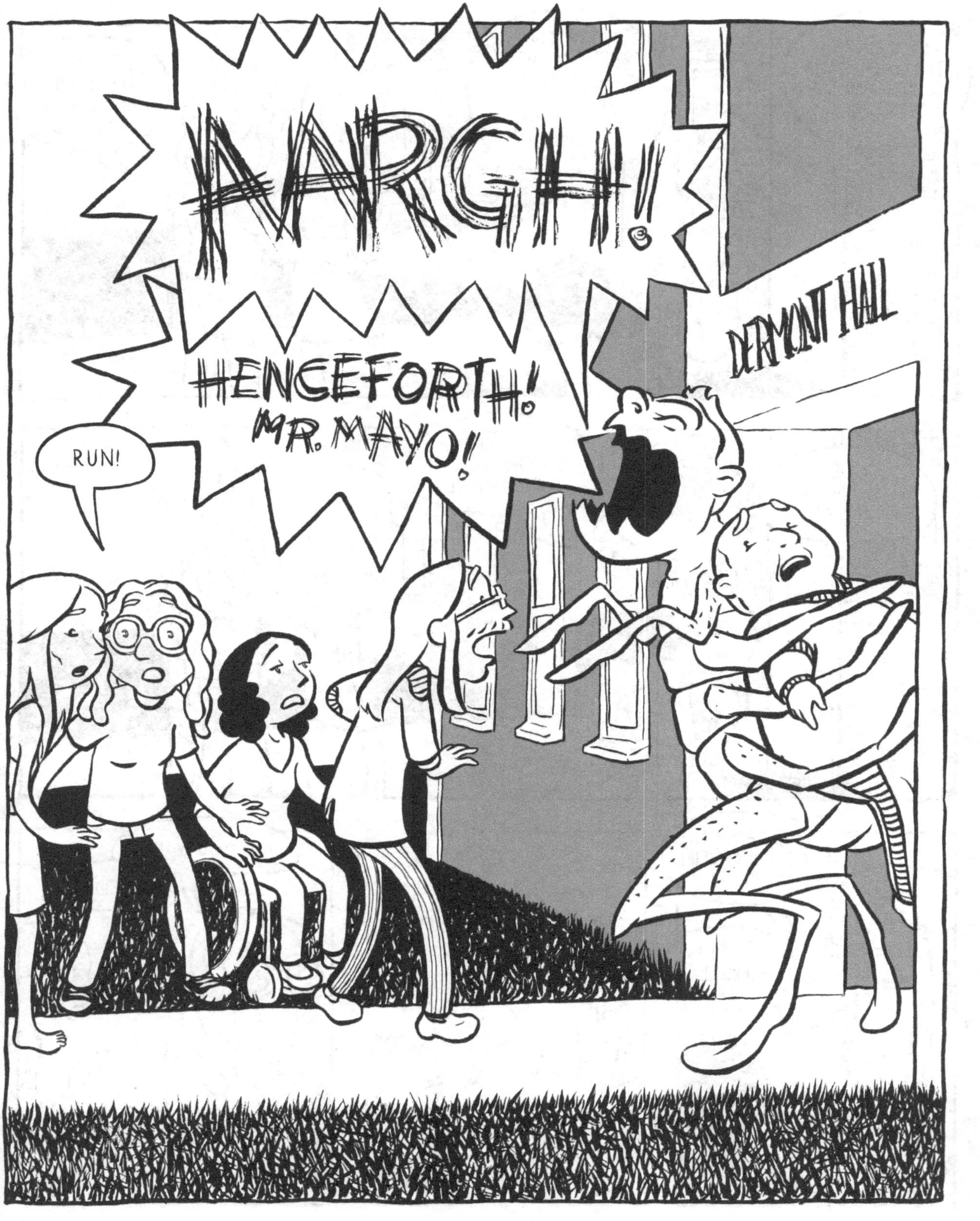
AARGH!
HENCEFORTH! MR. MAYO!
RUN!
DERMONT HALL

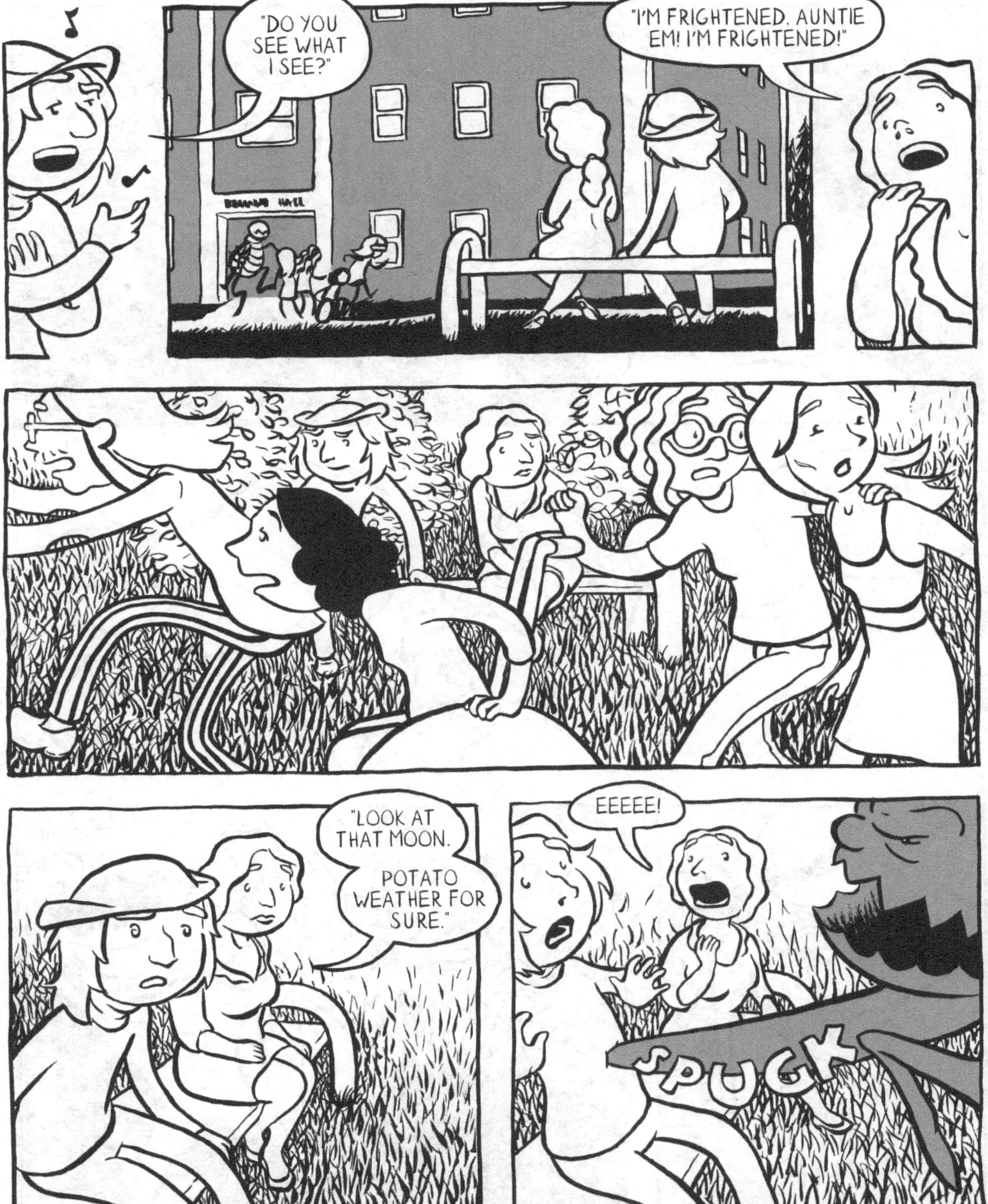
"DO YOU SEE WHAT I SEE?"
"I'M FRIGHTENED, AUNTIE EM! I'M FRIGHTENED!"
"LOOK AT THAT MOON.
POTATO WEATHER FOR SURE."
EEEEE!
SPUCK

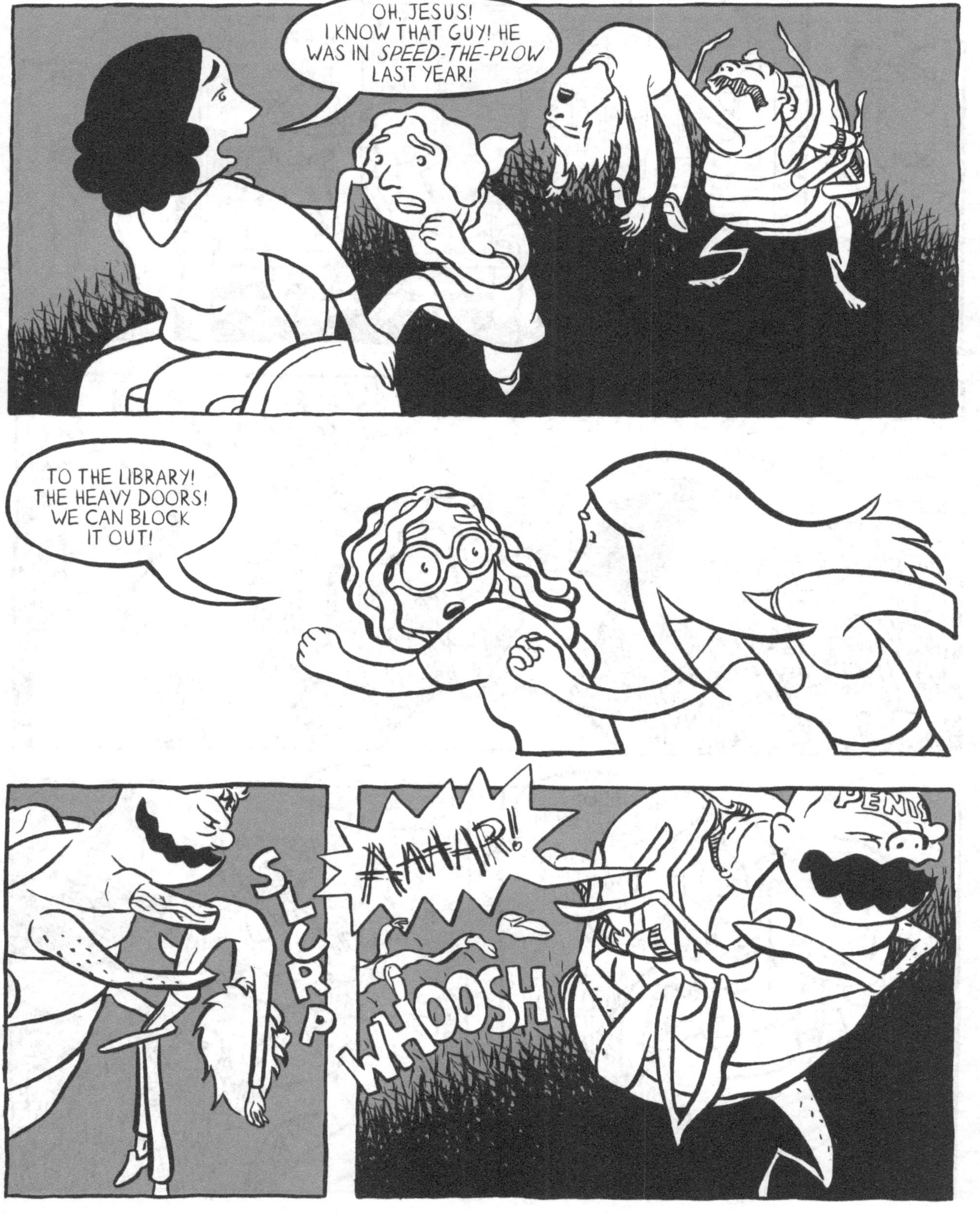
OH, JESUS! I KNOW THAT GUY! HE WAS IN *SPEED-THE-PLOW* LAST YEAR!
TO THE LIBRARY! THE HEAVY DOORS! WE CAN BLOCK IT OUT!
SLURP
AAAAR!
WHOOSH

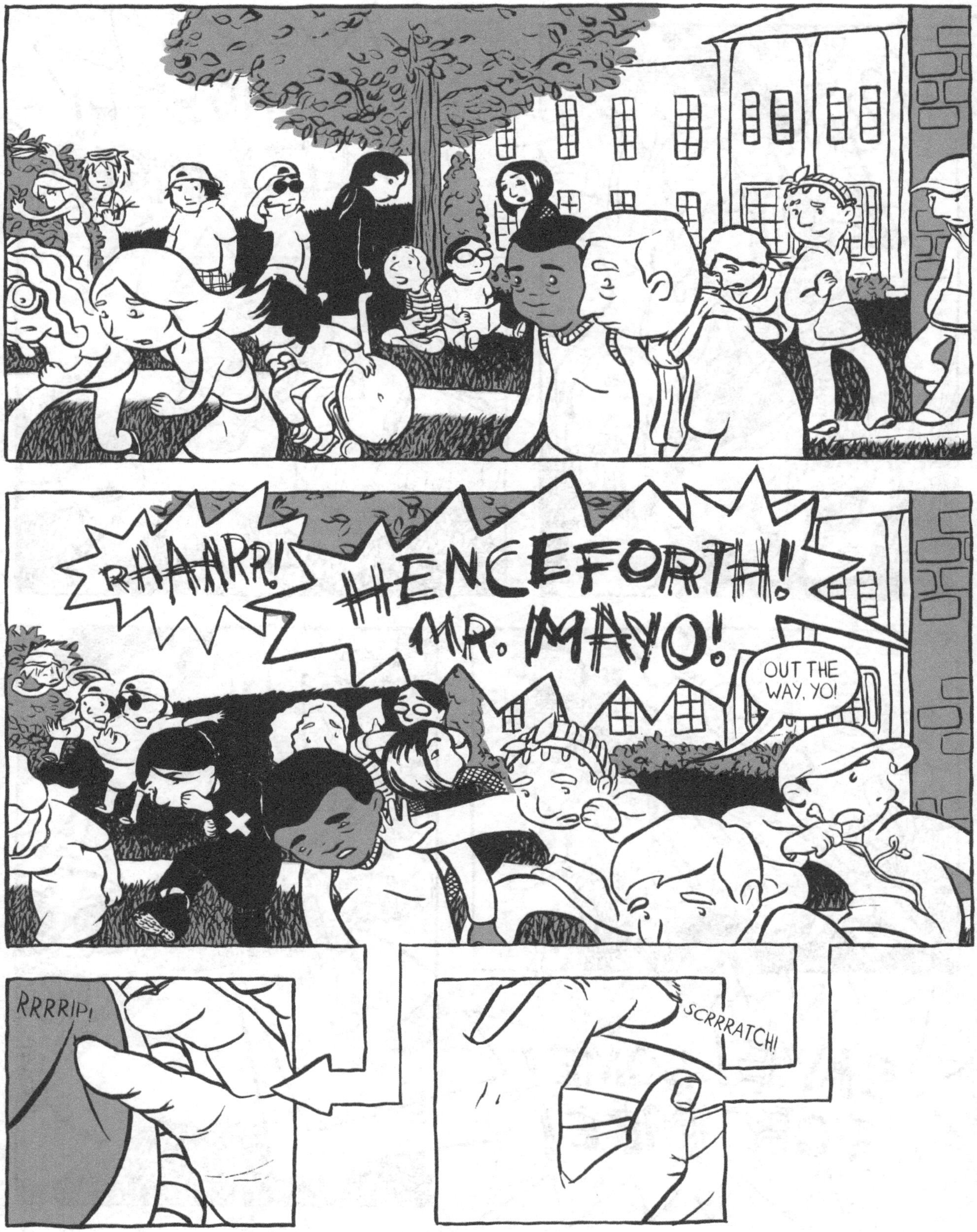
RAAARR!
HENCEFORTH! MR. MAYO!
OUT THE WAY, YO!
RRRRIP!
SCRRRATCH!

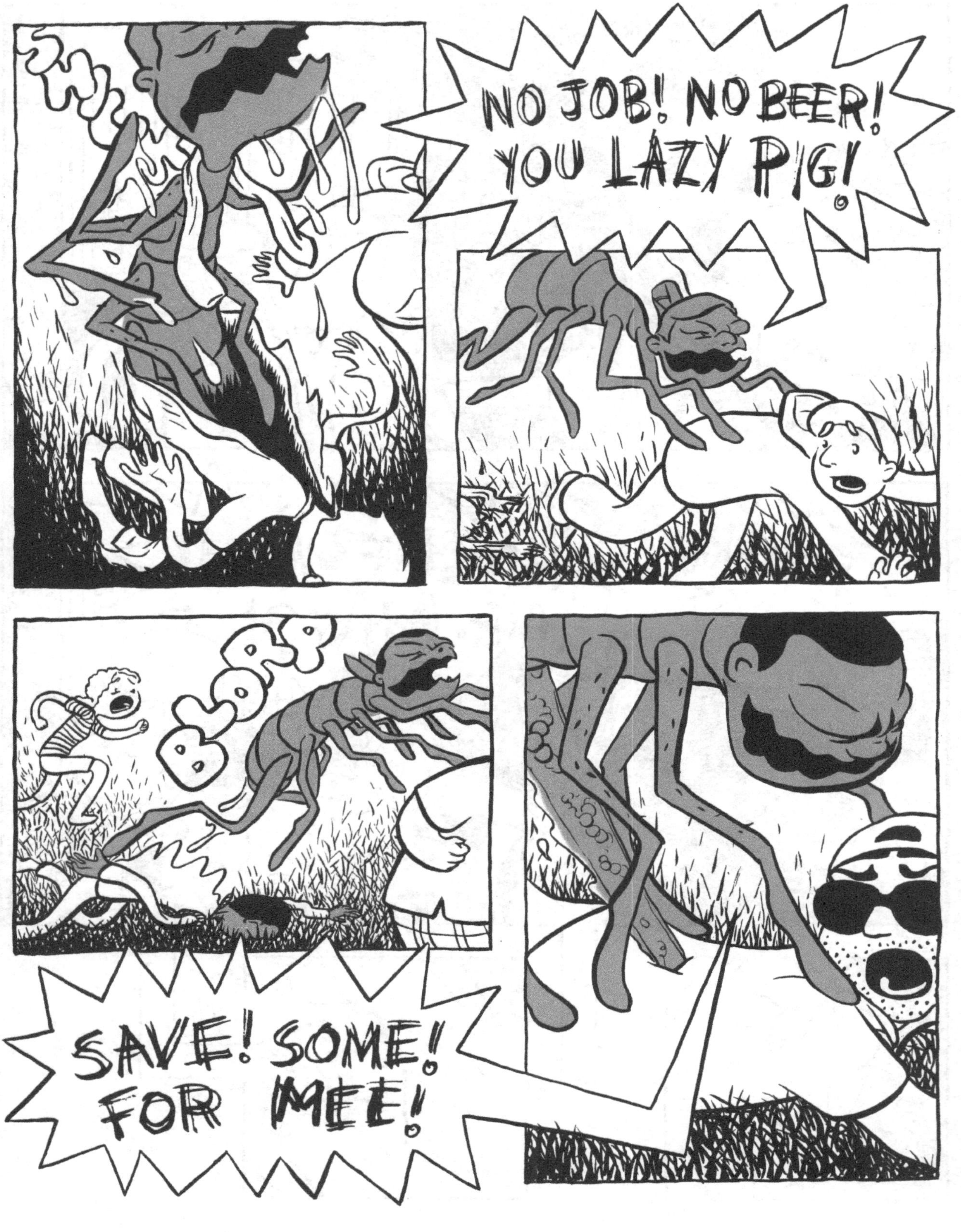
NO JOB! NO BEER! YOU LAZY PIG!
BLORP
SAVE! SOME! FOR MEE!

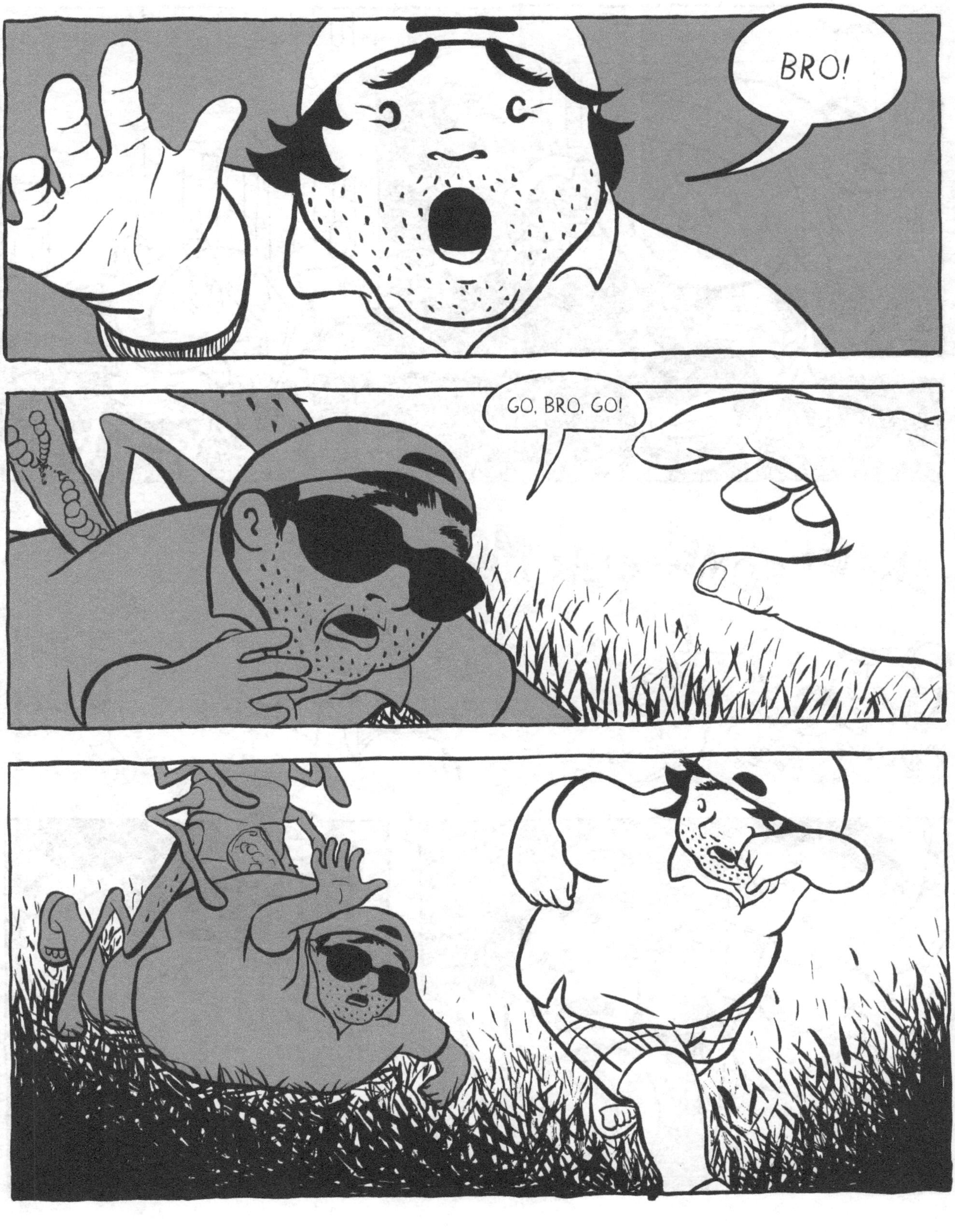
BRO!
GO, BRO, GO!

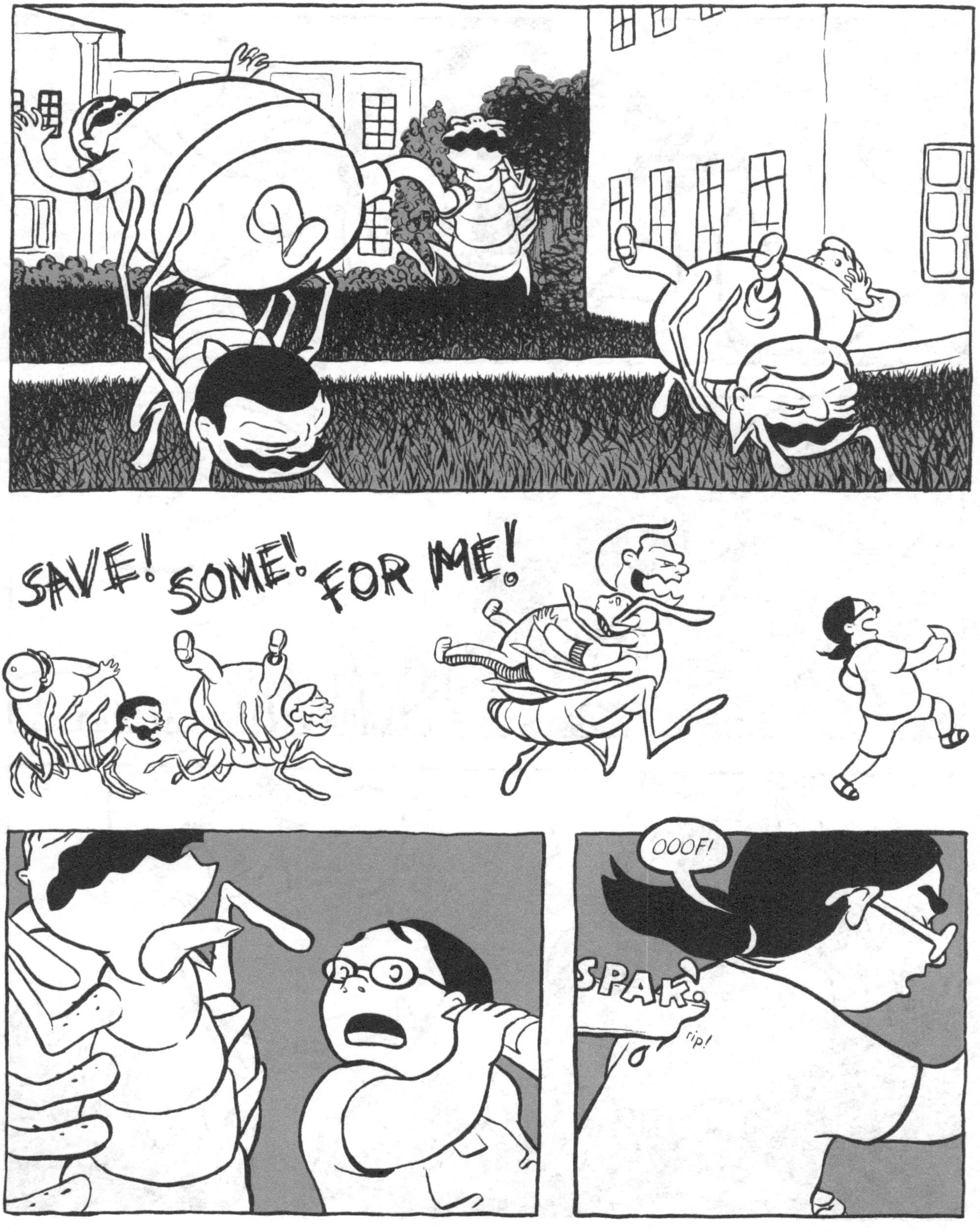
SAVE! SOME! FOR ME!
OOOF!
SPAK!
rip!

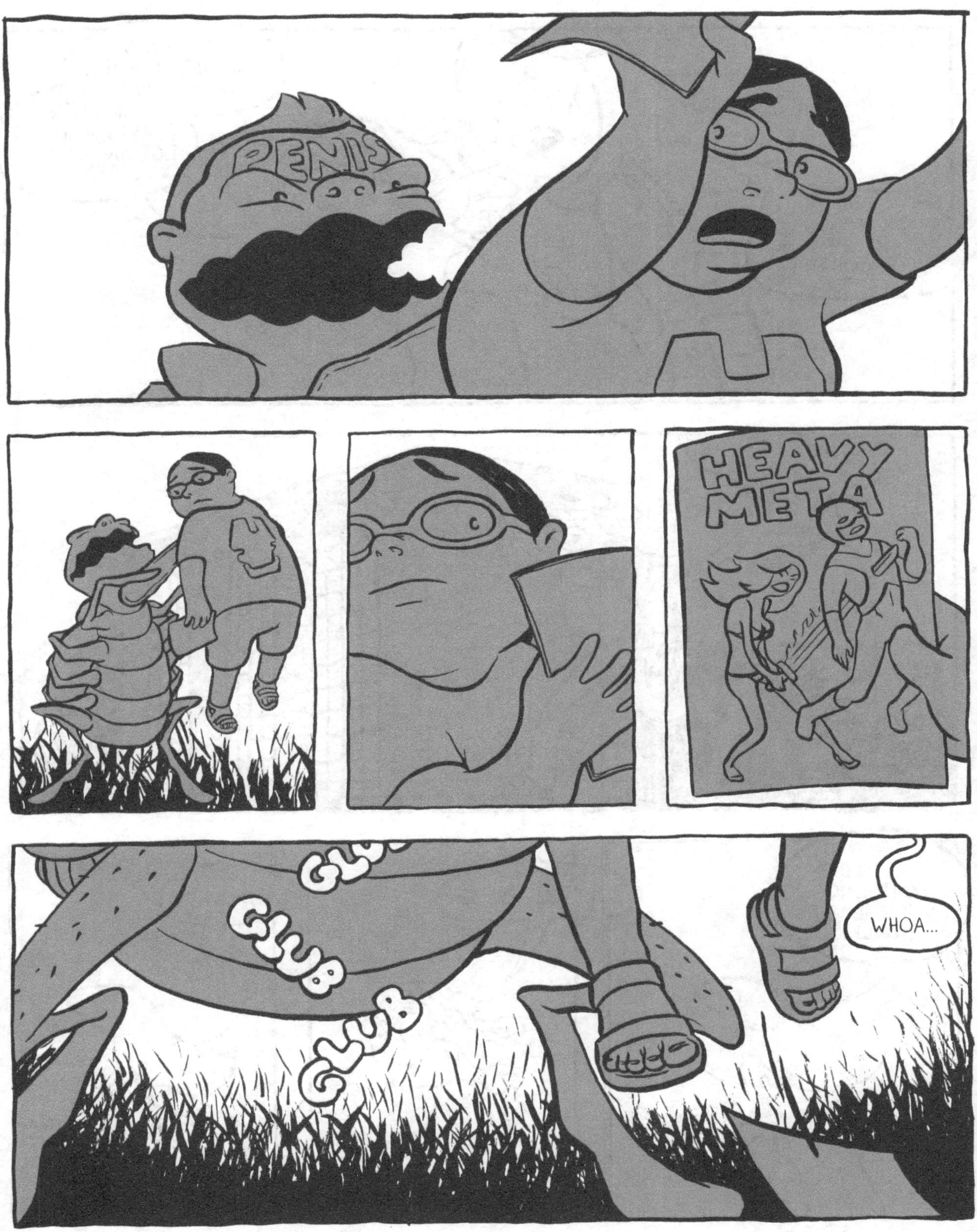
PENIS
HEAVY META
GLUB
GLUB
GLUB
WHOA...

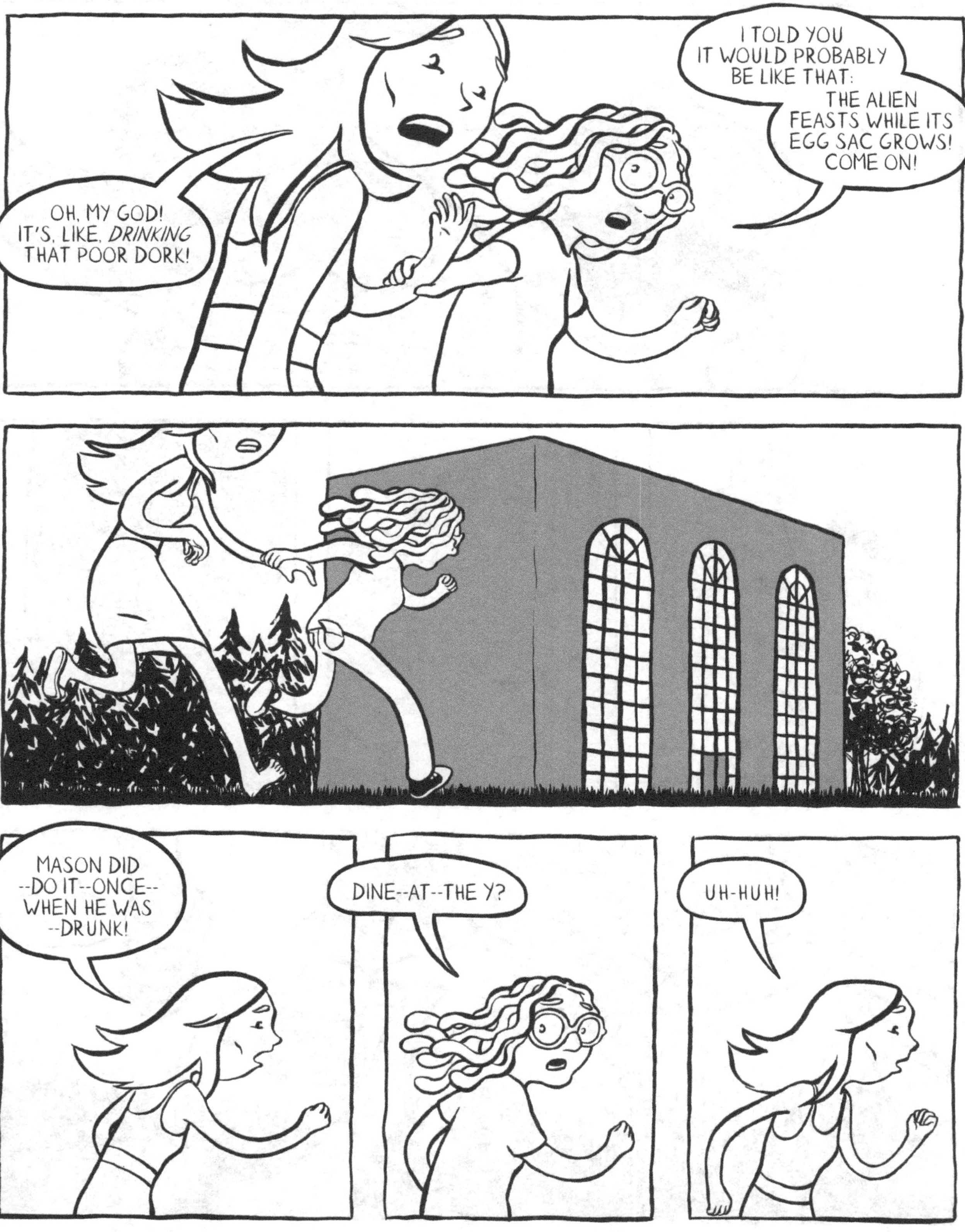
OH, MY GOD! IT'S, LIKE, *DRINKING* THAT POOR DORK!
I TOLD YOU IT WOULD PROBABLY BE LIKE THAT:
THE ALIEN FEASTS WHILE ITS EGG SAC GROWS! COME ON!
MASON DID --DO IT--ONCE-- WHEN HE WAS --DRUNK!
DINE--AT--THE Y?
UH-HUH!

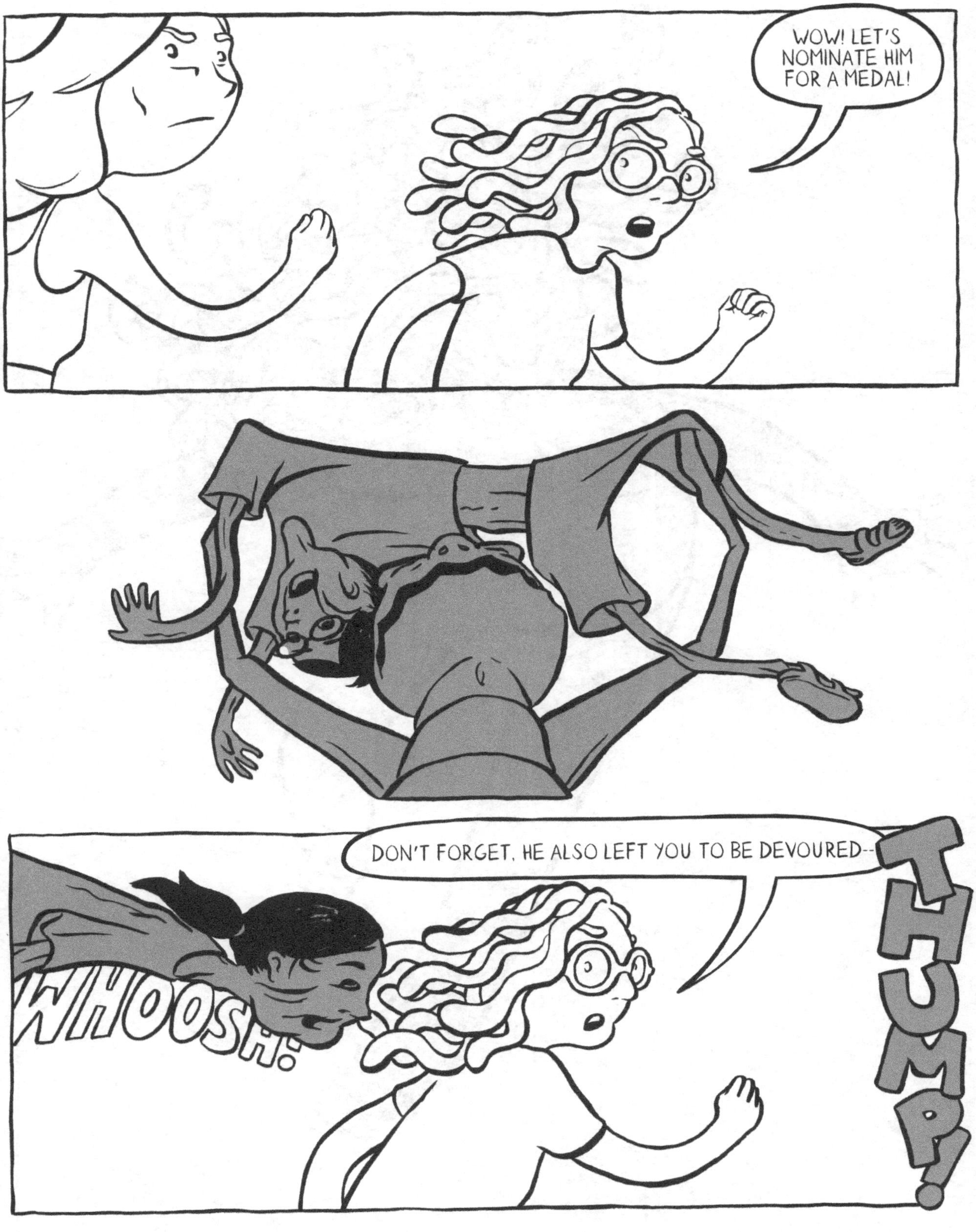
WOW! LET'S NOMINATE HIM FOR A MEDAL!
DON'T FORGET, HE ALSO LEFT YOU TO BE DEVOURED--
WHOOSH!
THUMP!

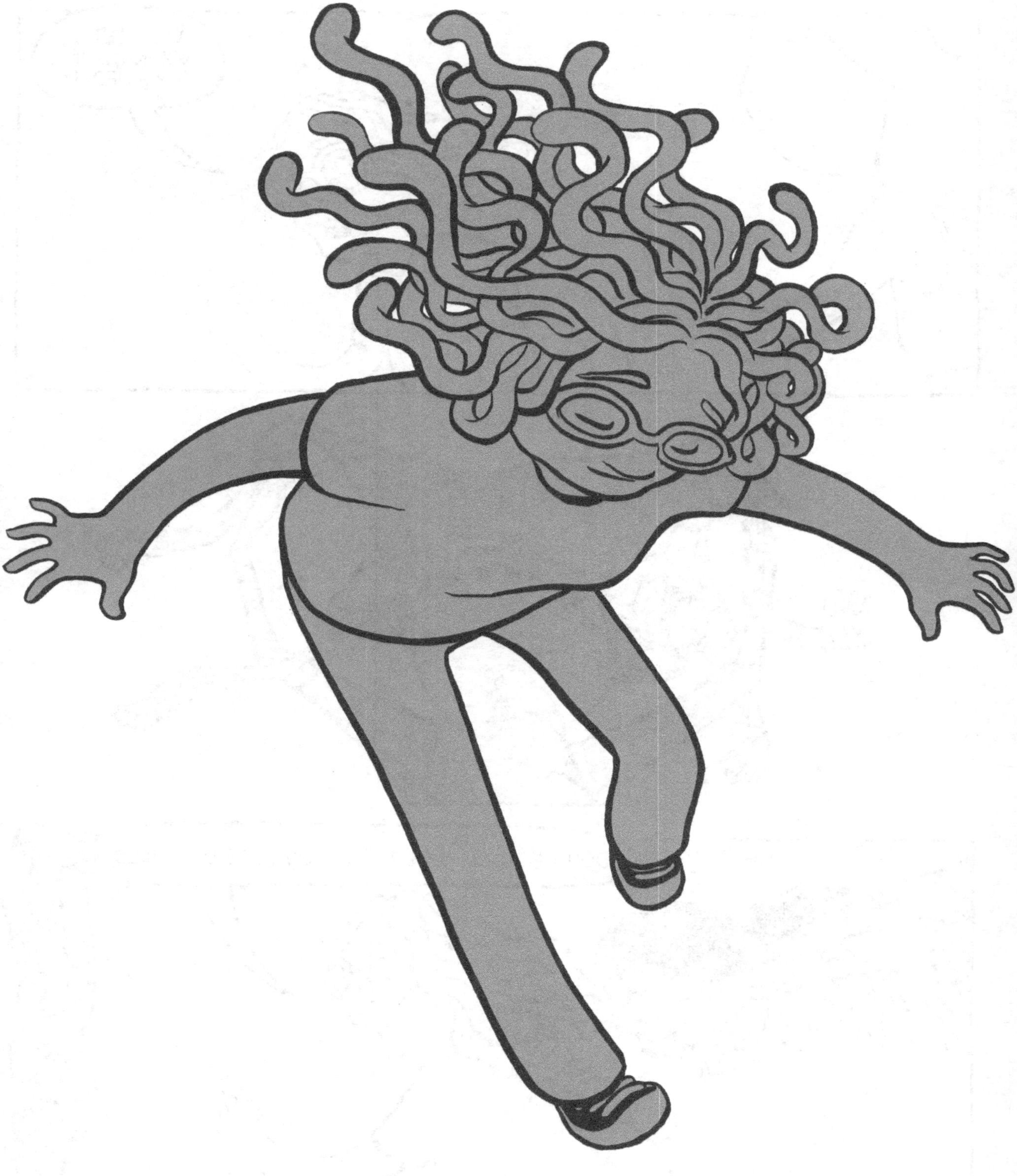

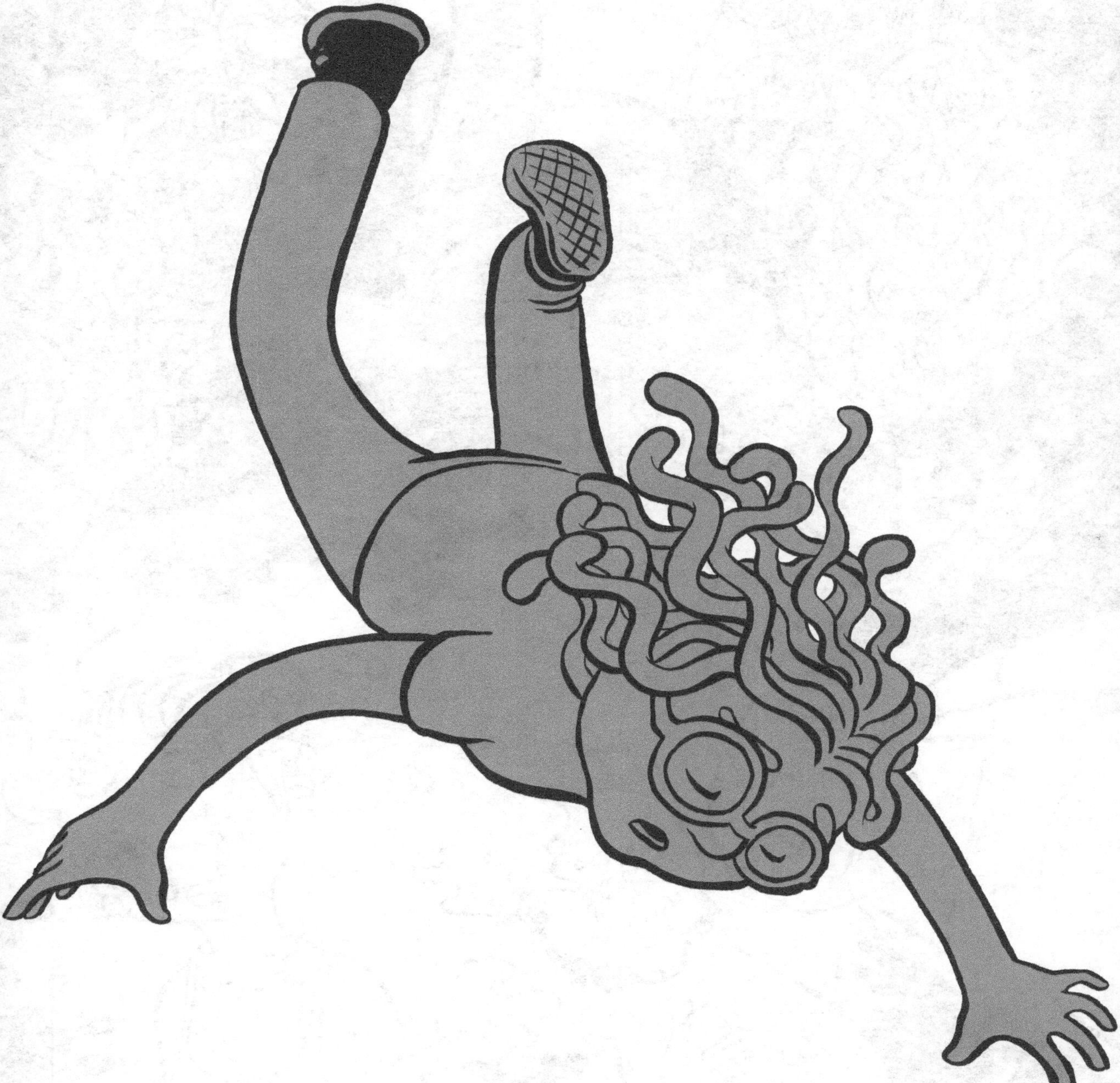

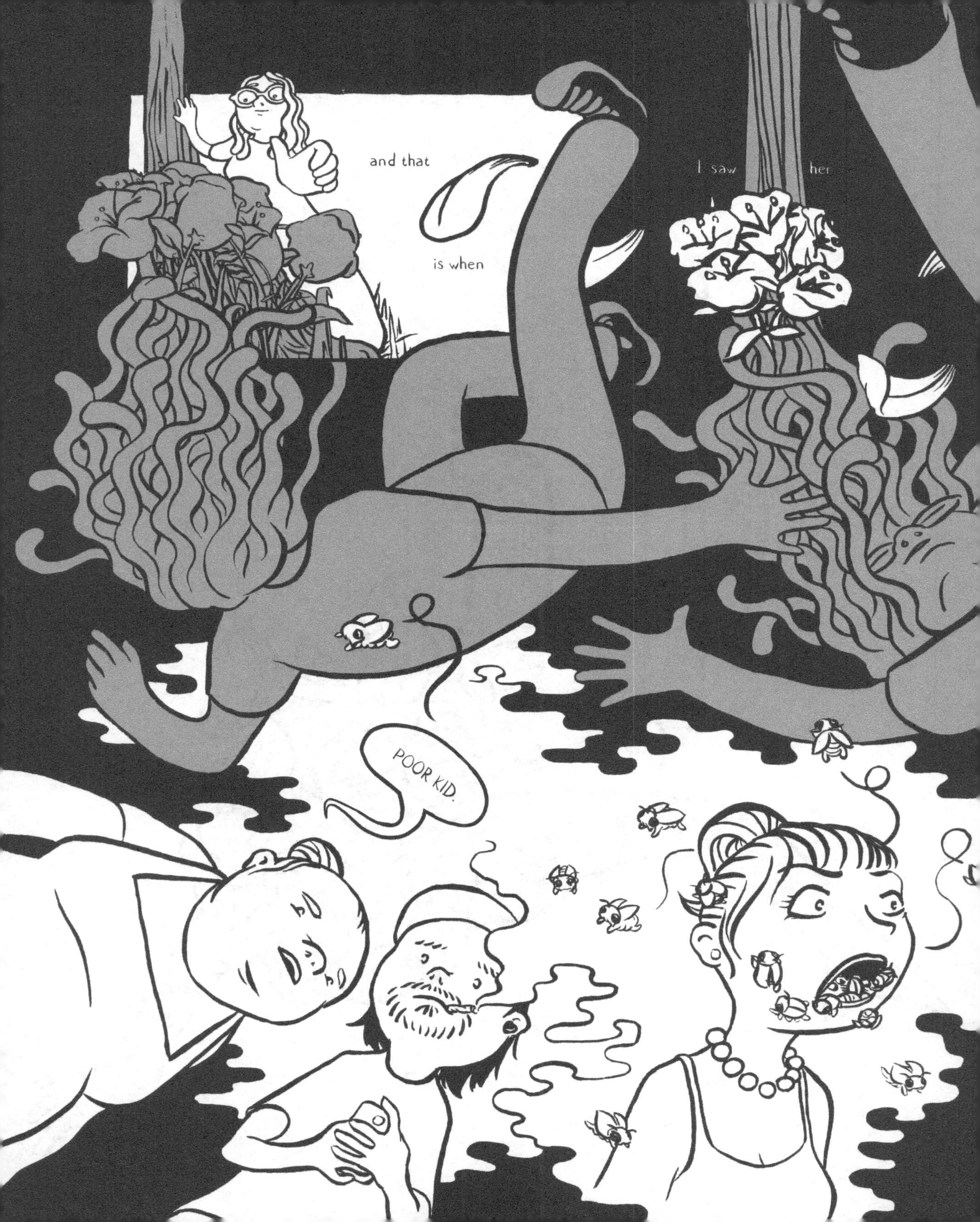
and that
is when
I saw
her
POOR KID.

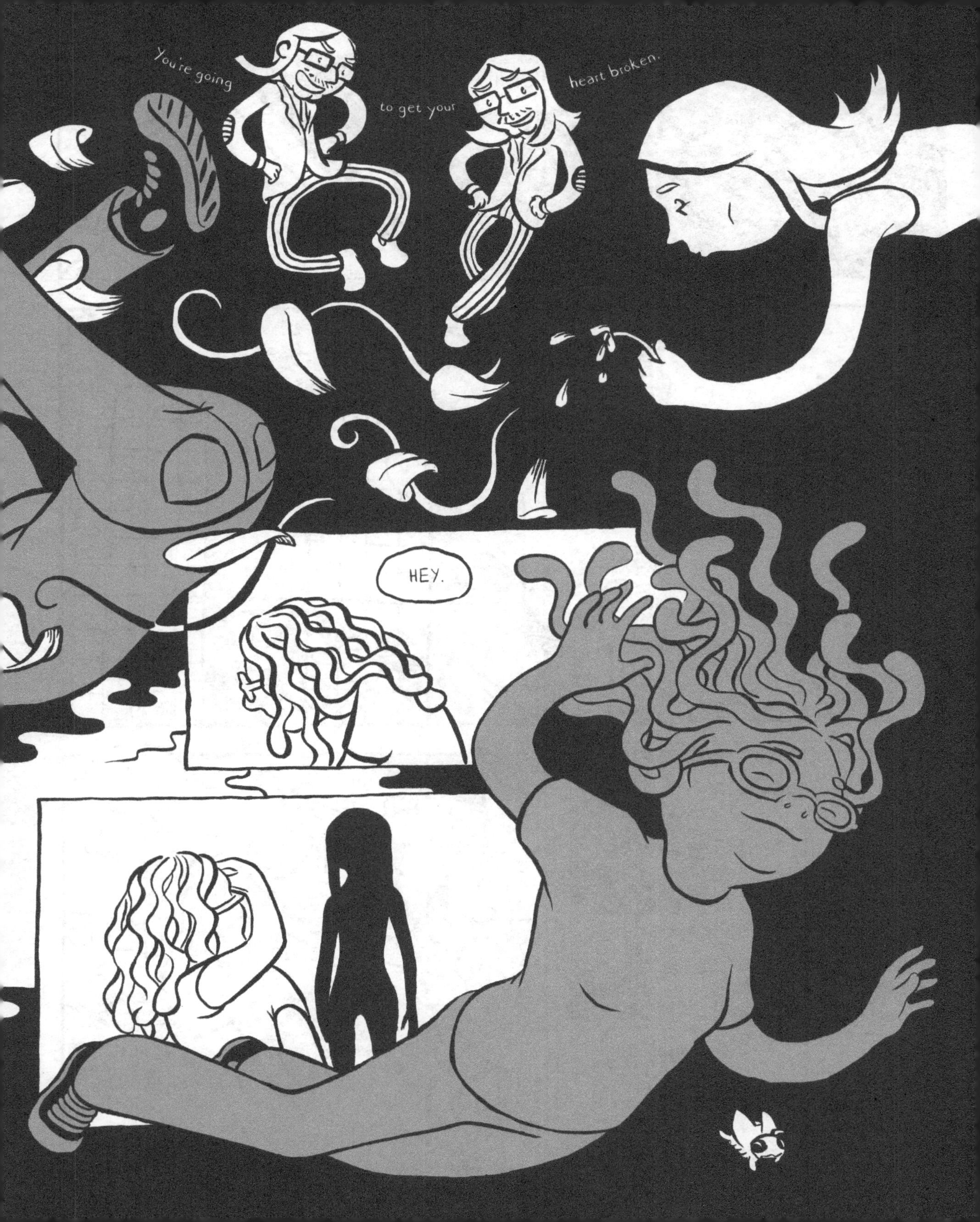
You're going
to get your
heart broken.
HEY.

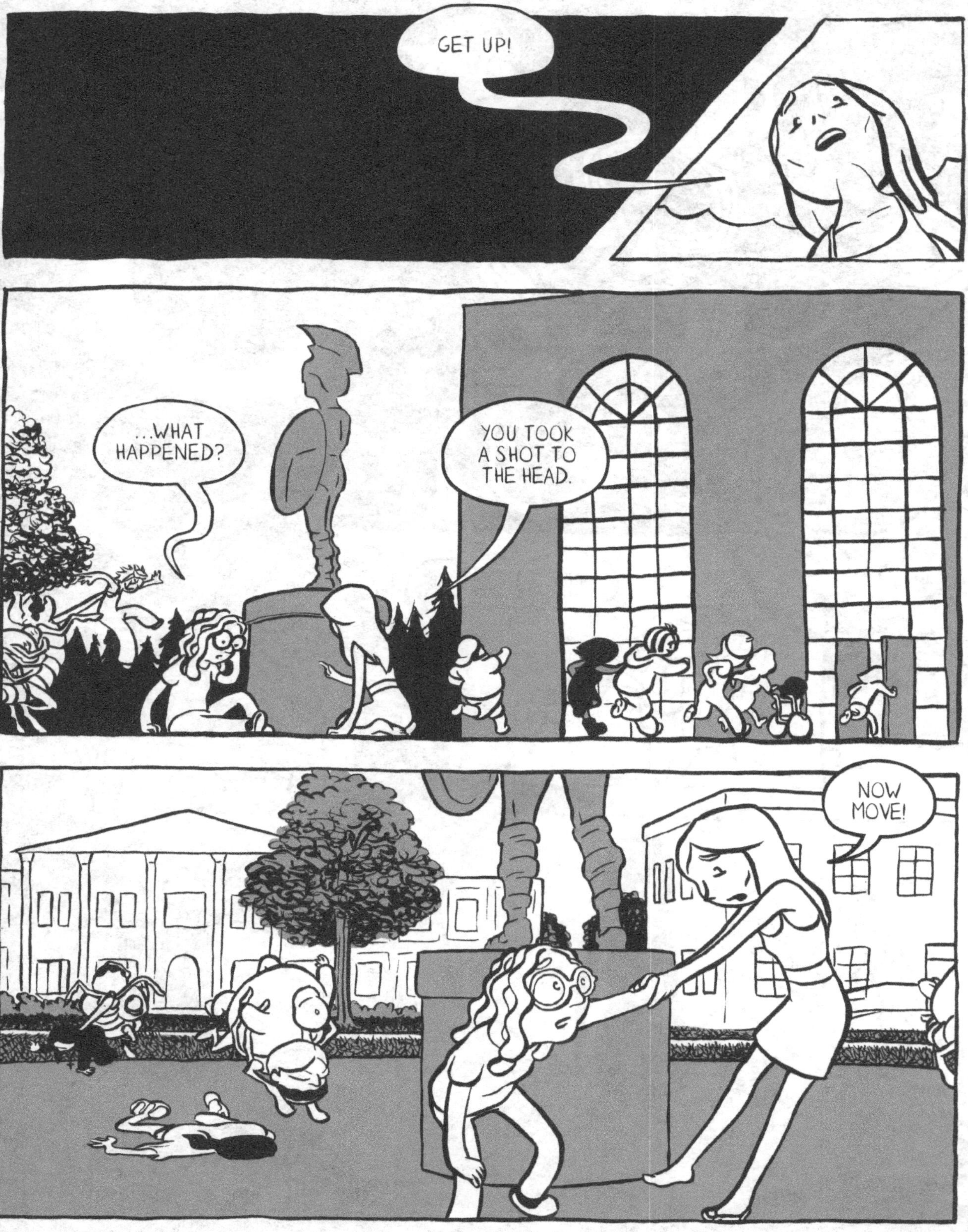
GET UP!
...WHAT HAPPENED?
YOU TOOK A SHOT TO THE HEAD.
NOW MOVE!

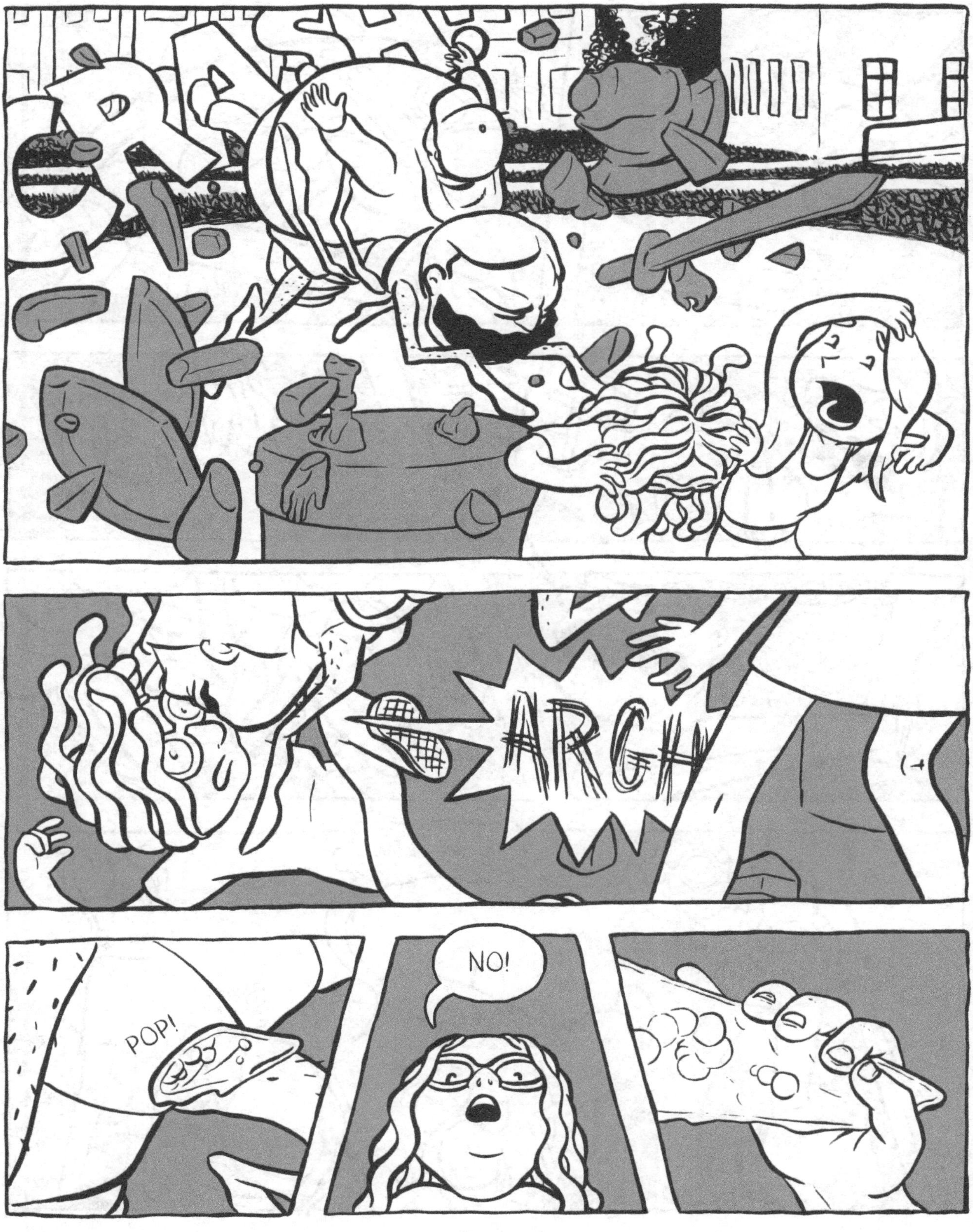
ARGH
POP!
NO!

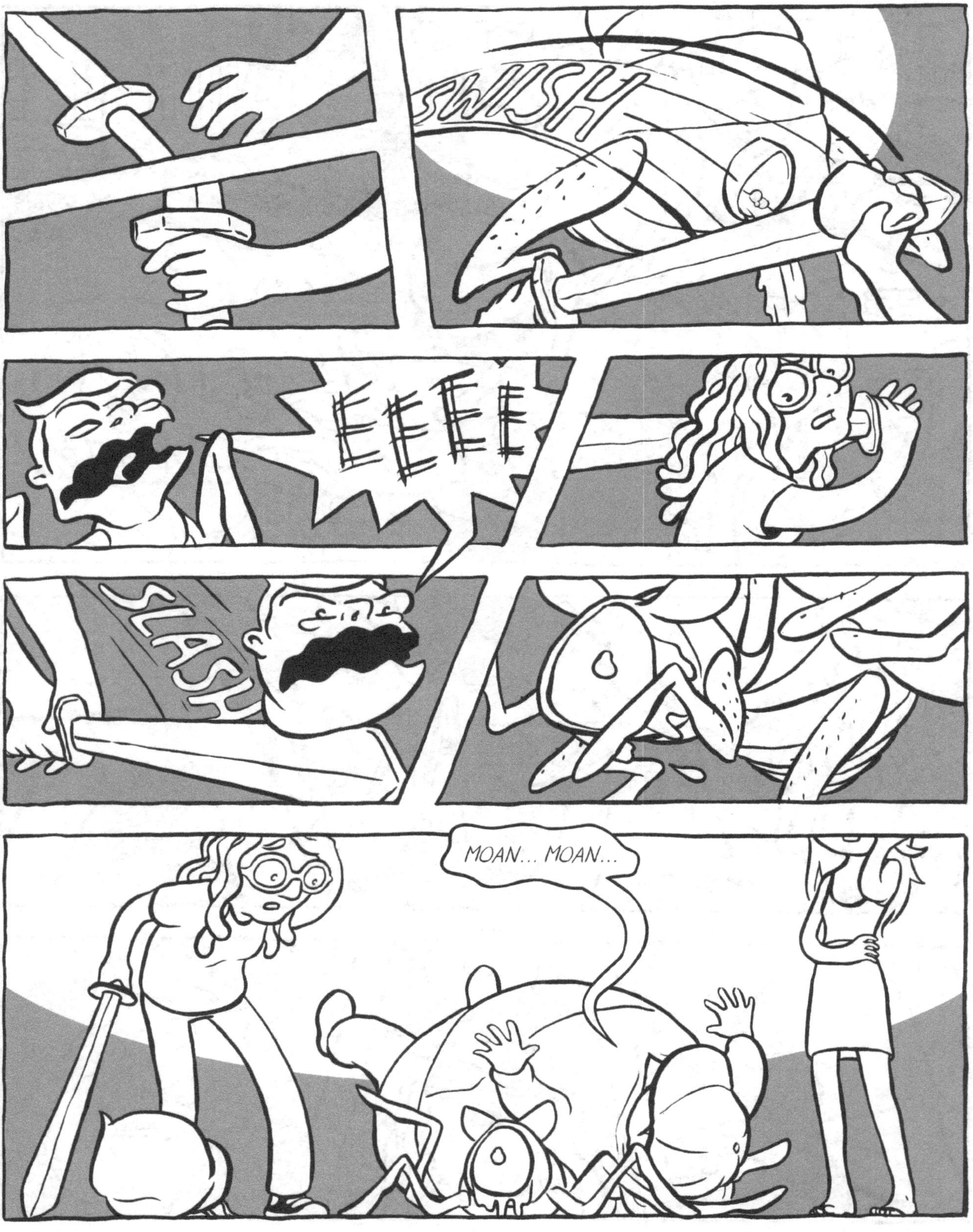
SWISH
EEEEE
SLASH
MOAN... MOAN...

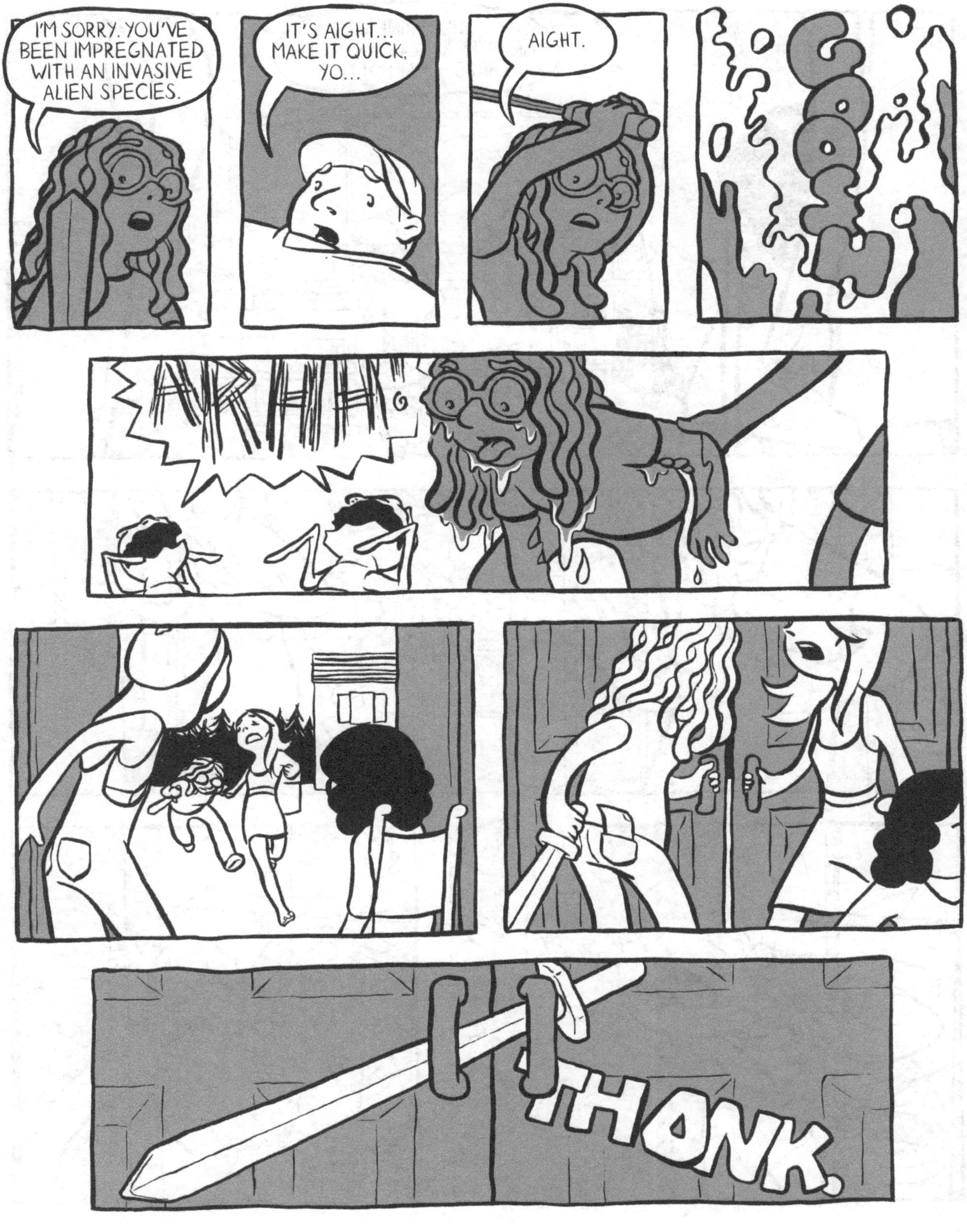
I'M SORRY. YOU'VE BEEN IMPREGNATED WITH AN INVASIVE ALIEN SPECIES.
IT'S AIGHT... MAKE IT QUICK, YO...
AIGHT.
THONK.

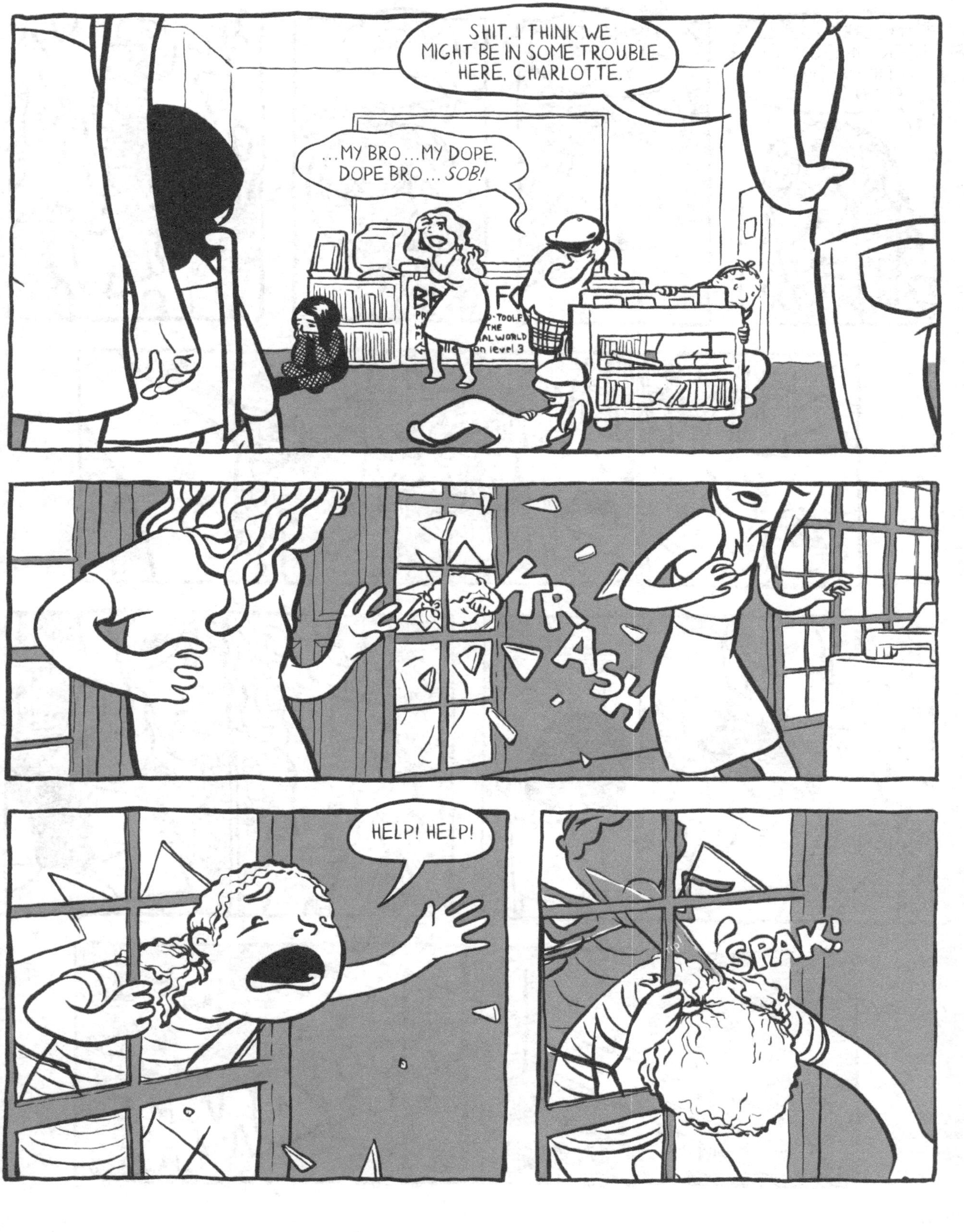
SHIT. I THINK WE MIGHT BE IN SOME TROUBLE HERE, CHARLOTTE.
...MY BRO...MY DOPE, DOPE BRO... *SOB!*
KRASH
HELP! HELP!
SPAK!

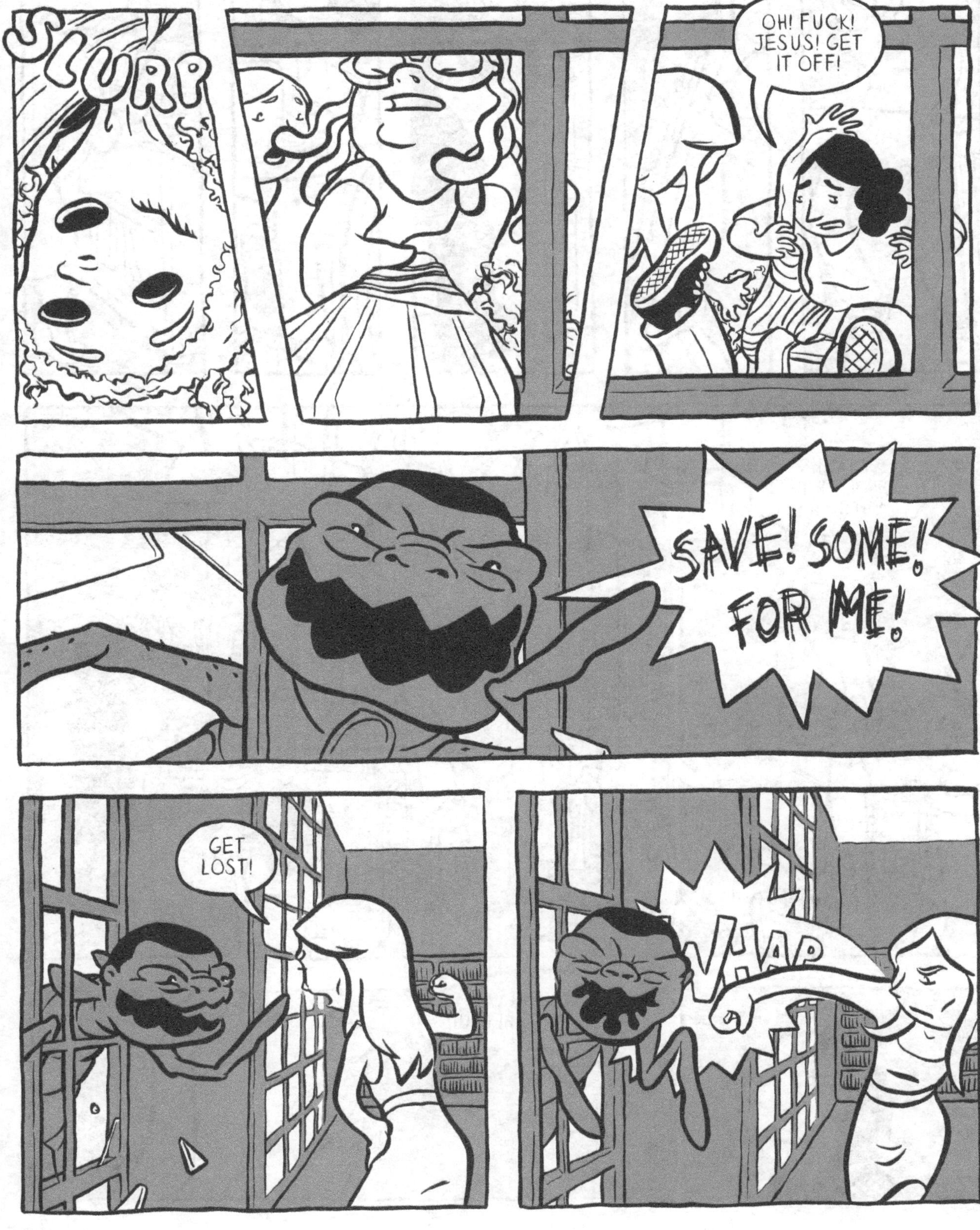
SLURP
OH! FUCK! JESUS! GET IT OFF!
SAVE! SOME! FOR ME!
GET LOST!
WHAP

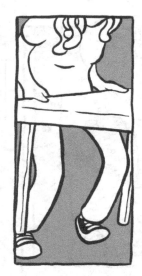

THANKS FOR YOUR HELP WITH THIS.

ARRHH!

I JUST WISH WE COULD SHUT THEM UP.

LET THE HELLBEAST SCREAM.

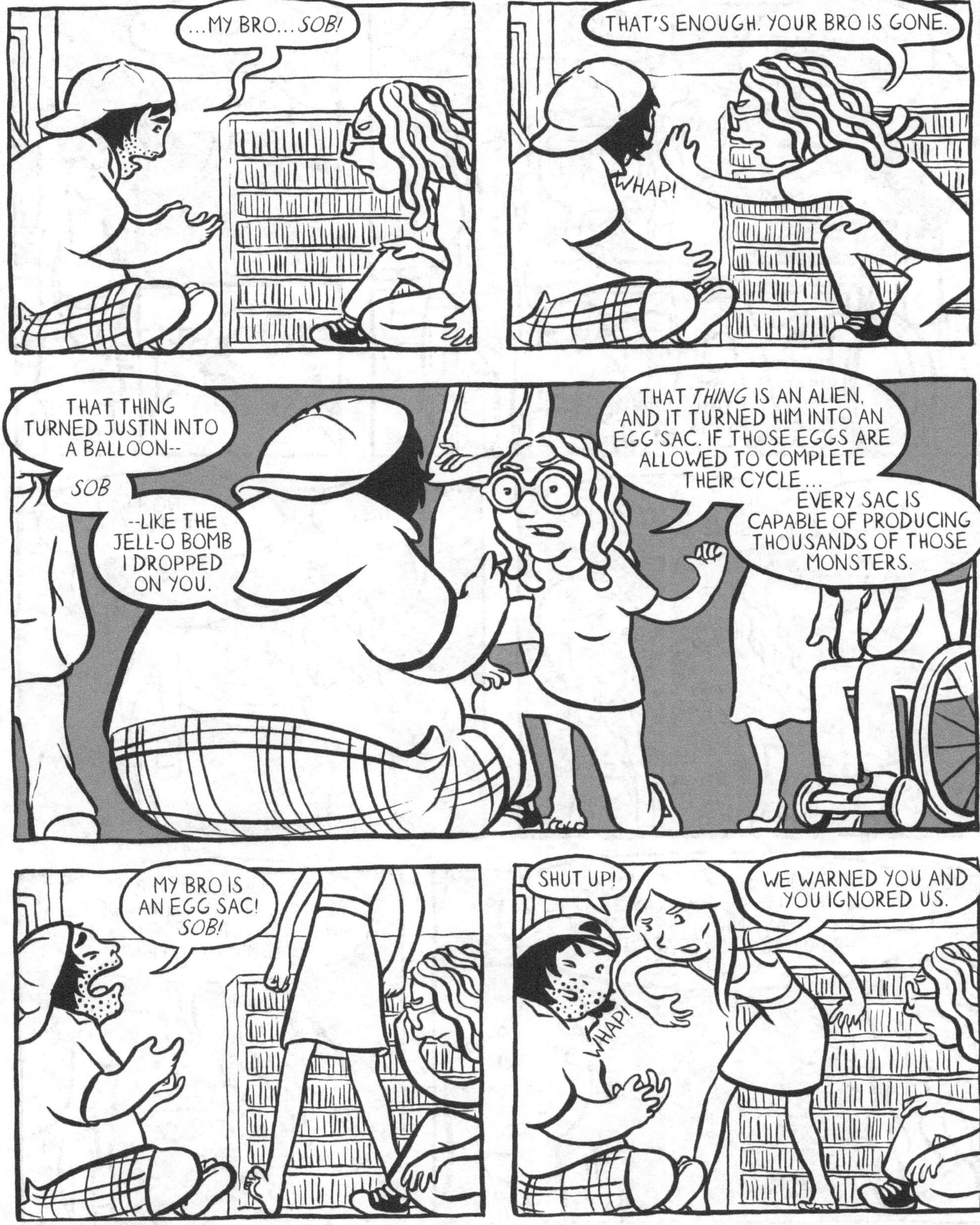

...MY BRO... SOB!
THAT'S ENOUGH. YOUR BRO IS GONE.
WHAP!
THAT THING TURNED JUSTIN INTO A BALLOON--
SOB
--LIKE THE JELL-O BOMB I DROPPED ON YOU.
THAT THING IS AN ALIEN, AND IT TURNED HIM INTO AN EGG SAC. IF THOSE EGGS ARE ALLOWED TO COMPLETE THEIR CYCLE...
EVERY SAC IS CAPABLE OF PRODUCING THOUSANDS OF THOSE MONSTERS.
MY BRO IS AN EGG SAC! SOB!
SHUT UP!
WE WARNED YOU AND YOU IGNORED US.
WHAP!

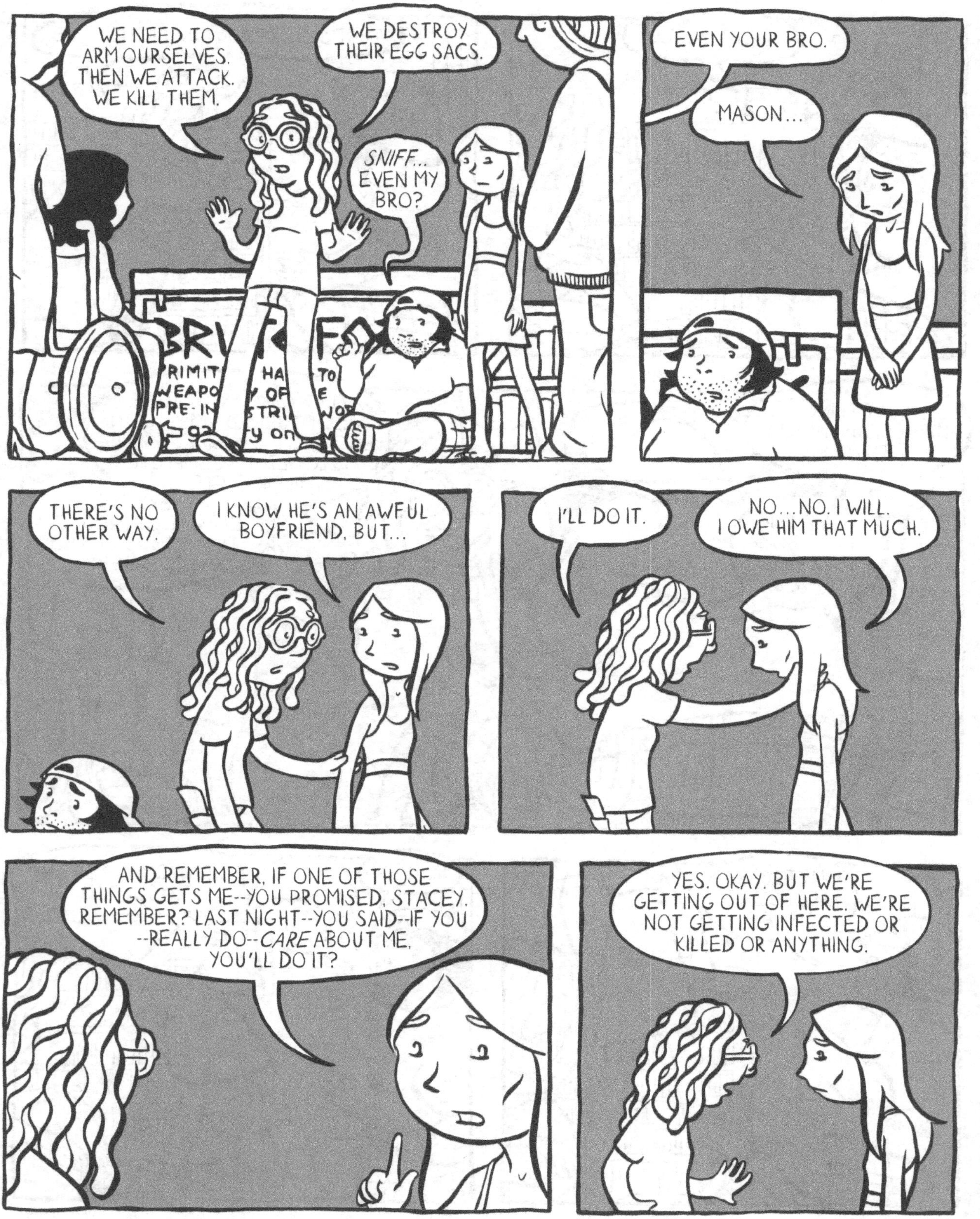
WE NEED TO ARM OURSELVES. THEN WE ATTACK. WE KILL THEM.
WE DESTROY THEIR EGG SACS.
SNIFF... EVEN MY BRO?
EVEN YOUR BRO.
MASON...
THERE'S NO OTHER WAY.
I KNOW HE'S AN AWFUL BOYFRIEND, BUT...
I'LL DO IT.
NO...NO. I WILL. I OWE HIM THAT MUCH.
AND REMEMBER, IF ONE OF THOSE THINGS GETS ME--YOU PROMISED, STACEY. REMEMBER? LAST NIGHT--YOU SAID--IF YOU --REALLY DO--*CARE* ABOUT ME, YOU'LL DO IT?
YES. OKAY. BUT WE'RE GETTING OUT OF HERE. WE'RE NOT GETTING INFECTED OR KILLED OR ANYTHING.

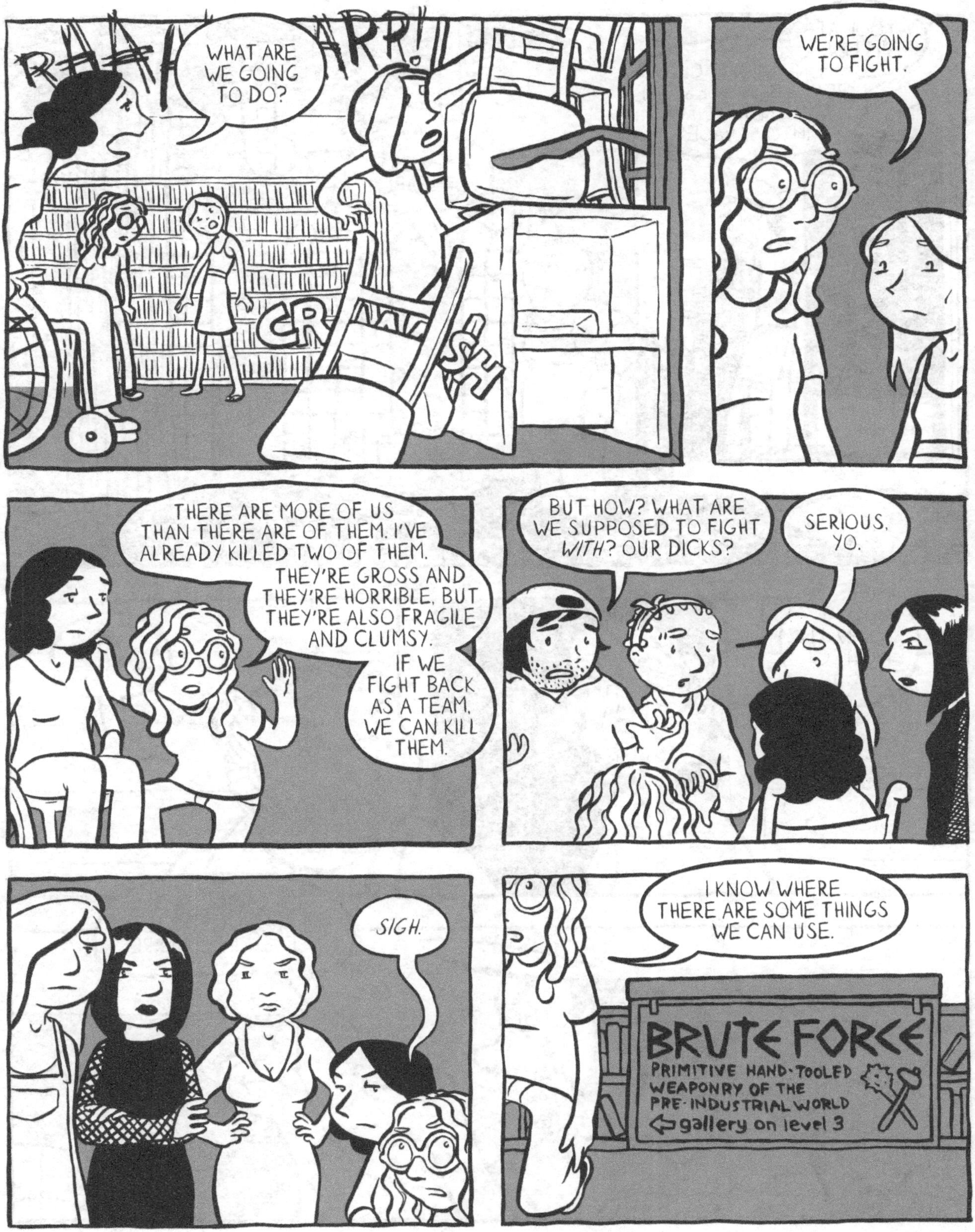
RAAAARR!
WHAT ARE WE GOING TO DO?
CRAAASH
WE'RE GOING TO FIGHT.
THERE ARE MORE OF US THAN THERE ARE OF THEM. I'VE ALREADY KILLED TWO OF THEM.
THEY'RE GROSS AND THEY'RE HORRIBLE, BUT THEY'RE ALSO FRAGILE AND CLUMSY.
IF WE FIGHT BACK AS A TEAM, WE CAN KILL THEM.
BUT HOW? WHAT ARE WE SUPPOSED TO FIGHT *WITH*? OUR DICKS?
SERIOUS, YO.
SIGH.
I KNOW WHERE THERE ARE SOME THINGS WE CAN USE.
BRUTE FORCE
PRIMITIVE HAND-TOOLED WEAPONRY OF THE PRE-INDUSTRIAL WORLD
gallery on level 3

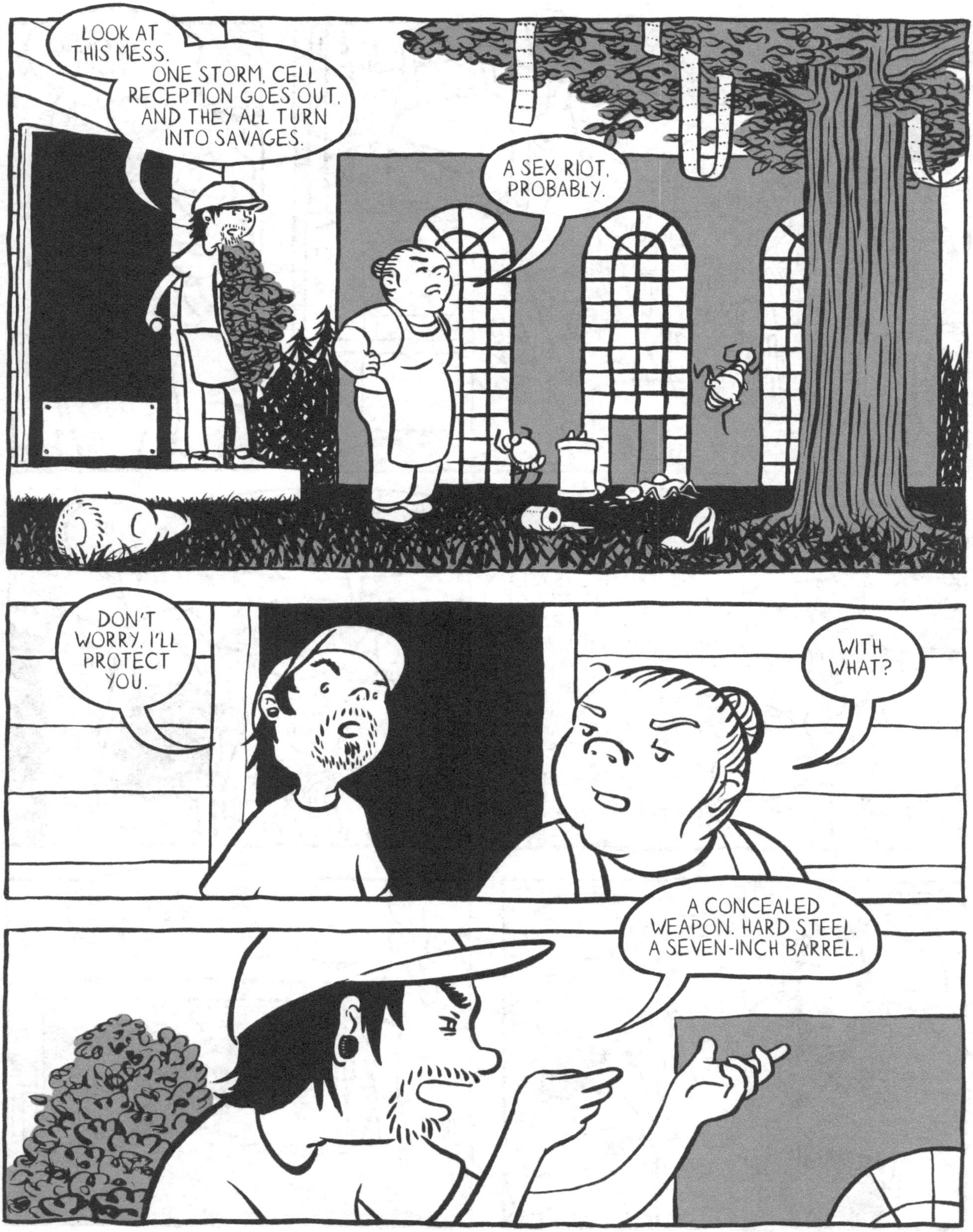
LOOK AT THIS MESS. ONE STORM, CELL RECEPTION GOES OUT, AND THEY ALL TURN INTO SAVAGES.
A SEX RIOT, PROBABLY.
DON'T WORRY, I'LL PROTECT YOU.
WITH WHAT?
A CONCEALED WEAPON. HARD STEEL. A SEVEN-INCH BARREL.

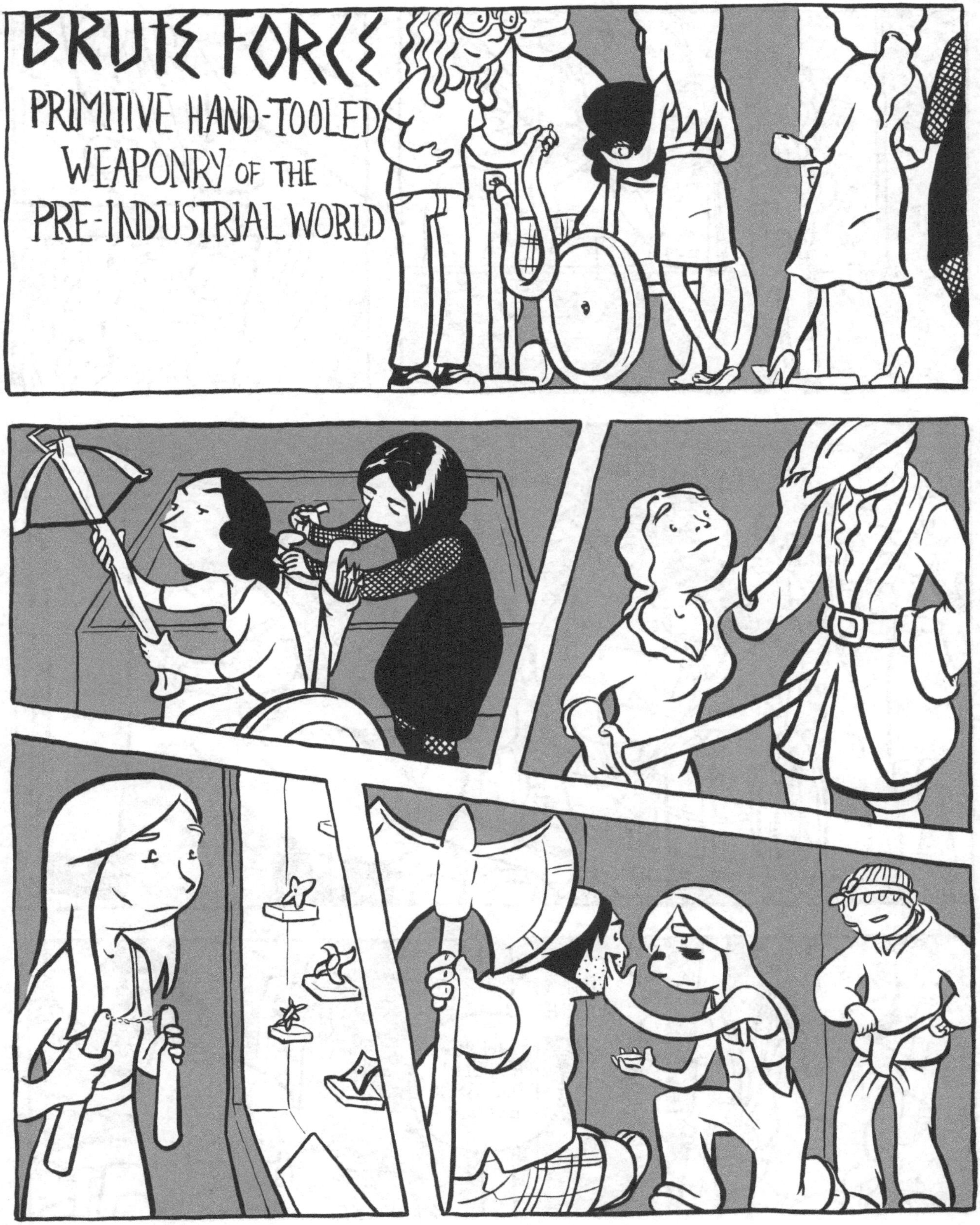
BRUTE FORCE
PRIMITIVE HAND-TOOLED WEAPONRY OF THE PRE-INDUSTRIAL WORLD

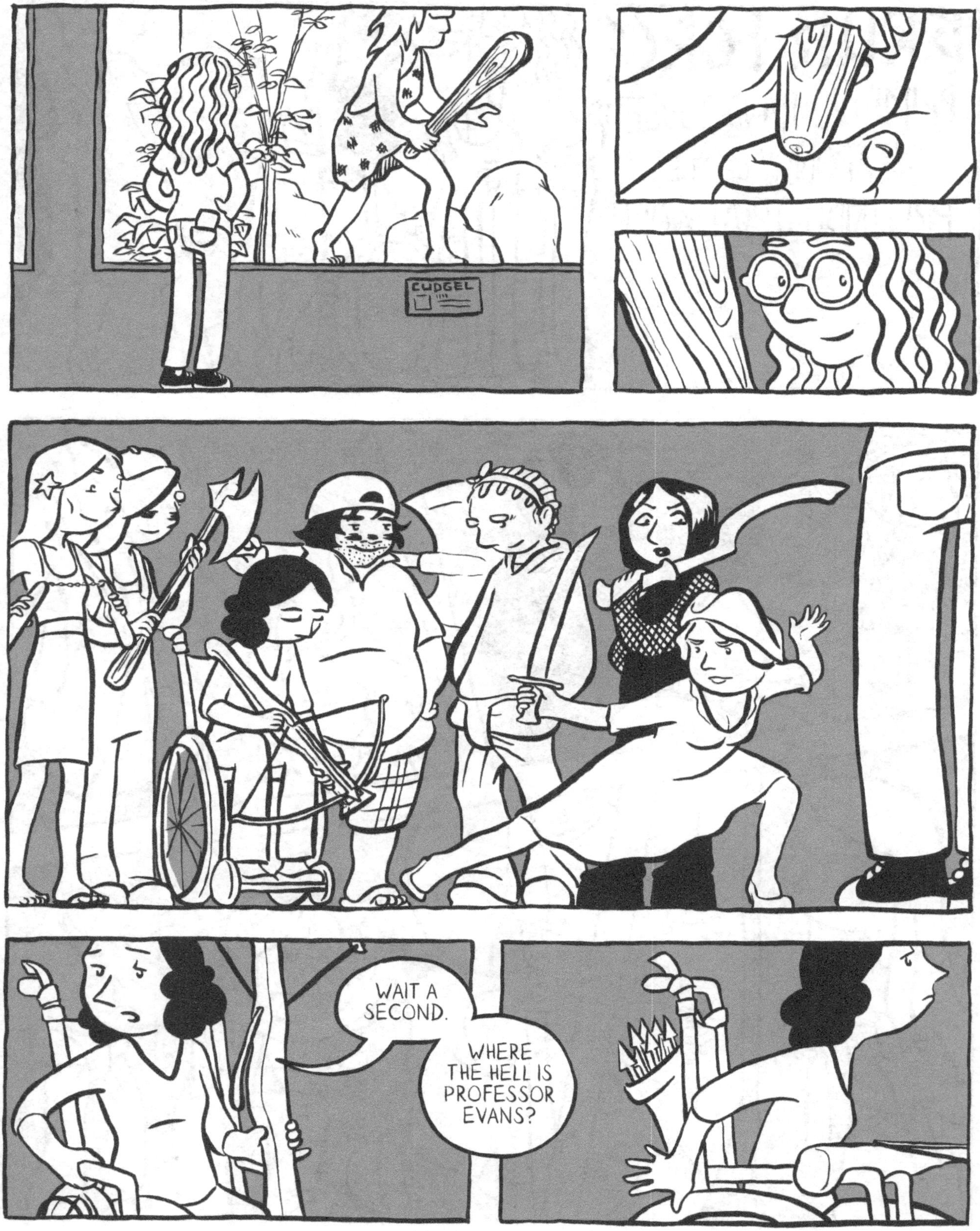
CUDGEL
WAIT A SECOND.
WHERE THE HELL IS PROFESSOR EVANS?

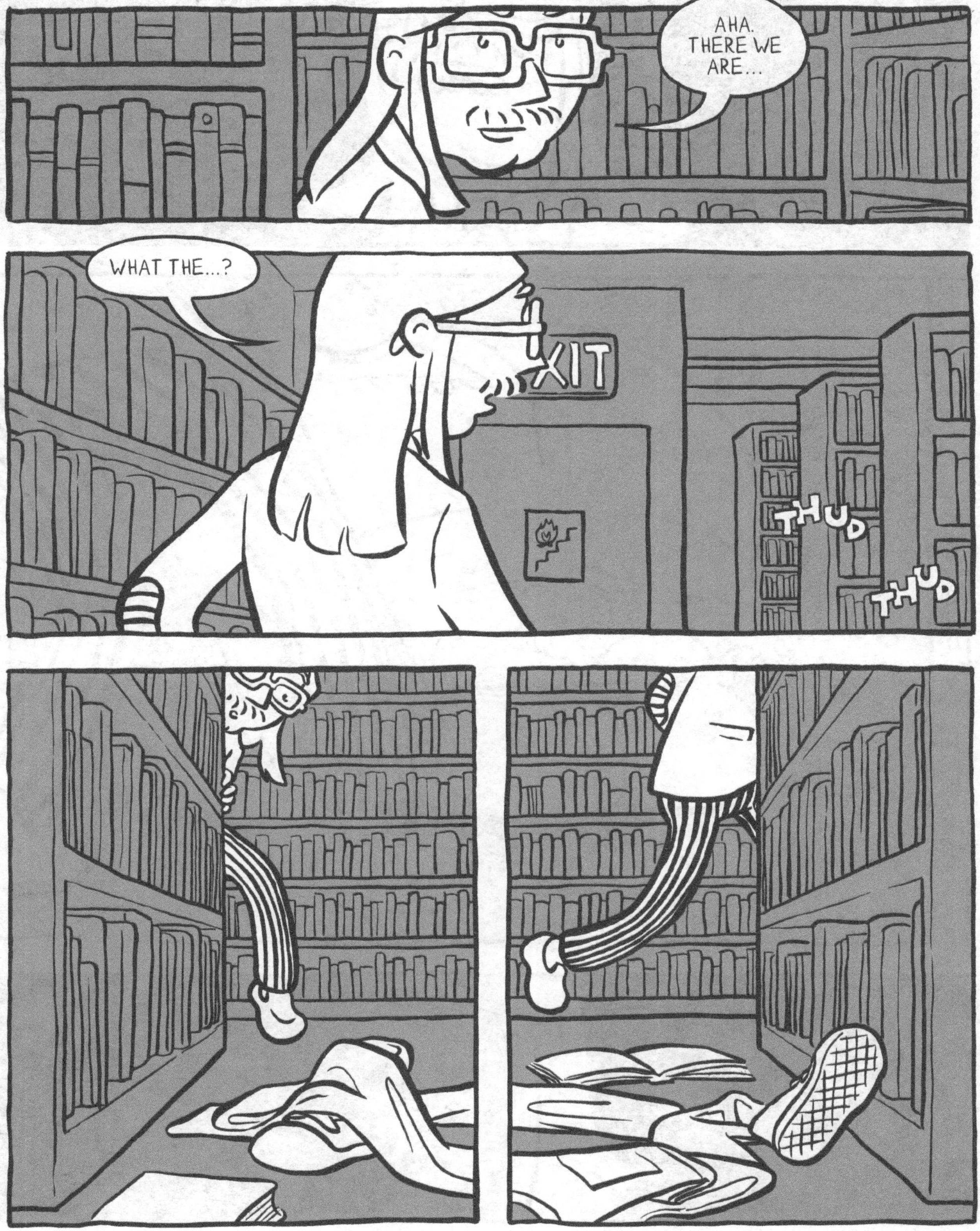
AHA. THERE WE ARE...
WHAT THE...?
EXIT
THUD
THUD

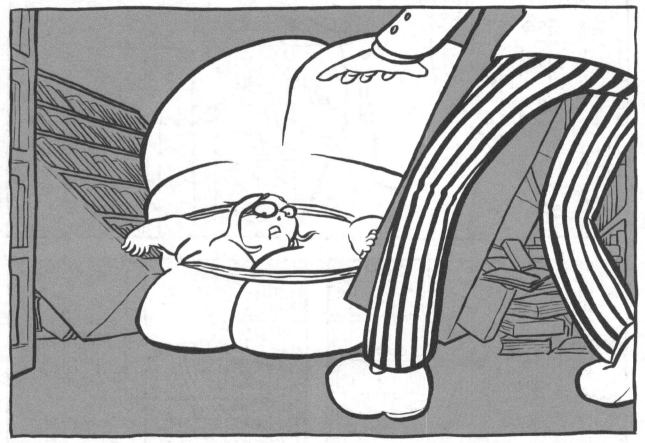

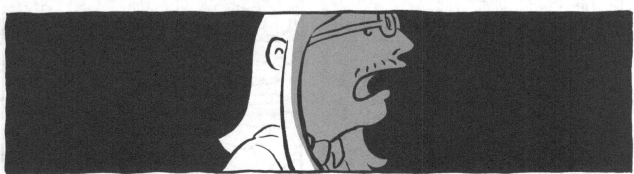

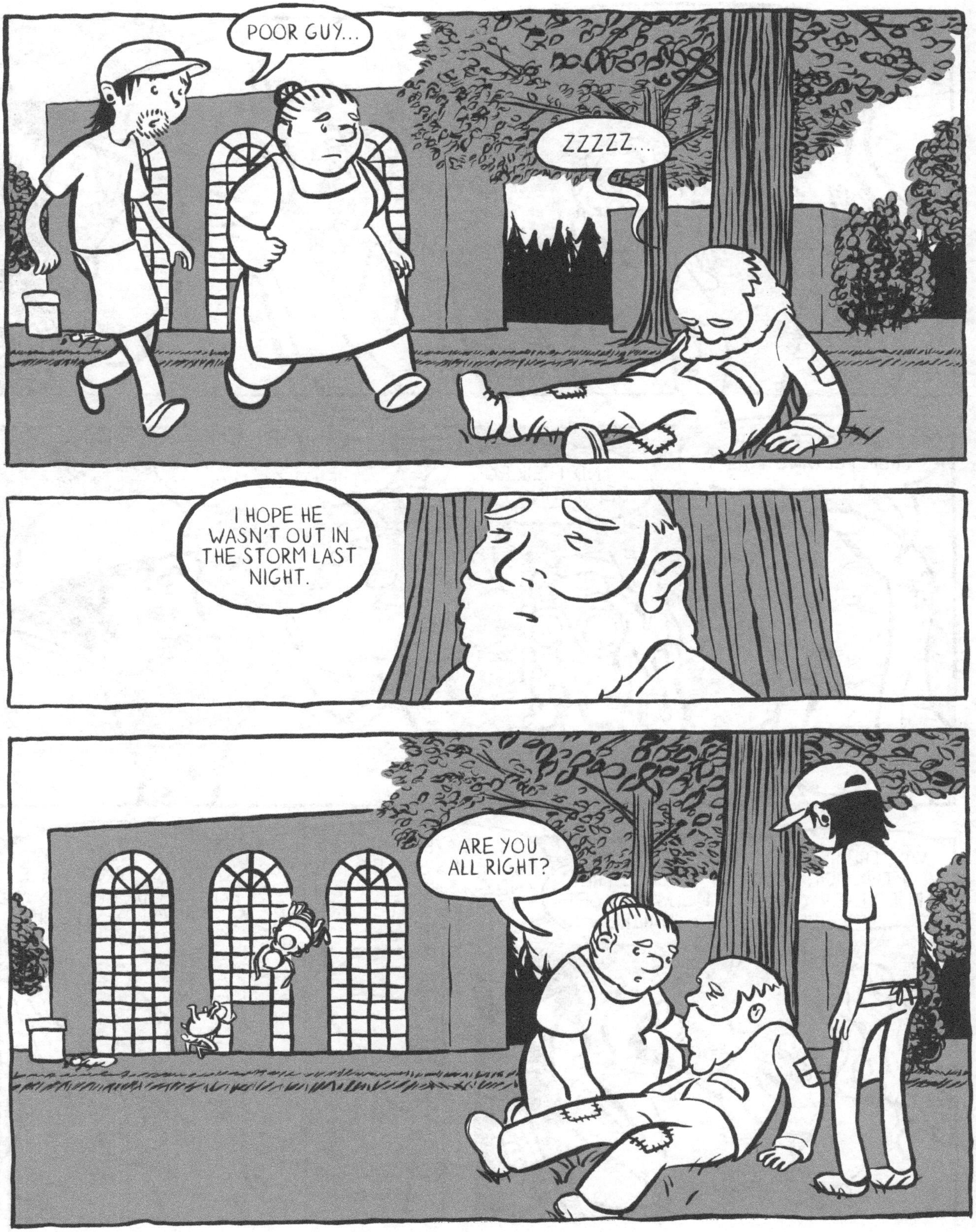
POOR GUY...
ZZZZZ...
I HOPE HE WASN'T OUT IN THE STORM LAST NIGHT.
ARE YOU ALL RIGHT?

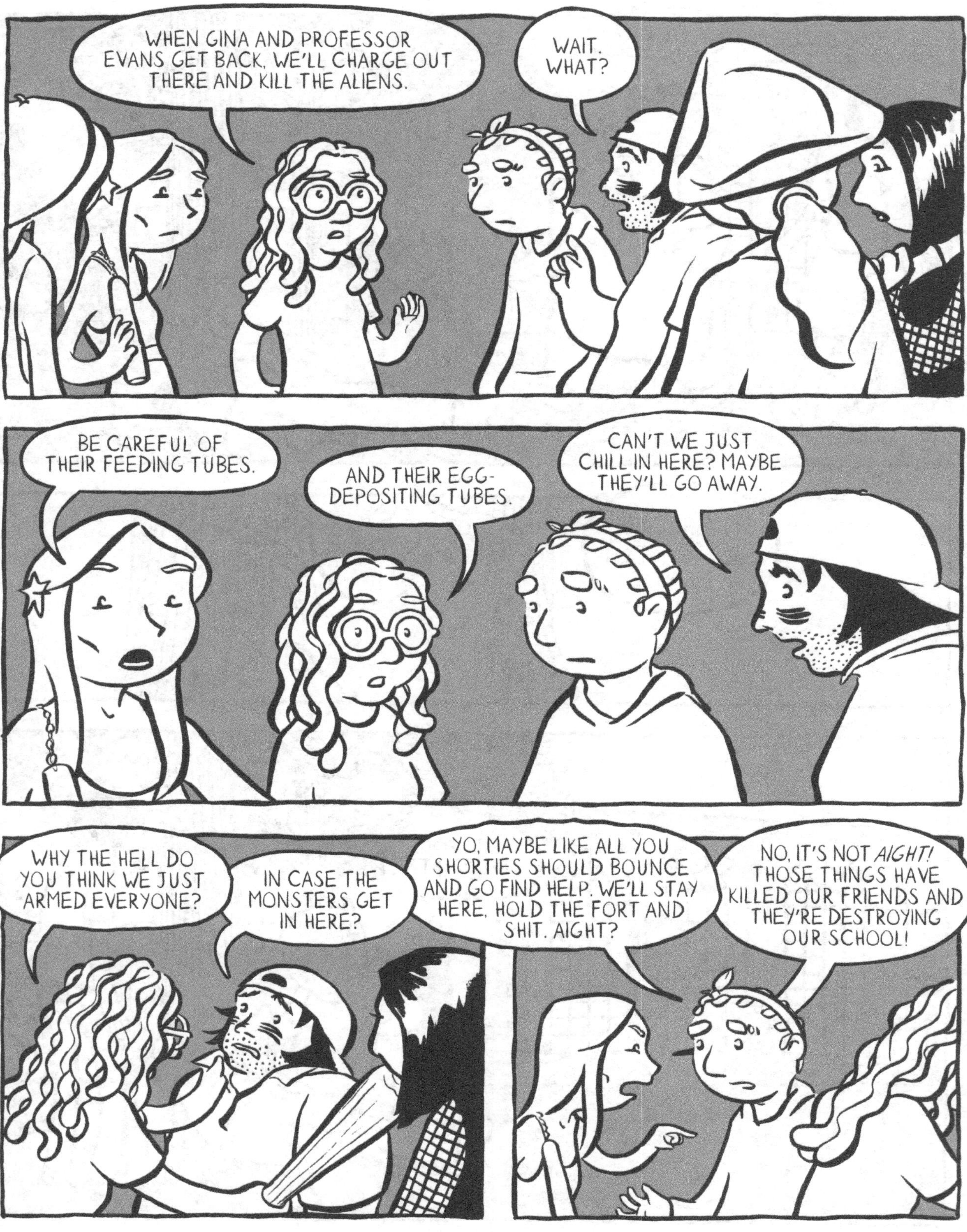
WHEN GINA AND PROFESSOR EVANS GET BACK, WE'LL CHARGE OUT THERE AND KILL THE ALIENS.
WAIT. WHAT?
BE CAREFUL OF THEIR FEEDING TUBES.
AND THEIR EGG-DEPOSITING TUBES.
CAN'T WE JUST CHILL IN HERE? MAYBE THEY'LL GO AWAY.
WHY THE HELL DO YOU THINK WE JUST ARMED EVERYONE?
IN CASE THE MONSTERS GET IN HERE?
YO, MAYBE LIKE ALL YOU SHORTIES SHOULD BOUNCE AND GO FIND HELP. WE'LL STAY HERE, HOLD THE FORT AND SHIT. AIGHT?
NO, IT'S NOT *AIGHT!* THOSE THINGS HAVE KILLED OUR FRIENDS AND THEY'RE DESTROYING OUR SCHOOL!

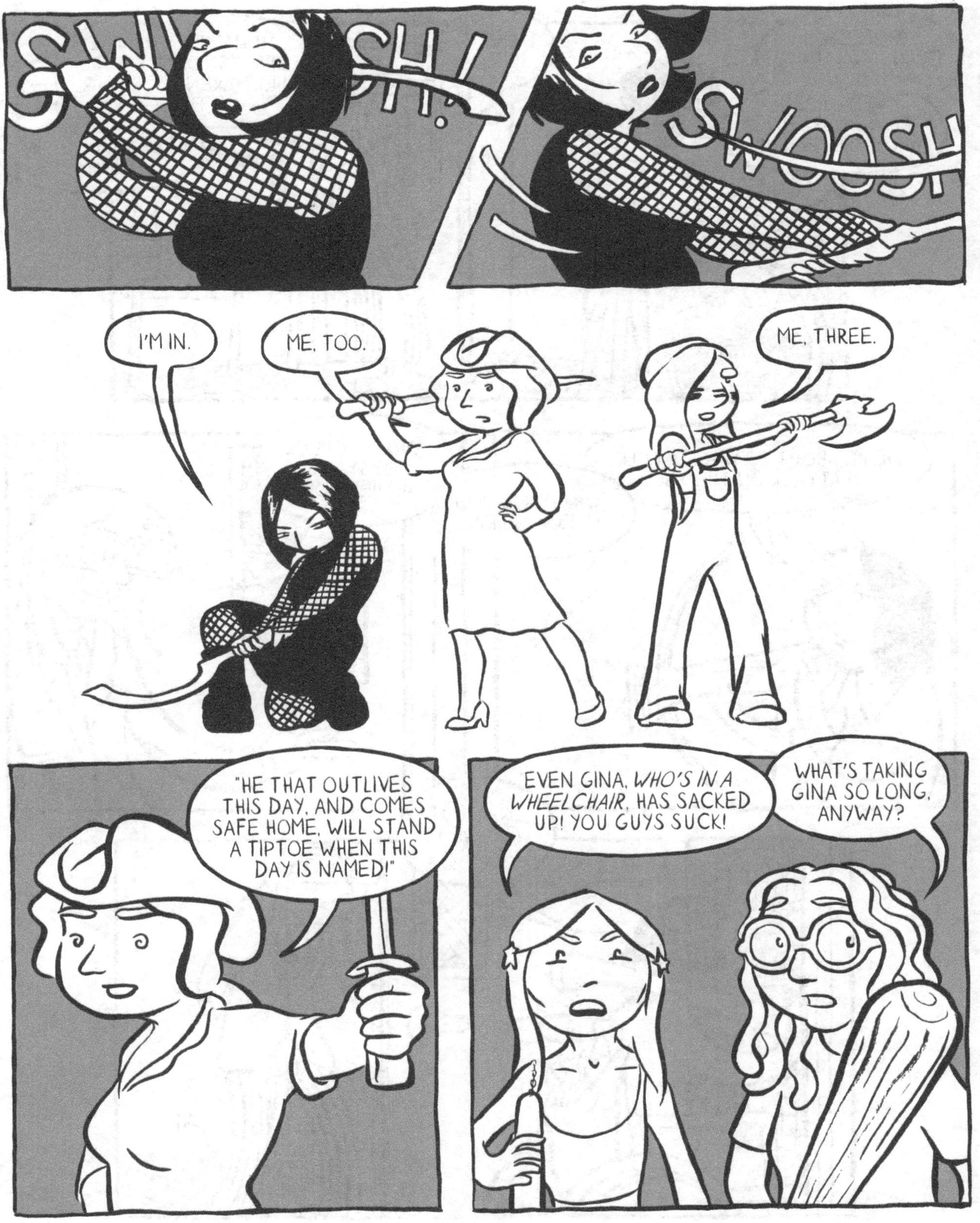
SWOOSH!
SWOOSH
I'M IN.
ME, TOO.
ME, THREE.
"HE THAT OUTLIVES THIS DAY, AND COMES SAFE HOME, WILL STAND A TIPTOE WHEN THIS DAY IS NAMED!"
EVEN GINA, *WHO'S IN A WHEELCHAIR*, HAS SACKED UP! YOU GUYS SUCK!
WHAT'S TAKING GINA SO LONG, ANYWAY?

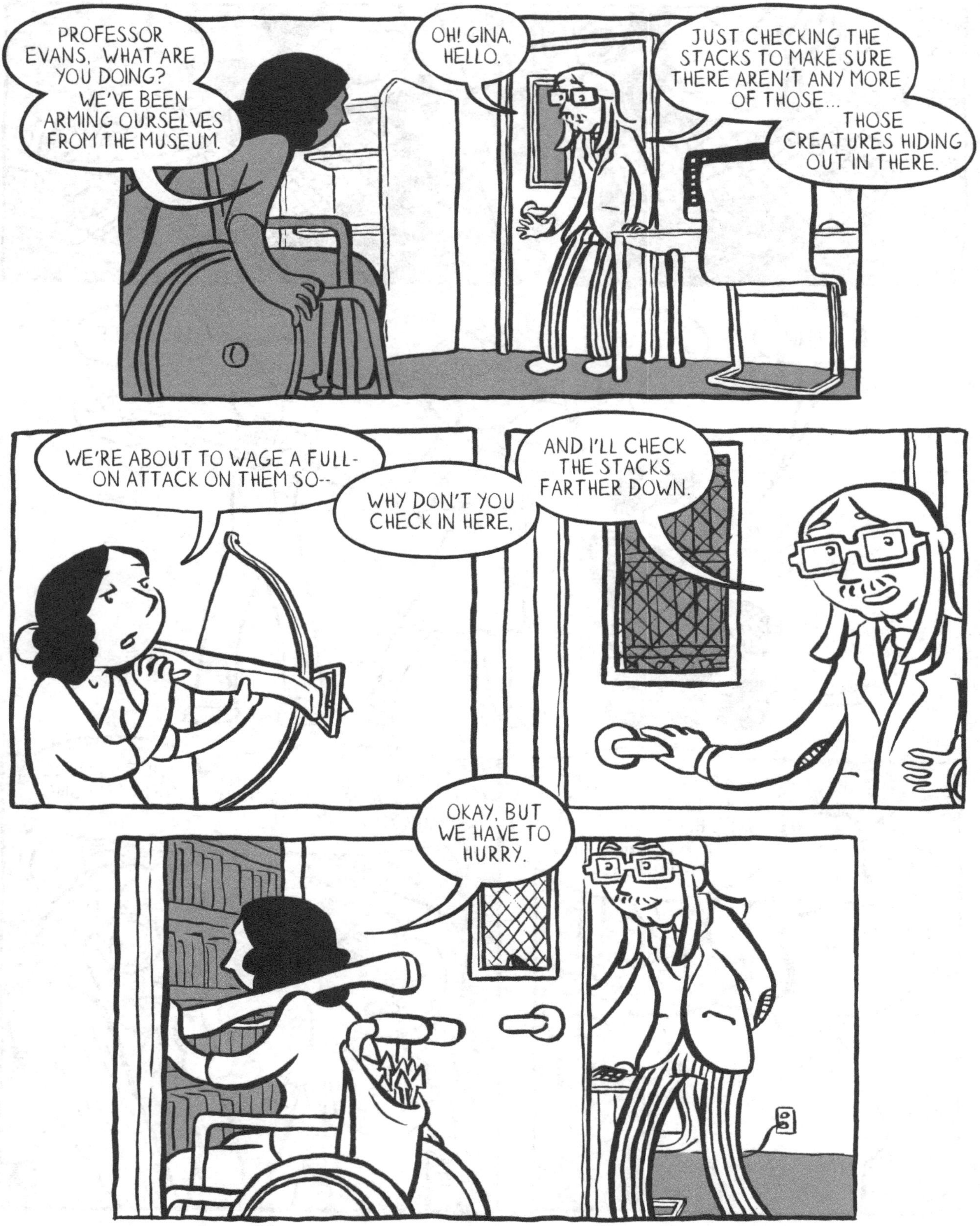
PROFESSOR EVANS, WHAT ARE YOU DOING? WE'VE BEEN ARMING OURSELVES FROM THE MUSEUM.
OH! GINA, HELLO.
JUST CHECKING THE STACKS TO MAKE SURE THERE AREN'T ANY MORE OF THOSE... THOSE CREATURES HIDING OUT IN THERE.
WE'RE ABOUT TO WAGE A FULL-ON ATTACK ON THEM SO--
WHY DON'T YOU CHECK IN HERE,
AND I'LL CHECK THE STACKS FARTHER DOWN.
OKAY, BUT WE HAVE TO HURRY.

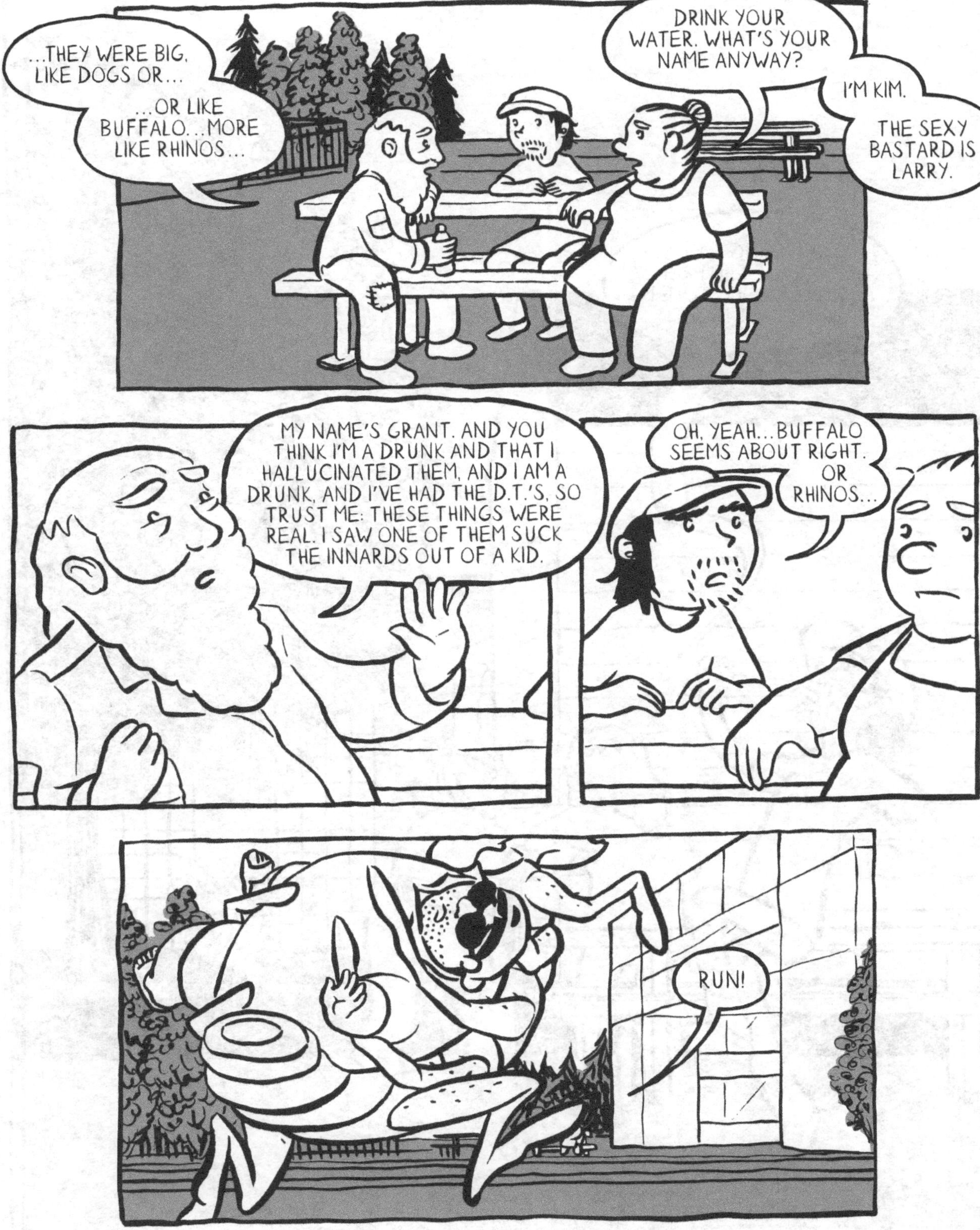
...THEY WERE BIG, LIKE DOGS OR...
...OR LIKE BUFFALO...MORE LIKE RHINOS...
DRINK YOUR WATER. WHAT'S YOUR NAME ANYWAY?
I'M KIM.
THE SEXY BASTARD IS LARRY.
MY NAME'S GRANT. AND YOU THINK I'M A DRUNK AND THAT I HALLUCINATED THEM, AND I AM A DRUNK, AND I'VE HAD THE D.T.'S, SO TRUST ME: THESE THINGS WERE REAL. I SAW ONE OF THEM SUCK THE INNARDS OUT OF A KID.
OH, YEAH...BUFFALO SEEMS ABOUT RIGHT.
OR RHINOS...
RUN!

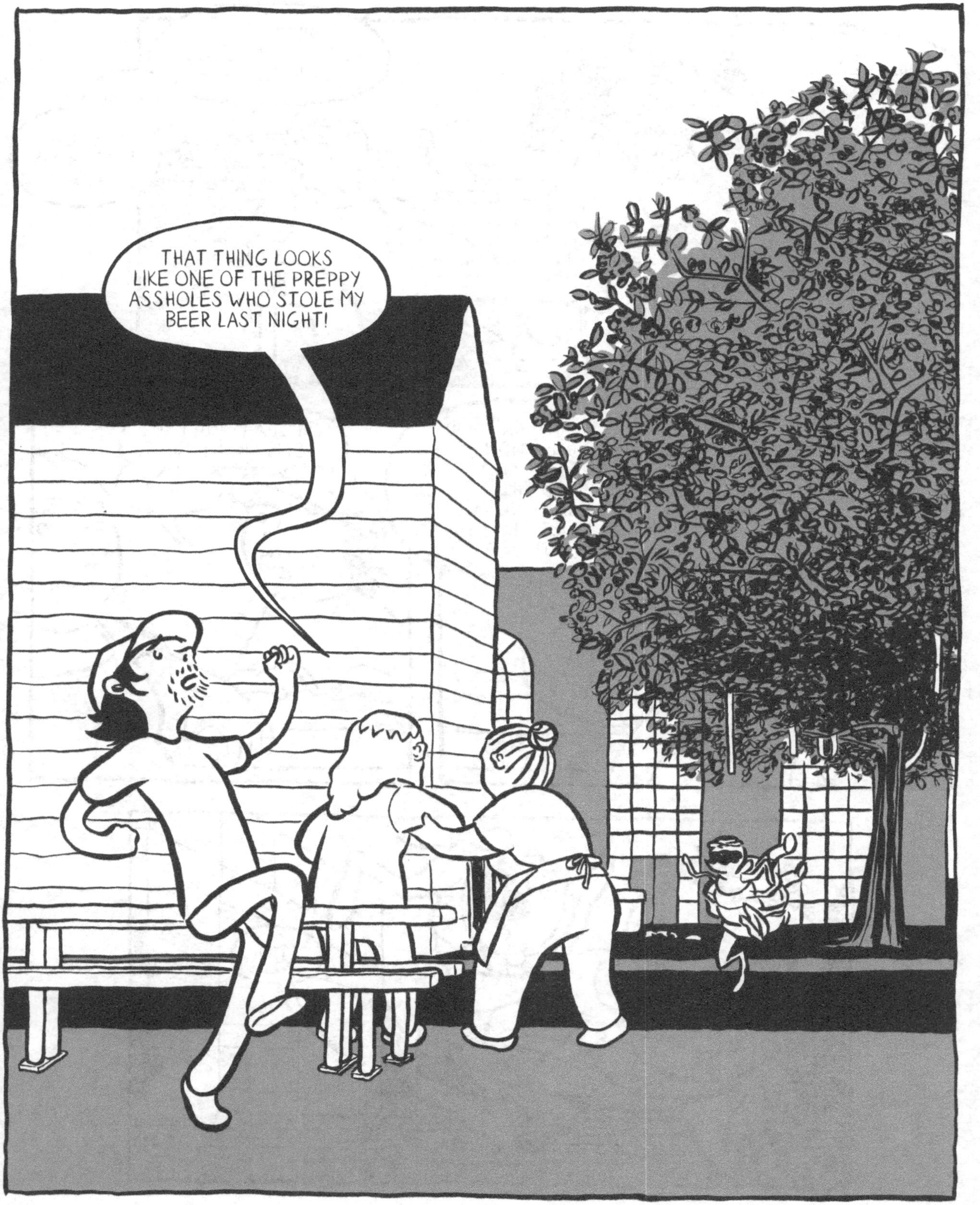
THAT THING LOOKS LIKE ONE OF THE PREPPY ASSHOLES WHO STOLE MY BEER LAST NIGHT!

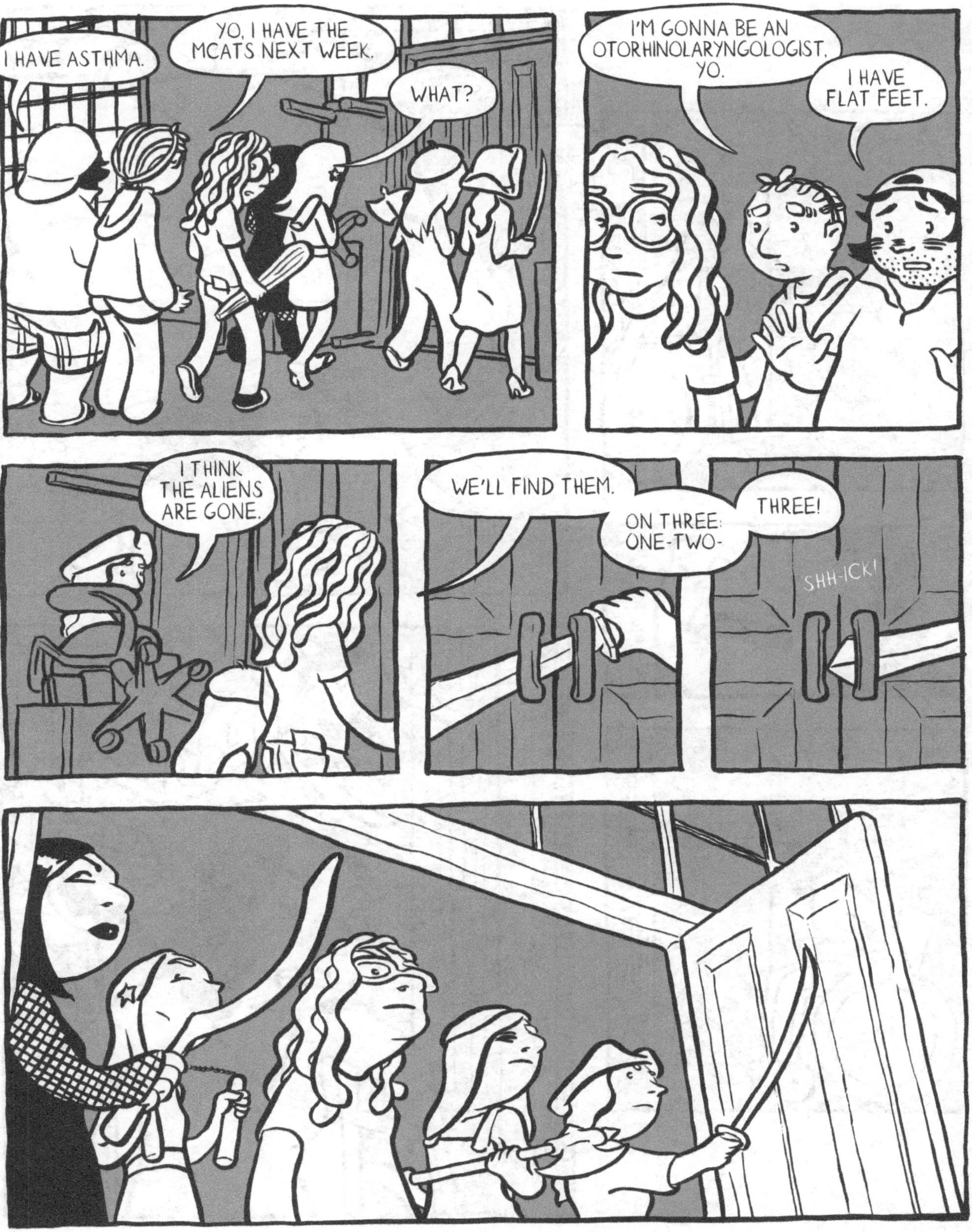
I HAVE ASTHMA.
YO, I HAVE THE MCATS NEXT WEEK.
WHAT?
I'M GONNA BE AN OTORHINOLARYNGOLOGIST, YO.
I HAVE FLAT FEET.
I THINK THE ALIENS ARE GONE.
WE'LL FIND THEM.
ON THREE: ONE-TWO-
THREE!
SHH-ICK!

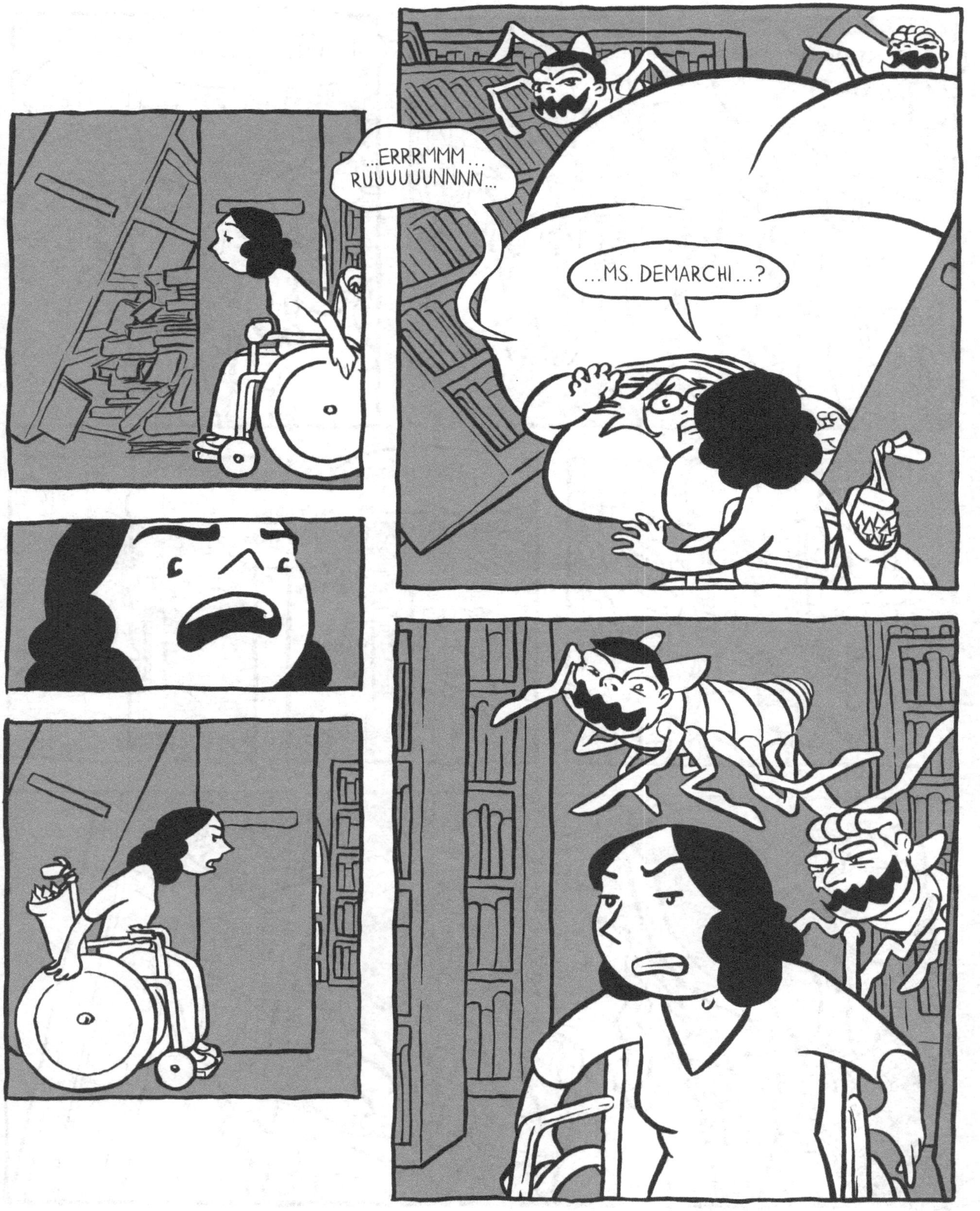
...ERRRMMM...
RUUUUUUNNNN...
...MS. DEMARCHI...?

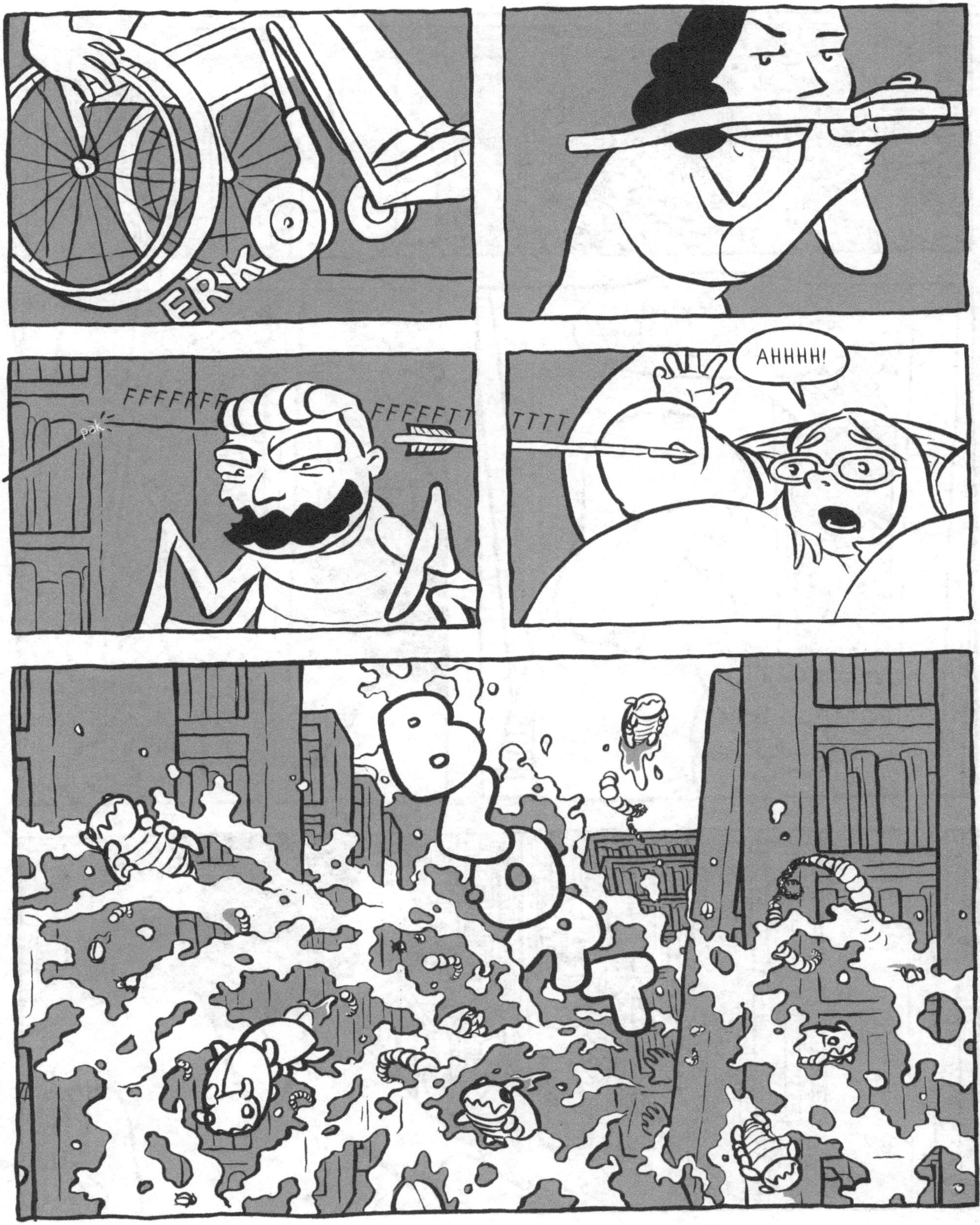
ERK
FFFFFFF
pak
FFFFFFTT
TTTT
AHHHH!

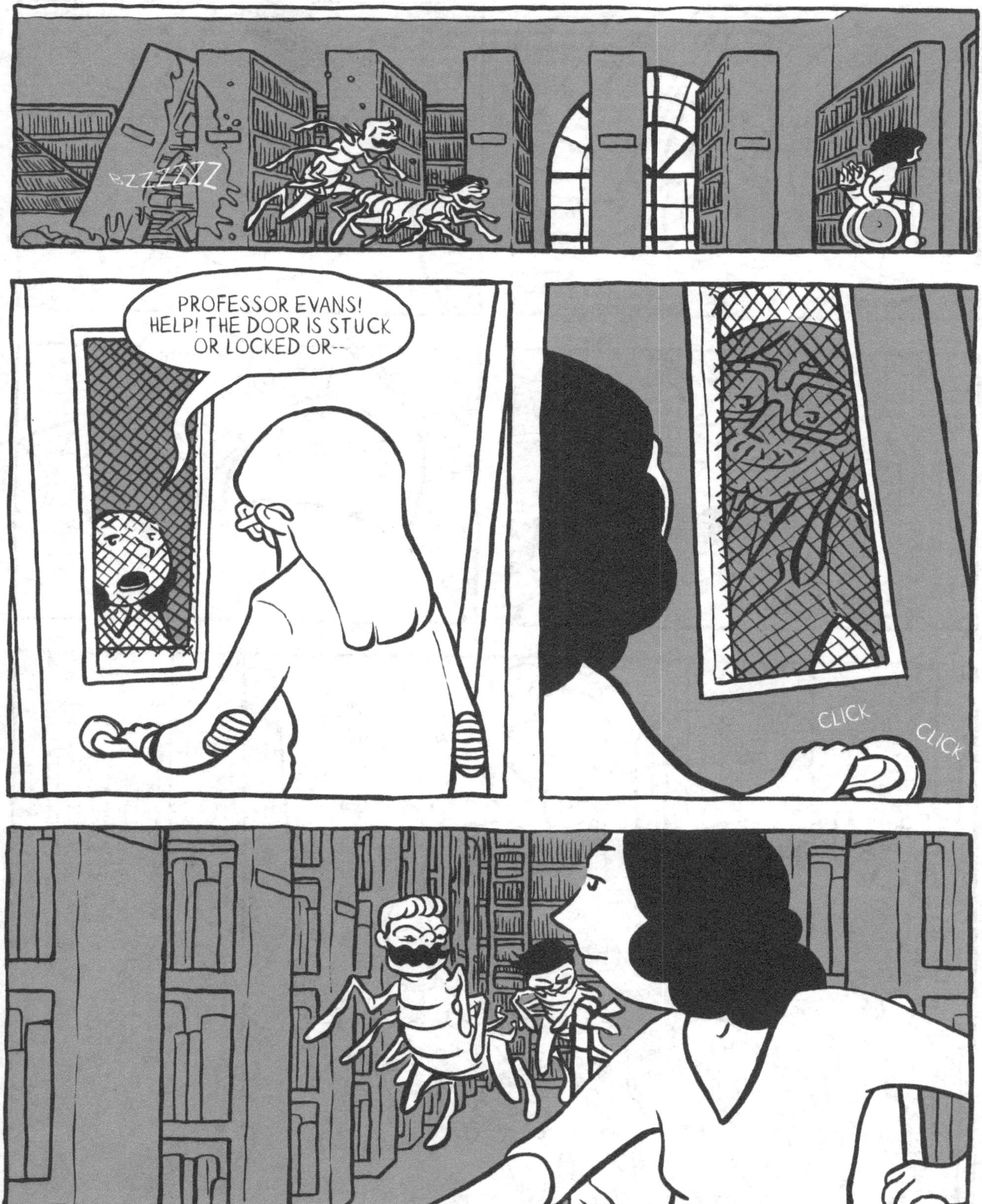
BZZZZZZZ
PROFESSOR EVANS! HELP! THE DOOR IS STUCK OR LOCKED OR--
CLICK
CLICK

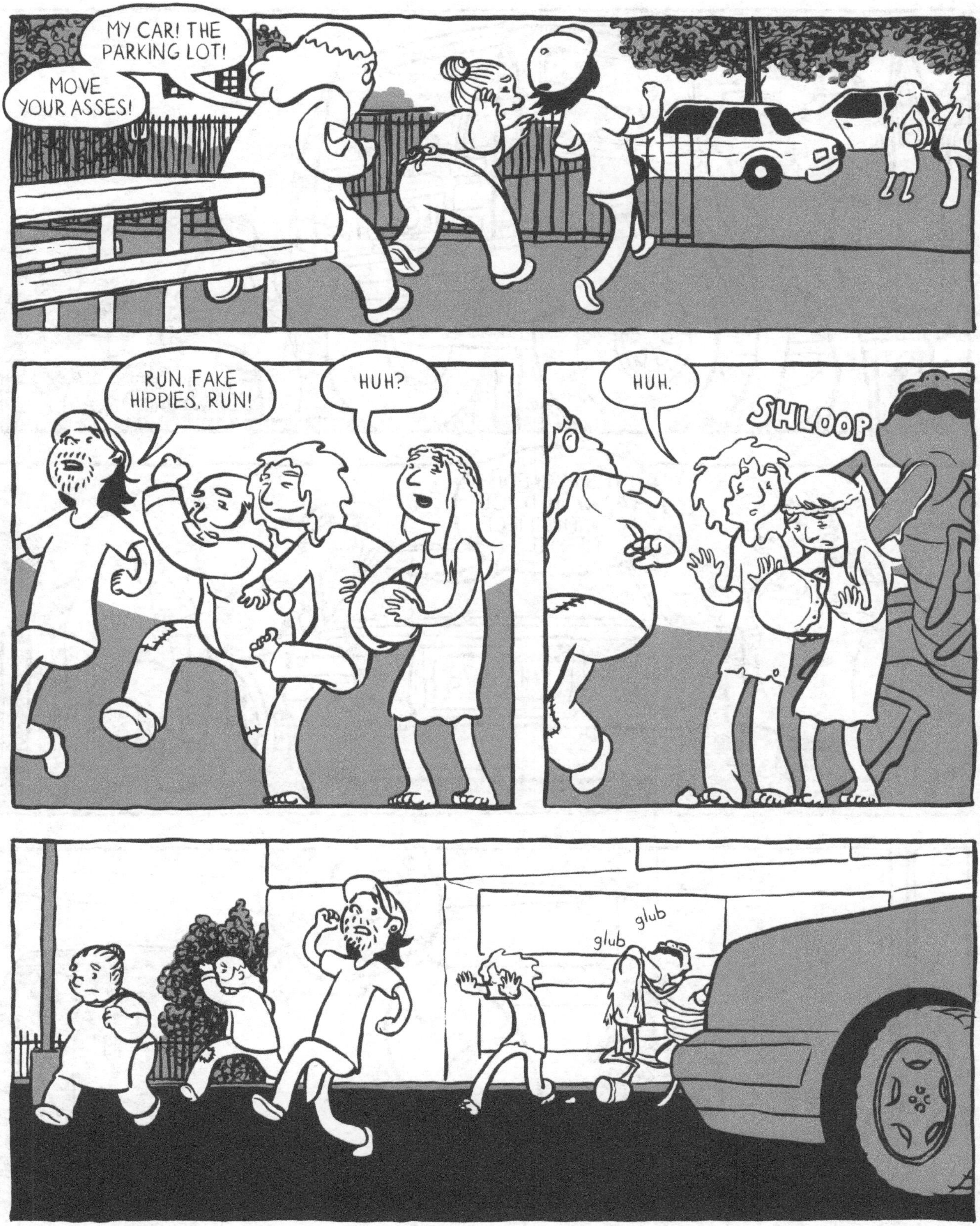
MY CAR! THE PARKING LOT!
MOVE YOUR ASSES!
RUN, FAKE HIPPIES, RUN!
HUH?
HUH.
SHLOOP
glub
glub

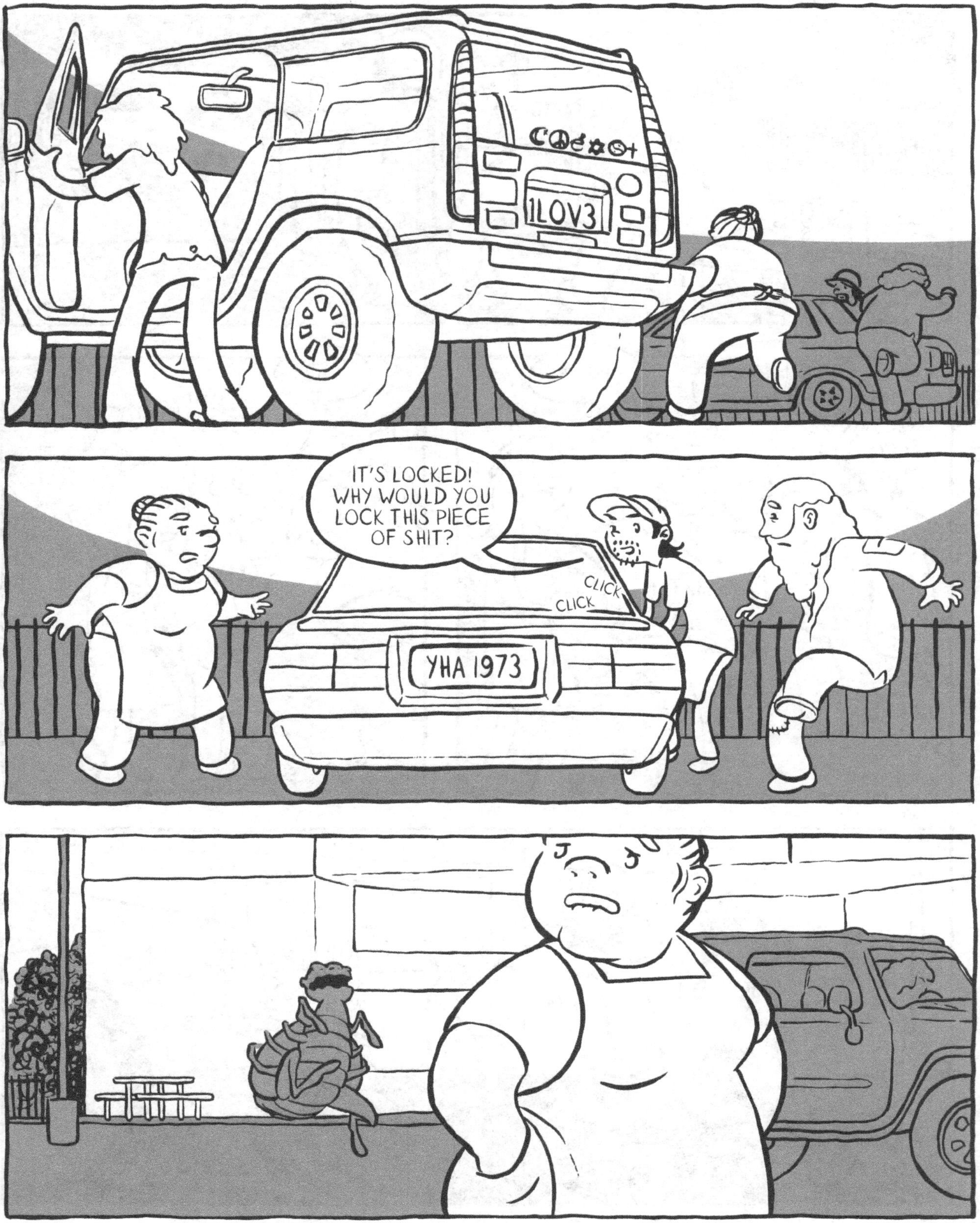
1LOV3
IT'S LOCKED! WHY WOULD YOU LOCK THIS PIECE OF SHIT?
CLICK
CLICK
YHA 1973

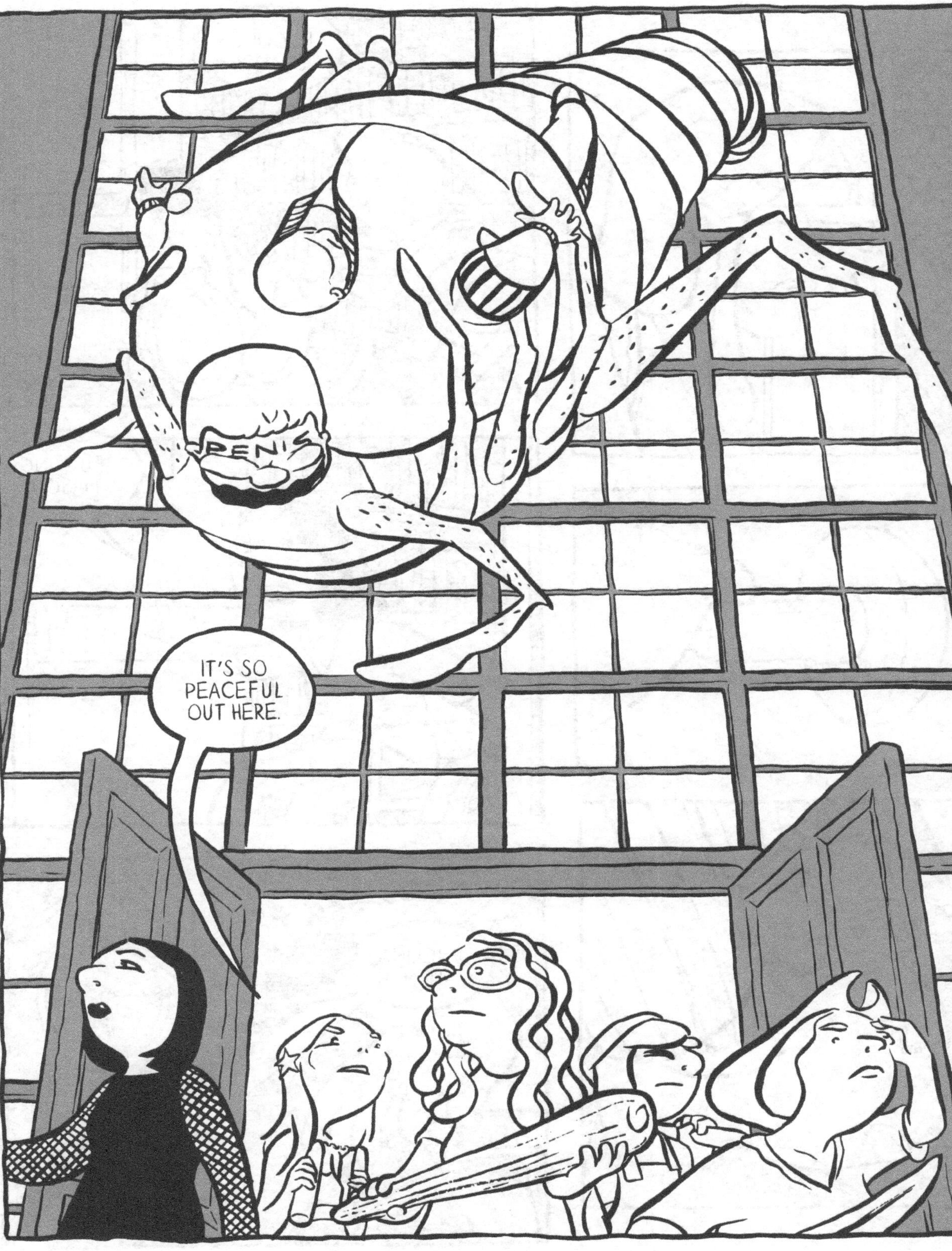
PENIS
IT'S SO PEACEFUL OUT HERE.

FUCKING EVANS!
FUCKING MASON!
FUCKING ALIENS!
THUD
CLICK
CLICK
THU

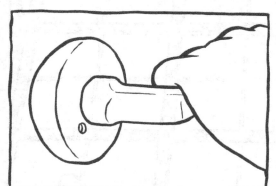

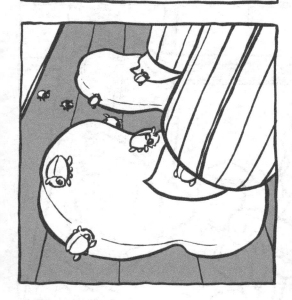

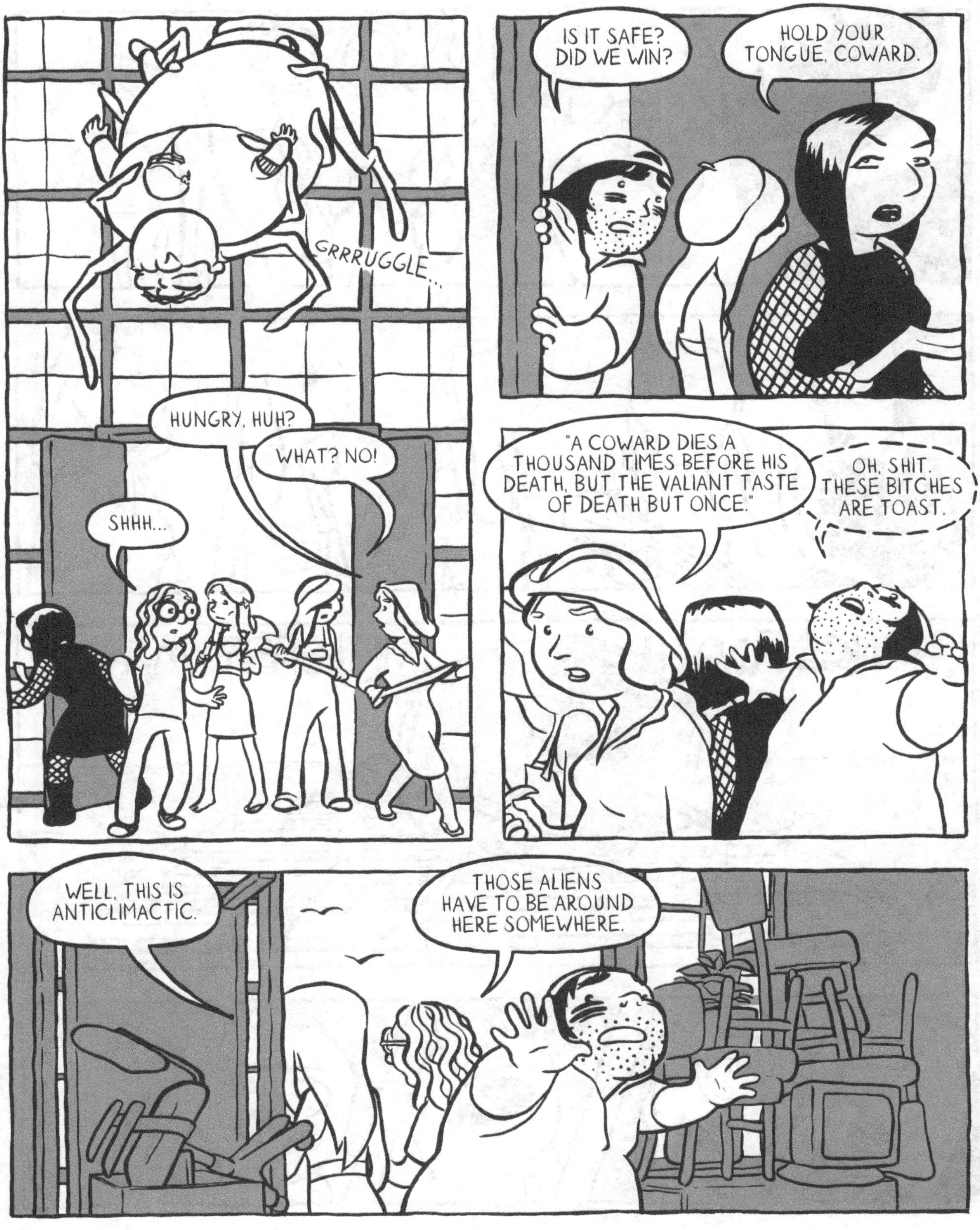
GRRRUGGLE...
IS IT SAFE? DID WE WIN?
HOLD YOUR TONGUE, COWARD.
HUNGRY, HUH?
WHAT? NO!
SHHH...
"A COWARD DIES A THOUSAND TIMES BEFORE HIS DEATH, BUT THE VALIANT TASTE OF DEATH BUT ONCE."
OH, SHIT. THESE BITCHES ARE TOAST.
WELL, THIS IS ANTICLIMACTIC.
THOSE ALIENS HAVE TO BE AROUND HERE SOMEWHERE.

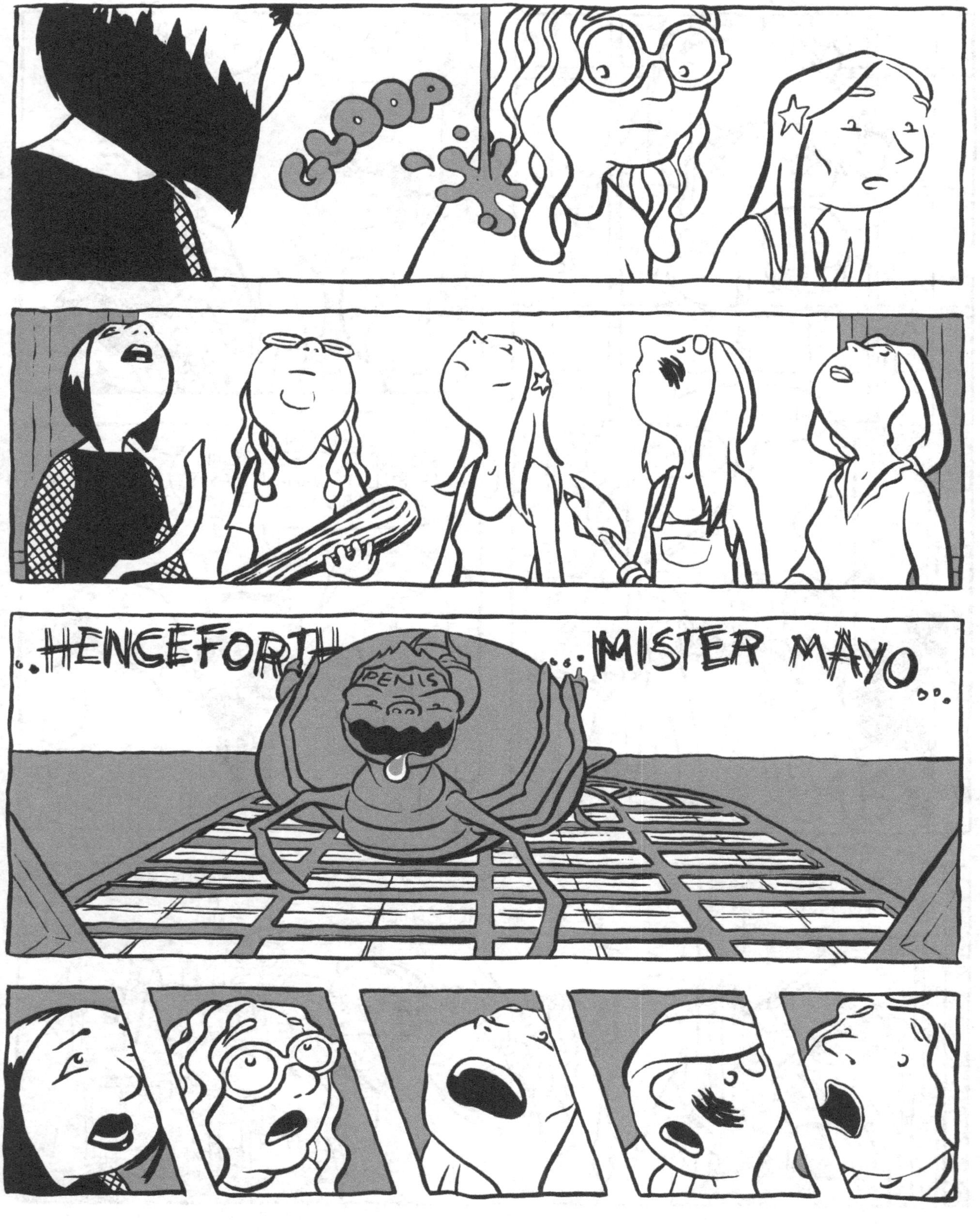
GLOOP
..HENCEFORTH
PENIS
...MISTER MAYO...

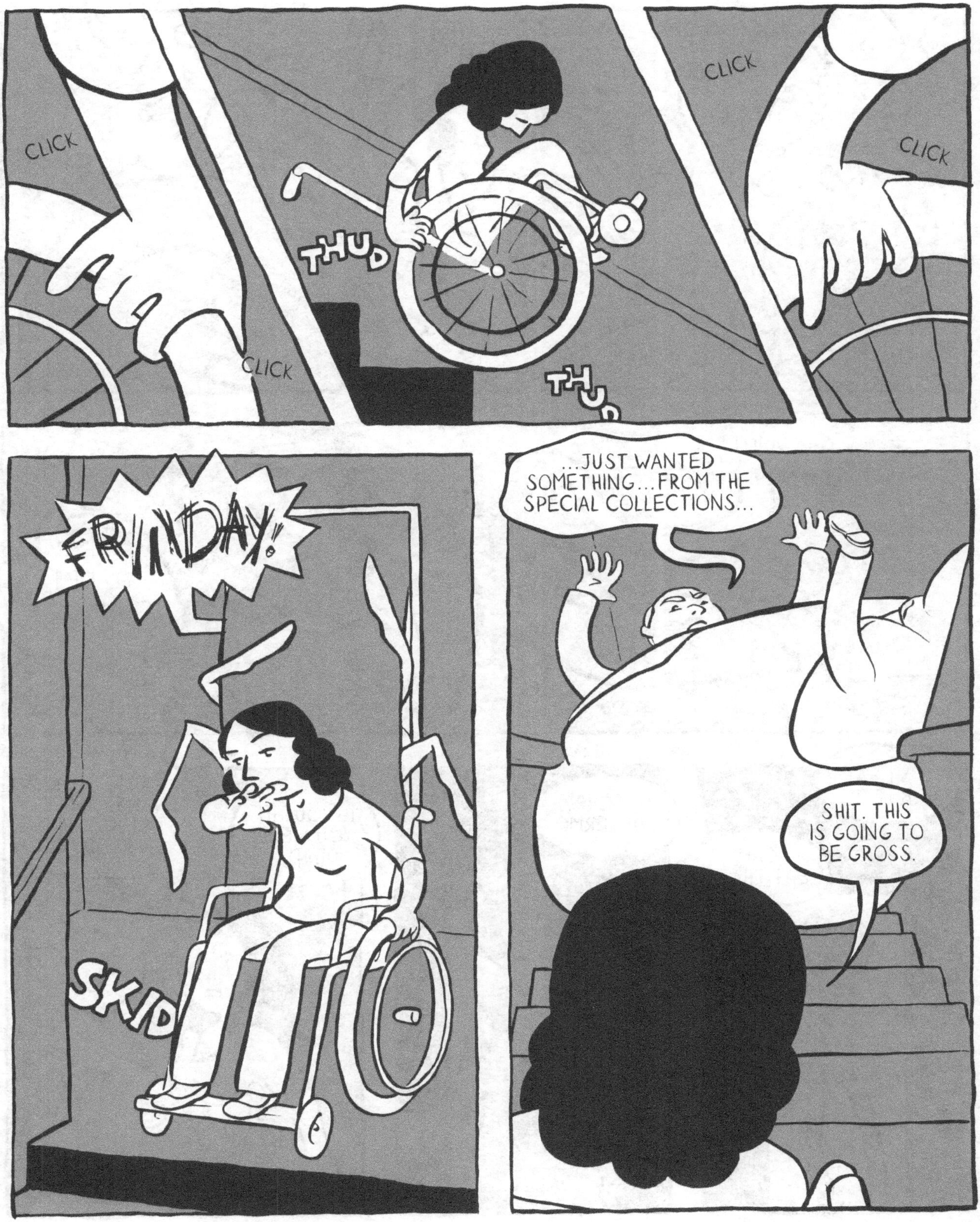
CLICK
CLICK
THUD
THUD
CLICK
CLICK
FRIDAY!
SKID
...JUST WANTED SOMETHING...FROM THE SPECIAL COLLECTIONS...
SHIT. THIS IS GOING TO BE GROSS.

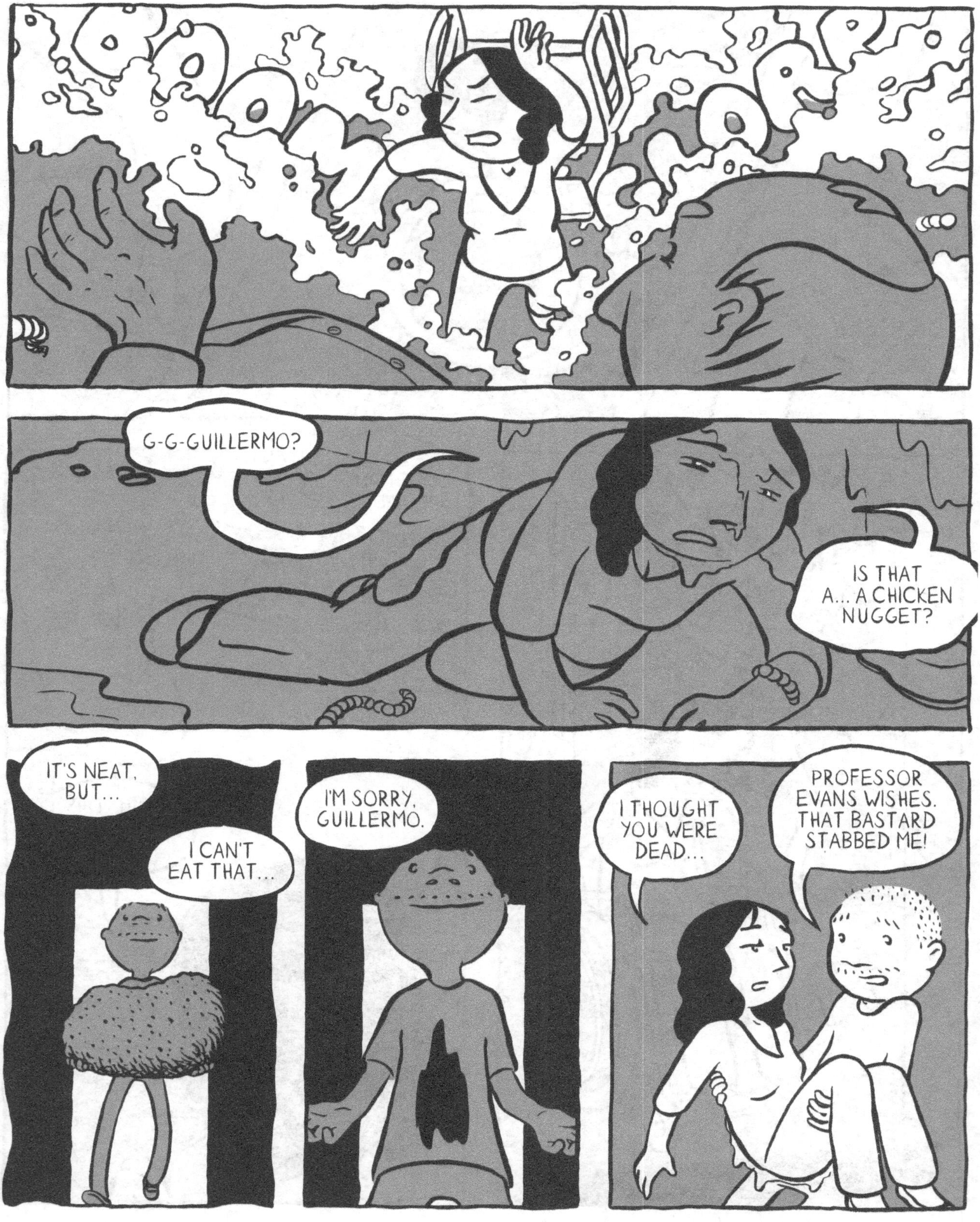
G-G-GUILLERMO?
IS THAT A... A CHICKEN NUGGET?
IT'S NEAT, BUT...
I CAN'T EAT THAT...
I'M SORRY, GUILLERMO.
I THOUGHT YOU WERE DEAD...
PROFESSOR EVANS WISHES. THAT BASTARD STABBED ME!

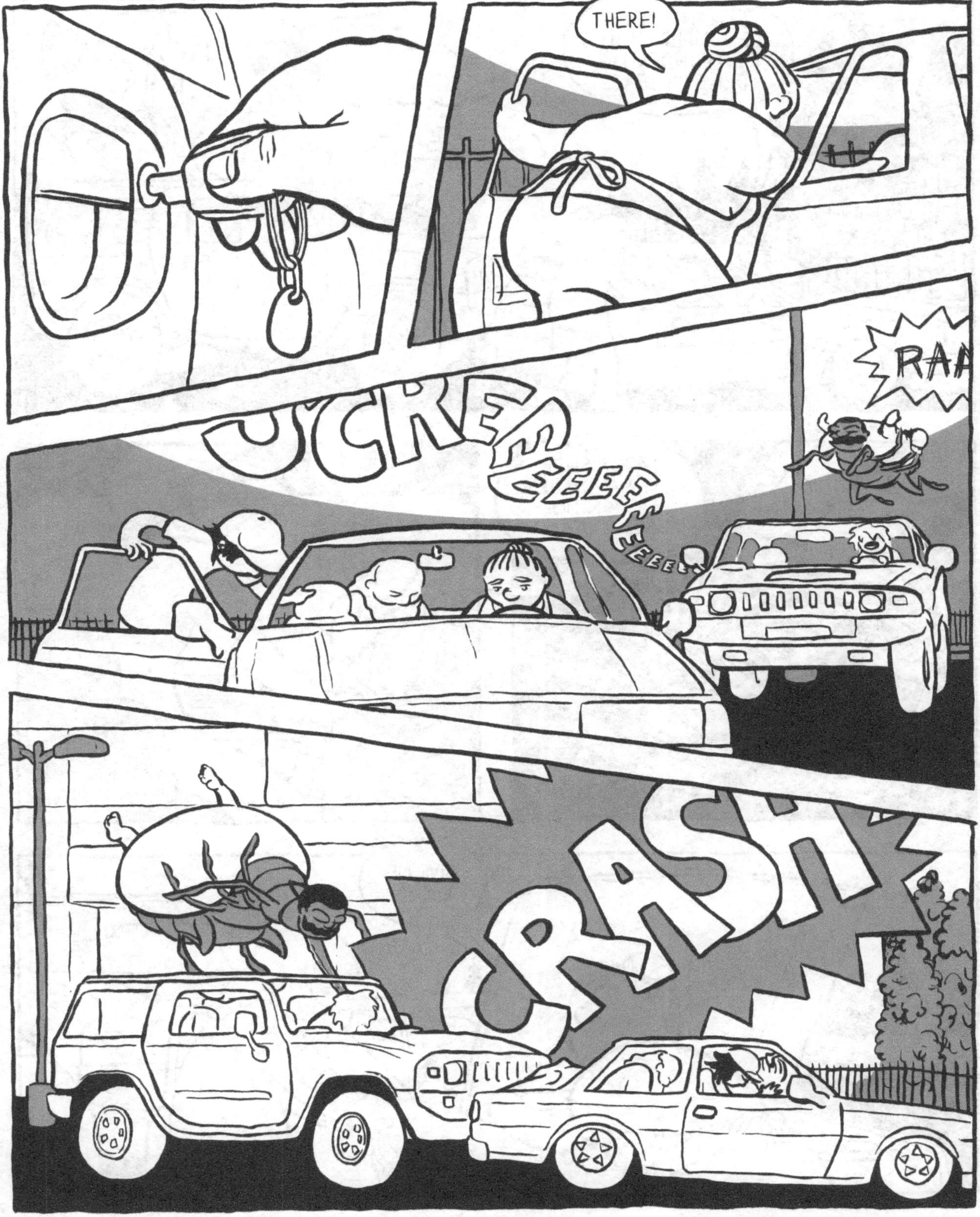

THERE!
RAA
SCREEEEEEEEEEEEEE
CRASH

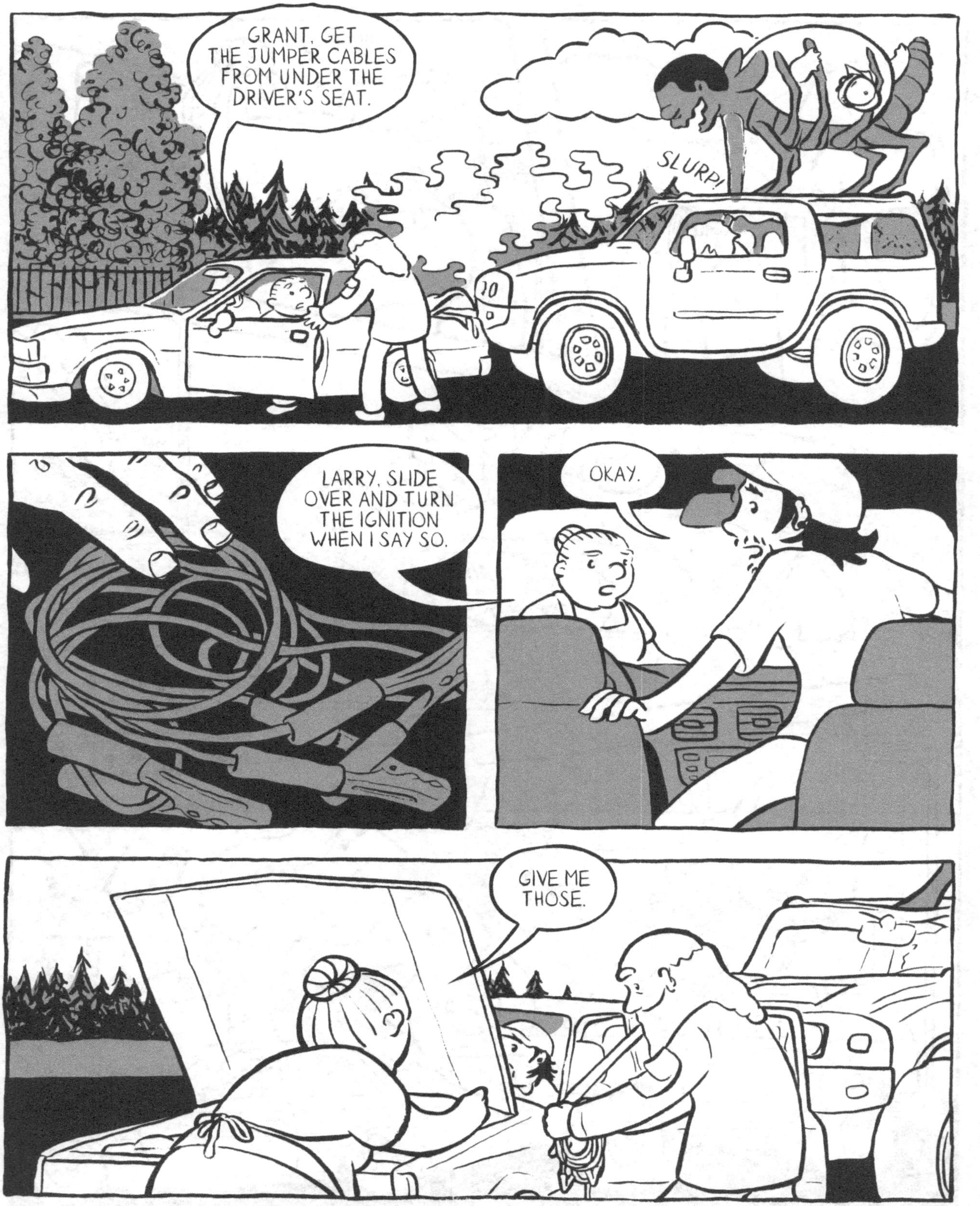
GRANT, GET THE JUMPER CABLES FROM UNDER THE DRIVER'S SEAT.
SLURP!
LARRY, SLIDE OVER AND TURN THE IGNITION WHEN I SAY SO.
OKAY.
GIVE ME THOSE.

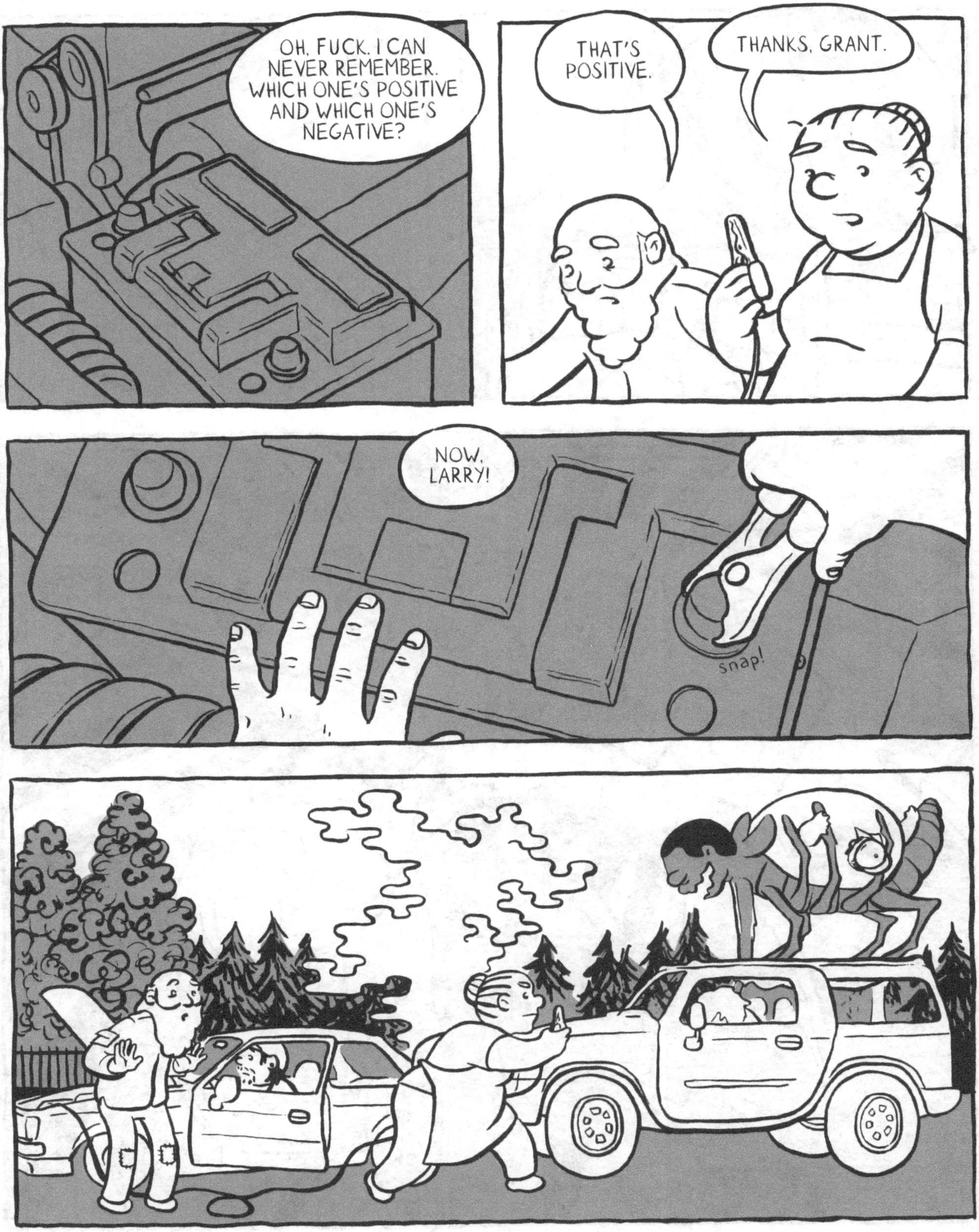
OH, FUCK. I CAN NEVER REMEMBER. WHICH ONE'S POSITIVE AND WHICH ONE'S NEGATIVE?
THAT'S POSITIVE.
THANKS, GRANT.
NOW, LARRY!
snap!

CRACKLE

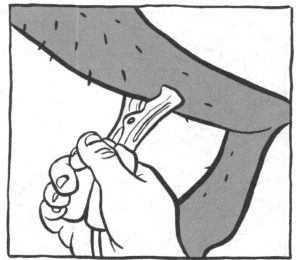

ZZZZZ BLAM!

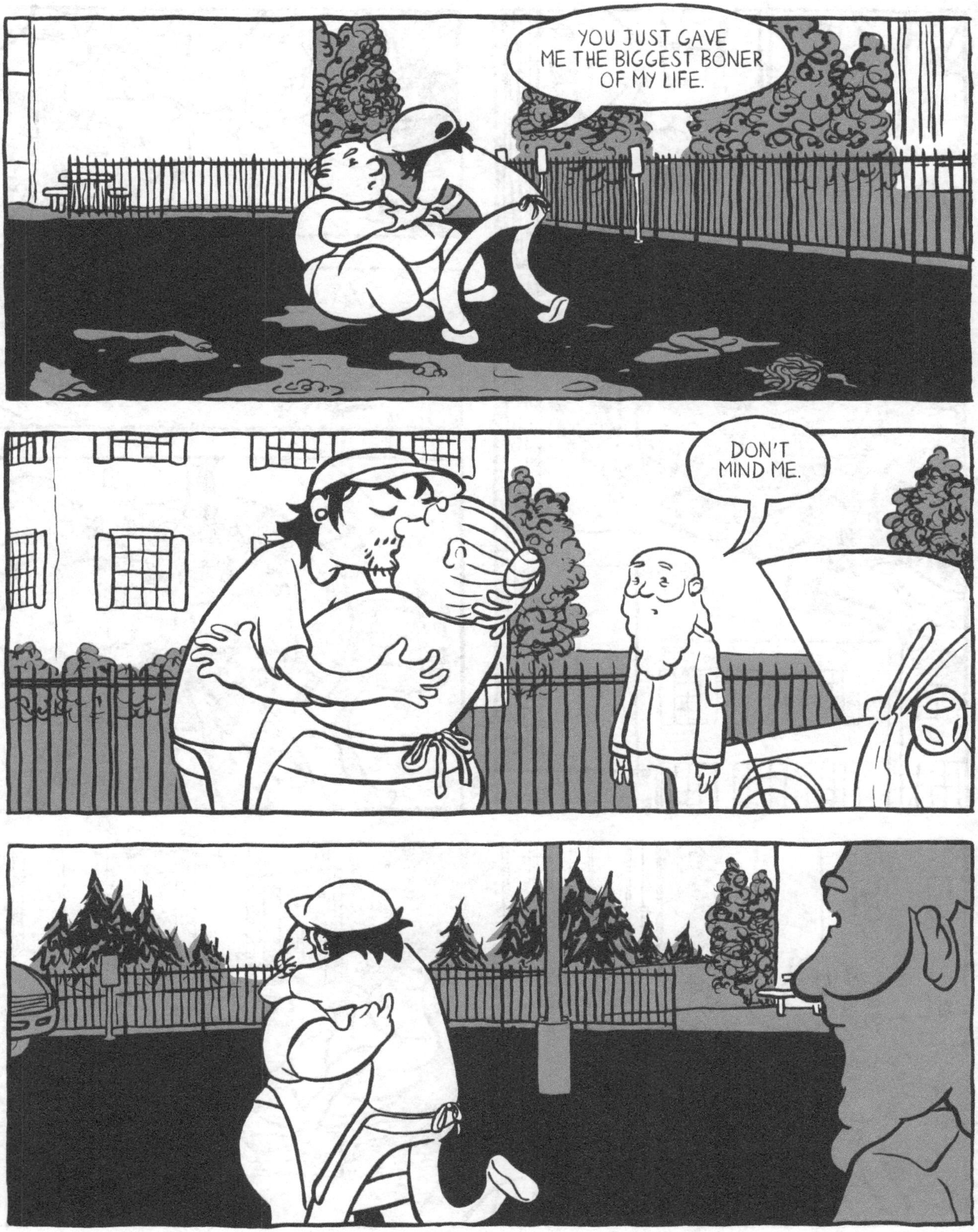
YOU JUST GAVE ME THE BIGGEST BONER OF MY LIFE.
DON'T MIND ME.

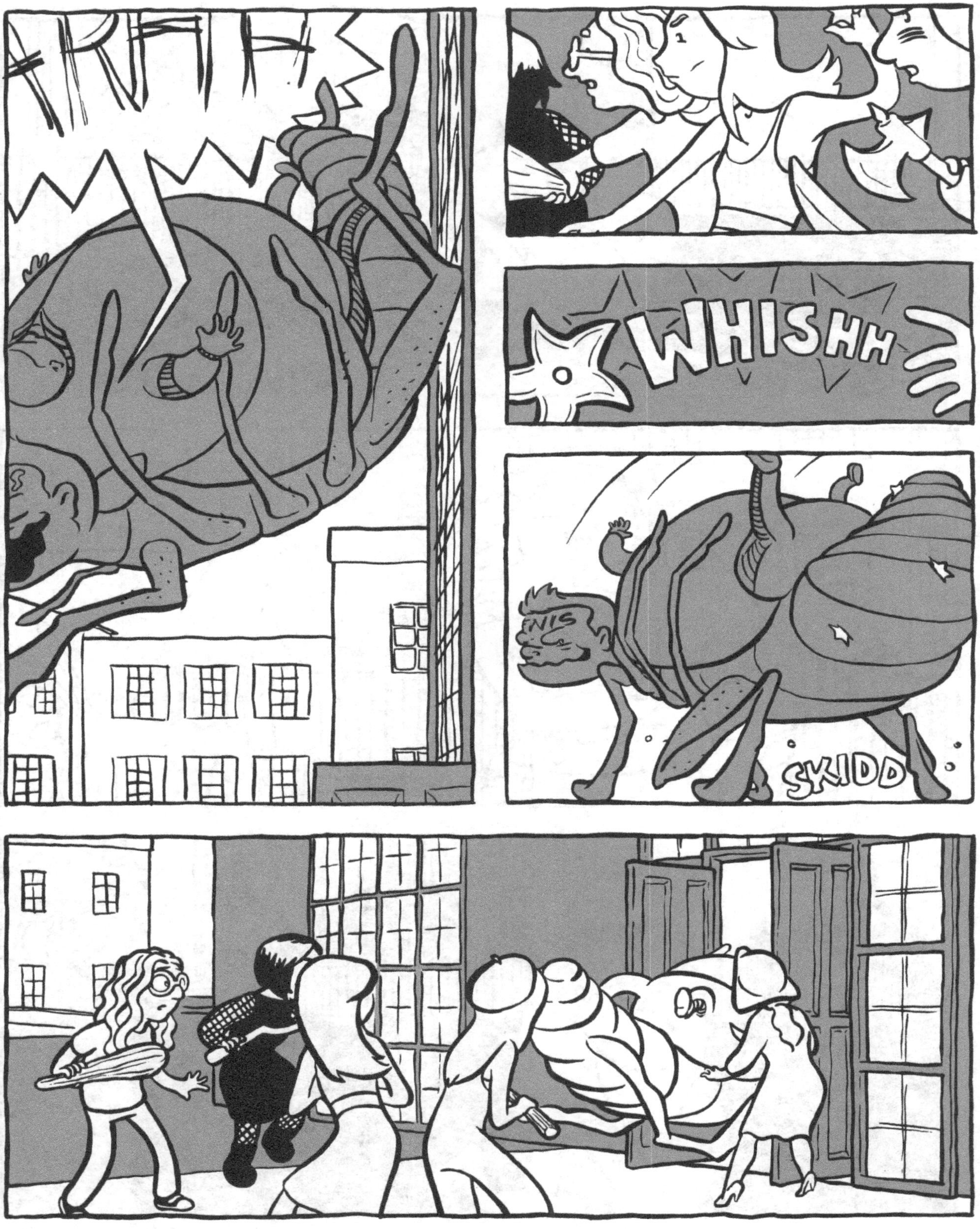
WHISHH
SKIDD

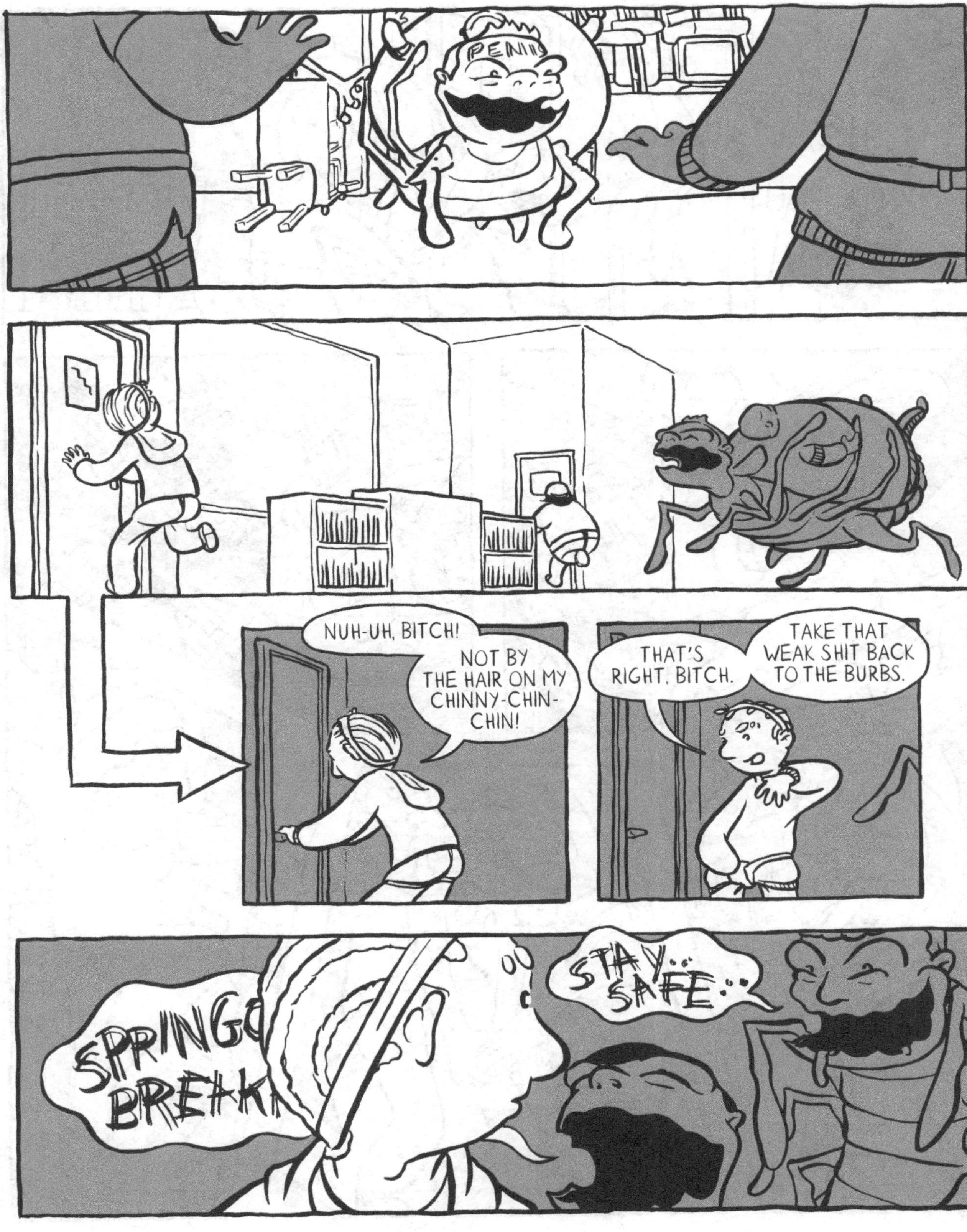
NUH-UH, BITCH!
NOT BY THE HAIR ON MY CHINNY-CHIN-CHIN!
THAT'S RIGHT, BITCH.
TAKE THAT WEAK SHIT BACK TO THE BURBS.
SPRING BREA
STAY... SAFE...

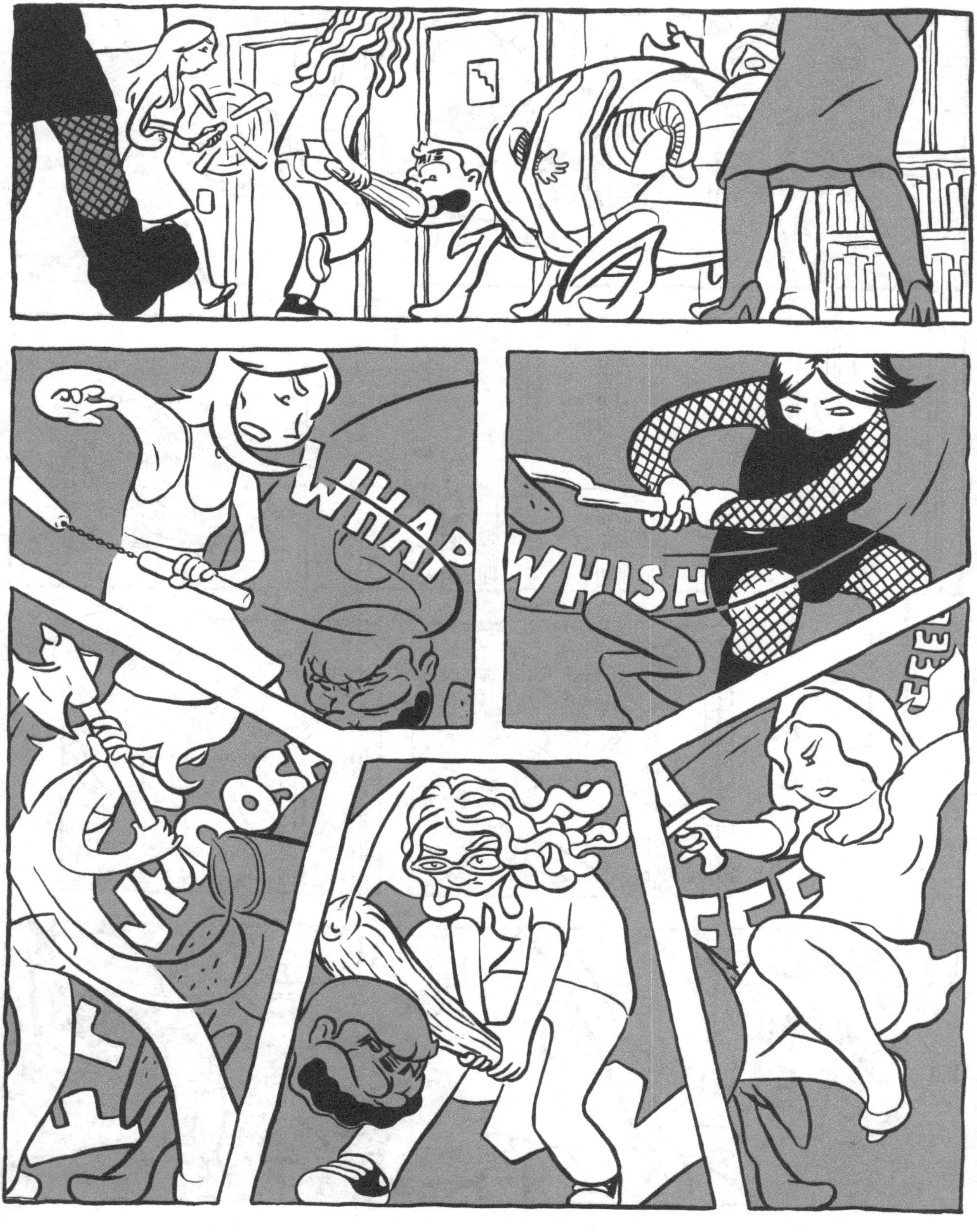
WHAP
WHISH

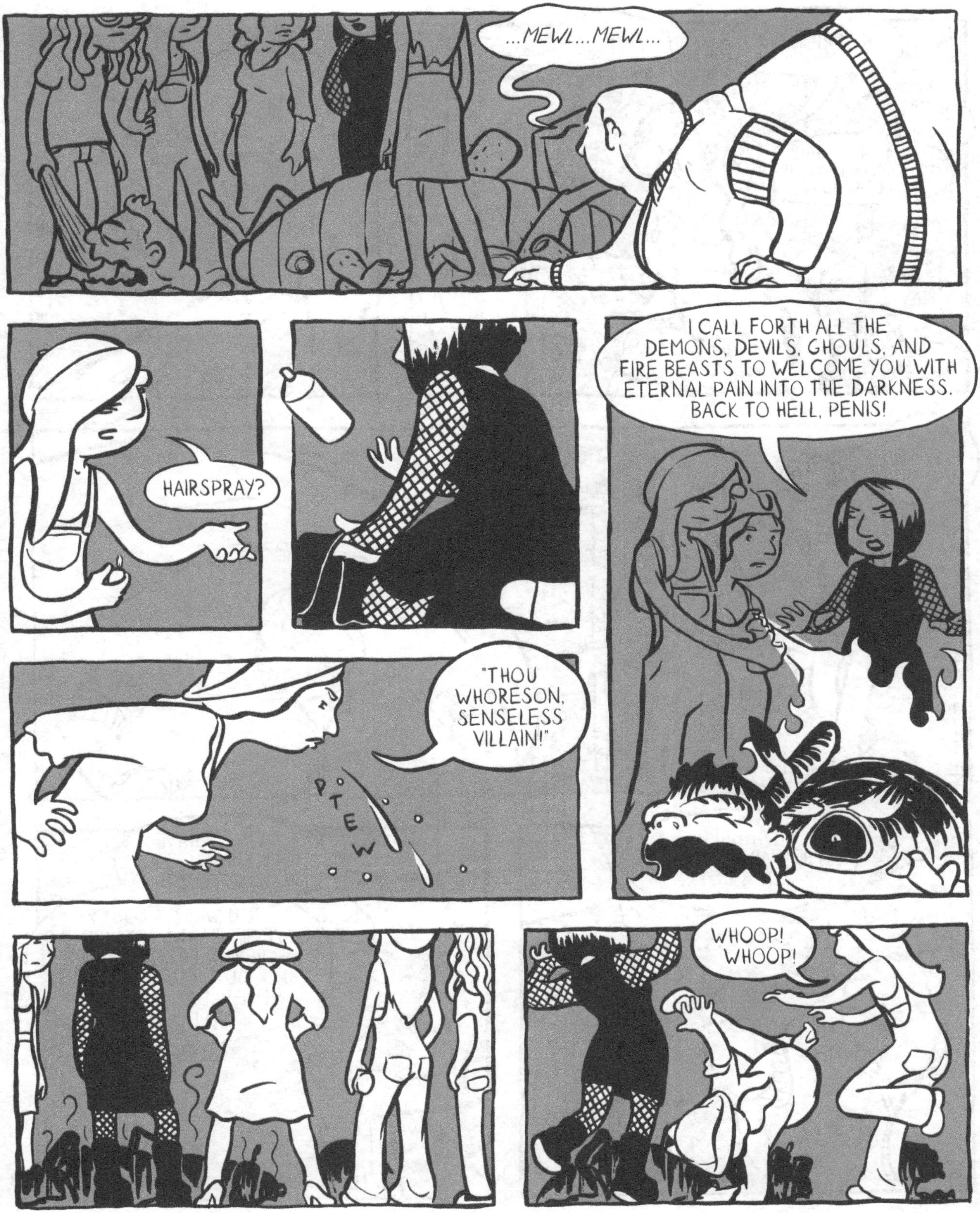
...MEWL...MEWL...
HAIRSPRAY?
I CALL FORTH ALL THE DEMONS, DEVILS, GHOULS, AND FIRE BEASTS TO WELCOME YOU WITH ETERNAL PAIN INTO THE DARKNESS. BACK TO HELL, PENIS!
"THOU WHORESON, SENSELESS VILLAIN!"
PTEW
WHOOP! WHOOP!

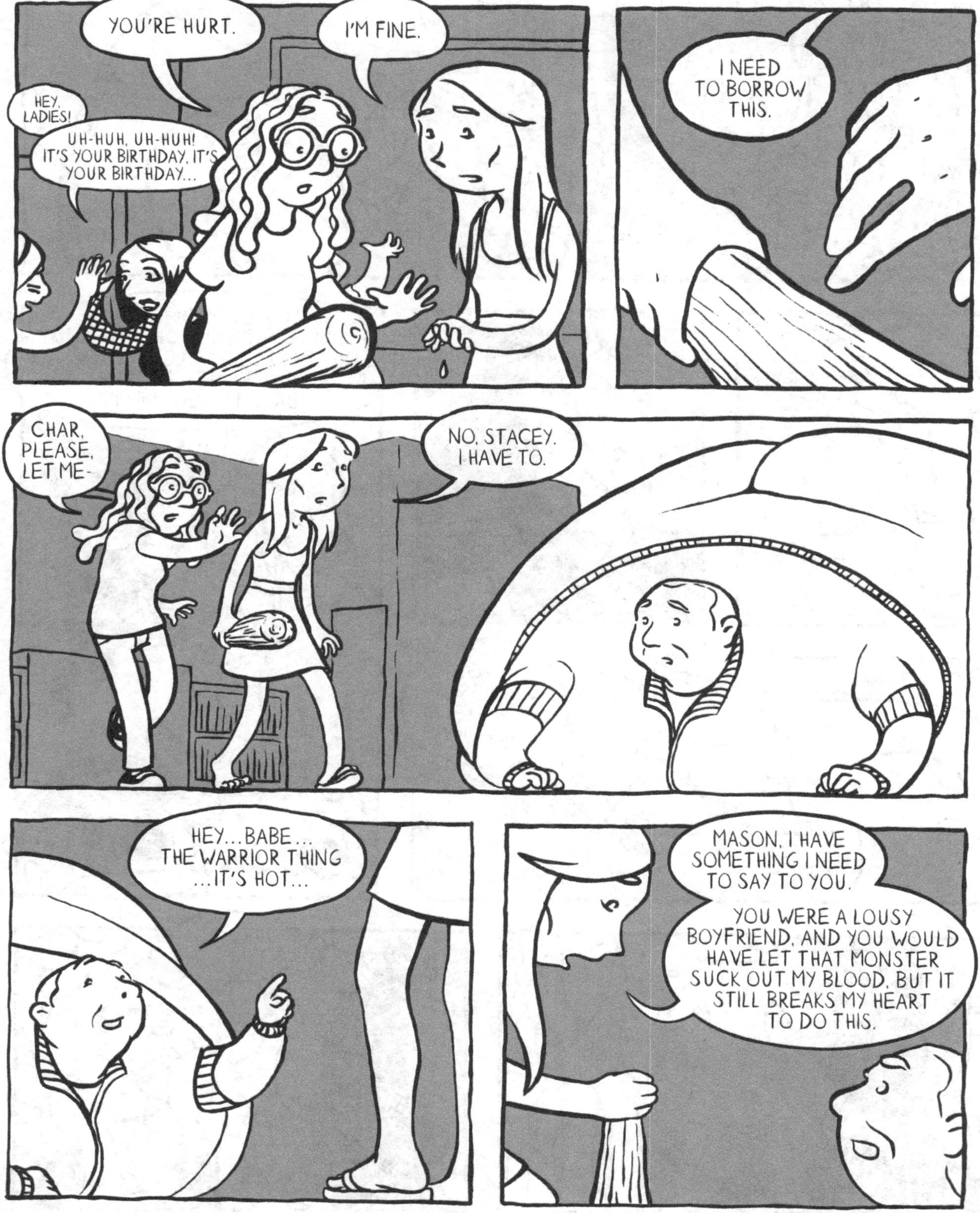
YOU'RE HURT.
I'M FINE.
HEY, LADIES!
UH-HUH, UH-HUH! IT'S YOUR BIRTHDAY, IT'S YOUR BIRTHDAY...
I NEED TO BORROW THIS.
CHAR, PLEASE, LET ME-
NO, STACEY. I HAVE TO.
HEY...BABE... THE WARRIOR THING ...IT'S HOT...
MASON, I HAVE SOMETHING I NEED TO SAY TO YOU.
YOU WERE A LOUSY BOYFRIEND, AND YOU WOULD HAVE LET THAT MONSTER SUCK OUT MY BLOOD, BUT IT STILL BREAKS MY HEART TO DO THIS.

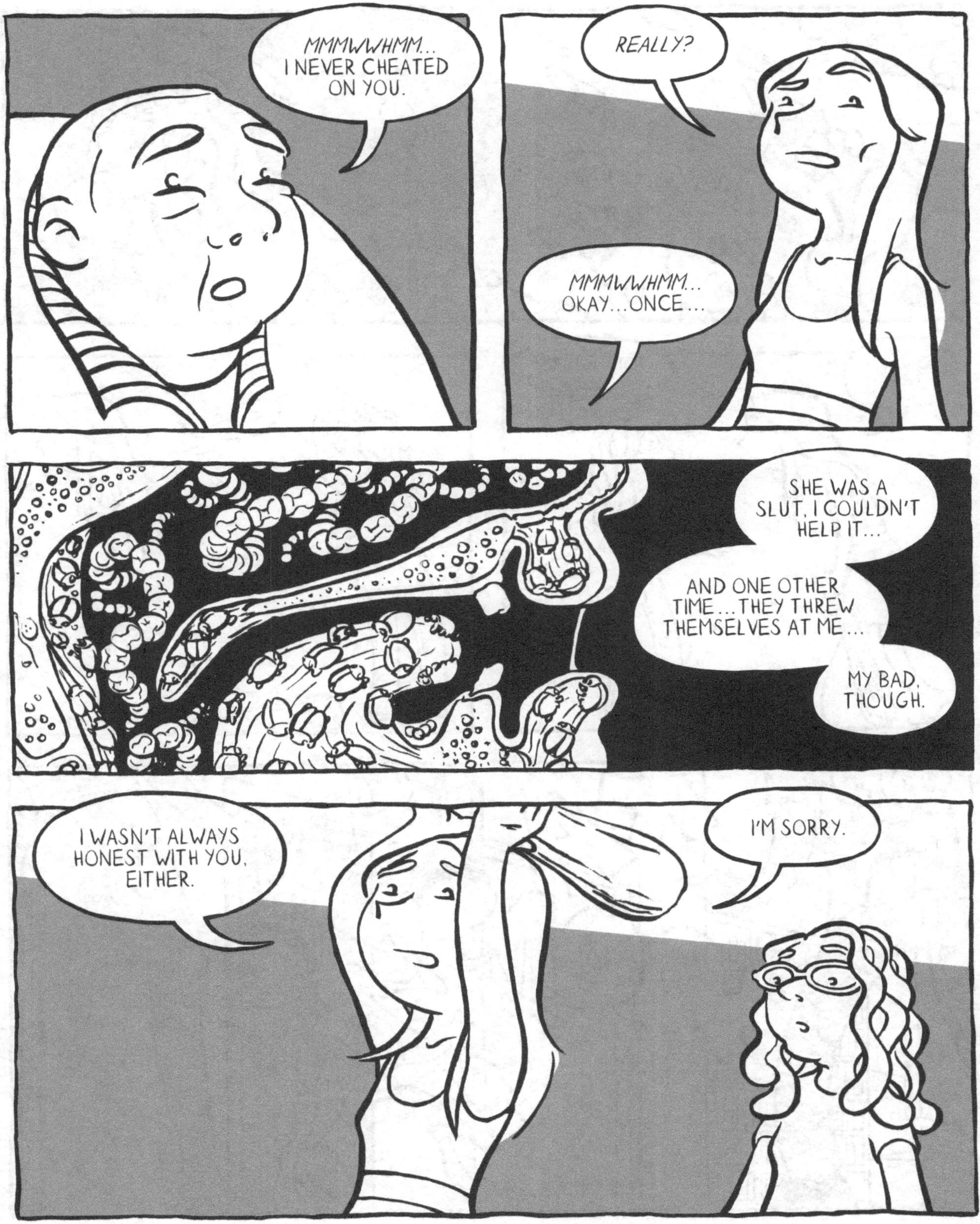
MMMWWHMM... I NEVER CHEATED ON YOU.
REALLY?
MMMWWHMM... OKAY...ONCE...
SHE WAS A SLUT, I COULDN'T HELP IT...
AND ONE OTHER TIME...THEY THREW THEMSELVES AT ME...
MY BAD, THOUGH.
I WASN'T ALWAYS HONEST WITH YOU, EITHER.
I'M SORRY.

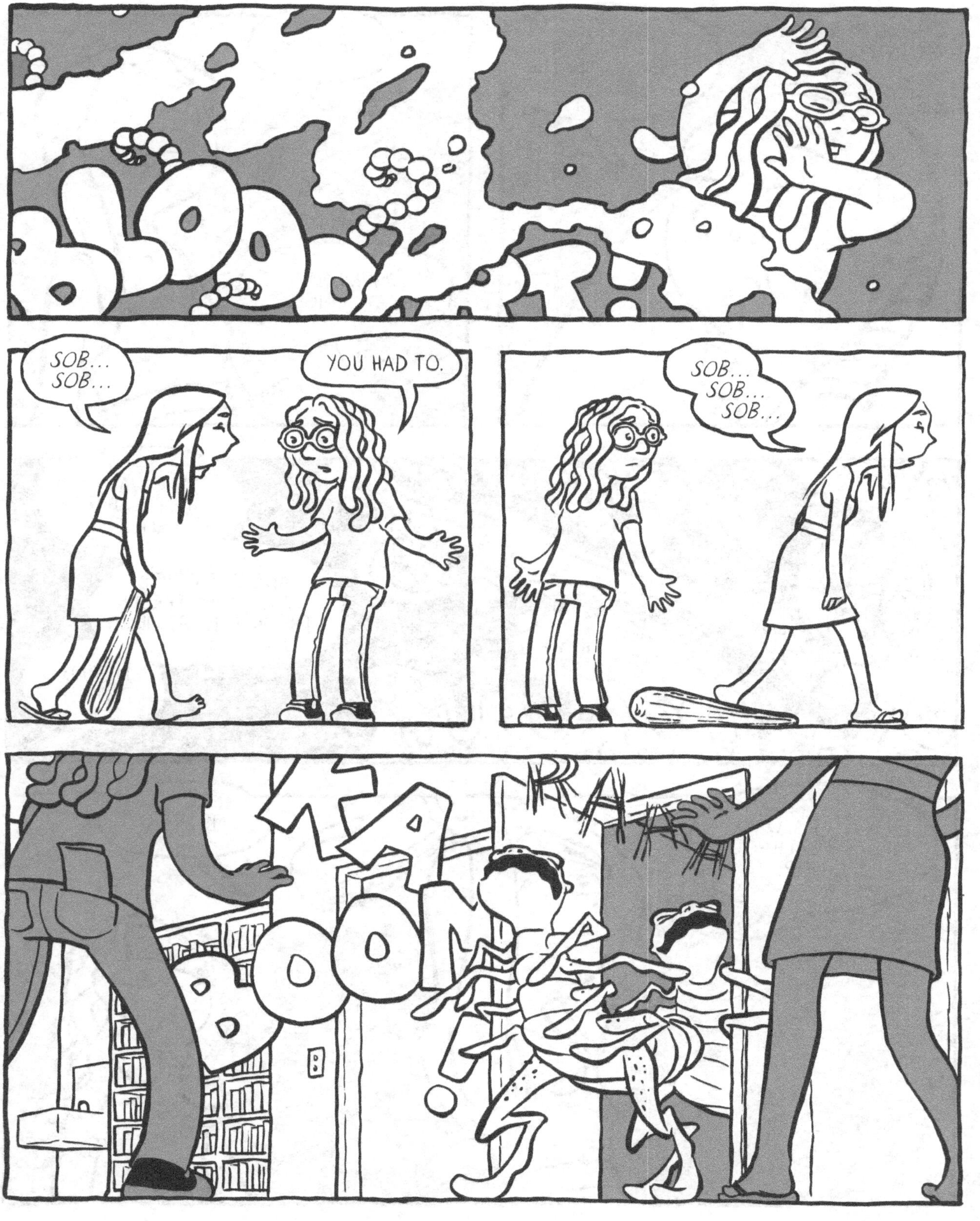
SOB... SOB...
YOU HAD TO.
SOB... SOB... SOB...

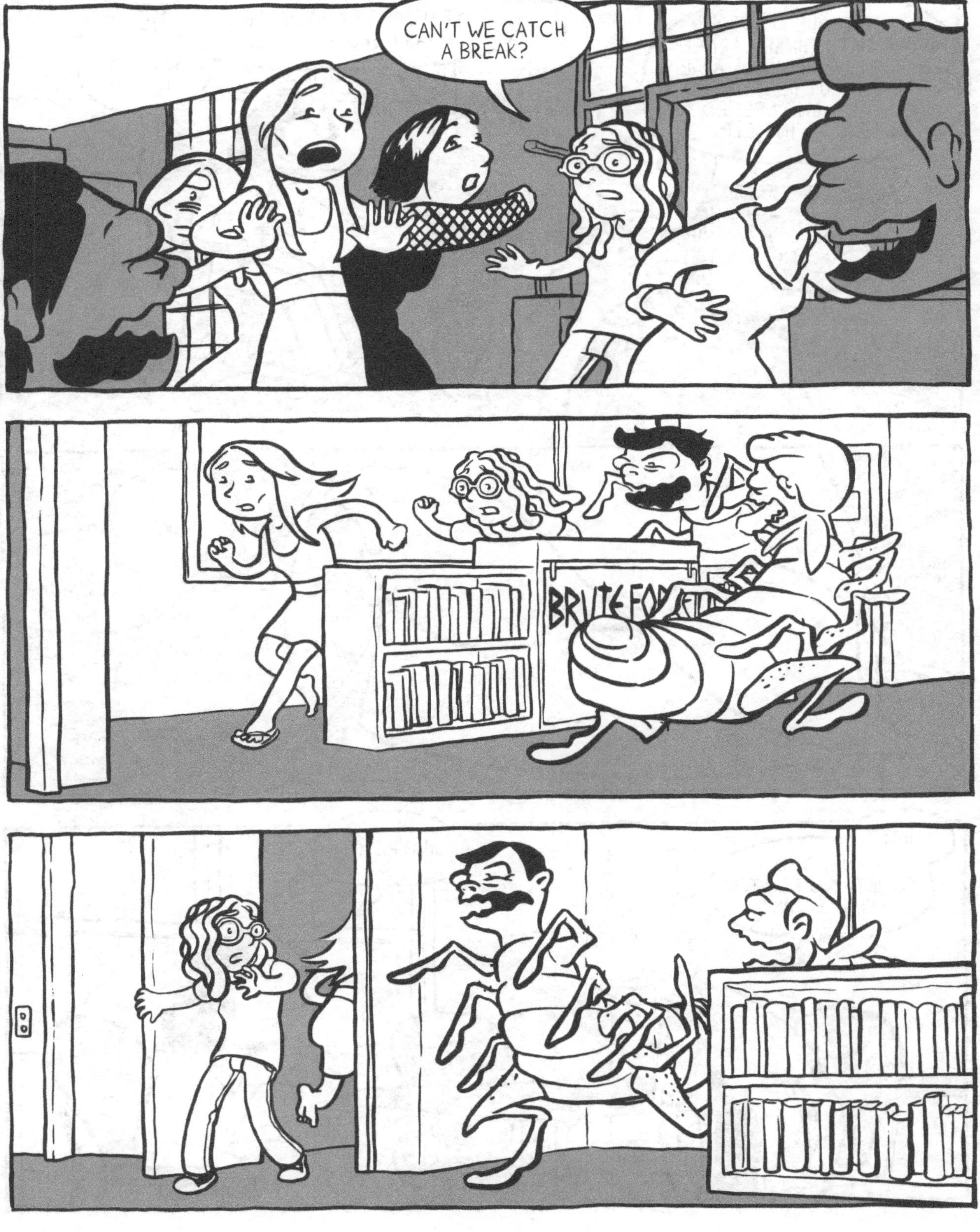
CAN'T WE CATCH A BREAK?

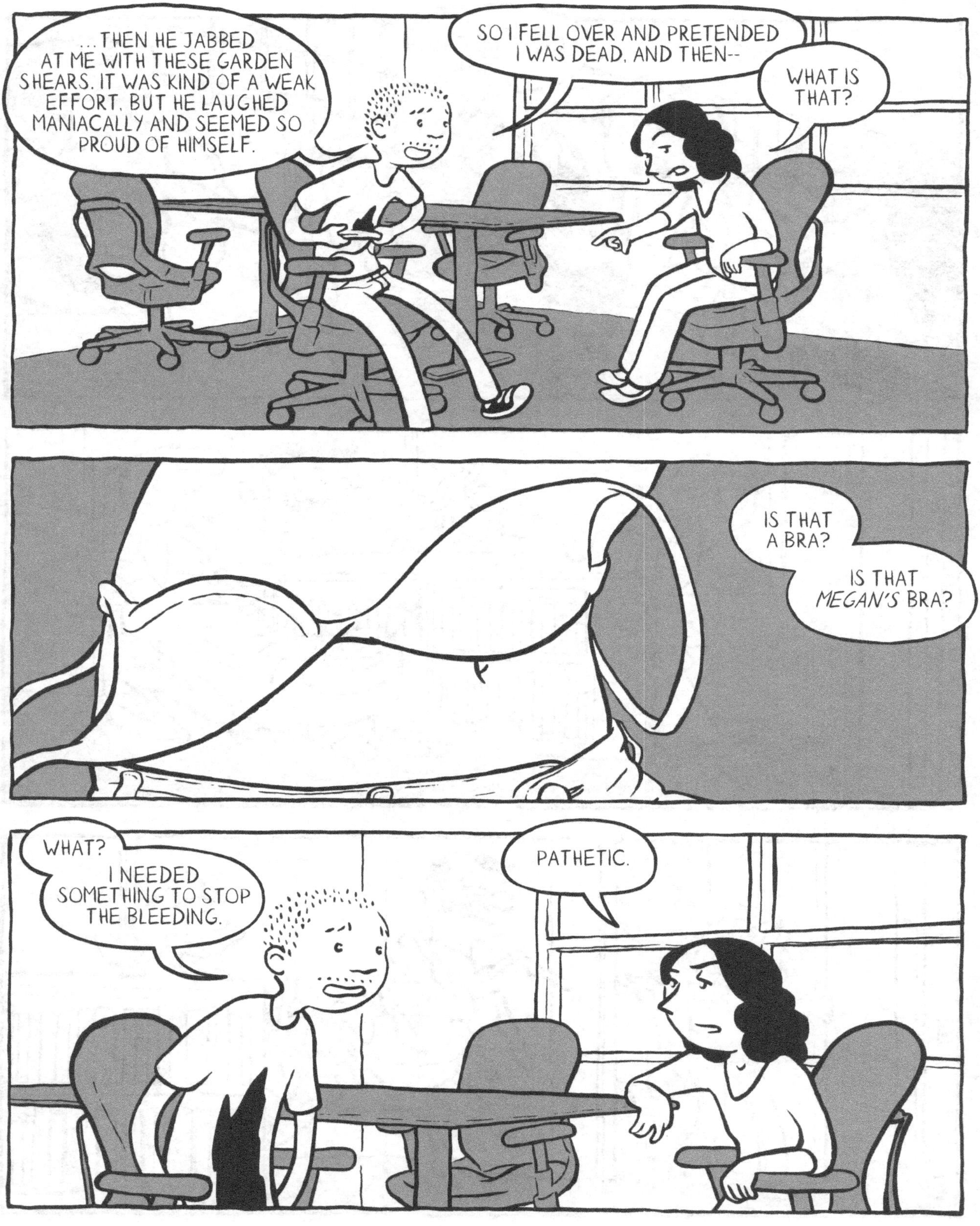
...THEN HE JABBED AT ME WITH THESE GARDEN SHEARS. IT WAS KIND OF A WEAK EFFORT, BUT HE LAUGHED MANIACALLY AND SEEMED SO PROUD OF HIMSELF.
SO I FELL OVER AND PRETENDED I WAS DEAD, AND THEN--
WHAT IS THAT?
IS THAT A BRA?
IS THAT *MEGAN'S* BRA?
WHAT?
I NEEDED SOMETHING TO STOP THE BLEEDING.
PATHETIC.

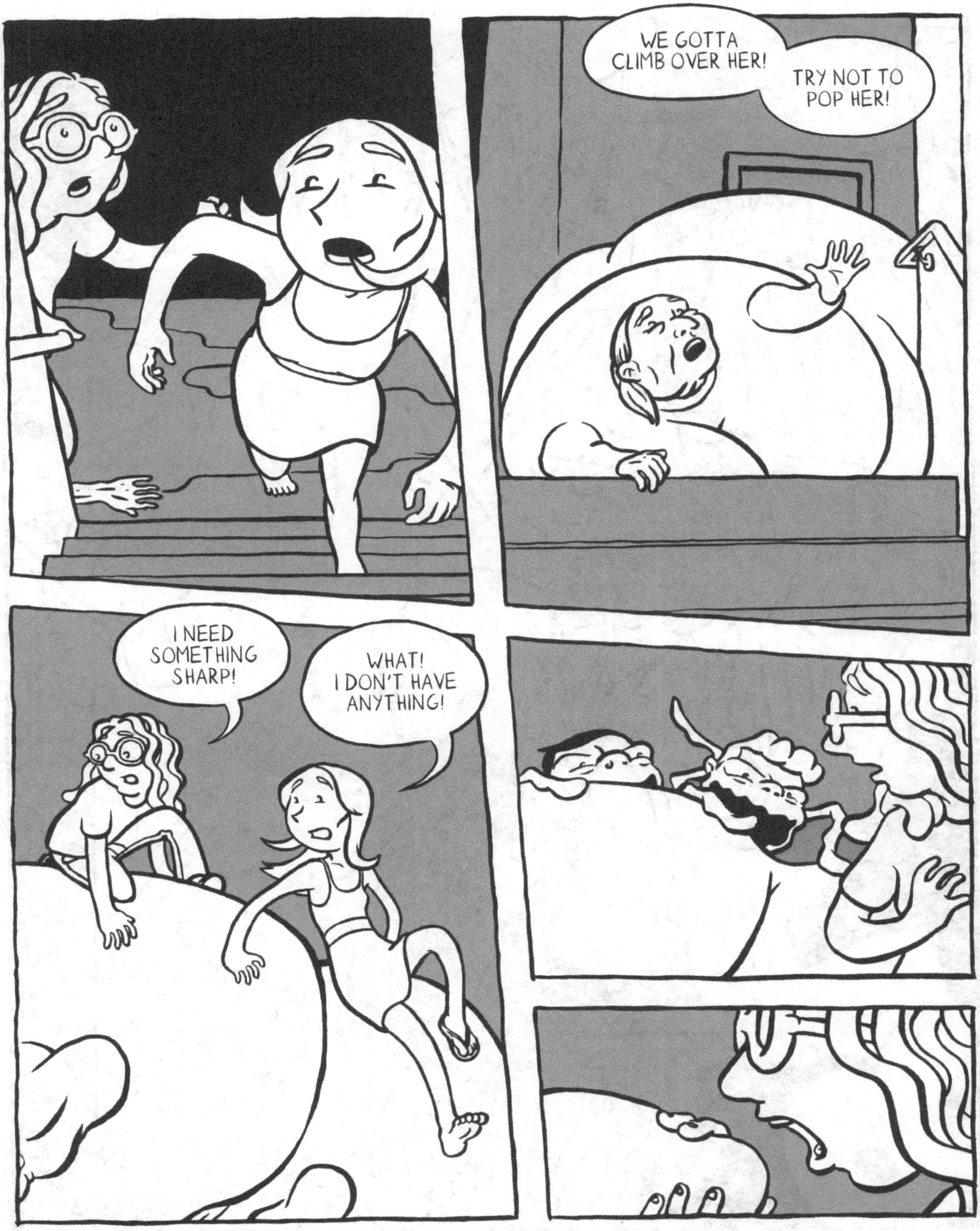
WE GOTTA CLIMB OVER HER!
TRY NOT TO POP HER!
I NEED SOMETHING SHARP!
WHAT! I DON'T HAVE ANYTHING!

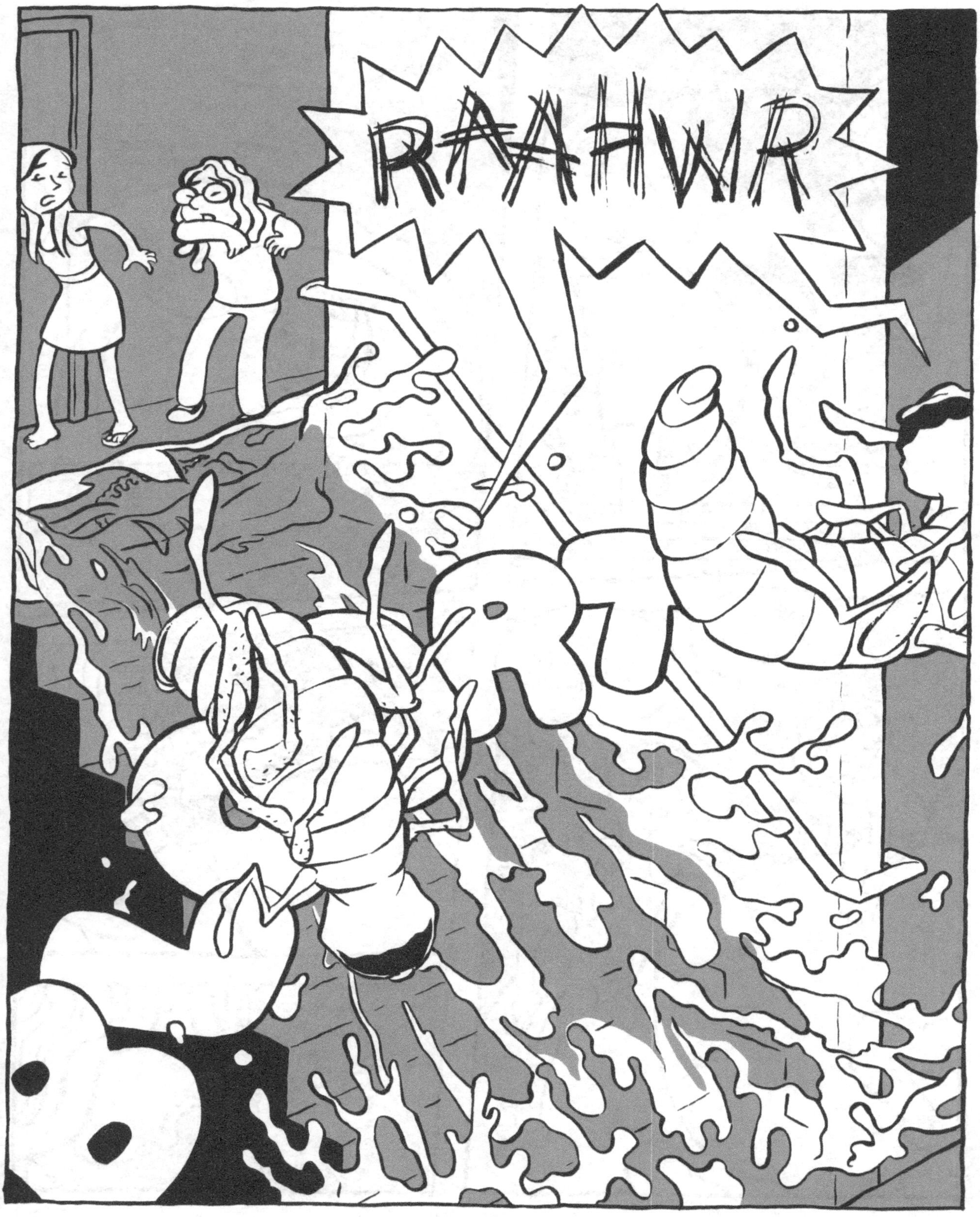
RAAHWR
RT

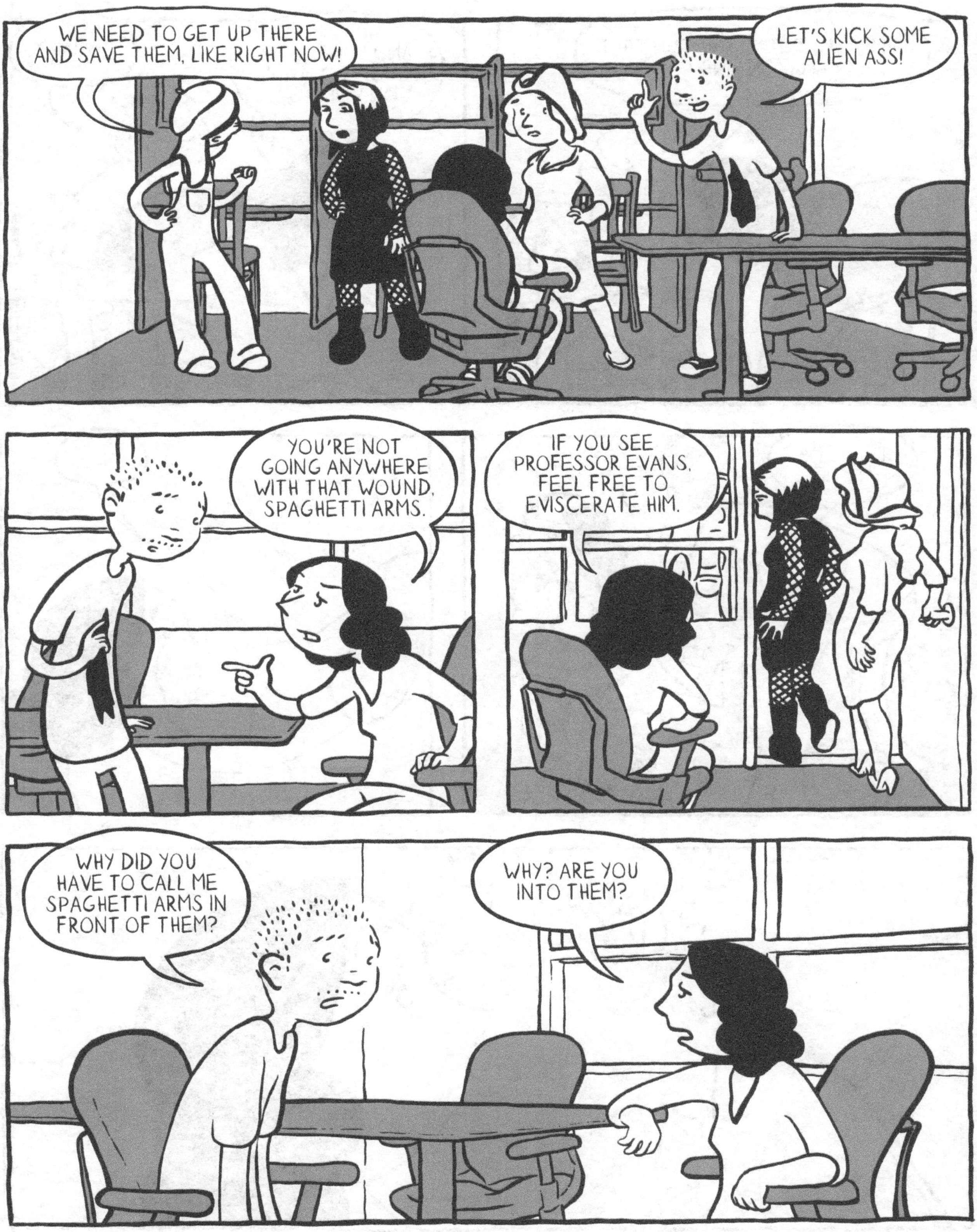
WE NEED TO GET UP THERE AND SAVE THEM, LIKE RIGHT NOW!
LET'S KICK SOME ALIEN ASS!
YOU'RE NOT GOING ANYWHERE WITH THAT WOUND, SPAGHETTI ARMS.
IF YOU SEE PROFESSOR EVANS, FEEL FREE TO EVISCERATE HIM.
WHY DID YOU HAVE TO CALL ME SPAGHETTI ARMS IN FRONT OF THEM?
WHY? ARE YOU INTO THEM?

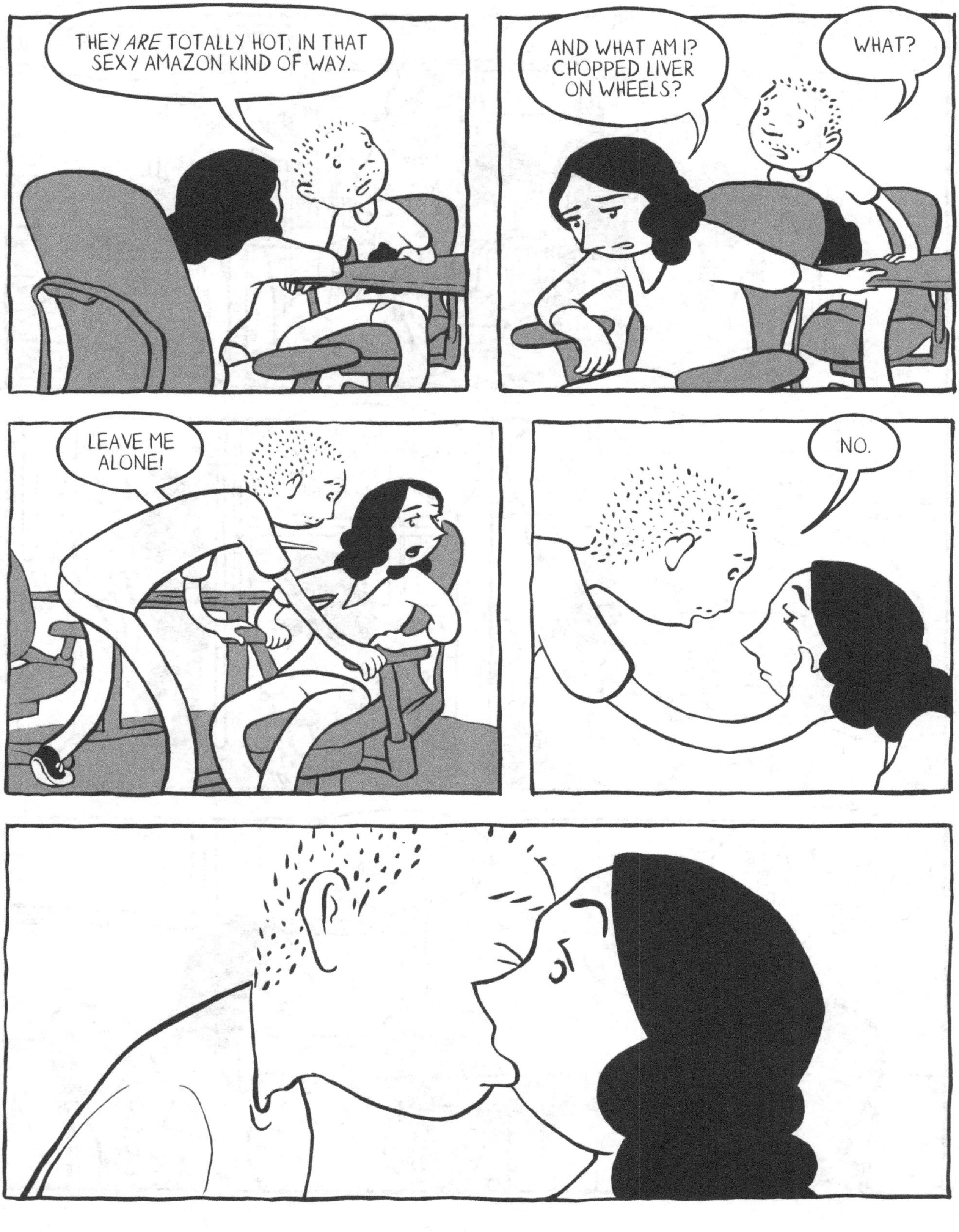
THEY *ARE* TOTALLY HOT, IN THAT SEXY AMAZON KIND OF WAY.
AND WHAT AM I? CHOPPED LIVER ON WHEELS?
WHAT?
LEAVE ME ALONE!
NO.

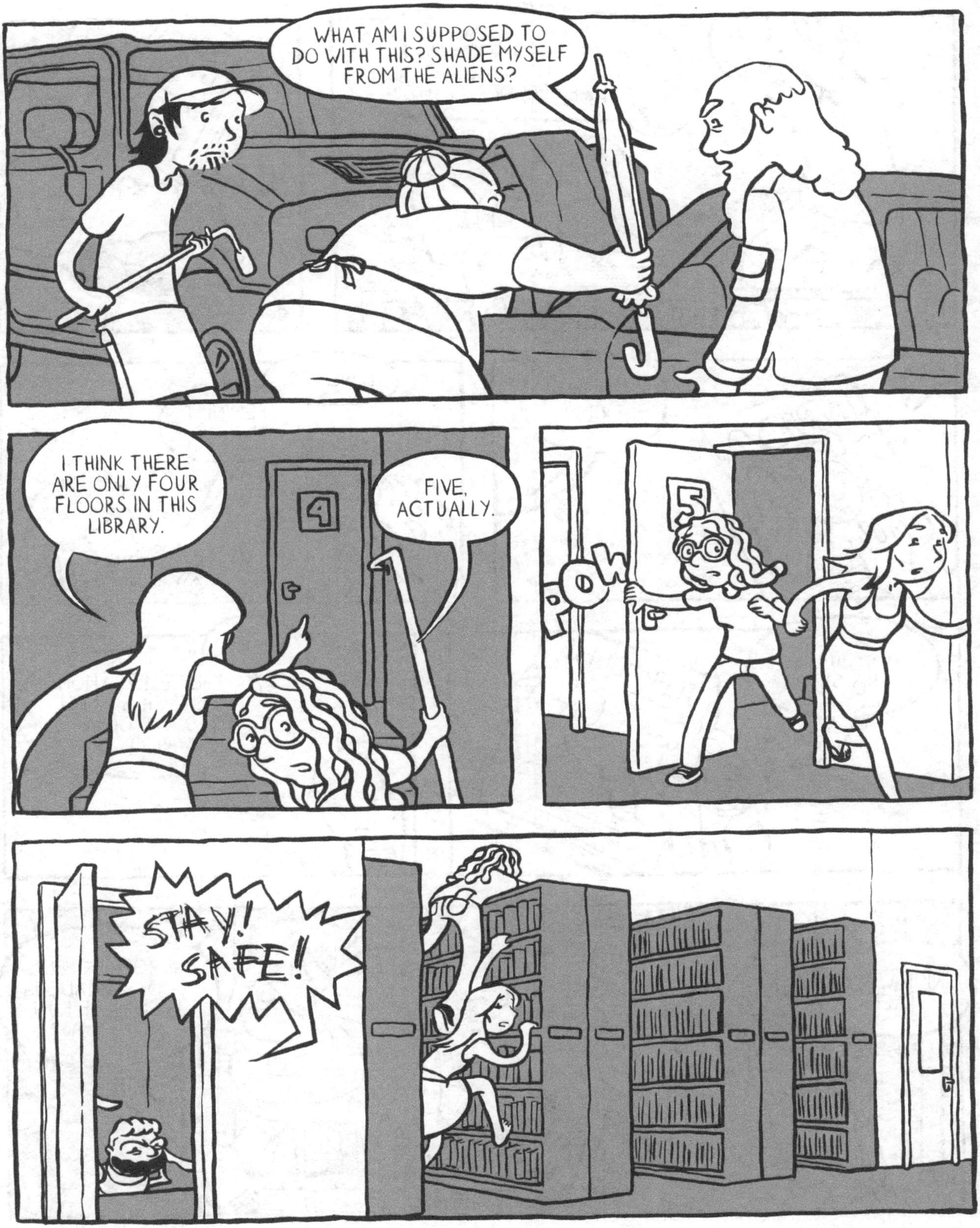
WHAT AM I SUPPOSED TO DO WITH THIS? SHADE MYSELF FROM THE ALIENS?
I THINK THERE ARE ONLY FOUR FLOORS IN THIS LIBRARY.
4
FIVE, ACTUALLY.
5
POW
STAY! SAFE!

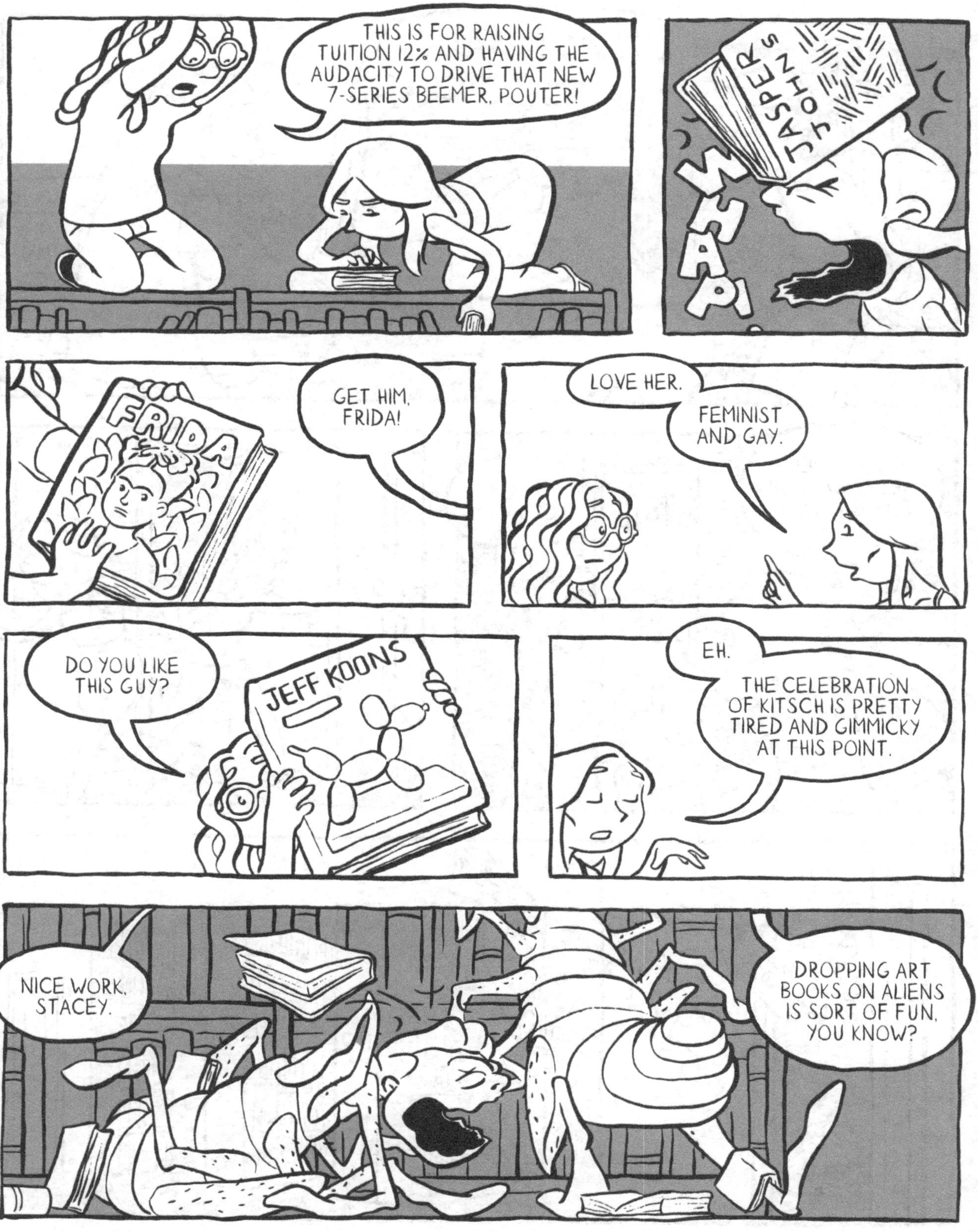
THIS IS FOR RAISING TUITION 12% AND HAVING THE AUDACITY TO DRIVE THAT NEW 7-SERIES BEEMER, POUTER!
JASPER JOHNS
WHAP!
FRIDA
GET HIM, FRIDA!
LOVE HER.
FEMINIST AND GAY.
DO YOU LIKE THIS GUY?
JEFF KOONS
EH.
THE CELEBRATION OF KITSCH IS PRETTY TIRED AND GIMMICKY AT THIS POINT.
NICE WORK, STACEY.
DROPPING ART BOOKS ON ALIENS IS SORT OF FUN, YOU KNOW?

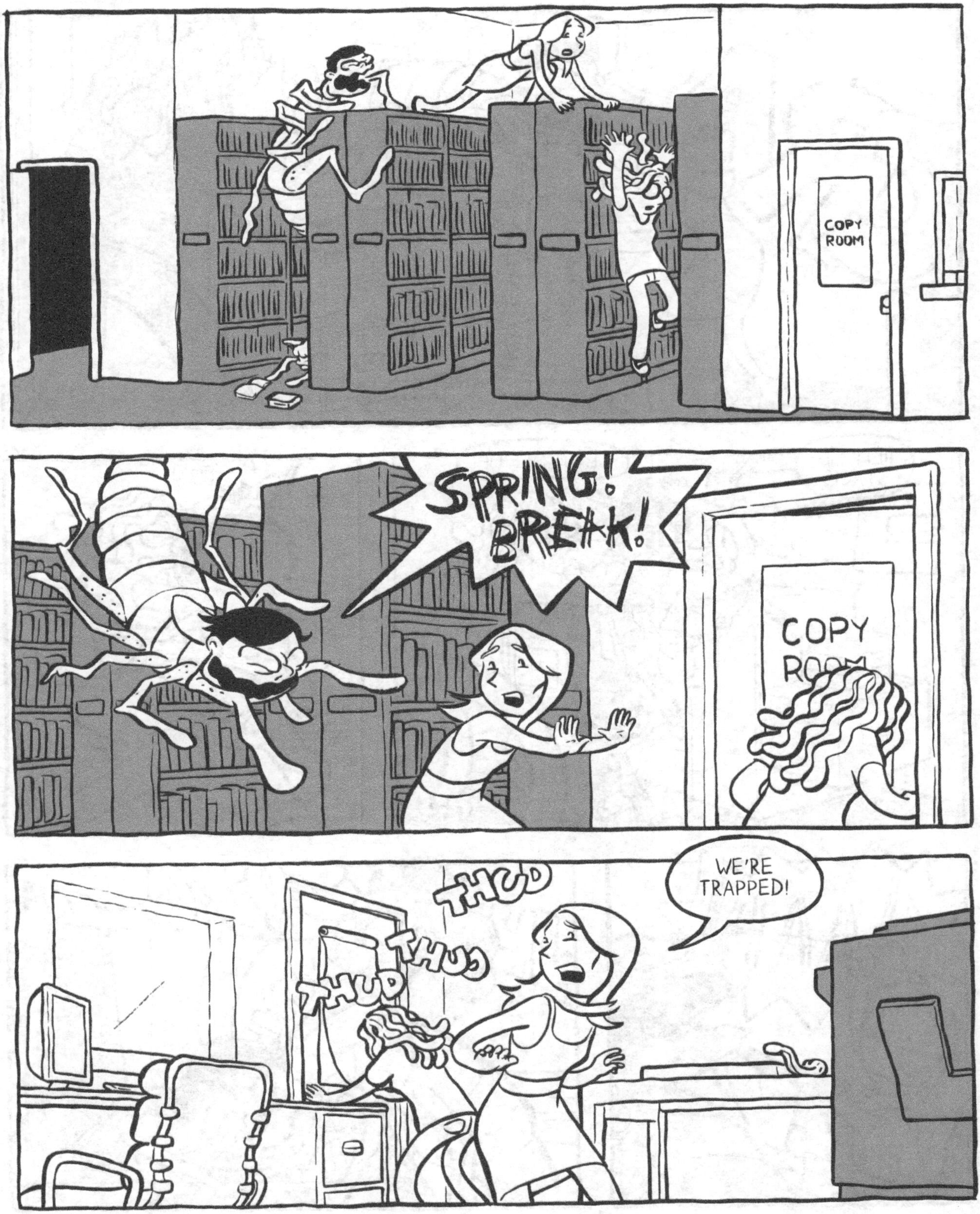
COPY ROOM
SPRING! BREAK!
COPY ROOM
THUD
THUD
THUD
WE'RE TRAPPED!

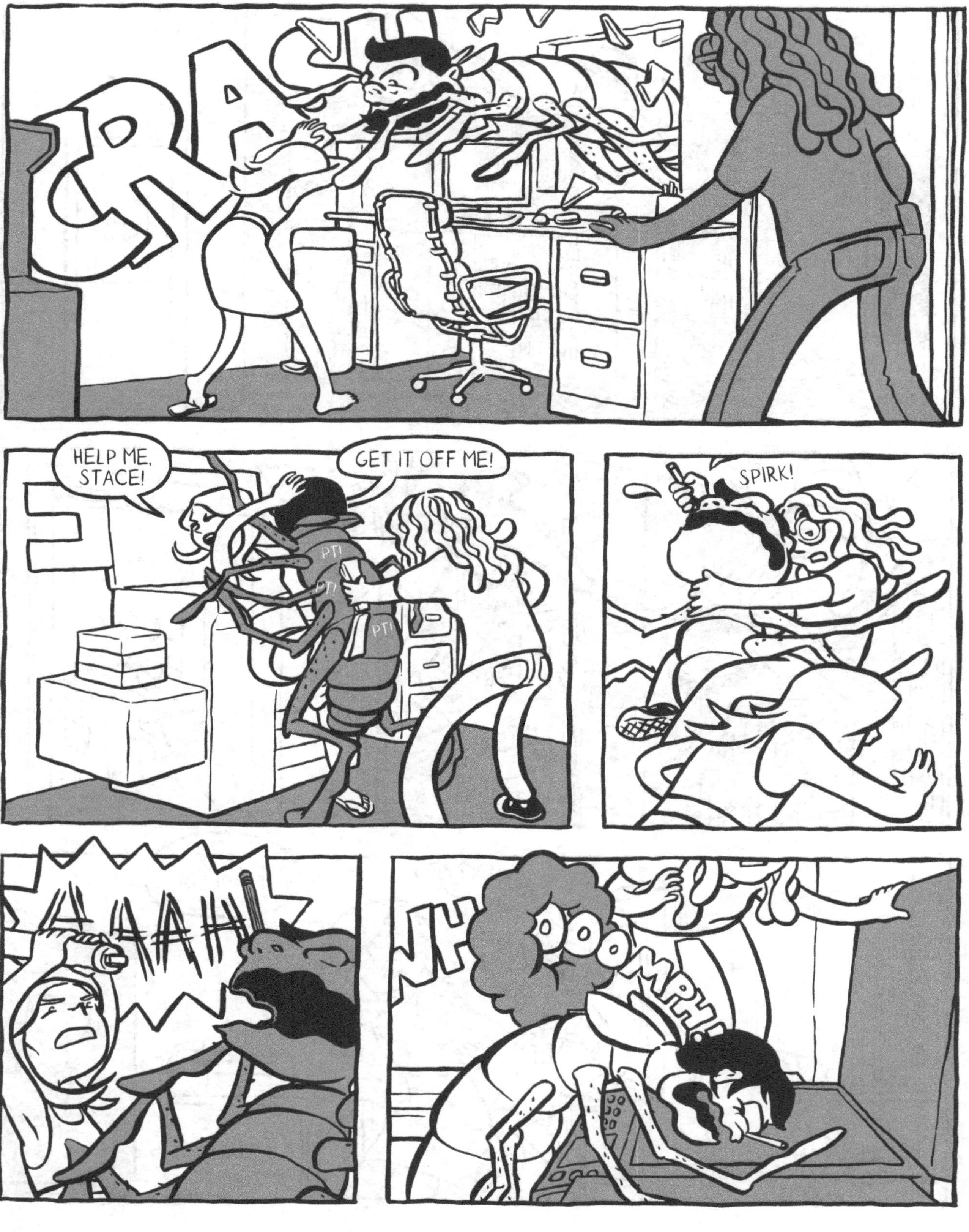
CRASH
HELP ME, STACE!
GET IT OFF ME!
PT!
PT!
PT!
SPIRK!
AAAH!
WHOOOOMPH!

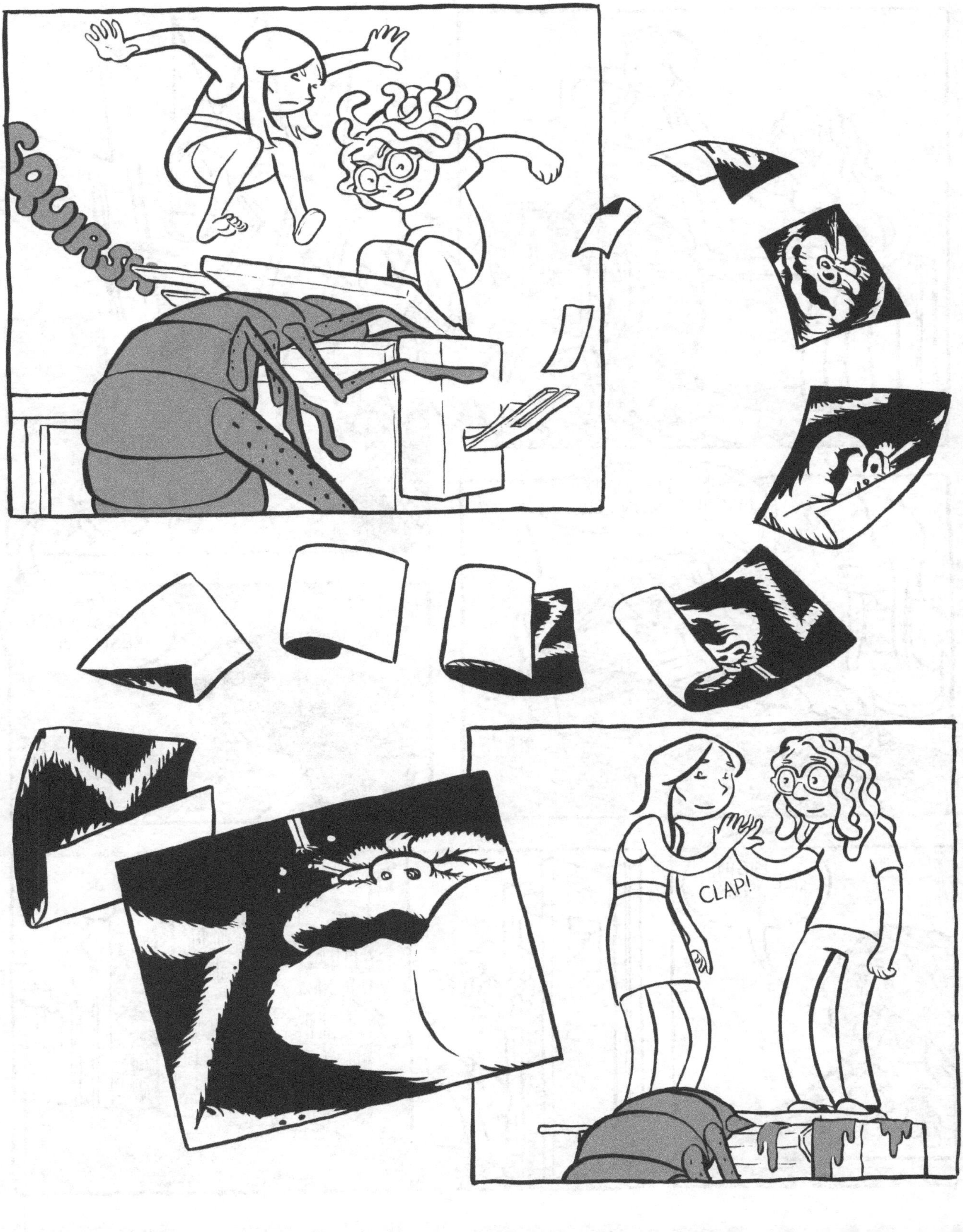
SQUIRSH
CLAP!

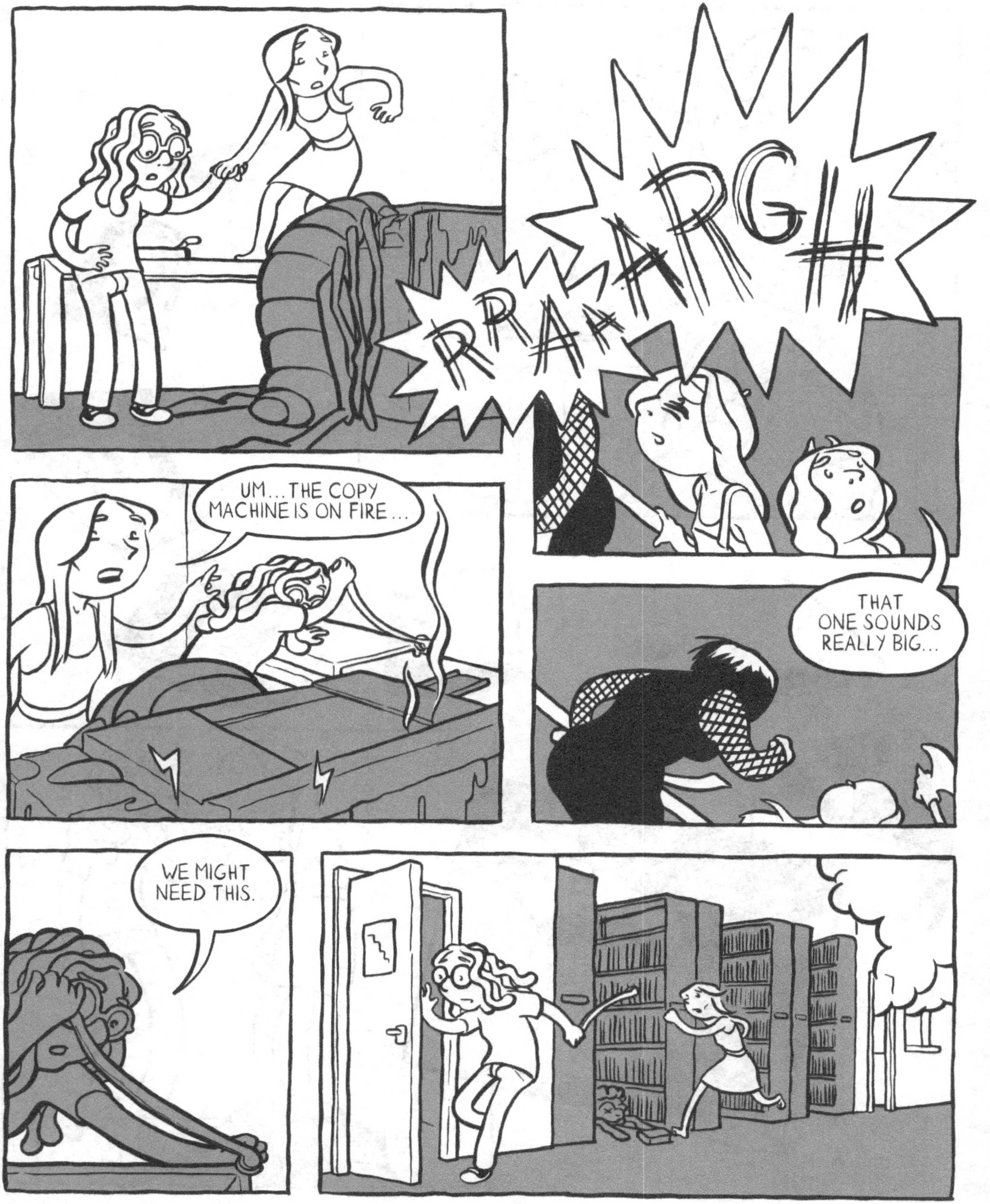
RRAAARGH
UM... THE COPY MACHINE IS ON FIRE...
THAT ONE SOUNDS REALLY BIG...
WE MIGHT NEED THIS.

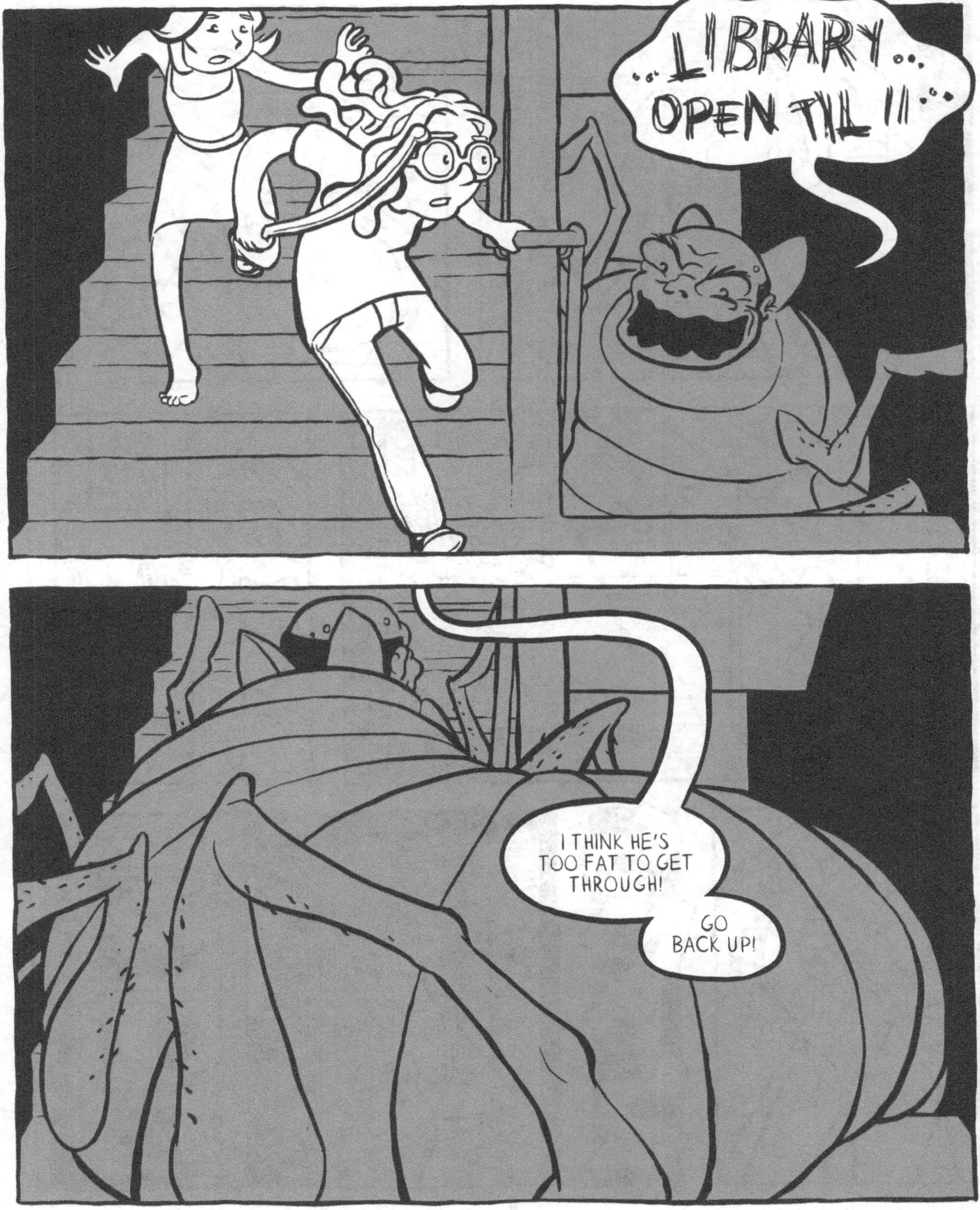

LIBRARY... OPEN TIL 11...
I THINK HE'S TOO FAT TO GET THROUGH!
GO BACK UP!

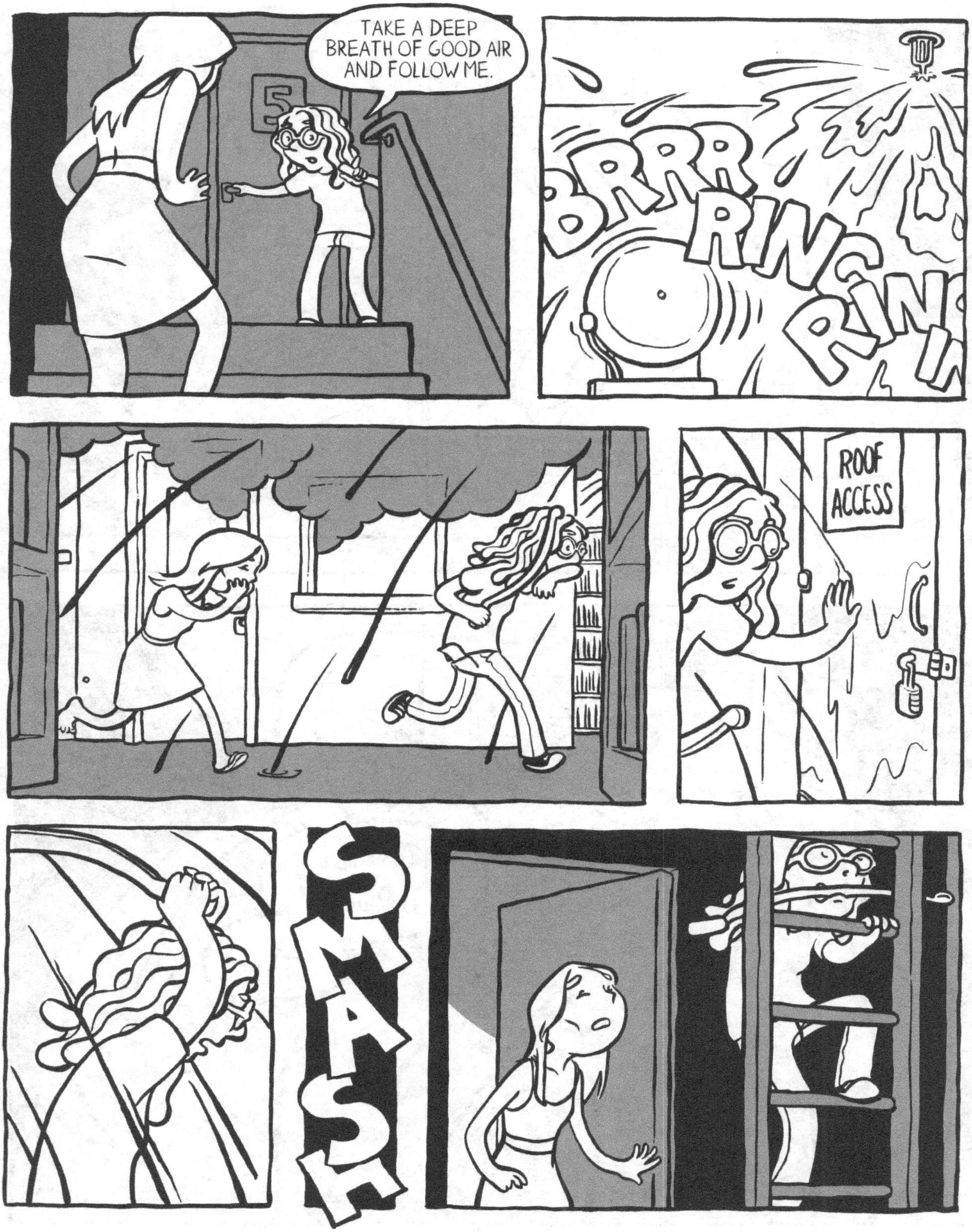
TAKE A DEEP BREATH OF GOOD AIR AND FOLLOW ME.
BRRRRING RING RIN
ROOF ACCESS
SMASH

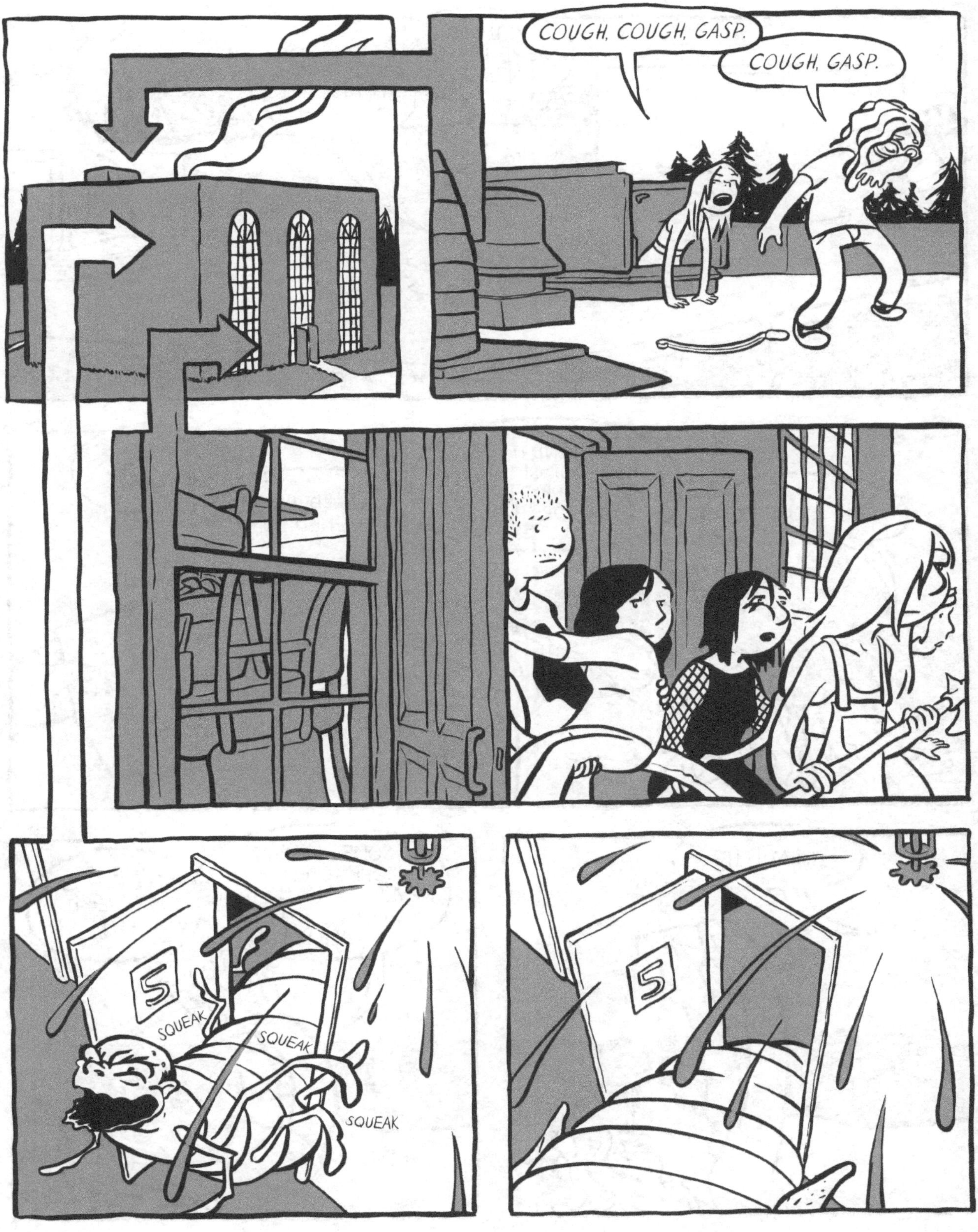
COUGH, COUGH, GASP.
COUGH, GASP.
SQUEAK
SQUEAK
SQUEAK

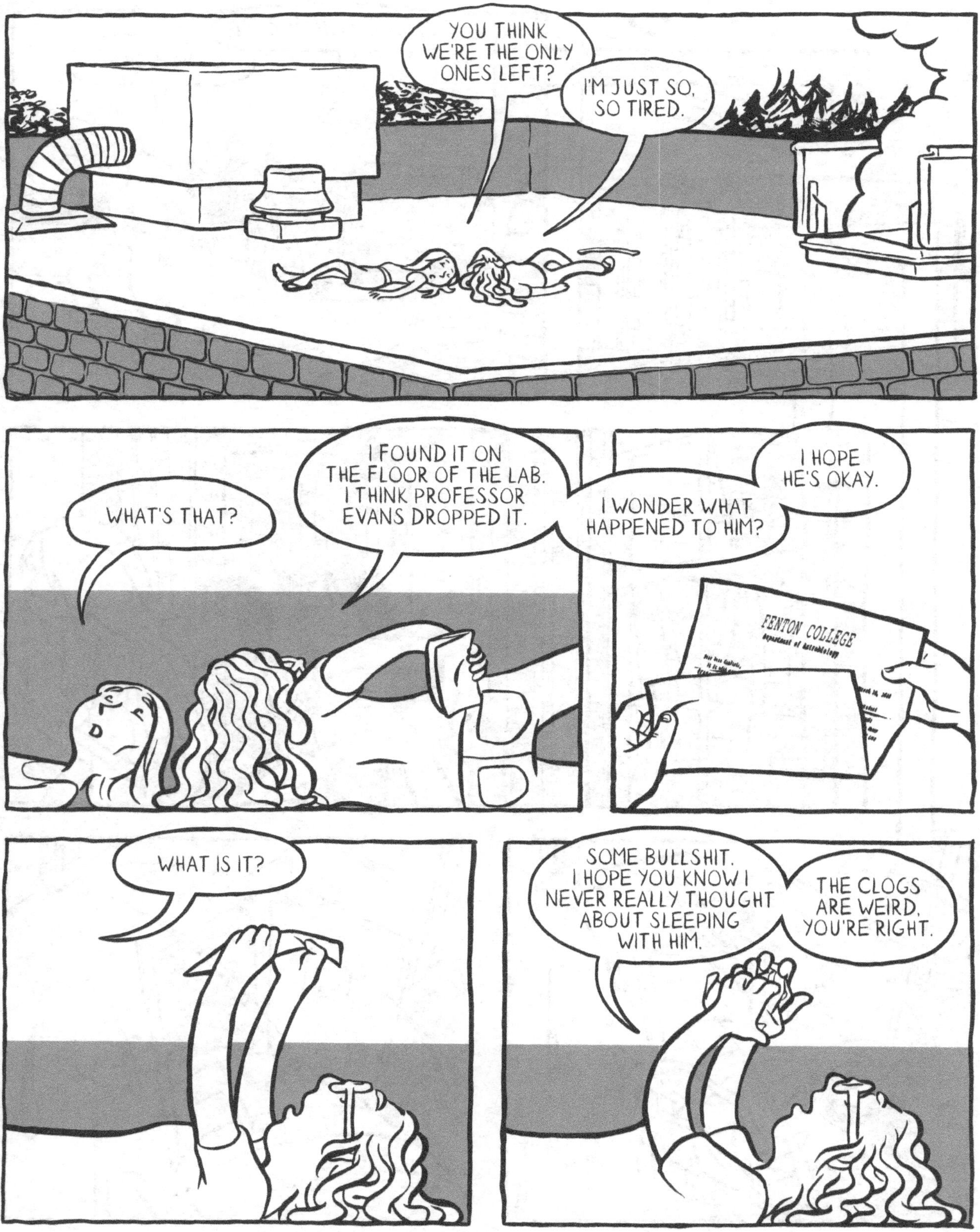

YOU THINK WE'RE THE ONLY ONES LEFT?
I'M JUST SO, SO TIRED.
WHAT'S THAT?
I FOUND IT ON THE FLOOR OF THE LAB. I THINK PROFESSOR EVANS DROPPED IT.
I WONDER WHAT HAPPENED TO HIM?
I HOPE HE'S OKAY.
FENTON COLLEGE
WHAT IS IT?
SOME BULLSHIT. I HOPE YOU KNOW I NEVER REALLY THOUGHT ABOUT SLEEPING WITH HIM.
THE CLOGS ARE WEIRD, YOU'RE RIGHT.

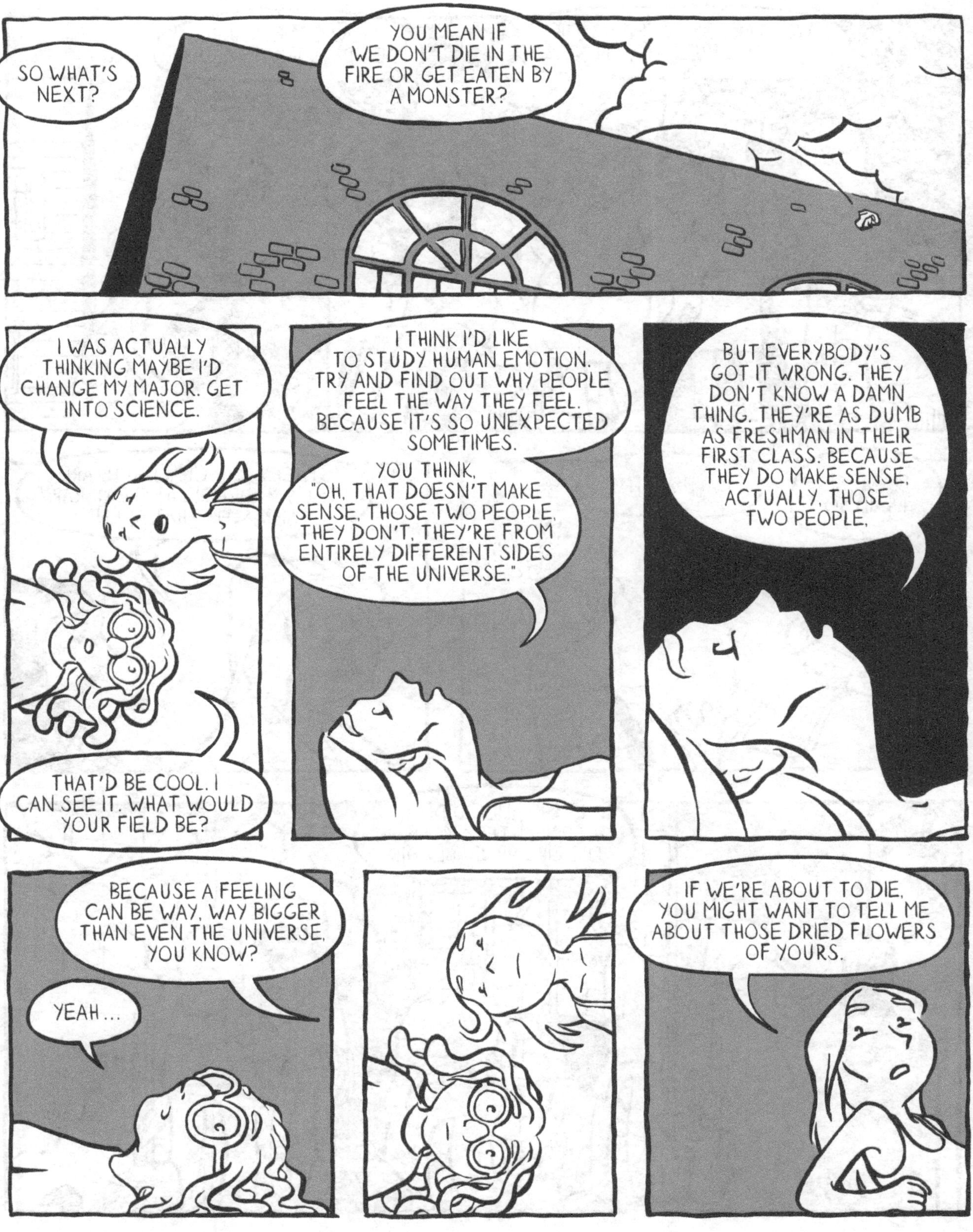
SO WHAT'S NEXT?
YOU MEAN IF WE DON'T DIE IN THE FIRE OR GET EATEN BY A MONSTER?
I WAS ACTUALLY THINKING MAYBE I'D CHANGE MY MAJOR. GET INTO SCIENCE.
THAT'D BE COOL. I CAN SEE IT. WHAT WOULD YOUR FIELD BE?
I THINK I'D LIKE TO STUDY HUMAN EMOTION. TRY AND FIND OUT WHY PEOPLE FEEL THE WAY THEY FEEL. BECAUSE IT'S SO UNEXPECTED SOMETIMES.
YOU THINK, "OH, THAT DOESN'T MAKE SENSE, THOSE TWO PEOPLE, THEY DON'T, THEY'RE FROM ENTIRELY DIFFERENT SIDES OF THE UNIVERSE."
BUT EVERYBODY'S GOT IT WRONG. THEY DON'T KNOW A DAMN THING. THEY'RE AS DUMB AS FRESHMAN IN THEIR FIRST CLASS. BECAUSE THEY DO MAKE SENSE, ACTUALLY, THOSE TWO PEOPLE.
BECAUSE A FEELING CAN BE WAY, WAY BIGGER THAN EVEN THE UNIVERSE, YOU KNOW?
YEAH...
IF WE'RE ABOUT TO DIE, YOU MIGHT WANT TO TELL ME ABOUT THOSE DRIED FLOWERS OF YOURS.

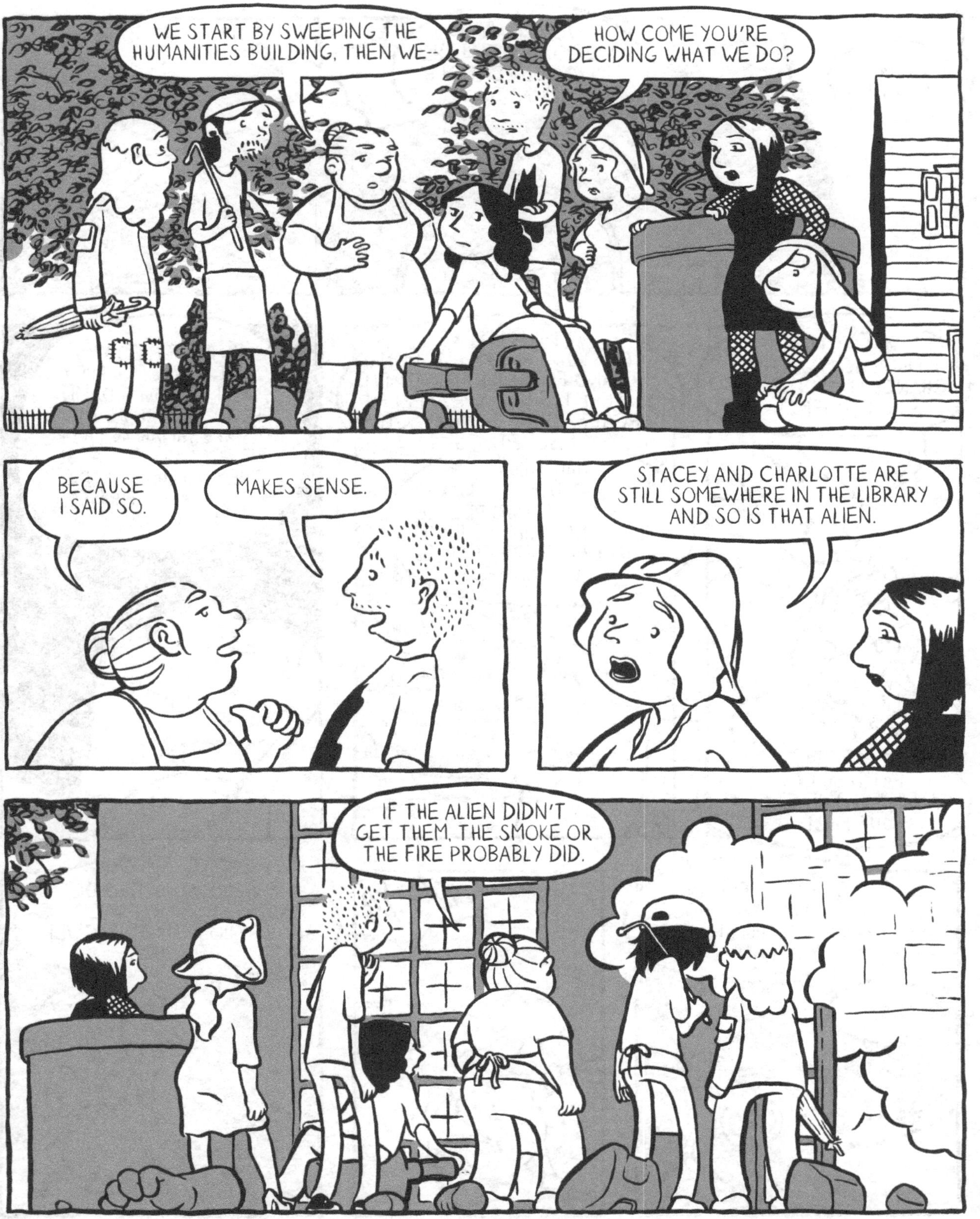
WE START BY SWEEPING THE HUMANITIES BUILDING, THEN WE--
HOW COME YOU'RE DECIDING WHAT WE DO?
BECAUSE I SAID SO.
MAKES SENSE.
STACEY AND CHARLOTTE ARE STILL SOMEWHERE IN THE LIBRARY AND SO IS THAT ALIEN.
IF THE ALIEN DIDN'T GET THEM, THE SMOKE OR THE FIRE PROBABLY DID.

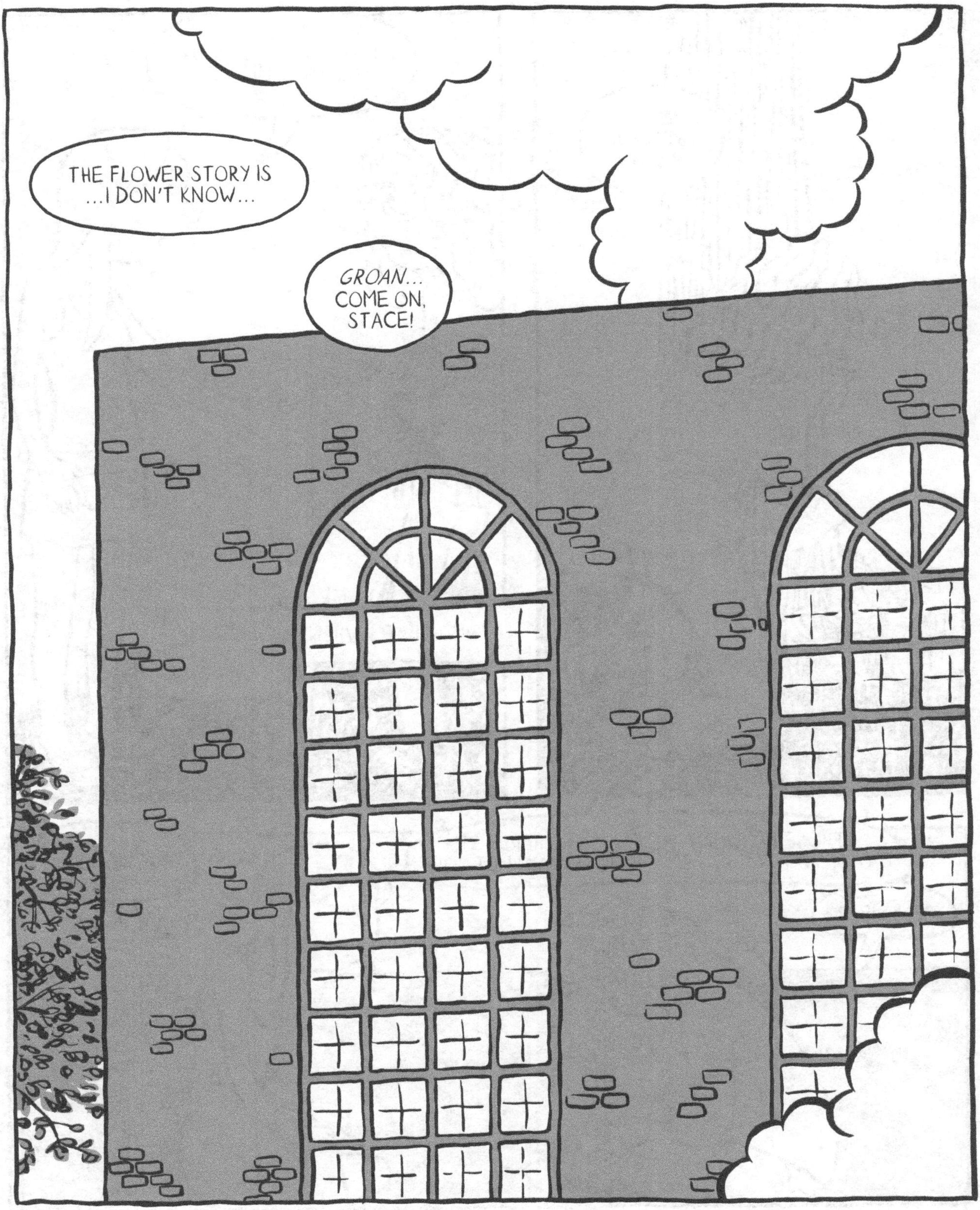
THE FLOWER STORY IS ...I DON'T KNOW...
GROAN... COME ON, STACE!

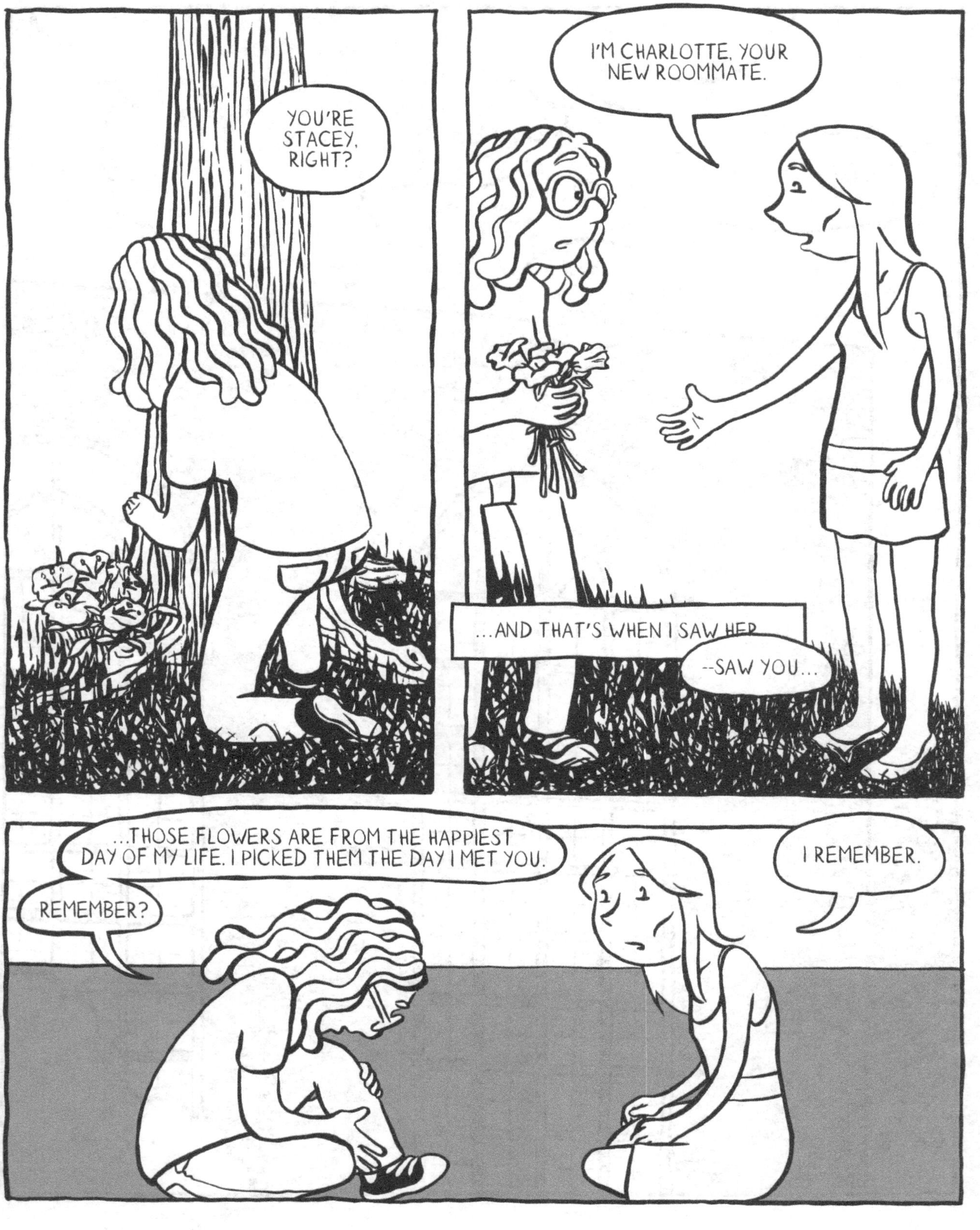
YOU'RE STACEY, RIGHT?
I'M CHARLOTTE, YOUR NEW ROOMMATE.
...AND THAT'S WHEN I SAW HER
--SAW YOU...
...THOSE FLOWERS ARE FROM THE HAPPIEST DAY OF MY LIFE. I PICKED THEM THE DAY I MET YOU.
REMEMBER?
I REMEMBER.

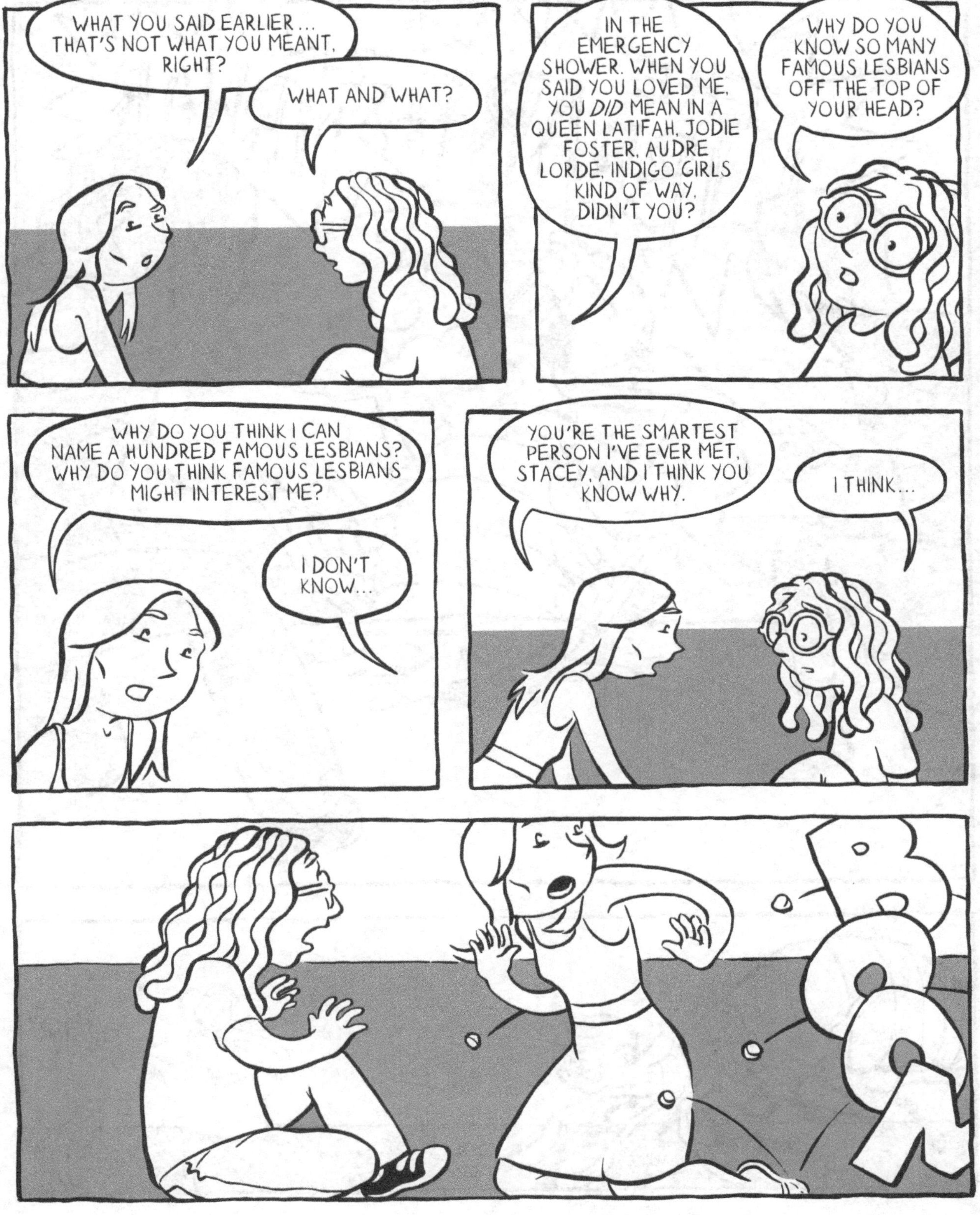
WHAT YOU SAID EARLIER... THAT'S NOT WHAT YOU MEANT, RIGHT?
WHAT AND WHAT?
IN THE EMERGENCY SHOWER. WHEN YOU SAID YOU LOVED ME, YOU *DID* MEAN IN A QUEEN LATIFAH, JODIE FOSTER, AUDRE LORDE, INDIGO GIRLS KIND OF WAY, DIDN'T YOU?
WHY DO YOU KNOW SO MANY FAMOUS LESBIANS OFF THE TOP OF YOUR HEAD?
WHY DO YOU THINK I CAN NAME A HUNDRED FAMOUS LESBIANS? WHY DO YOU THINK FAMOUS LESBIANS MIGHT INTEREST ME?
I DON'T KNOW...
YOU'RE THE SMARTEST PERSON I'VE EVER MET, STACEY, AND I THINK YOU KNOW WHY.
I THINK...

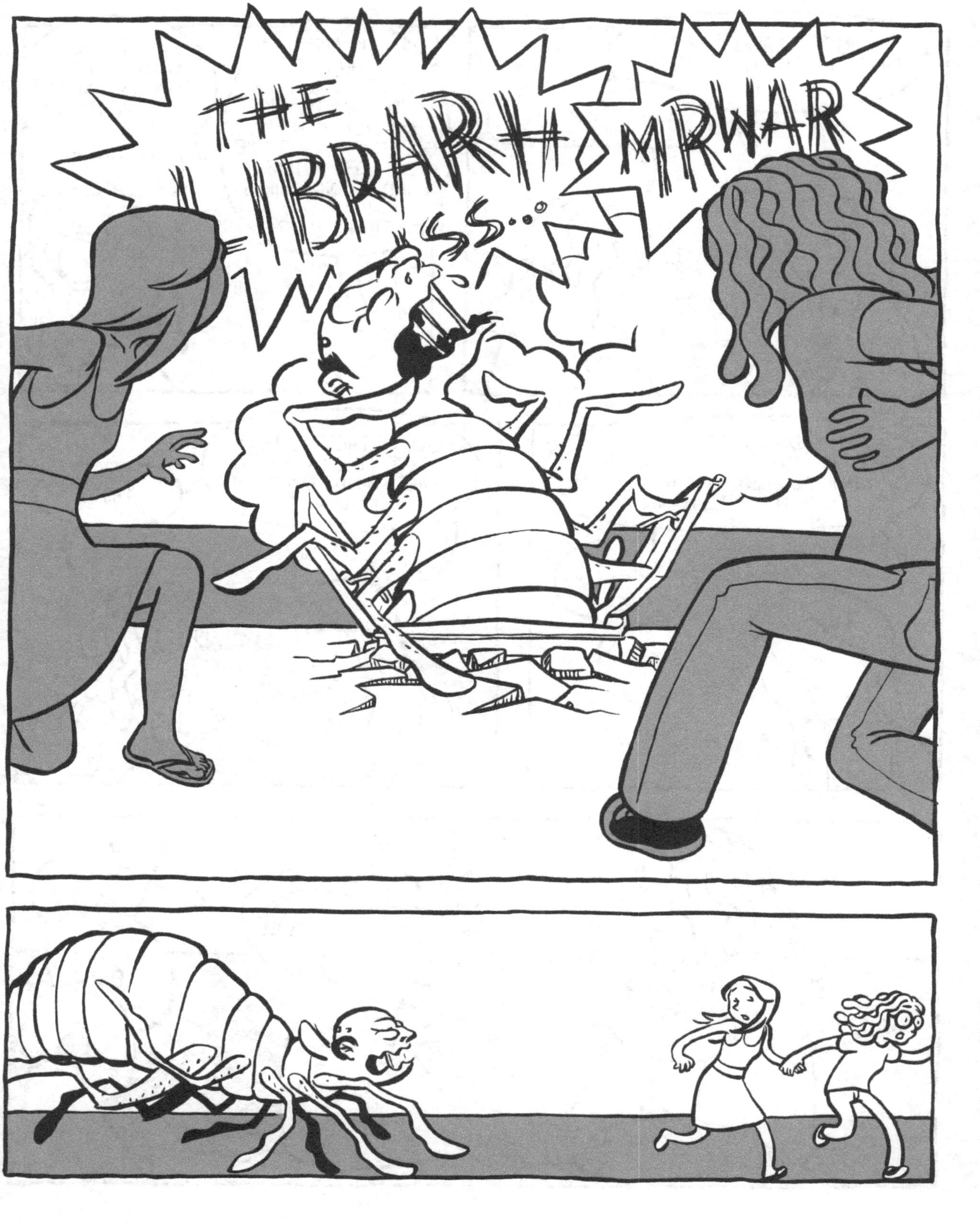
THE LIBRARH
MRWAR
SS...

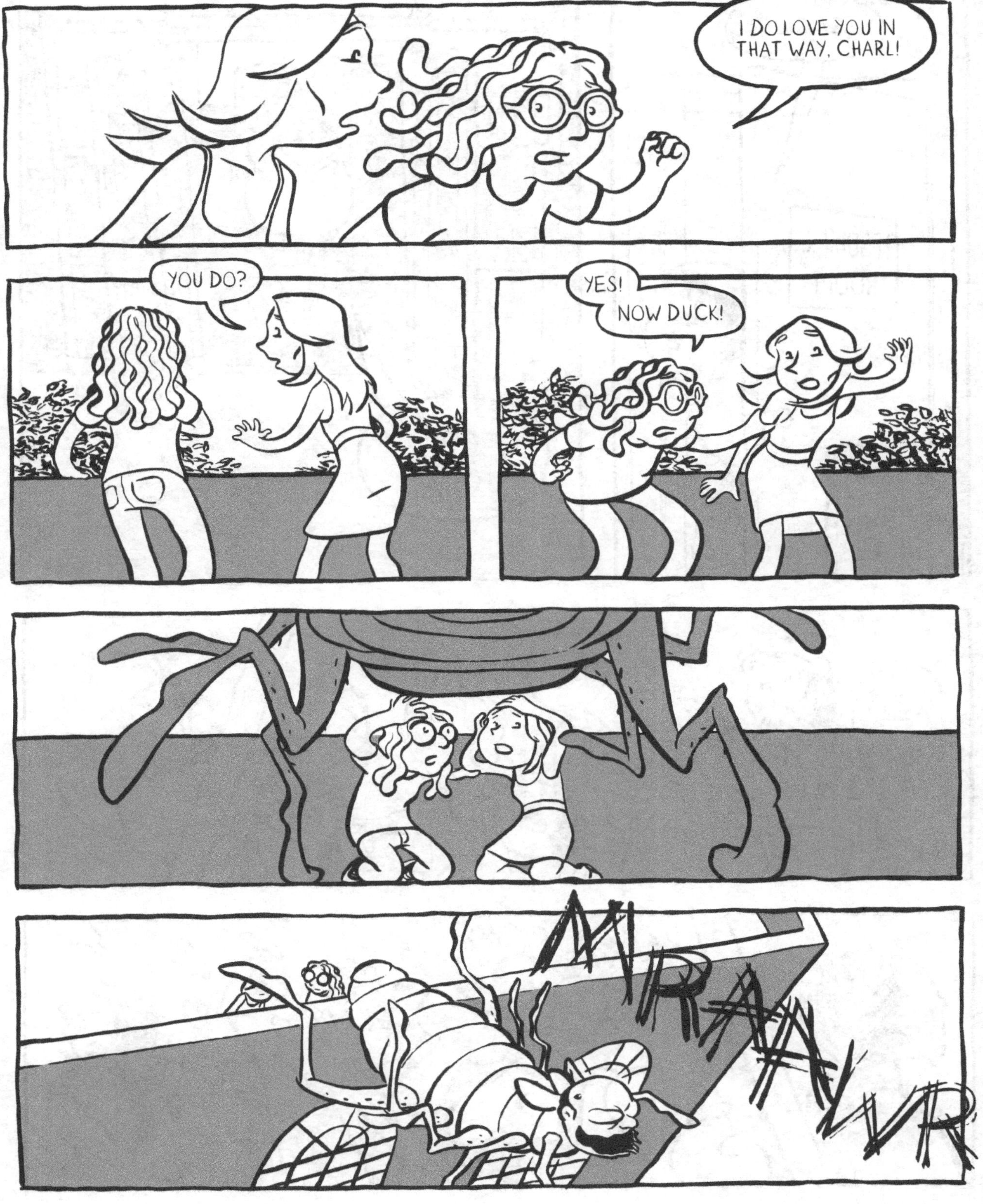
I DO LOVE YOU IN THAT WAY, CHARL!
YOU DO?
YES!
NOW DUCK!
MRAAWR

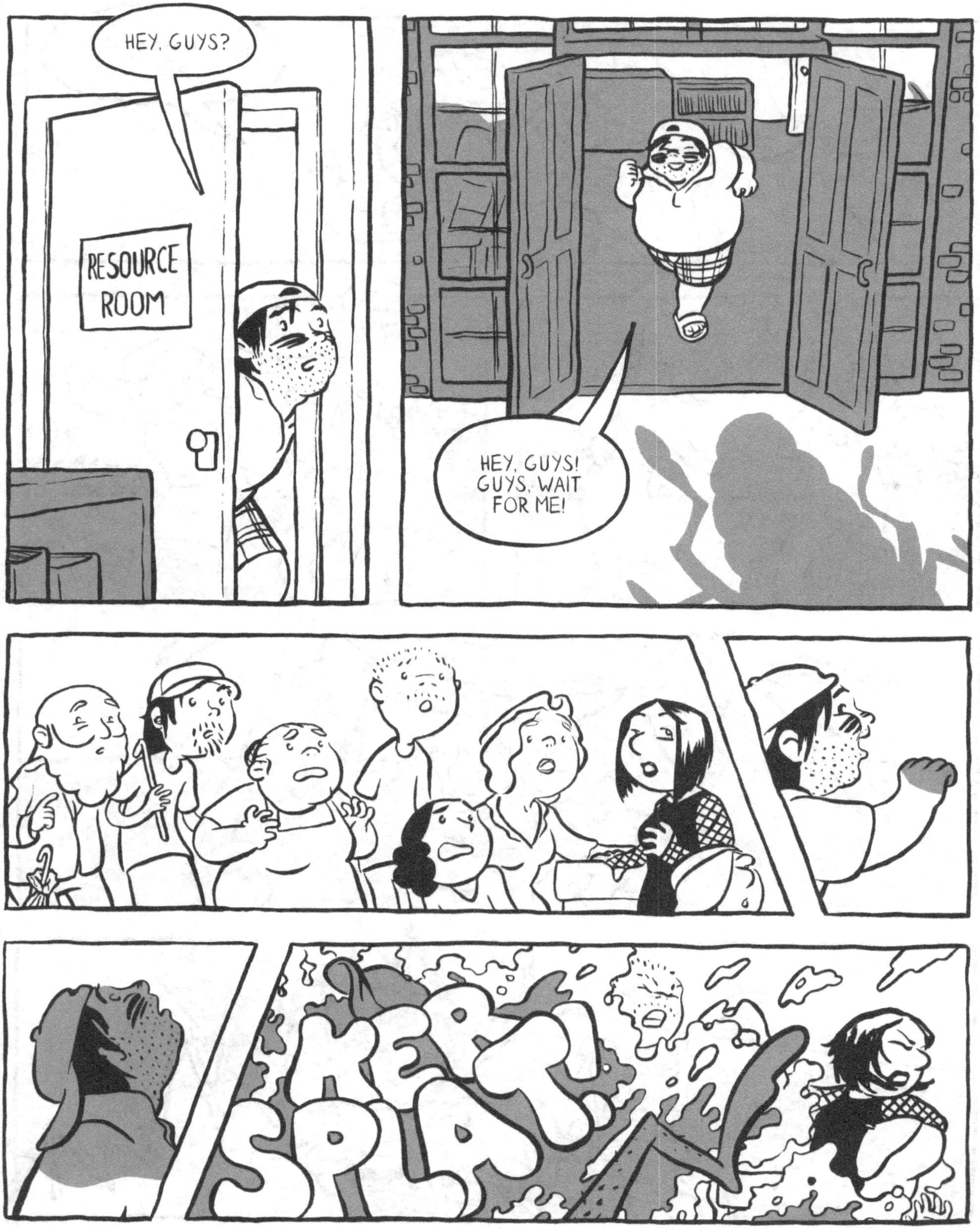
HEY, GUYS?
RESOURCE ROOM
HEY, GUYS! GUYS, WAIT FOR ME!
SPLAT!

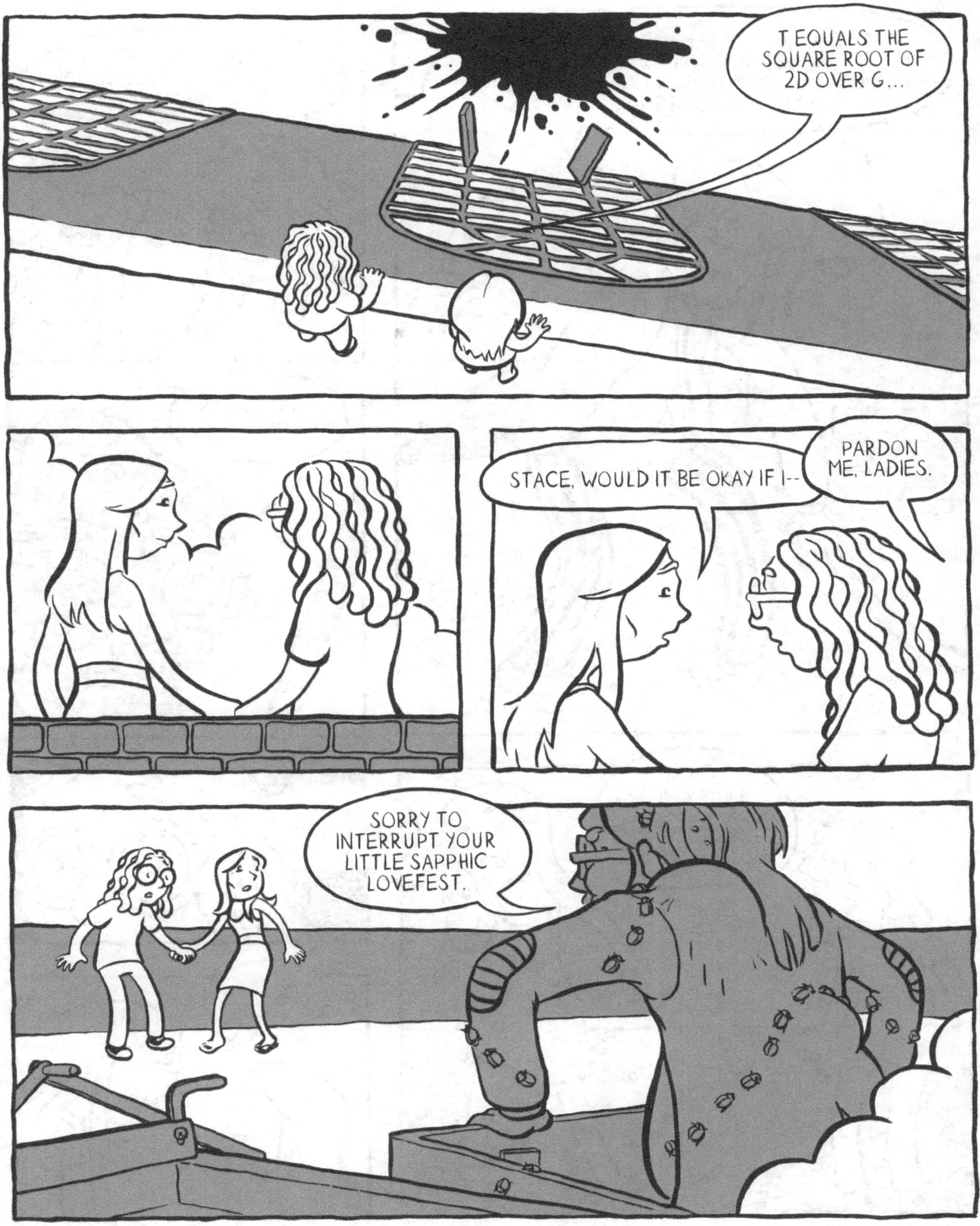
T EQUALS THE SQUARE ROOT OF 2D OVER G...
STACE, WOULD IT BE OKAY IF I--
PARDON ME, LADIES.
SORRY TO INTERRUPT YOUR LITTLE SAPPHIC LOVEFEST.

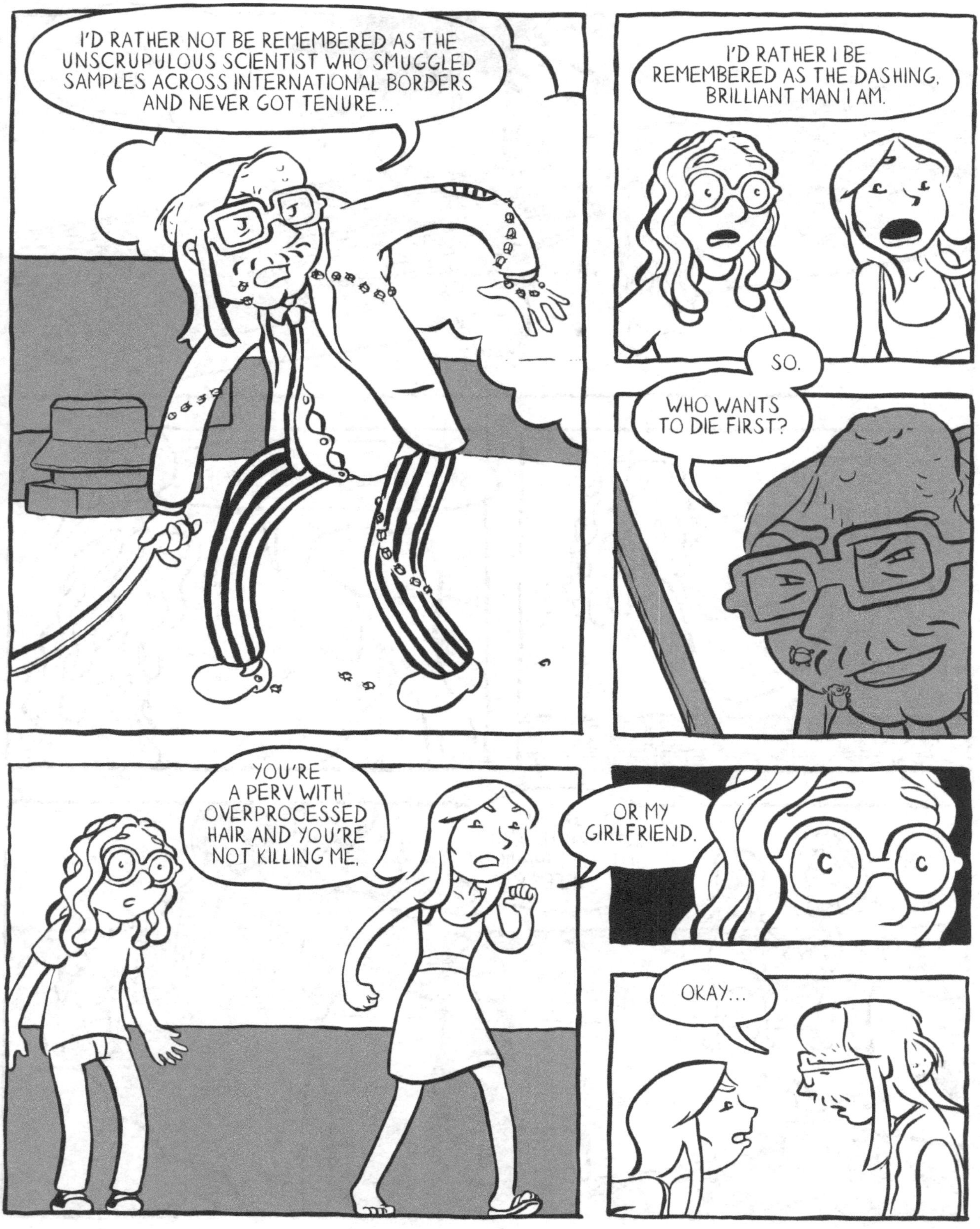
I'D RATHER NOT BE REMEMBERED AS THE UNSCRUPULOUS SCIENTIST WHO SMUGGLED SAMPLES ACROSS INTERNATIONAL BORDERS AND NEVER GOT TENURE...
I'D RATHER I BE REMEMBERED AS THE DASHING, BRILLIANT MAN I AM.
SO.
WHO WANTS TO DIE FIRST?
YOU'RE A PERV WITH OVERPROCESSED HAIR AND YOU'RE NOT KILLING ME.
OR MY GIRLFRIEND.
OKAY...

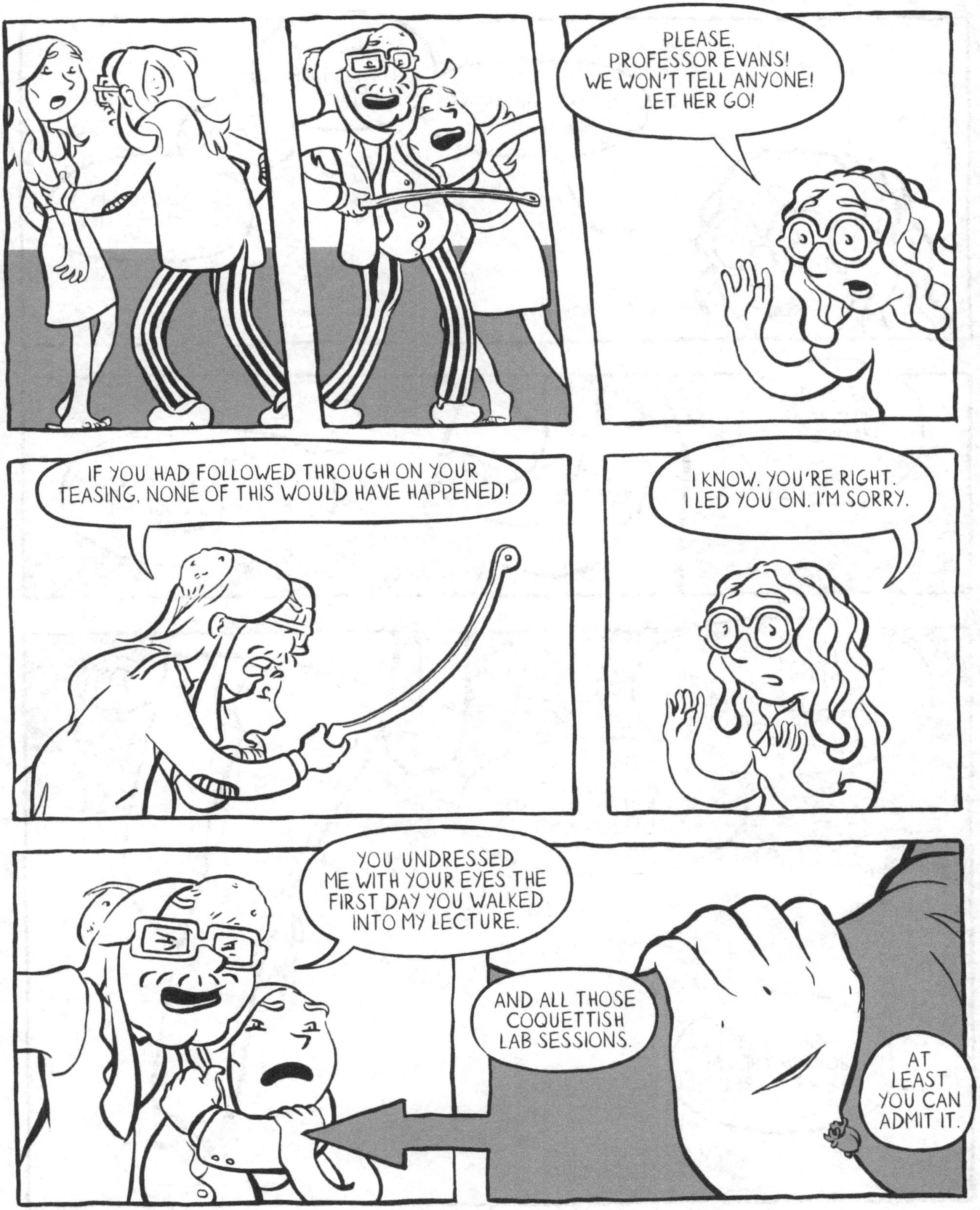
PLEASE, PROFESSOR EVANS! WE WON'T TELL ANYONE! LET HER GO!
IF YOU HAD FOLLOWED THROUGH ON YOUR TEASING, NONE OF THIS WOULD HAVE HAPPENED!
I KNOW. YOU'RE RIGHT. I LED YOU ON. I'M SORRY.
YOU UNDRESSED ME WITH YOUR EYES THE FIRST DAY YOU WALKED INTO MY LECTURE.
AND ALL THOSE COQUETTISH LAB SESSIONS.
AT LEAST YOU CAN ADMIT IT.

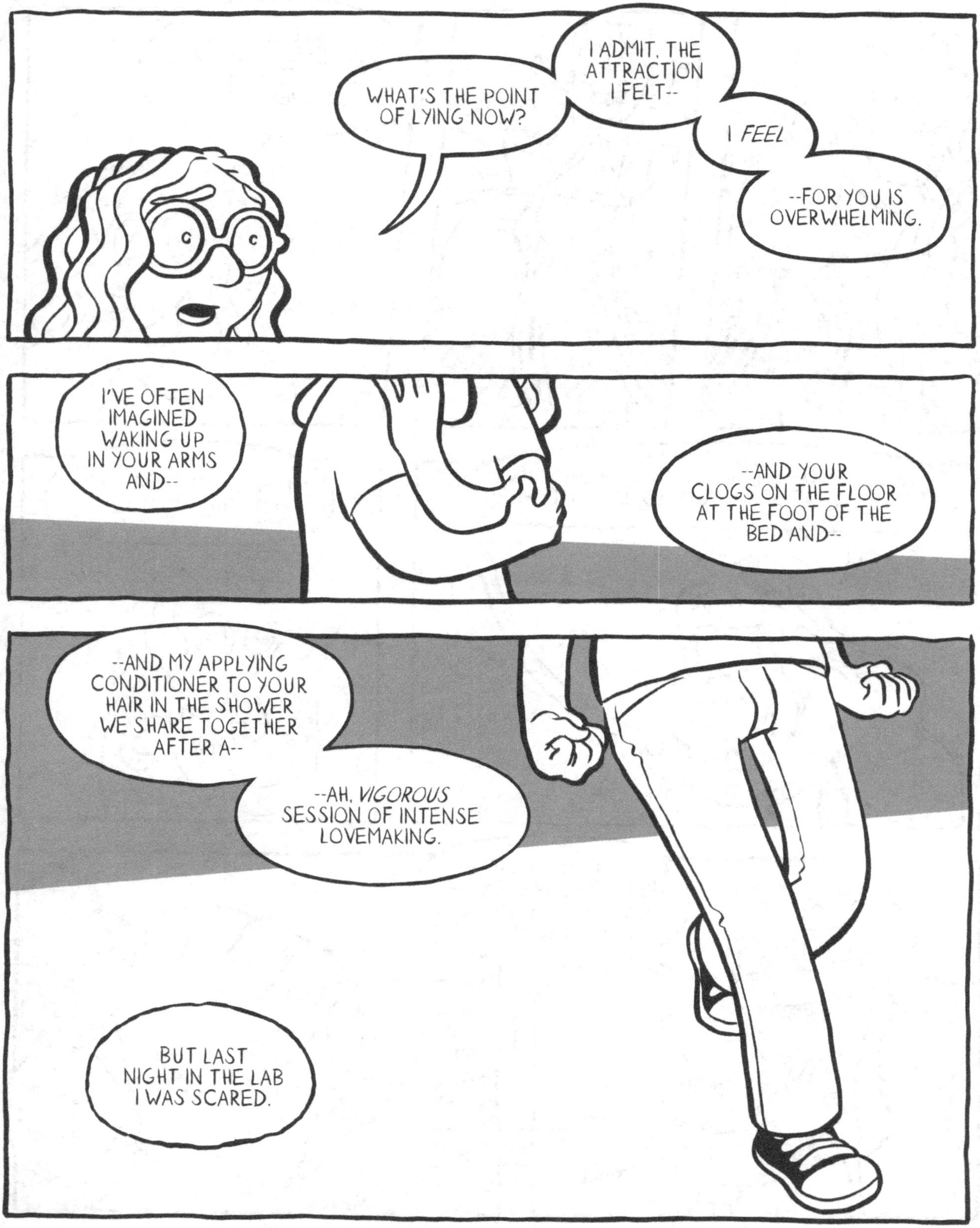
WHAT'S THE POINT OF LYING NOW?
I ADMIT, THE ATTRACTION I FELT--
I *FEEL*
--FOR YOU IS OVERWHELMING.
I'VE OFTEN IMAGINED WAKING UP IN YOUR ARMS AND--
--AND YOUR CLOGS ON THE FLOOR AT THE FOOT OF THE BED AND--
--AND MY APPLYING CONDITIONER TO YOUR HAIR IN THE SHOWER WE SHARE TOGETHER AFTER A--
--AH, *VIGOROUS* SESSION OF INTENSE LOVEMAKING.
BUT LAST NIGHT IN THE LAB I WAS SCARED.

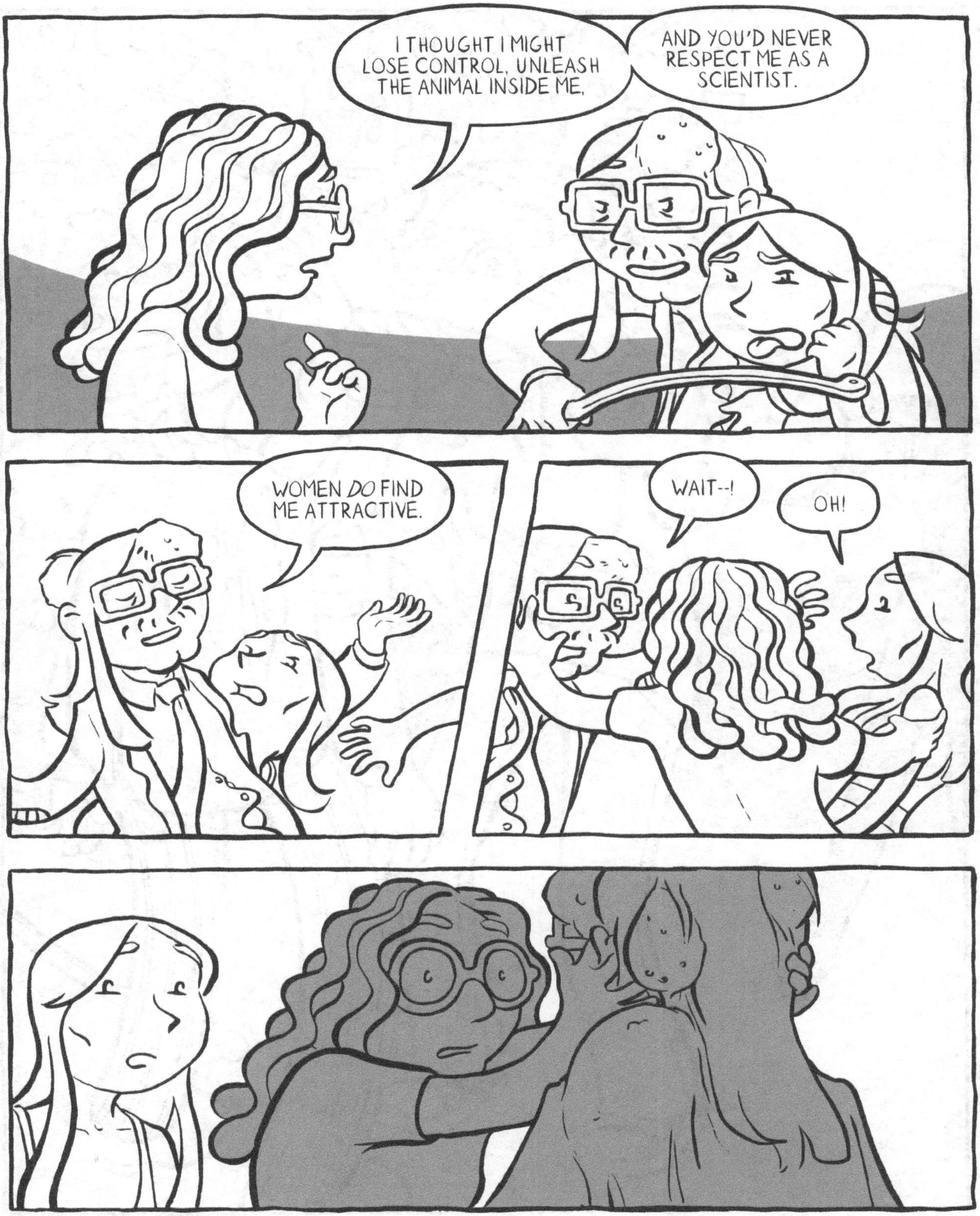
I THOUGHT I MIGHT LOSE CONTROL, UNLEASH THE ANIMAL INSIDE ME,
AND YOU'D NEVER RESPECT ME AS A SCIENTIST.
WOMEN *DO* FIND ME ATTRACTIVE.
WAIT--!
OH!

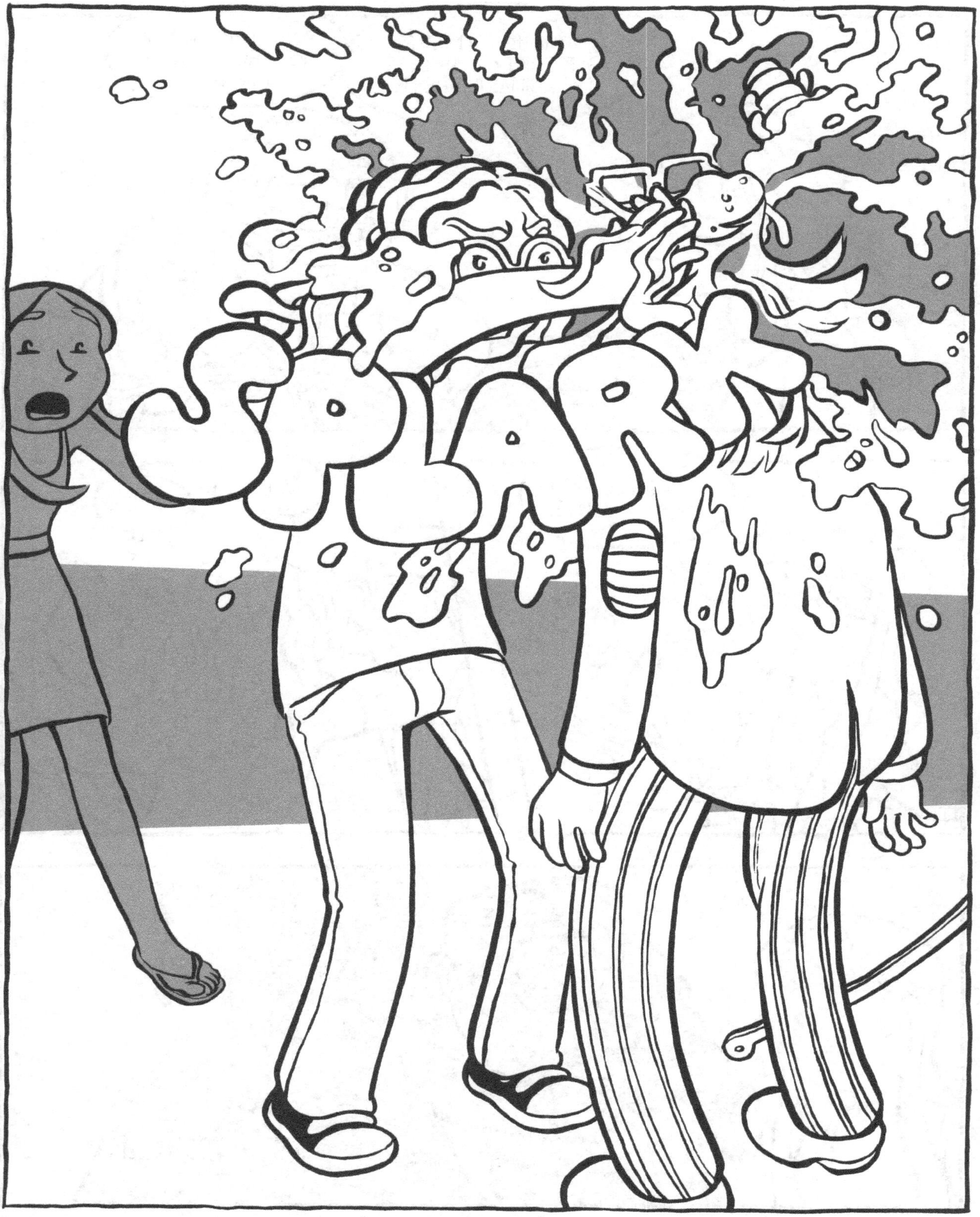
SPLART

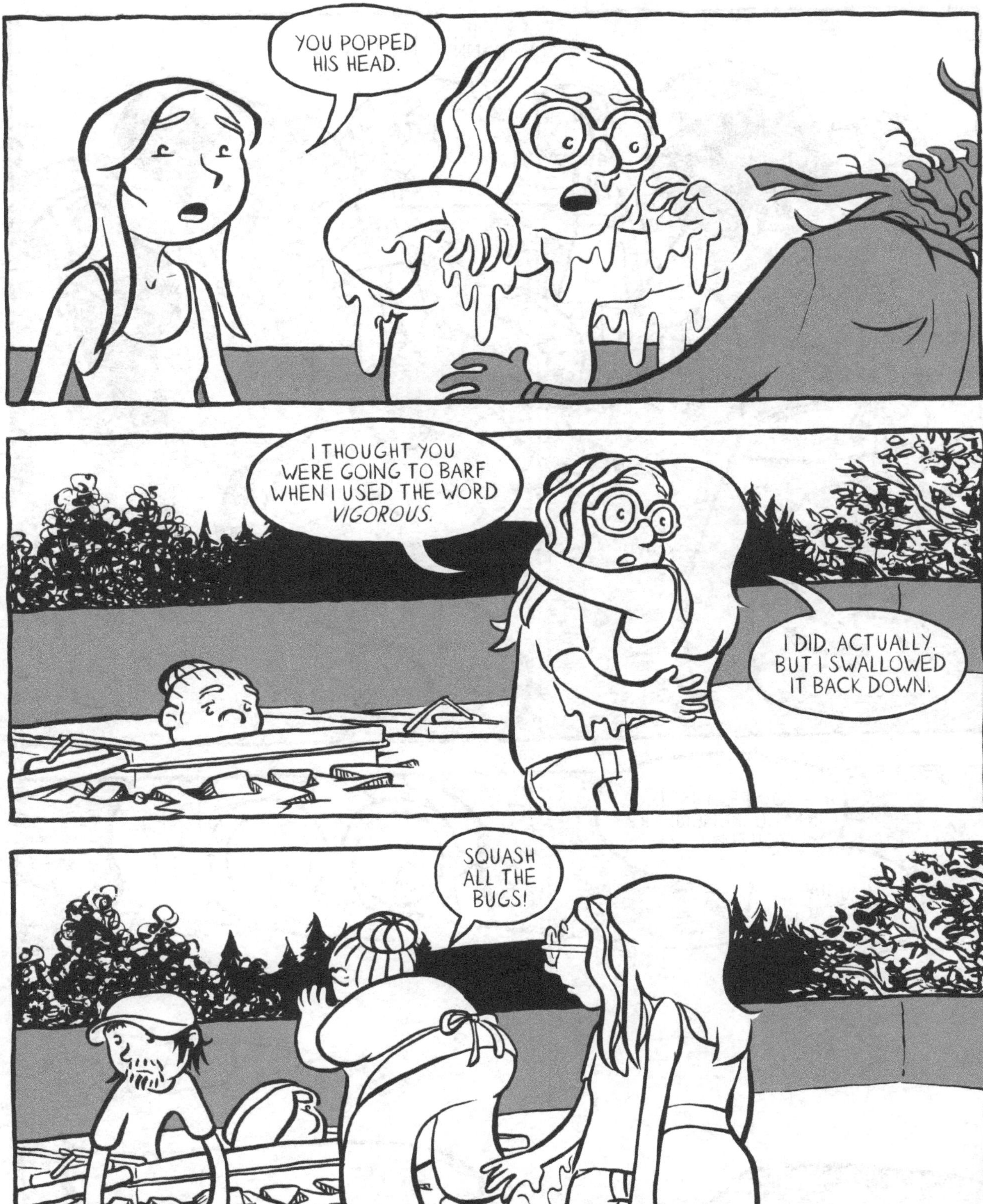
YOU POPPED HIS HEAD.
I THOUGHT YOU WERE GOING TO BARF WHEN I USED THE WORD *VIGOROUS*.
I DID, ACTUALLY, BUT I SWALLOWED IT BACK DOWN.
SQUASH ALL THE BUGS!

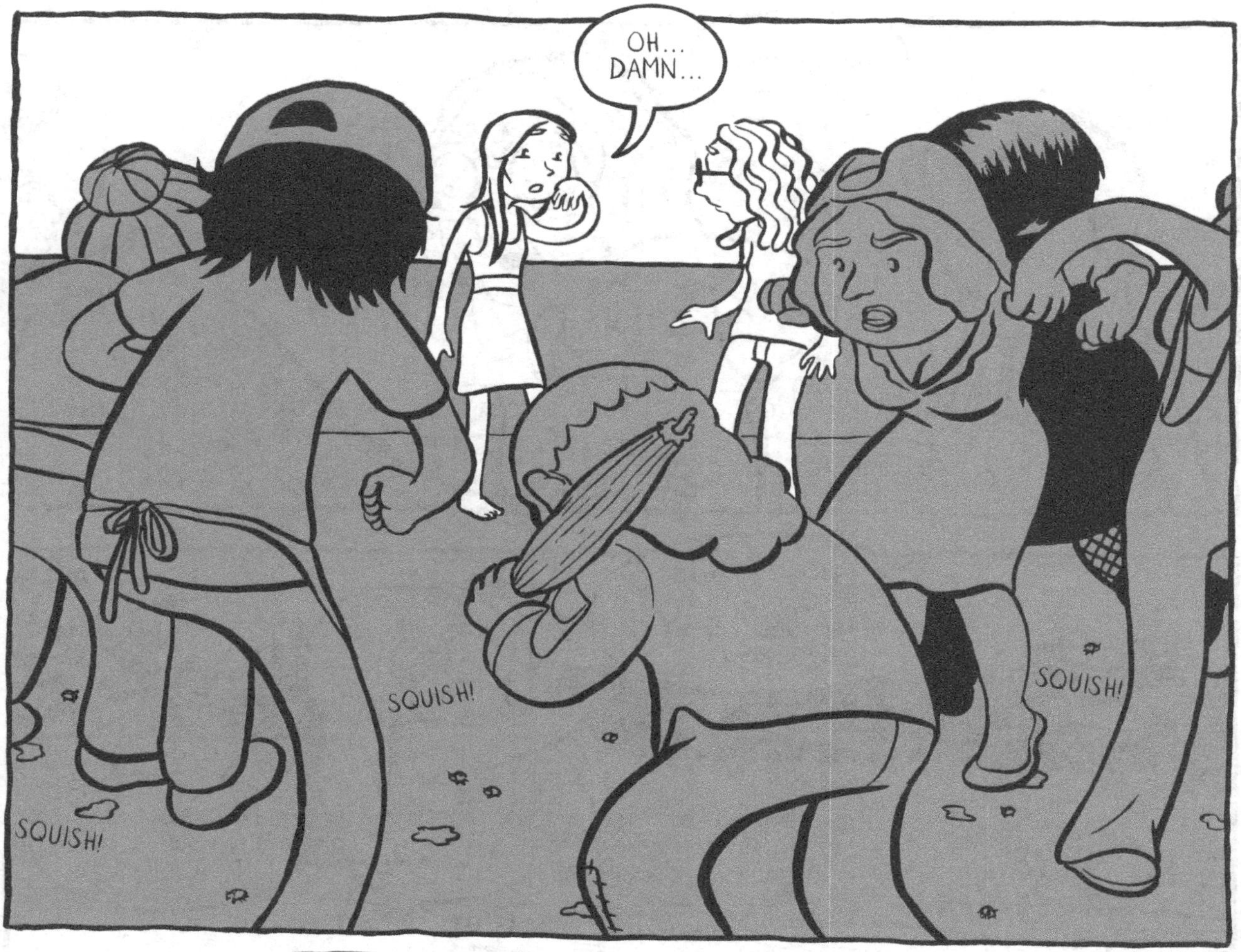
OH... DAMN...
SQUISH!
SQUISH!
SQUISH!

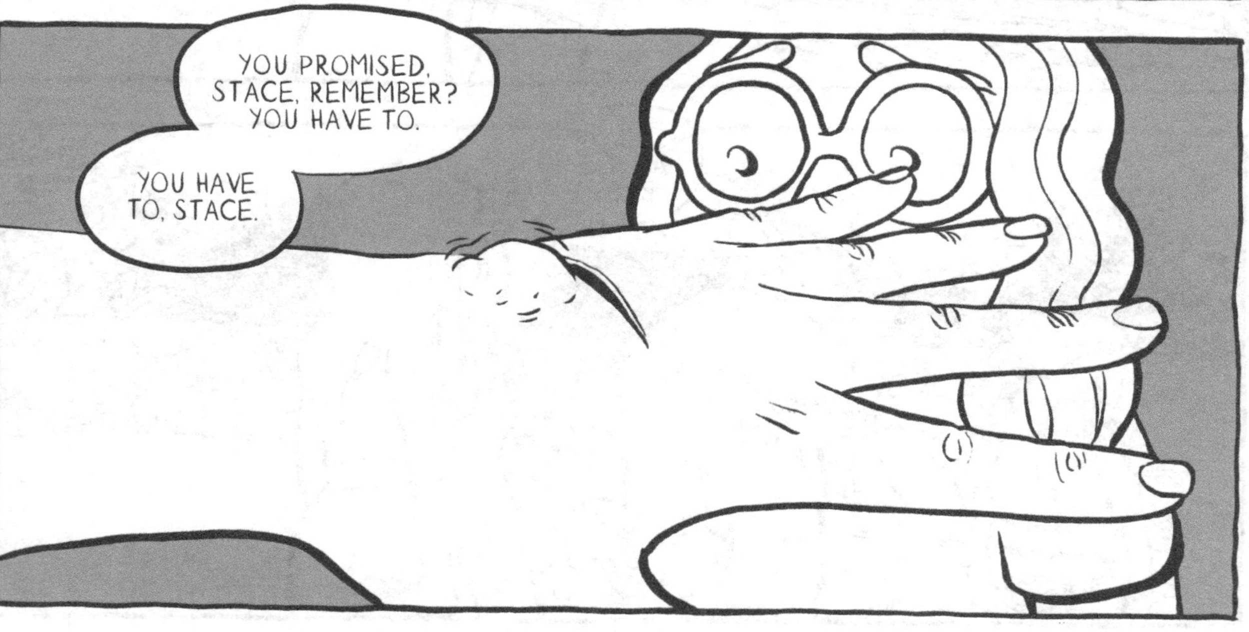
YOU PROMISED, STACE, REMEMBER? YOU HAVE TO.
YOU HAVE TO, STACE.

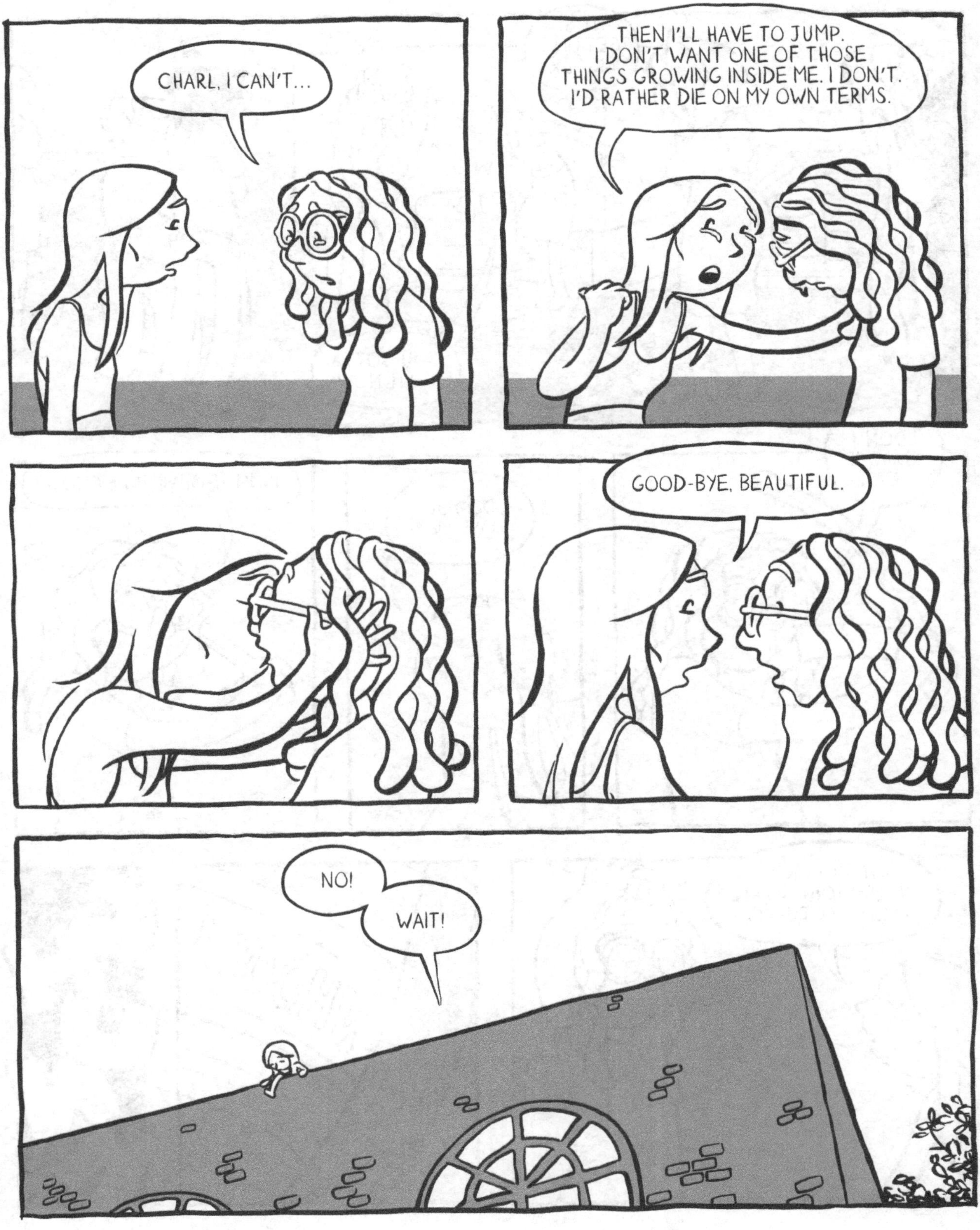
CHARL, I CAN'T...
THEN I'LL HAVE TO JUMP. I DON'T WANT ONE OF THOSE THINGS GROWING INSIDE ME. I DON'T. I'D RATHER DIE ON MY OWN TERMS.
GOOD-BYE, BEAUTIFUL.
NO!
WAIT!

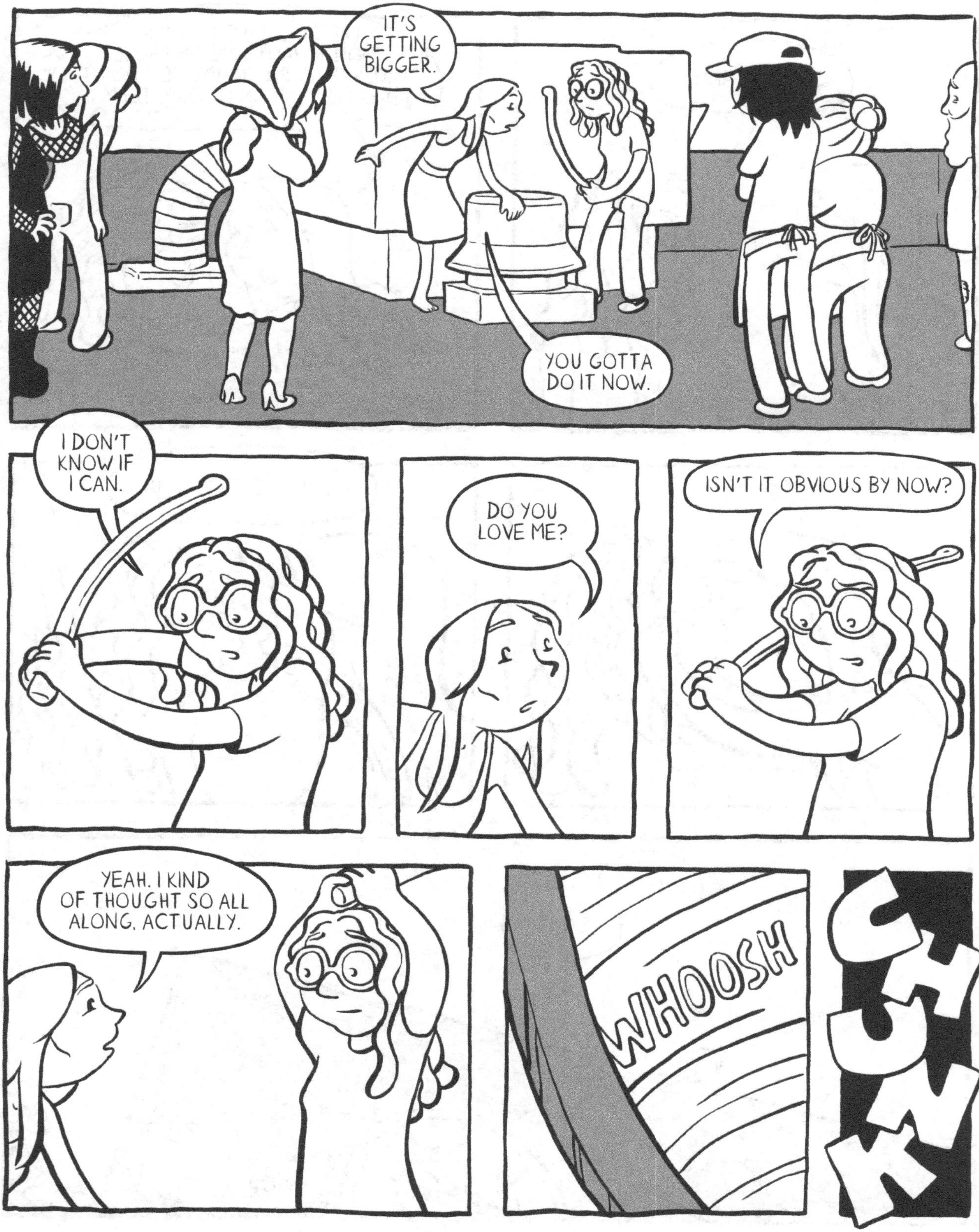
IT'S GETTING BIGGER.
YOU GOTTA DO IT NOW.
I DON'T KNOW IF I CAN.
DO YOU LOVE ME?
ISN'T IT OBVIOUS BY NOW?
YEAH. I KIND OF THOUGHT SO ALL ALONG, ACTUALLY.
WHOOSH
CHUNK

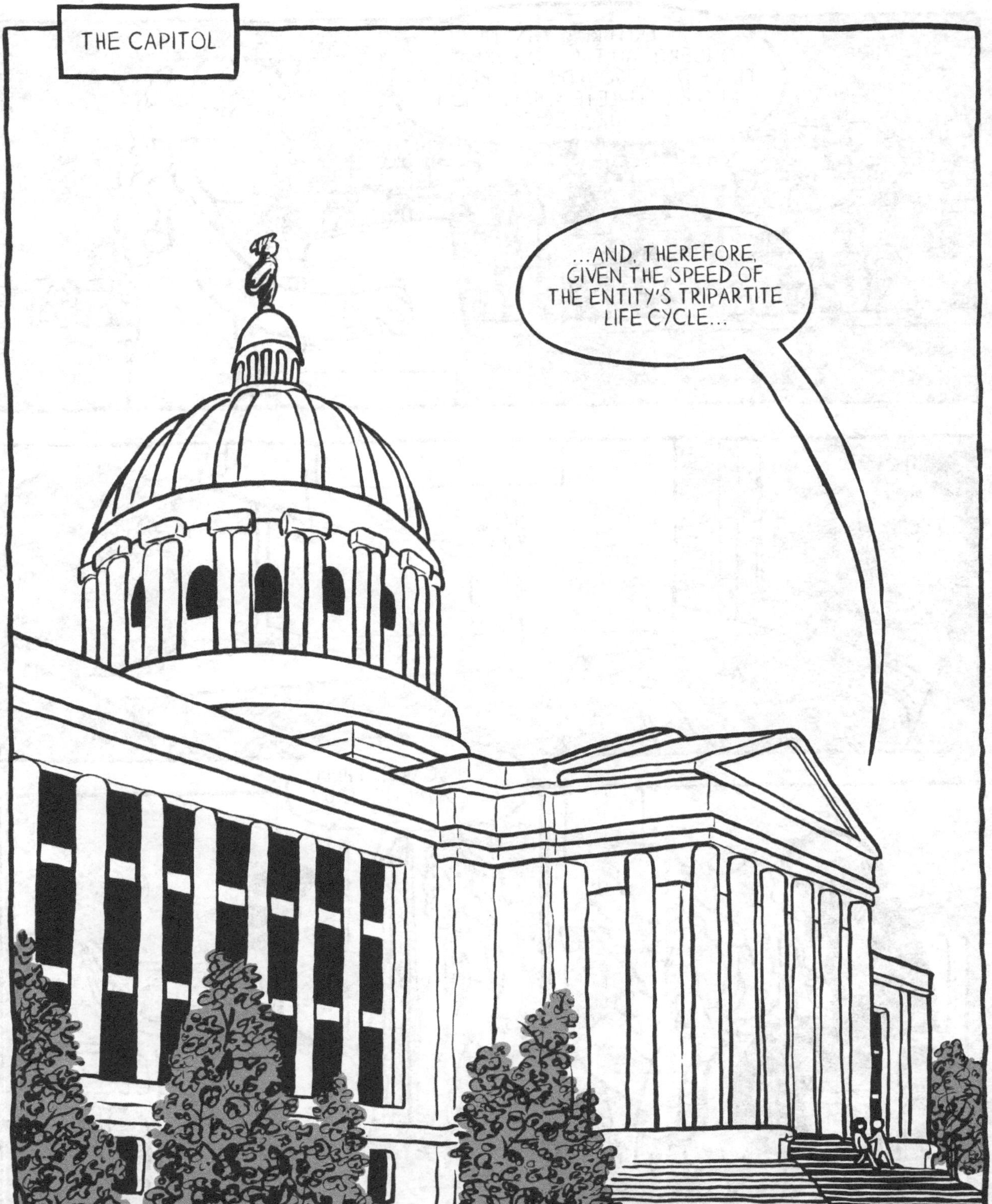
THE CAPITOL
...AND, THEREFORE, GIVEN THE SPEED OF THE ENTITY'S TRIPARTITE LIFE CYCLE...

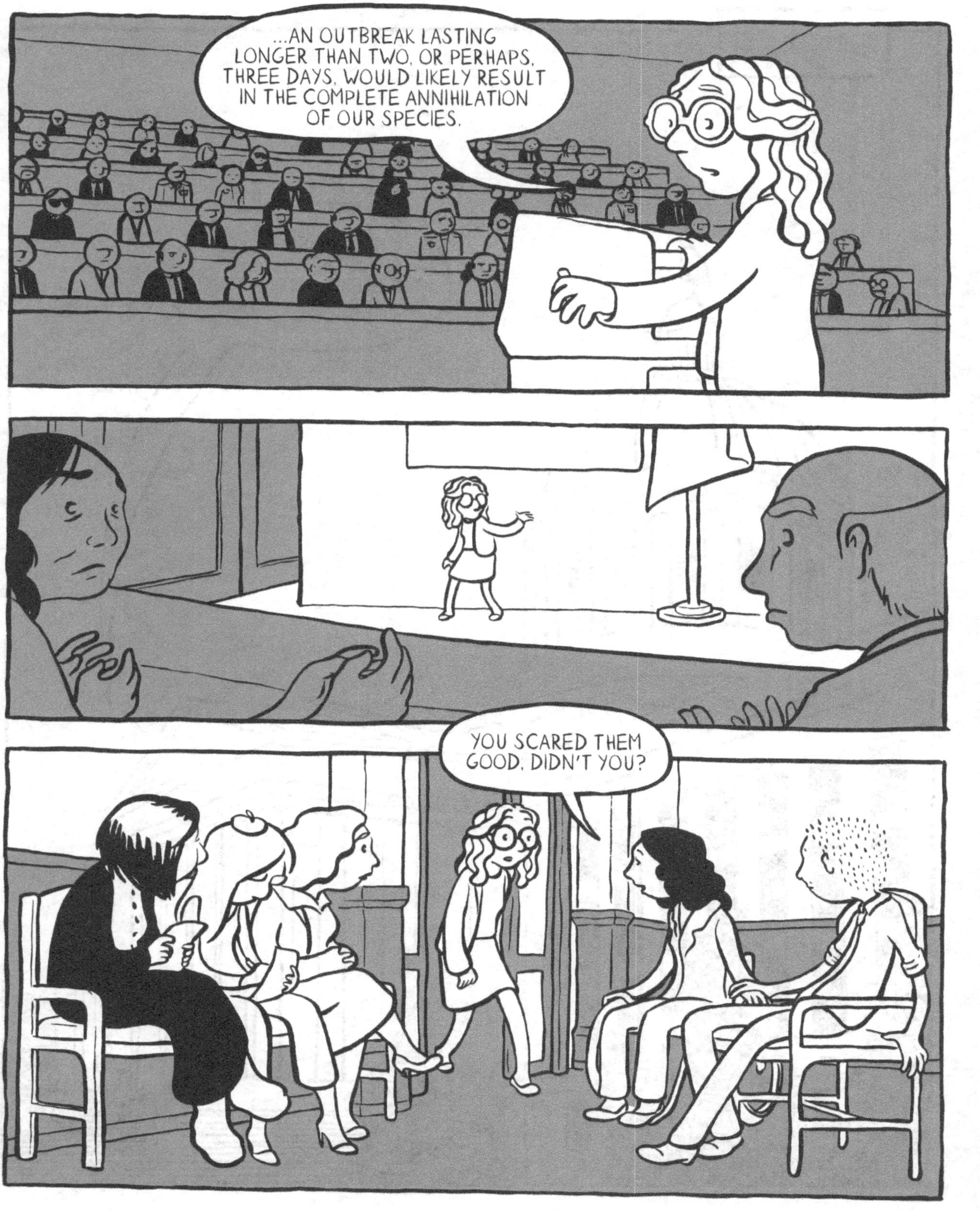
...AN OUTBREAK LASTING LONGER THAN TWO, OR PERHAPS, THREE DAYS, WOULD LIKELY RESULT IN THE COMPLETE ANNIHILATION OF OUR SPECIES.
YOU SCARED THEM GOOD, DIDN'T YOU?

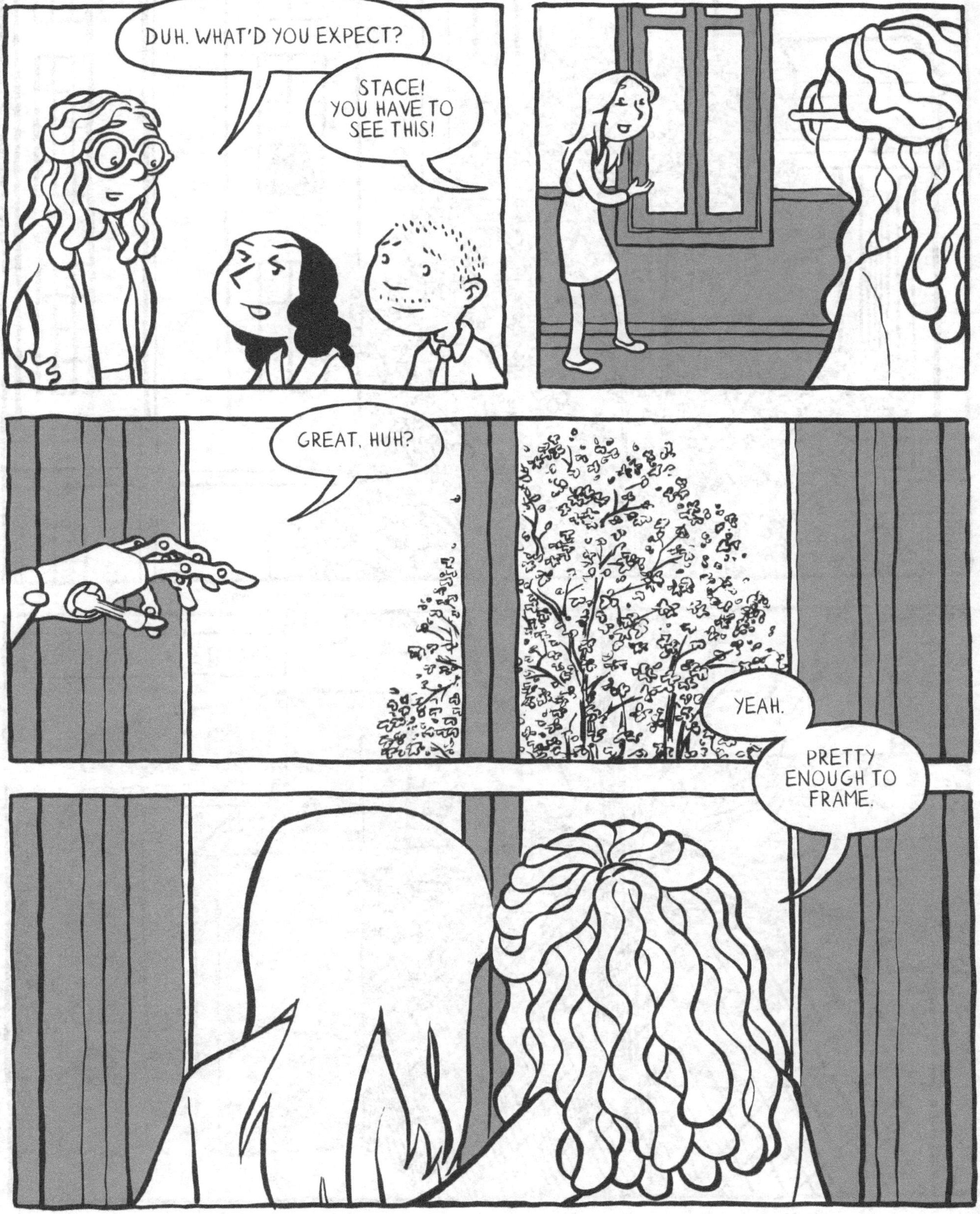
DUH. WHAT'D YOU EXPECT?
STACE! YOU HAVE TO SEE THIS!
GREAT, HUH?
YEAH.
PRETTY ENOUGH TO FRAME.

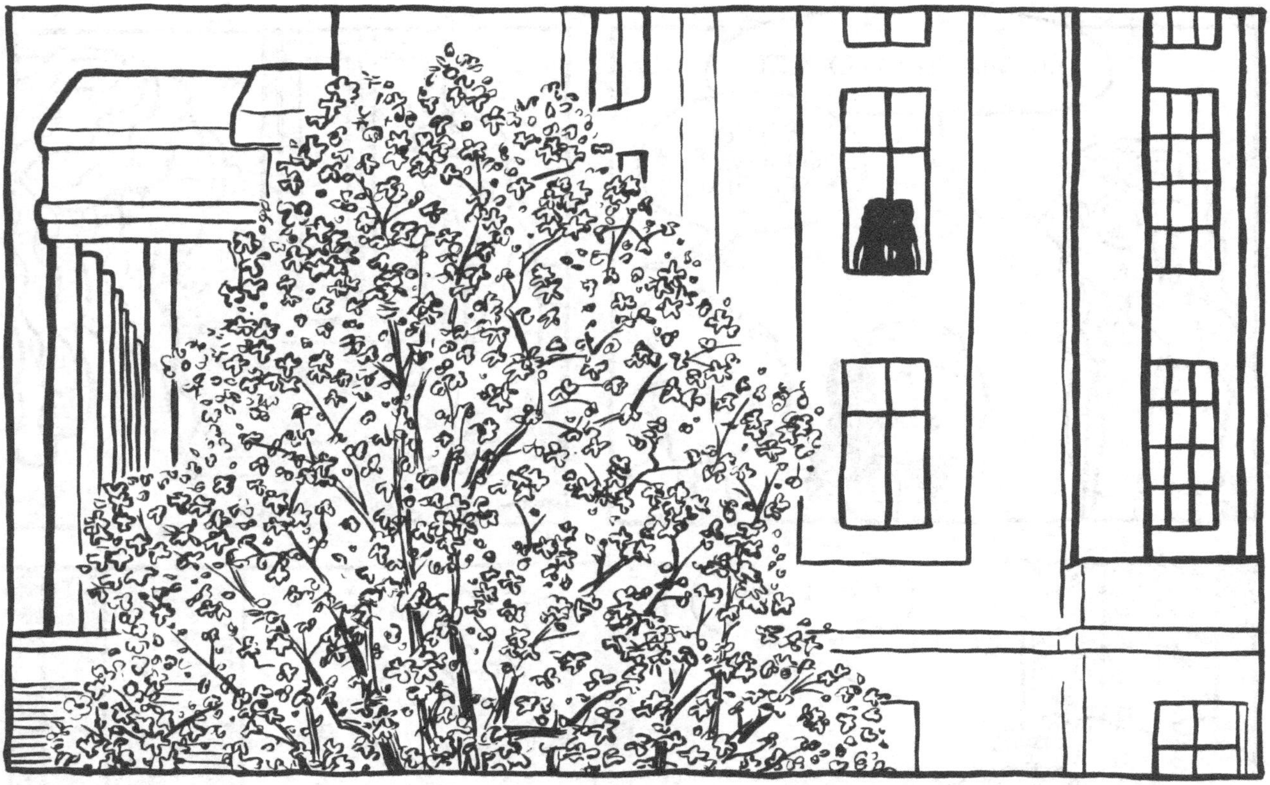

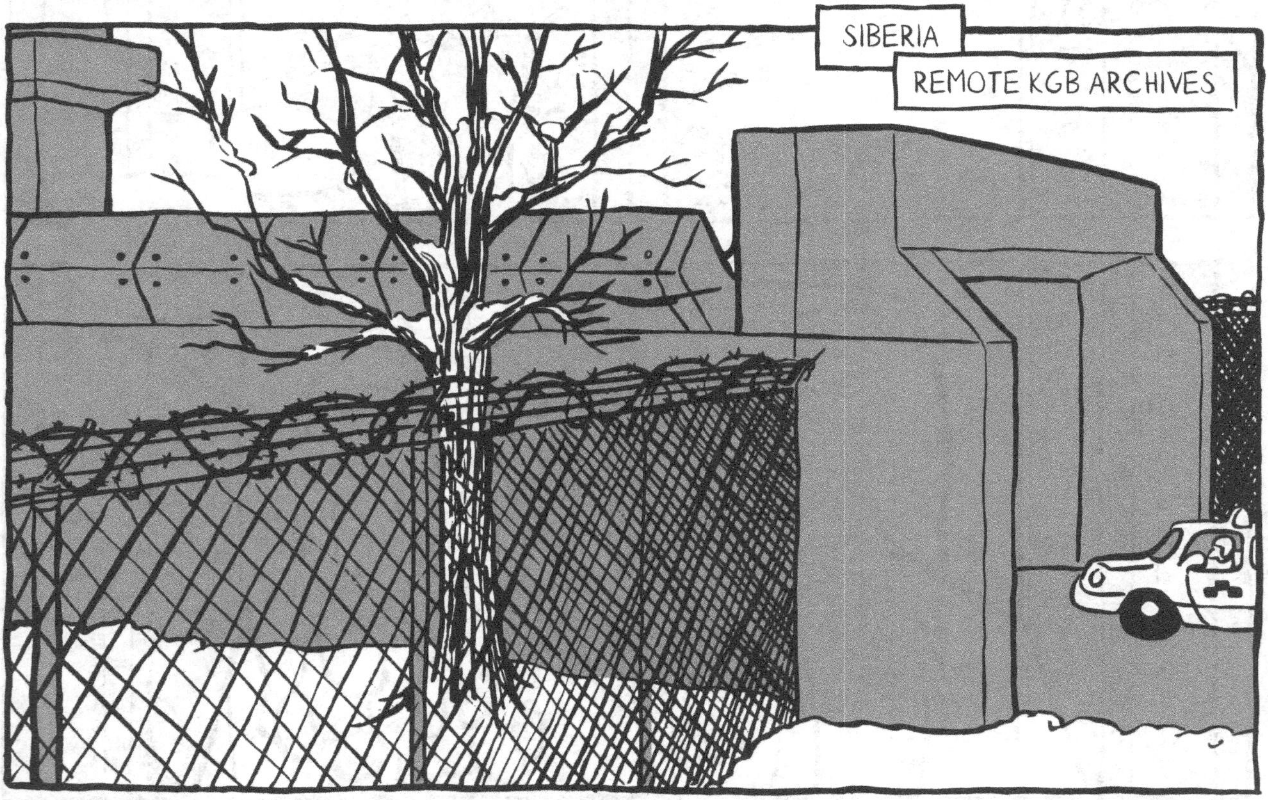
SIBERIA
REMOTE KGB ARCHIVES

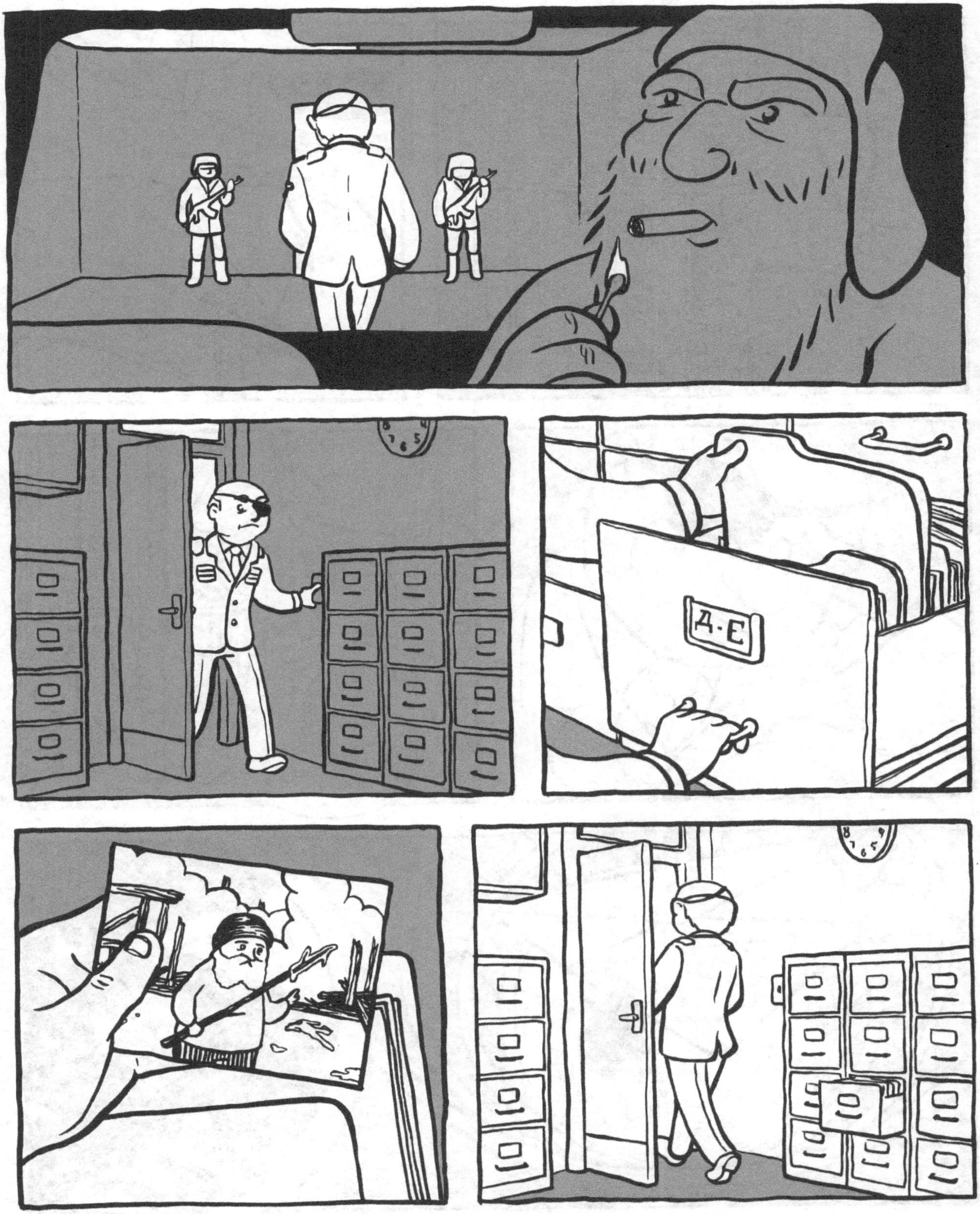
Д-Е

HM?

TRASH.

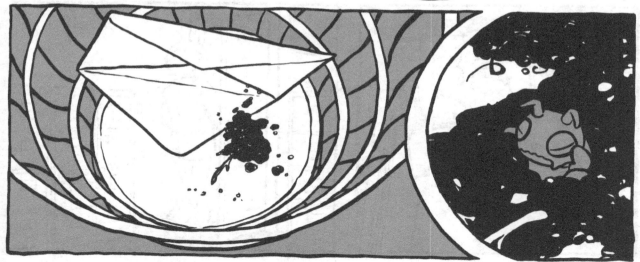

Central Intelligence Agency

TOP SECRET

JANUARY 7, 1983

TO: [redacted]
FROM: [redacted]
RE: Defector Yuri P

[redacted] and following yesterday afternoon's debrief session Agent [redacted] told the subject, Yuri P, that he was going to get some burgers and fries. The subject asked if he could have some. Agent [redacted] explained that it is strictly against CIA regulations to give Communist spies tasty grub.

The subject became upset and began to threaten us in Russian and also to cast aspersions on the character of Agent [redacted]'s wife. The subject claimed that the KGB has in its possession photographs showing Agent [redacted]'s wife and a person believed to be a ranch hand, who is distinguished by a heavy beard and a tattoo on his [redacted]. [redacted] on a horse farm in Warrenton on the evening of [redacted] and by the light of a three-quarter moon in the stables.

To our surprise a cross-check with the National Weather Service shows that, indeed, on the evening of [redacted] there was a three-quarter moon, and a contact in the real estate office where Agent [redacted]'s wife works confirmed that she had the keys to [redacted] estate in Warrenton. Nonetheless, we are skeptical of the subject's truthfulness here.

****Please see attached FILE C-1 for advisable protocol on determining the identity of the ranch hand with the heavy beard and the tattoo of [redacted] in order to bring him in for questioning.****

At this point, Agent [redacted] announced that he was no longer hungry.

I raised the possibility that we might let Yuri P have Agent [redacted]'s share of the burgers and fries if he told us something new. The subject asked us what we knew about the "Siberian Meteor Incident of 1923." We had no idea what the subject was talking about, but Agent [redacted] cunningly told him that what we did have was "strictly classified."

According to Yuri P a meteor of unknown origin and mysterious properties fell in far-eastern Siberia in the winter of 1923. When authorities reached the nearest neighboring village, [redacted], every structure was in ruins and only a single survivor remained, an elderly woodcutter. The woodcutter professed that monsters had attacked. His bizarre, verbatim testimony was, Yuri P said, "They made us pregnant! They filled us with jelly!" The authorities did the logical thing and quickly assigned this madman to a mental facility.

However, Yuri P indicated that further investigations had uncovered inexplicable evidence, some biological in nature. We pressed him on this point and the subject claimed that he had seen in the KGB archives at [redacted], as well as soil samples.

In this agent's opinion the entire story sounded fanciful to say the least, although another cross-check with the National Weather Service did correlate part of the story: a significant meteor impact was recorded as having fallen in Siberia in early 1923.

****Please see attached FILE D-1 for advisable protocol on developing resources on Siberian history and opening lines of communication with astrobiology scholars.****

At this point, the subject asked if he could have the hamburgers and fries, but unfortunately for him Agent [redacted] had regained his appetite.

See attached recording for complete exchange. *

Replaced by Agents [redacted] and [redacted] at 1500.

Signed [redacted]

FENTON COLLEGE

Department of Astrobiology

March 20, 2015

Dear Dean Kaminski,

It is with great disappointment that I must notify you of a very serious student transgression. Stacey Kepler, a junior in my Astrobiology Seminar, was caught attempting to cheat on the midterm. I overheard her offering sexual favors to Mason Korda, another junior, in exchange for quiz answers. Moreover, it was clear that this was not the first time they had made such an arrangement.

My recommendation is for immediate expulsion of this despicable whore.

On another note, I was wondering if you ever received my request for a course reduction. Did you? My current responsibility of two classes per semester is onerous and is greatly interfering with my important research—research, I might add, that will unquestionably put Fenton College's Astrobiology Department on the map. Last time I checked, we were ranked #178 in US News and World Report, above only the University of Phoenix's online astrobiology certificate program (whatever that is). In fact, we're ranked below Bucknell, which doesn't even have an astrobiology department!

My recommendation is that I teach one class in the fall and zero classes in the spring. Thank you in advance for accommodating me.

As long as I have your attention, I'd like to register a formal complaint against Amber Bryant, a creative-writing professor. I have heard from several of her students that she used the following as an in-class writing prompt: "With his ridiculous bobbed haircut swinging to and fro, and the clogs on his feet echoing through the quad, the astrobiology professor marched into the library." Clearly, Professor Bryant is referring to me. I'm the only astrobiology professor at Fenton who wears clogs. And I wouldn't call my hair "ridiculous." Many women find my hair very attractive. I condition it daily and use a special cream rinse that I order from Portugal. I've been told by complete strangers that my hair is "beautiful," "disturbingly stunning," and "sexy." One woman in the drugstore in town actually offered to pay me to let her brush it. Of course, I declined her offer.

My recommendation is that you send Professor Bryant a formal cease-and-desist letter and relay to her that I can and will sue her for defamation of character and slander if she continues to use me as the subject of her writing prompts.

With Sincere Gratitude and Admiration,

Stanley Evans, PhD

FENTON COLLEGE

Colbrook, VT
Total Enrollment: 1,123
Male/Female Ratio: 45/55
SAT: 630 CR, 680 M, 720 W

History

Founded in 1913 by wealthy agronomist and radical education pioneer Forsythe Fenton II, Fenton College in its early years represented, by all accounts, something of a shock to the American collegiate system. Laid out across twelve hundred acres of bucolic Vermont woodland, the college had all the modern amenities of the time, as well as a top-notch faculty. But along with a dedication to developing a background in the humanities and the hard sciences for the youth of tomorrow, Forsythe Fenton II believed that human beings were destined to develop supramental powers—such as telekinesis, ESP, and the ability to communicate with animals and plants. In accordance with these convictions Fenton II was beloved by students and faculty for his acceptance of nontraditional pedagogical approaches, particularly the use of psychedelics in a classroom environment. Conversely, government authorities viewed the unique Fenton curriculum and atmosphere much less positively, and J. Edgar Hoover was said to have taken a personal interest in "cleaning up" the iconoclastic college before its founder's death of natural causes in 1954. While the college has gradually evolved into a more conventional liberal arts environment, every April 20 high-spirited students still pay tribute to their founder's mission by going "Full Fenton": stripping naked and using homemade dowsing rods to search for water in the forest surrounding the campus— while tripping on mushrooms, of course. Regarded, unfairly, as a fallback school for Bard and Sarah Lawrence applicants, Fenton College, with its impressive neo-Gothic buildings and lush campus, is a fine option for serious students and searchers alike.

Academics: 7 laurel leaves (out of 10)

- "I chose Fenton over Yale because of its intimate size and Astrobiology Department."—Stacey, Sophomore, Astrobiology Major
- "I told my parents I'm premed, but I don't like to study so I'm probably switching to something really easy like Public Relations, which is a new major that some rich girl's parents insisted on. I'd like to work for Riff Raff when I graduate, promoting him and shit."—Stevie, Sophomore, Undeclared
- "The arts here are strong. We did an acclaimed performance of *Speed-the-Plow* last spring."—Dawn, Junior, Dramatic Arts Major

- "I turned in a graphic novel for my final project in my algebraic geometry class. It was about Cassini ovals. My professor thought it was stupid, but I still got a C."
  —Tyler, Junior, Math Major, Art Minor
- "It's a cliché to say that people here study and party hard, so I'll say that I study a little and smoke a lot of weed."—Kirk, Freshman, Undeclared

Life and Community: 5 laurel leaves (out of 10)

- "Vassar and Brown didn't want me, so I came to Fenton. It's okay here, but socially it's very cliquey."—Dawn, Junior, Dramatic Arts Major
- "I came here because I knew I could be high for four years and still graduate. Plus, my dad went here and so did my grandfather and great-grandfather."
  —Ethan, Junior, Premed
- "Fenton gave me better financial aid than Bennington, so I can't complain, and I've met some really cool girls at the lab. Also, I tried mushrooms for the first time, but don't print that."—Guillermo, Sophomore, Biology Major
- "I hate it here. It's too far from New York or any decent shopping. I'm transferring to NYU as soon as my father makes the donation."
  —Megan, Junior, Public Relations Major
- "There's nothing to do here unless you like wandering in the woods. I wish I had gone to Barnard, but I'm a dude, so they didn't let me in."
  —Brian, Sophomore, History Major
- "Fenton is not like it used to be. A lot of kids from public schools go here now. There are students on financial aid. It seems unfair that my father's tuition dollars are subsidizing other students' educations because their parents didn't work hard enough to save any money. It's socialism, is what it is."
  —Landon, Junior, Economics Major

Athletics: 1 laurel leaf (out of 10)

- "The weight room blows, but at least the nerds know to stay away."
  —Mason, Junior, Business Major
- "I saw some trustafarians playing hacky sack once."—Doug, Senior, English Major
- "There are sports here?"—Susan, Junior, Philosophy

Dorms: 6 laurel leaves (out of 10)

- "My first year they stuck me in a double with this awful geek who smelled like vitamins. It was a nightmare. Then they closed my sorority because we were honest about not letting fat girls in, so now I'm back in the dorms with my

best friend, who has the worst fake tits I've ever seen. I can't wait to transfer to NYU when my father makes the donation."
—Megan, Junior, Public Relations Major

- "My roommate and I hit it off from the get-go. They did a great job matching us up by our interests. We actually get along so great we started, like, our own small business."—Kirk, Freshman, Undeclared
- "The dorms are about as wheelchair accessible as the Grand Canyon, and all the lounges smell like pizza barf. On the other hand, the bathroom graffiti is always fascinating. I mean that earnestly."—Gina, Sophomore, Physics Major
- "I don't mind the dorms. I have earplugs if people are being loud and I need to concentrate on my work. My freshman-year roommate wasn't so great. I like the roommate I have now, though. We've become good friends."
—Stacey, Sophomore, Astrobiology Major

Food Services: 4 laurel leaves (out of 10)

- "If you've ever dreamed of eating fart stew made by ex-convicts, you'll love the Fenton cafeteria. I can't wait to transfer to NYU when my father makes the donation."—Megan, Junior, Public Relations Major
- "The people who work in the dining hall hate Fenton students. Wait. One girl is nice. Stacey. She's nice."—Charlotte, Sophomore, English Major
- "After a while, it all tastes the same."—Gina, Sophomore, Physics Major
- "I found a Band-Aid in my rigatoni last night."—Susan, Junior, Philosophy

Coolest Professor: Amber Bryant, Creative Writing

- "I wrote a short story about this beautiful girl who's a genius, but kind of defensive, and how she falls in love with this laid-back guy from Fullerton who works at a genetic-design firm but is also a superhero vigilante who fights skinheads in his extra time. I had never written a story before that, and she was really encouraging overall."—Guillermo, Sophomore, Biology Major

Lamest Professor: Stanley Evans, Astrobiology

- "He's the whole package: speaks directly to your boobs, corpse hair, stupid clogs, pop quizzes. Also, all that stuff in the catalog about 'life in the stars'? Completely false advertising. We haven't talked about the zodiac once. I can't wait to transfer to NYU when my father makes the donation."
—Megan, Junior, Public Relations Major

Fun Facts

- All twenty-seven members of the inaugural class of 1913 were personally gifted gray parrots by Forsythe Fenton II.
- In the fall of 2003, all but seven Fenton students had visible cold sores.
- On September 17, 1971, Mark King, then president of the college, was revealed to be the infamous "Fenton Flasher." At ninety-eight, he still teaches Psychology of Human Sexuality.
- The first meal served at Fenton was squirrel pie.
- Fenton's mascot, Forsythe III, is a snarling squirrel pie.
- Ke$ha considered attending Fenton, but her application was denied.

Famous Alumni

- Sarah Palin (former governor of Alaska, one semester, asked to leave), Toru Watanabe (creator of Puc-Man, a Pac-Man rip-off), Fred LoBiondo (lunch-box artist), Jason Willis-Barber (poet, and son of poetess Phyliss Willis-Barber), Jennifer Wiswell ("Goofy," *Disney on Ice*), Michael Bontarte (Cher's assistant, 2007–8), Thomas R. Snuggie (inventor of the Snuggie).

ACKNOWLEDGEMENTS

We'd like to express our everlasting, collective gratitude to Brant Rumble, who got this train rolling, and John Glynn, who ably piloted it into the station.

Nan Graham and Susan Moldow: thank you. There are a lot of exploding aliens in this book—some might even say too many—but you never asked us to pull back.

Ken Sommer and George Kokkinidis provided invaluable guidance on the illustration and design of this book. Erich Hobbing completed the layout, and we really appreciate it.

Owen wants to give a shout-out to the following family, friends and accomplices: Mom, Dad, Joe, Naomi, Kelly, Z, Michael Cendejas, Lynn Pleschette, Chris Ryall, Scott Snyder, and Amy Williams. Also, and most of all, his coconspirators, Mark and Nancy.

Nancy profusely thanks Alice, Youngho, and Oksoon Ahn for their quiet support; her Bennington and Brooklyn families for their loud support; and Mark and Owen for being so cool.

Mark thanks Owen for calling him one day to suggest they write something like this. He thanks Nancy for not ignoring the Facebook message from her former professor. He thanks Ed Cahill for reading early drafts and offering his ideas, and Jin Auh for taking care of business. Mark is especially grateful to Rose Davis (1970–2003), who helped cultivate his love of kitsch and the absurd.